THE SHAAR PRESS

THE JUDAICA IMPRINT FOR THOUGHTFUL PEOPLE

A novel by
CHAIM ELIAV

© *Copyright 2002 by* Shaar Press

First edition – First impression / Febuary 2002

ALL RIGHTS RESERVED

No part of this book may be reproduced **in any form,** *photocopy, electronic media, or otherwise without* **written** *permission from the copyright holder, except by a reviewer who wishes to quote brief passages in connection with a review written for inclusion in magazines or newspapers.*

> This is a work of fiction. Names, characters, places, and incidents are either the product of the author's imagination or are used fictitiously. Any resemblance to actual persons, living or dead, or locales is entirely coincidental.

THE RIGHTS OF THE COPYRIGHT HOLDER WILL BE STRICTLY ENFORCED.

Published by **SHAAR PRESS**
Distributed by MESORAH PUBLICATIONS, LTD.
4401 Second Avenue / Brooklyn, N.Y 11232 / (718) 921-9000

Distributed in Israel by SIFRIATI / A. GITLER
10 Hashomer Street / Bnei Brak 51361

Distributed in Europe by J. LEHMANN HEBREW BOOKSELLERS
20 Cambridge Terrace / Gateshead, Tyne and Wear / England NE8 1RP

Distributed in Australia and New Zealand by GOLD'S BOOK & GIFT SHOP
36 William Street / Balaclava 3183, Vic., Australia

Distributed in South Africa by KOLLEL BOOKSHOP
Shop 8A Norwood Hypermarket / Norwood 2196, Johannesburg, South Africa

ISBN: 1-57819-780-5 Hard Cover
ISBN: 1-57819-781-3 Paperback

Printed in the United States of America by Noble Book Press
Custom bound by Sefercraft, Inc. / 4401 Second Avenue / Brooklyn N.Y. 11232

THE ENVELOPE

A SHAAR PRESS PUBLICATION

Carefully — and curiously — Avraham Rosenbaum opened the cardboard file.

It was brown, medium sized, and unmarked. Near the edges, the color was beginning to fade with age. Peering inside, Avraham saw three envelopes lying in a pile. They were large, old envelopes, once white but yellowed now with the years. The uppermost envelope bore the number 1.

Lifting it, Avraham saw that the envelope beneath was marked with a 2. It did not take brilliant guesswork to conclude that the third one, at the bottom of the pile, would be 3. He checked anyway; it was.

"Avraham! Avraham, where are you?"

Avraham did not answer. With mounting interest, he studied the envelopes. *What,* he wondered, *did they contain?*

He had come upon the cardboard file in the top drawer of his father's desk. His father, may his memory be blessed, had always kept the drawer locked. To Avraham's surprise, it held nothing at all except this file.

He had just returned from the cemetery, at the conclusion of the week of mourning for his father. A *minyan* from the *shtiebel* had come along. Avraham had recited *Kaddish*, after which one of his father's close friends had said the *Kel Malei Rachamim* prayer and then eulogized the departed man. Then they had returned — Avraham, the only son, and his mother — to the apartment on Jerusalem Street in Bnei Brak, still reeling from the shock of the unexpected death. It was only now that they were beginning to feel the true weight of their pain, and to sense the frightening emptiness of the small apartment. R' Elimelech Rosenbaum, a chassid who had worked as an accountant in a local food business, had passed away on *Rosh Chodesh* Tammuz, 5750 (1990). He had been relatively young — no more than 65 years old. A sudden heart attack had sent him to Beilinson Hospital, where he had suffered for two weeks before finally returning his soul to his Creator.

"Avraham, come to the kitchen!"

Avraham did not hear his mother's call. The envelopes had totally captured his attention. He turned them over, and then over again, not yet daring to open them. He was filled with a sudden fear, which he recognized as emanating from his reverence for his father. He had the uneasy feeling that he was intruding into an intimate area of his departed father's life. There was a sense, almost, of sacrilege.

He was face-to-face with a secret that his father had kept from him. In general, his father had talked a great deal to him, on just about any topic. But never, during his lifetime, had he revealed the existence of this cardboard file or its contents. This drawer had always been securely locked, with the key resting in Elimelech Rosenbaum's pocket.

Now, with the envelopes in his hand, Avraham suddenly recalled the startled expression on his father's face when he had entered the room and the drawer had been open. With a quick motion of his wrist, the elder Rosenbaum had shut the drawer and locked it. The movement had been accompanied by a brief glance at his son, as though to assure himself that Avraham had noticed nothing unusual.

Avraham had assumed that his father kept personal secrets locked in that drawer, but he had never given the matter too much thought. By nature, he was not overly curious. Besides, what was at issue here? Every man has secret drawers in his heart, and he is not obligated to reveal them to another soul.

"Avraham! What happened to you? Why aren't you coming to eat?"

But now, the drawer was unlocked. The cardboard file stood open to his scrutiny. Only the envelopes remained sealed. Avraham hesitated, and then slit open the first of them.

He opened it very carefully, almost reverently. A shower of newspaper clippings fell out of the envelope. Avraham spread the clippings over the desk and studied them.

After a moment, he realized that the articles had one thing in common: Most of them had been clipped from daily newspapers. A further examination also revealed a common theme. The articles, collected from many different years, were dated either 27 Nissan, the date of Israel's *Yom HaZikaron L'Shoah U'Legevurah* — the Remembrance Day for the Holocaust and its martyrs — or 10 Teves. There were articles, too, from Adolf Eichmann's trial. All the articles were about the Polish cities of Radomsk and Pinchov.

Pinchov, Avraham knew, had been his father's hometown, where he had lived until the Nazi Holocaust. And his father's family had been numbered among the Radomsker chassidim.

"*Avraham!*"

This time, he heard her. His mother sounded impatient, even a little angry. He heard her turn on the gas stove in the kitchen.

"Yes!" he called back.

"What are you doing in there?"

"Nothing special."

Avraham moved the clippings from place to place over the desk's surface, as though trying to put together pieces in a jigsaw puzzle.

"Then come to the kitchen already, and let's eat something."

"Coming," he replied absently, eyes glued to the clippings. The aroma of frying eggs wafted from the kitchen into the living room of the tiny apartment.

Rapidly scanning the articles, Avraham found that all of them were about the towns of Pinchov and Radomsk, during the Holocaust. One

The Envelope / 9

dealt with the day the SS entered Pinchov. Another described the time the Radomsker Rebbe was taken out by the Nazis to be killed. A third pinpointed the precise date of the *aktion* in which Pinchov's residents were deported to the death camps. This last included, apparently, his father's parents and grandparents. Avraham's father had never spoken much on this topic. Elimelech Rosenbaum, Avraham knew, had also been sent to Auschwitz, but his father had not volunteered any details. In fact, the entire subject of the Holocaust had been shrouded in a deep, heavy silence in the Rosenbaum home.

Avraham had always hoped that his father would one day open up and provide a glimpse of his world before the war overturned it. Now, his heart constricted painfully as he realized that that time would never come. The opportunity had slipped away forever.

"Avraham!"

"All right, I'm coming."

He quickly swept the clippings back into the envelope. Before he joined his mother, he wanted to peek into the other two envelopes.

His eager fingers opened the second envelope, and several photographs fell out onto the desk. They were family photos, unfamiliar to him. Avraham studied them attentively.

The photos featured a tall man, a woman, and a small girl. All three bore the confident smiles of youth. They stood in the shade of a spreading tree but Avraham could not identify the setting. Neither did he recognize the people in the photos. Judging by the way they were dressed, they were not observant Jews — or, at most, observant in a very lukewarm way. A pity he could not ask his father to explain the photographs to him. On the other hand, had his father been living, Avraham would not be studying the contents of the envelope in the first place. At the right moment, he decided, he would show the photographs to his mother and see if she could identify them. Right now, he did not want her to know that he had breached his father's privacy.

"Avraham, your omelette's getting cold. Come already!"

Absently, he called back, "I know, I know. I'll be right there. Just a minute!"

He hurriedly gathered together the photographs and stuffed them back into their envelope. Then he picked up the third envelope and carefully opened it.

Once again, a shower of newspaper clippings slid onto the desk's polished surface. Avraham glanced through them with widening eyes. Here was a mystery!

The first clipping featured a picture of an armed man with black hair, a thick mustach, and eyes that were hard, dark, and deepset. Beneath the picture was a caption: *The death of a terrorist*. And under that, in smaller letters, the text read that that the terrorist Abu Daoud al-Razak, long wanted by Israel's General Security Service (the G.S.S., or *Shabak* in Hebrew), had broken out of prison. After a difficult and heroic chase, the security men had caught up with the terrorist and killed him in the Shomron hills.

Why in the world, Avraham wondered, staring at the clipping and photo, *is this in my father's drawer?*

To his astonishment, he found two words, written by his father, at the very bottom of the article: *Baruch Hashem*. His surprise grew as he scanned the remaining articles. They all dealt with acts of terror, chases, roadblocks, kidnappings, and the like. All of them involved the same terrorist: Abu Daoud al-Razak.

What was this about?

No matter how long Avraham stared at the strange collection, he could still make no sense of it. No answer to the mystery presented itself. What possible connection could a chassid from Bnei Brak who had, in the last years of his life, even begun to wear the *spuhdik* that had been customary among Poland's chassidim, have to this terrorist?

Had his father known him? Had he perhaps even met this Abu Daoud in person? If so, where had this strange meeting taken place — in the *shtiebel*? On Rabbi Akiva Street? At his workplace? Perhaps the terrorist had once been employed at his father's business — Who knew?

And who was the secular-looking family in the photographs in the other envelope? His father's brother, killed in the Holocaust? Elimelech had once told Avraham about an older brother in Poland who had not been Torah observant.

Absorbed in the mystery, Avraham did not hear his mother's footsteps. She had grown weary of sitting in the kitchen waiting for her son to eat the light meal she had prepared for him.

"What are you doing?" Her voice was sharp.

He was startled, but quickly recovered. "Nothing. Just looking at some stuff Abba left."

All at once, she noticed the open folder on her husband's desk, and the envelopes scattered beside it. Her eyes darted from the envelopes to her son and back again. Avraham thrust the picture of the terrorist at her. "Imma, what is this? Who is it?"

He had asked the question impulsively, never dreaming it would unleash a storm. Suddenly, he noticed that his mother's face had gone very white and her eyes had filled with fear. It seemed to him that she was on the verge of fainting.

"Imma!" He sped around the desk to support his mother before she fell. "What happened? Have I said something to hurt you?"

He led her to an armchair and gently lowered her into it. His mother's left hand reached up to rub her creased forehead in a nervous gesture. She burst out, "And *how* you've hurt me!"

"But what did I do?" Avraham was at his wits' end.

His mother did not hurry to reply. Finally, when she had calmed down somewhat, she wriggled out of his grasp and said, "You did not do anything! Not a thing!" Her tone was not very convincing.

With difficulty, she rose from the armchair and darted toward the kitchen. Avraham followed, pleading, "Imma, please explain this to me! How did I hurt you, and what are those pictures of a terrorist doing in Abba's desk?"

His mother turned and looked directly at him. Her gaze held a mixture of pain and determination. After a moment she went toward the kitchen without saying anything.

Avraham persisted. "Why don't you answer me?"

"I don't want to. I don't want to answer you."

"Why not?"

"Just because! Understand?"

"I *don't* understand."

"All right. You don't have to understand everything."

Confused, Avraham said, "Even so —"

"Even so — even nothing! I am not prepared to talk to you about this. I *can't* talk to you. Period, end of sentence!"

"But can you at least explain why? Why can't you talk to me about it? Why won't you tell me what's going on? Who else do you have in the world except me?"

He thought he heard her sigh. She moved closer to him, took his hands in her own trembling ones, and gripped them firmly. Bringing her face close to that of her only son, she whispered, "Don't ask me any more questions on this topic. I won't tell you anything. Don't keep trying, because I can't talk about it. *I — simply — cannot — talk about it.* Do you understand, Avraham? Do me a favor and don't bring this up again. Remember, I have suddenly become a widow. I am already hurting enough." Her voice shook.

"And I am an orphan, Imma. Do you think it's any easier for me?" Avraham's own voice was none too steady.

"There's no comparison!"

A sudden silence fell between them. Mother and son stood for a long moment, staring at one another in anguish. Her eyes held a question, a pleading; at last, Avraham nodded his head in reply. He would not ask her again.

She let go of his hands and turned back to the kitchen, not asking him to follow. Avraham stood where he was, frozen in place. He heard the faucet turned on in the sink, then off again, and understood that his mother had washed her hands to eat — alone. That hurt.

With halting footsteps, he made his way to the kitchen. He washed his hands, recited the blessing over bread, and ate the omelette his mother had prepared for him. Silence reigned for the entirety of the small, sad meal. Not a word passed between Avraham and his mother, except when she asked, "Do you want coffee?" and he muttered, "Yes, please."

Afterwards, his mother rose, murmured something softly, and went to her bedroom.

Avraham remained at the table for some time, toying with his knife and fork. His thoughts were disorganized, flitting aimlessly from one subject to the next. He knew only one thing for sure: He was burning with curiosity to solve the mystery of the envelopes — especially the one containing the photo of the Arab terrorist. He felt that he could find no peace until he had unraveled the riddle. He must know the secret that had been hidden from him in his own home by both his father and his mother.

He knew himself. He tended to wax enthusiastic over things, to make grandiose plans and resolutions, and then to become mired after a day or two in the routine stream of life. Angrily, he pictured this happening again now. But — maybe not? Maybe this time he would remain determined to the very end?

After the week's absence, he felt obliged to make an appearance at Mad-Kal, where he was employed. The firm imported medicines from abroad. At his desk, he dealt with various matters that fell under his sphere of responsibility, and from which his sudden plunge into mourning had not excused him.

It was very late by the time he returned home to Petach Tikvah.

Avraham opened the door of his apartment slowly. The hour was late and he had no wish to disturb anyone. As he crossed the threshold of his home, he was greeted by total silence.

His wife, Rachel, was sitting at the corner of the sofa, absorbed in a book. The living room was dark aside from a single lamp casting a faint yellow light. She lifted her head at his entrance and greeted him with a nod. She knew that his father's sudden death had had a deep impact on her husband and she had tried, all through the week of mourning, to figuratively walk on tiptoe around him. Now, with the week behind them, she hoped that their home would gradually begin to function normally once more.

Their young daughters, Tamar and Rivky, had sensed it, too. All last week, their father had slept at Savta's house. Tonight was the first night that Abba would be back home with them. They were excited at the prospect — and yet, when he walked into the house, the little girls did not pounce on him happily the way they usually did on his return from work.

Tonight, they satisfied themselves with a sleepy but curious peek from their bedroom doorway. Abba, they knew, was very sad.

Avraham's reply to his wife's greeting was a similar, wordless nod. Still without speaking, he went into the kitchen, turned on the light, and opened the refrigerator. For a long moment he stood in front of the open door, searching its contents for something to satisfy his sudden hunger.

"What do you want to eat?"

He had not heard Rachel get up or follow him. The fact that he had gone into the kitchen without asking her to fix supper troubled her. A single lucid thought floated among the turmoil she felt: *Something's happened.*

"It doesn't matter what. Just food."

"But tell me what you want," she persisted gently.

"It really doesn't matter."

"All right, then. Sit down, please, and I'll prepare something."

In silence, Avraham obeyed. He stared sightlessly at the wall in front of him while Rachel washed and chopped vegetables for a small salad. As she worked, she asked over her shoulder, "How is your mother feeling?"

"So-so. She's all right."

Rachel spread a cloth on the table, set out some bread, butter, and cheese, and then placed the salad before her husband. "That poor woman," she murmured, almost to herself. Avraham said nothing.

He ate in silence. Rachel sat opposite him, watching him attentively. She wanted to continue the conversation, but did not know how.

He reached to switch on the electric kettle. Rachel opened the coffee jar and placed a teaspoonful into a mug. "What is she going to do now, all alone?"

Avraham's mind had been miles away. "Who?" he asked.

"What do you mean, 'Who'? Your mother! I asked you what she will do now that she's on her own. You're not paying attention, Avraham."

Impatiently, Avraham answered, "What will my mother do now? She'll do what all widows do."

Rachel was quiet. Avraham had never before spoken to her in this abrupt and dismissive way. Why was he in such an impatient mood tonight? Was it all because of the sudden tragedy?

Leaning her head on the palm of one hand, she regarded her husband. "Avraham?"

"Yes? What do you want?"

She drew a deep breath, then ventured, "Is something bothering you?"

He had betrayed some of his inner turmoil, he knew. Forcing a smile, he said, "Why do you think that?"

She shrugged. "It's just a feeling I have."

Avraham took tiny sips of hot coffee from his mug. After a few minutes of somewhat strained silence, she spoke again. "Am I mistaken?"

He hesitated. Finally, he answered, "Not completely."

"Not completely — or completely not?"

Smiling more naturally now, Avraham said, "I don't know the difference. My English is not as good as yours. In your school in New York they spent more time teaching grammar and sentence structure than in the Talmud Torah where I was educated."

He finished his coffee. Rachel removed the dishes from the table while her husband recited the Grace after Meals. When he was done, she broke the silence to say, "Maybe she'll come to us for Shabbos?"

"Don't bother inviting her. She won't come."

"How can you know that ahead of time? Have you already asked her?"

"No — but I know. I know *her*."

"Then what? Does she stay home all alone?"

Avraham did not answer.

"Or maybe we can spend Shabbos at her place. We can't just leave her alone!"

"She won't agree."

"Have you suggested it already and know that she won't agree?"

"No. But, as I told you, I think that she specifically wants to be alone on the first Shabbos after —"

In the renewed silence that fell after this declaration, Rachel had enough time to wash the dishes and clear away a few pots. Avraham rose. He was standing at the kitchen door, preparing to leave, when Rachel

The Envelope / 17

suddenly exclaimed, "The truth, Avraham! Has something happened between you and your mother?"

Avraham stopped in his tracks. After a moment, he turned his head and said abruptly, "Yes. Something happened with my mother!"

"Did you quarrel?"

"Almost."

"Why?"

"It's a long story —"

"Tell it to me. I love stories."

Avraham looked away. "Maybe tomorrow."

"What's wrong with today?"

"It's nearly midnight. I want to go to bed."

"If you don't tell me now, I'll be too curious to sleep!"

Avraham burst into laughter. "And if I *do* tell you, you certainly won't sleep!"

Rachel turned off the faucet, dried her hands on a dishcloth, untied the apron from around her waist, and once again sat down at her place at the table.

"If that's the case, then you must certainly tell me now. You have to!"

With a deep sigh, Avraham gave in. He, too, sat down again, and told her about the envelopes that he had found in his father's locked drawer that morning. As he had expected, Rachel focused at once on the third envelope — the one dealing with the terrorist killed by the Israeli security forces.

"That's a strange story!" she said, shivering. "Strange and fascinating. The more strange, the more fascinating!"

Avraham grinned, appreciating her American enthusiasm. "I agree," he said. "Fascinating, strange — but even more confusing."

The sound of their voices had roused one of their daughters. Tamar stood in the kitchen doorway yawning.

"What do you want now?" her mother asked impatiently. Absorbed in her husband's story, Rachel wanted to hear more. The little girl rubbed her eyes and said, "I want a drink."

Rachel hurriedly filled a glass for her, then sent her off to her room. Returning to the table, she said to Avraham, "I want to understand: What was so confusing? Did you ask your mother what those clippings were all about?"

"Of course I asked her. And that's exactly where the trouble started."

"Meaning?"

"Her reaction was terse. It was — weird."

"What did she say?"

"I asked her for the meaning of that envelope."

"And what did she say?" Rachel repeated patiently.

Looking suddenly a bit frightened, Avraham answered, "She grew very pale. My mother nearly fainted. Then she warned me, very emotionally, never to talk to her about it again. After a very uncomfortable meal, she disappeared into her bedroom. It seemed to me that I heard her crying."

Rachel paid close attention. She was unsure how to react to this surprising information. At last, she asked, "So what do you think? What's it all about?"

He spread his hands in a gesture of helplessness. "I wish I knew. I've been breaking my head over it for hours, trying to understand."

"And you've had no ideas?"

"Nothing!"

Silence.

"Avraham."

"Yes?"

"You do realize that we have to do something about this?"

"Of course."

"We have to know what this whole business is about."

In a teasing tone, he asked, "Why? To satisfy your curiosity?"

She took him seriously. Forgetting that it was after midnight, Rachel raised her voice indignantly. "What do you mean, 'curiosity'? We have a puzzle here. I love solving puzzles and riddles!"

"I'll buy you a book of crossword puzzles, then, if that's the problem."

"No, Avraham. Why won't you understand? There's some strange secret here — a mystery in your family. And I don't like secrets and unsolved riddles. Who knows — Maybe there's something in your father's past? Isn't it possible? I think it's important for us to know what lies behind all this. If only for the girls —"

After a moment, she added with a smile, "You know what? I admit it. I'm also a little curious!"

Husband and wife sat at the small kitchen table, each sunk in private thought. Rachel broke the silence first.

"Avraham?"

"Yes?"

"What do you actually know about your parents?"

"I don't understand the question."

"I'm just trying to help you. To provide direction for your thoughts."

"Okay — but what does that have to do with my parents?"

"I don't know. Maybe something in their past ties in with all this. I don't know *what* to think! Anyway, what do you know about them?"

He stared at her. "What should I know about them? Do you think they're involved with Arab terrorists? Maybe there was a terrorist cell in the Radomsker *shtiebel* in Bnei Brak?"

"Don't exaggerate! But, between you and me, are you familiar with their life history from the time they moved to Eretz Yisrael after the war? Do you know where they lived? Were they always in Bnei Brak? What did they do when they were younger? You're practically a *ben zekunim*, a child of their old age — and also an only son. Admit it — you don't have the answers to all these questions!"

Avraham closed his eyes. "First of all, I do think I know everything about them. My father was open with me. Apart from that, anything we might learn about them would not give us an explanation for the envelope dealing with Arab terrorists."

Quickly, Rachel asked, "What about your mother's reaction — and her tears? Doesn't that tell you anything?"

"It's true. My mother's strong reaction did arouse some interesting questions. But what can I do? Your suggestion that I dig into my family history doesn't seem useful. I don't believe that route holds the slightest chance of solving this mystery. I don't think my father hid anything from me. And —"

"No?" Rachel smiled. "But you see that he *did* hide something from you."

"What?"

Triumph danced in her eyes. "The envelopes, for example!"

Avraham was taken aback. "Yes. You're right."

After a moment's thought, he added, "You know what? I'm not so sure anymore. But what does all this do to help me understand what Abu Daoud al-Razak is doing in my father's drawer? It's still hard for me to say '*zichrono livrachah*' [may his memory be blessed]. My head is spinning already. Please fix me another cup of coffee. Thank you in advance."

"Okay. I'll make some for myself, too." She stood up. "And I do think I'm on the right track. I don't know what to tell you, exactly — but various ideas are already turning over in my mind!"

"What do you mean?"

"I don't want to talk about it yet. Give me some time to clarify my thoughts."

"Tell me *something*. The suspense is killing me!"

"There's no point. The picture is not yet clear to me — and I may be completely wrong. So why talk?"

Avraham was silent. He knew his wife. Opinionated and assertive, she was not likely to budge. If she chose not to speak, she would not speak. On the other hand, he was secretly glad she found the subject so intriguing. He could certainly use her help in unraveling this riddle. Rachel had a good head for solving puzzles.

"Let's give your mother a few days to rest," Rachel said presently. "Next week — early in the week — we'll go visit her."

"For sure. From now on we'll have to go see her more often than in the past. She has no one else in the world but us. But what are you planning?"

Rachel grinned. "I'm going to try to interrogate her."

Avraham set down his coffee cup. Fixing his wife with a keen gaze, he said firmly, "Rachel, it's a waste of time. Forget about it. If that's the big idea you've been turning over in your mind — it's a waste of time. You won't succeed."

"Trust me a little, won't you?"

Avraham observed his wife. More often than not, when she set her sights on a goal, she achieved it. This time, though, he knew it would turn out differently.

"I trust you implicitly," he said. "But I don't think you really know your mother-in-law."

"That's what you think."

"I think very well. I've known her many more years than you. And I tell you this: When my mother decides to dig in her heels about something, not even her energetic New York daughter-in-law will budge her."

Rachel merely smiled and shrugged her shoulders. Once again, Avraham predicted, "You won't succeed."

With a tactical retreat, Rachel murmured, "But a person's allowed to try, no?"

"Yes," Avraham conceded generously. "Yes, you're allowed to try."

She was the first to leave the kitchen. From the living room, where she was tidying up for the night, her voice floated back to him. "You're listening, Avraham?"

"Yes."

"When we visit your mother, I want to see those envelopes. Especially the one with that Arab. What did you say his name was?"

"Abu Daoud al —"

"Actually, his name doesn't matter. The main thing is that I see his picture."

Avraham smiled to himself. "Is this a part of your big plan?"

"No. It's part of my natural curiosity — or maybe not. It will also be useful with what I'm planning."

Suddenly, from sheer exhaustion, Avraham gave a mighty yawn. His eyes began to close of their own accord. He forced them open again. The idea of once again removing those envelopes from the drawer seemed almost impossible. If his mother noticed movement on his part toward his father's desk, she would react very angrily. This was definitely an issue of honoring one's parents — and his mother, now, was a widow, to boot.

But this was not the time to start thrashing out that point with his wife. With another yawn, he called back, "Okay, okay."

"Remember," Rachel said, poking her head back into the kitchen. "It's very important. I won't take no for an answer."

On Sunday night, Avraham and his wife arrived at his mother's apartment in Bnei Brak. They climbed the stairs to the third floor, each sunk in personal musings and feeling the weight of more than slight tension. This was their first visit to the new widow after her week of mourning, and they had no idea what mood she would be in.

And then there was the mystery of the envelope, whose secret they hoped to unveil on this visit.

They reached the apartment and stood before the door. As Avraham raised his hand to knock, Rachel whispered, "Remember, Avraham, act naturally. Don't let your mother sense our anxiety."

He nodded. She went on, "Remember where to sit at the table. And at the right moment, do what you have to do. Okay?"

Again, he nodded. Then he knocked.

The door opened. Mrs. Rosenbaum stood there, startled at the sight of her unexpected visitors. Joy suffused her face. "Hello! What a surprise!"

Rachel answered first. "Hello. Why are you so surprised?"

"First of all, come inside, please," the older woman invited warmly — albeit a trifle stilted. "I will tell you why I'm surprised. Neither of you has been here since Monday, the last day of the '*shivah*.' I'd begun to think you'd forgotten me." She paused. "Where are the girls?"

Rachel pretended to be insulted. "*Oy*, Imma, don't exaggerate. Why in the world should we forget you? There was a reason why we didn't come. As for the girls, they're with a babysitter!"

Avraham gazed around him at the familiar living room. He would never see his father within these walls again. The knowledge was a knife in his heart. The room appeared, for some reason, smaller and emptier than he remembered it. Glancing at the walls, he noticed that the mirror near the bookcase was still covered with a sheet. And the large painting hanging opposite — a group of chassidic children before the war — was turned to the wall. Avraham tried to reverse it. He had an urge to see the place restored to its normal order. But his mother stopped him.

"Leave it alone, Avraham. It's better for me this way."

"But, Imma —"

"No 'buts,'" she said sharply. "This is how I want it right now."

Avraham replaced the painting and stepped back. More important matters hung in the balance on this visit.

"Would you like something to drink?" she asked her son and daughter-in-law when they had seated themselves on the sofa.

"No, thank you," Rachel answered. "Please, sit down. Let's talk a little. Afterwards, we'll see."

Mrs. Rosenbaum did not sit down immediately. "Maybe you want some supper?" Her gaze sized them up, particularly her son.

"Don't trouble yourself over us. Now, sit down and talk with us a little."

A flicker of suspicion came and went in the older Mrs. Rosenbaum's eyes. She noticed that Avraham was silent, and that it was her daughter-in-law who kept insisting that she "sit down and talk."

"Has something happened?" she asked with a flicker of anxiety.

"Why do you think that?" It was Avraham who was speaking now.

She shrugged. "How do I know?"

Her mother-in-law, Rachel saw, was on the alert now. The suspicious light in the older woman's eyes was connected, she was sure, with the mysterious envelopes that Avraham had described to her. *This isn't going to be easy,* Rachel thought. *Have we come too soon? Maybe it would have been better to wait a few more days.*

Mrs. Rosenbaum stirred uneasily. "Anyway, tell me, was there a special reason you came over tonight?"

Avraham reacted instantly, asking again, "Why, Imma? Why do you think that?"

Rachel said, "Imma, I wanted to invite you to our house for Shabbos. But Avraham said that you'd definitely prefer to be alone on your first Shabbos," she breathed deeply before continuing, "after — what happened."

Mrs. Rosenbaum went to an armchair and sat down. With a sigh, she assented, "Yes. Avraham was right."

"Will you come next Shabbos, then?"

Mrs. Rosenbaum closed her eyes for a moment. Then, with another sigh, she said, "What do I know now? I'll see how I feel. In the meantime, I'm finding it hard. Especially —" She broke off.

"Especially — what?"

"Oh, it's not important." The older woman waved a dismissive hand. "Really, it's nothing."

Avraham and Rachel exchanged a quick but pointed glance — which Mrs. Rosenbaum noticed. An abrupt, strained silence descended on the room. Nervously, Avraham rapped out a light rhythm with his knuckles, while Rachel searched her mind for a way to reopen the conversation.

Suddenly, Mrs. Rosenbaum stood up and headed for the kitchen. "I'll bring you something to drink. I'm not comfortable otherwise. Make a *berachah* in my house, why not?"

Avraham and Rachel found themselves alone. From the kitchen came the rattle of glasses, the sound of the refrigerator door opening and shutting, then the click of a closing cabinet door. Rachel knew it was only a matter of seconds before her mother-in-law would be back. She turned to stare at her husband. There was a definite message in her eyes, but for a

The Envelope / 27

moment Avraham was at a loss to know what it was. Then Rachel hissed, "This is it. Now!"

"Now what?"

"This is our chance! Get the envelope out of the drawer!"

Avraham hesitated. "It won't work. I won't have enough time to show you the pictures before my mother gets back."

"Just hurry! Put the envelope in your pocket. Quick, before she comes!"

Avraham yielded to his wife's demand. He began to move toward his father's desk. He was nearly there — nearly close enough to put out a hand and touch the drawer — when his mother reappeared in the doorway. She held a tray containing a bottle of soda, a container of orange juice, several glasses, and a plate of cookies. Her eyes flew to Avraham, and a faint smile crossed her lips. She had caught her son in the act.

She placed the tray on the coffee table. "Help yourselves. Drink something. Make a *berachah*." She turned. "Avraham, please join us."

Avraham heard, quite clearly, the sting behind the innocuous words. Sheepishly, he returned to the sofa. Rachel looked chagrined. Her mother-in-law sat down beside her.

"Juice?" she asked Rachel.

Rachel nodded. Mrs. Rosenbaum poured a glassful of juice, sneaking surreptitious glances at her son and daughter-in-law. She sensed the tension in the atmosphere and could guess its general nature, but she was still unsure as to its exact meaning.

She held out the juice and turned to Avraham. "You?"

"No, thanks. I don't want anything."

"Are you sure?"

"I'm sure."

She leveled a long look at her son. "You seem nervous. What's wrong?"

"Nothing. I just don't feel like a drink at the moment. Maybe I'll have one later. We're not leaving yet."

Mrs. Rosenbaum shrugged. "Whatever you want. So why didn't you bring along the girls? They're the *nachas* that I have left after what happened."

"They'll be coming," Rachel promised. "Don't worry, Imma. We'll bring them over many times, and you'll come to us too. Tonight, though, we wanted to come by ourselves, and talk."

Her mother-in-law opened her eyes very wide. "Talk?"

"Yes," Rachel said firmly. "Talk!"

With a thin smile, Mrs. Rosenbaum said, "From the moment the two of you walked in here, you've been saying you want to talk. So talk already! Is there something special you want to discuss?"

Avraham and Rachel were taken aback by her directness. They had intended to lead up gradually to the topic in which they were interested. A frontal "attack" would, they knew, meet with a wall of stony silence. But the older woman had preempted them.

Rachel recovered first. "No, nothing special, Imma," she said airily. "We just thought it would be good for you to get things off your chest."

Her mother-in-law responded with a skeptical nod. "Maybe. But up until now, we've been talking only about the need to start talking!"

Avraham burst out, "That's right — because it's hard for us! Do you think that what happened was easy for Rachel or me?"

Mrs. Rosenbaum heaved a deep sigh. Pulling a handkerchief from her pocket, she wiped her nose to hide a trickling tear that had unknowingly found its way out of her eye.

"I understand. It's hard for you, and you're probably imagining how hard it is for me. Especially —"

"Especially *what?*" Rachel asked quickly.

"Oh, it doesn't matter. It really doesn't."

The suspicion in Mrs. Rosenbaum's mind became firmer. The young couple was after something specific. She had deliberately used the word "especially" once again, to see her daughter-in-law's reaction. Ten minutes earlier, she had innocently explained why she had wished to stay home alone on the first Shabbos since her husband's death, and she had used the word "especially —" She had noticed then the way Rachel pounced on the word. Now, Mrs. Rosenbaum said it again, and for a second time Rachel had reacted with definite curiosity.

The Envelope / 29

They want something, she thought. An alarm bell went off in her head. *This visit is not as innocent as it seems.*

She knew what it was that so interested them. She remembered Avraham's sauntering over to his father's desk — which she had interrupted by her reappearance in the living room with the drinks.

Abruptly, Mrs. Rosenbaum stood up. "You know what? I'm going to prepare some supper in any case. A light meal, nothing heavy. I see that it's difficult for you to talk. Maybe, at the table, as we're eating, it will be easier for you." She paused, then added with a small smile, "And maybe it will be easier for me, too."

Quickly, Rachel said, "Okay. I'll help."

Mrs. Rosenbaum's nod invited her daughter-in-law to join her in the kitchen.

Just before she entered, Rachel turned to urgently signal Avraham with her eyes. Here, the eyes seemed to say, is your chance!

The moment he was alone, Avraham leaped out of his seat and darted over to his father's desk. The desk stood near the bookcase, and Avraham pulled down a *sefer* to serve as camouflage in case his mother should surprise him again. It was the *Tiferes Shlomo* of R' Shlomo of Radomsk, which his father would peruse every Shabbos night. As Avraham pored over the pages, his hand snaked out toward the drawer.

To his astonishment, it was not locked. He opened it slowly — just a crack — and inserted a hand.

His hand groped around the drawer. There was no file folder there.

Dismayed, Avraham jerked the drawer completely open.

The drawer was empty. The folder with the three envelopes had disappeared.

Avraham stood staring into the empty drawer, disbelieving the evidence of his own eyes. All their carefully laid plans, his and his wife's, had gone up in smoke. The plans had focused on extracting the secrets of the envelopes; that the envelopes would be gone had never entered their minds.

Instinctively, he ran his hand along the drawer's inside walls, though he knew there was no chance he would find anything. It was an idea born of despair, telling him that perhaps the file folder had slipped into some corner that he had overlooked.

There was nothing there.

Deliberately ignoring the possibility that his mother might return at any moment to find him standing there, he yanked the drawer out of the desk. His eyes raked the drawer beneath. Perhaps the folder had slipped down, unseen?

Nothing.

With slightly trembling hands, he returned the drawer to its place in the desk. With the envelopes missing, the sense of mystery seemed suddenly heightened. Without a doubt, it was his mother who was responsible for the folder vanishing — and this only doubled, in his mind, the mystery of the envelopes. His mother obviously believed that, by hiding the envelopes, she could hold off her son's interest in their contents. She hoped to divert his mind from some secret that lay in his father's past.

Avraham could understand her reaction. From her perspective, she was absolutely correct. There was room to hope that, with the passage of time — weeks and months — his own interest in the envelopes would fade, and the image of Abu Daoud al-Razak along with it, until he ultimately forgot the entire episode. Without the envelopes, there were no questions. And — even better, from his mother's point of view — there was no need for her to avoid answering those questions.

Her action, however, had the opposite effect. It only served to strengthen the confusion and disquiet in Avraham's heart. He closed the *sefer* he had been holding and wearily returned it to its place on the bookshelf. Exhaustion threatened to overwhelm him. Still standing by the bookcase, he stared at the desk and wondered what his next step should be.

For a moment, he toyed with the idea of abandoning the matter entirely. He could learn to live with the fact that some strange and inexplicable secret hovered at the edges of his life. Perhaps, someday, the riddle would be unraveled. Perhaps his mother, at some unknown future date, would suddenly consent to talk about it. The answer might also come from a totally different source.

It was clear to Avraham that, from this day forward, the shadow of that secret would cast a shadow over his own life. It was decidedly unpleasant to think that his father, whom he had so admired, had hidden something from him. Still, there was no use embittering his present life because of an unexplained mystery from the past.

Then, on second thought, he realized that he was fooling himself. He could not rest until he found the solution to the mystery. Somehow, the absence of the envelopes made the mystery seem a bit threatening.

From the kitchen, Rachel called, "Avraham, come. The food's ready."

For Avraham, the call served as a lifesaver, dragging him out of the state of frozen bewilderment in which he had been standing. He turned from the bookcase and went to the kitchen at once. He wondered what, if anything, his wife had managed to talk about with his mother during his absence. Perhaps she had wrung some secrets from his mother as they set the table, tossed the salad, prepared the omelettes, or whatever they had done in there.

"Wash your hands," his mother requested the instant he set foot in the kitchen. Avraham noticed her penetrating look. She was testing him. *She's convinced that I've gone through the drawer and found that the envelopes are gone*, he thought. *Now she wants to see my reaction*. He tried with all his might to appear impassive.

Rachel, too, threw him a look — a questioning one. She wanted to know whether he had taken the envelopes. Avraham returned the look with the same calm impassivity, giving nothing away.

He washed his hands, recited the blessing, and sat at the table to say the blessing over the bread. Already, he could sense that the atmosphere between his mother and his wife was not an especially comfortable one. Despite his efforts, he could not guess what they had been discussing that had caused the strain. Or had they been silent the entire time they had been alone together?

The two women seated themselves at the table. The tension was palpable. The elder Mrs. Rosenbaum was the first to break the silence. "So, what's new?" she asked.

Avraham replied, "*Baruch Hashem*, as much as is possible, we're all right. I've returned to work. Hashem will help."

Rachel stirred. "Imma, I wish it were as simple as Avraham is making it sound. The truth is that Avraham is all broken up by what happened. He's very confused."

"I understand," her mother-in-law said quietly. "*Nu*, would you have it be any different? Such a sudden tragedy!" She sighed.

Rachel swallowed a piece of tomato, then said, "I think it's getting out of hand, Imma. Avraham has hardly been able to function since then."

The elder Mrs. Rosenbaum shot an anxious glance at her son. "Is this true, Avraham?"

Avraham hesitated. "Maybe. I'm not sure."

"Believe me, Imma," Rachel said earnestly. "That's the situation."

"But why? What's happened?"

Slowly, Rachel said, "There's something weighing on Avraham's mind. It won't give him any peace. Didn't you sense it the moment we walked in? I suspect depression. I'm really worried."

Avraham's mother put down the bread she'd been holding, and asked again, "Why? What's happened?"

"He won't say. That's the whole problem."

"But what do you think?"

Rachel twisted her fingers together nervously. "You want to hear the truth?"

"Yes!"

"Do you *really* want to hear the truth?" Rachel demanded.

"Of course! Why shouldn't I? Your husband is also my son!"

"Yes — I'll admit that's true. And that's exactly why I'm so worried about his state of mind."

Mrs. Rosenbaum straightened her back. Sharply, she asked, "What's the connection?"

Inhaling deeply, Rachel said softly, "It's a little because of you, Imma."

"Because of *me*?"

Rachel shrugged. "What can I do? That's the situation."

"Because of me? What have I done to him? Are you accusing me of something?"

"No, of course not! But that's the reality."

Her mother-in-law stared at her. "Look, Rachel, I want you to speak openly with me. What, exactly, are you talking about?"

"All right. Since you insist, I'll tell you. It's because of the envelopes."

Mrs. Rosenbaum was silent for a moment. "Because of *what*?"

"I told you — because of the envelopes!"

"What envelopes? I don't know what you're talking about." The older woman had apparently decided to play the innocent.

Rachel smiled wryly. "As if you don't know."

"I *don't* know."

Rachel exchanged a quick glance with Avraham. According to her game plan, this was the moment to produce the envelopes and place them dramatically in the center of the table. Her eyes told her husband, "It's your turn. Take the envelopes out of your pocket so your mother will stop pretending not to know what we're talking about."

But Avraham's eyes held only discouragement and helplessness. Rachel did not understand what he was trying to tell her. However, seeing that he was not coming through, she turned once more to her mother-in-law.

"Okay, I'll tell you the whole story. Avraham returned home at the end of the *shivah* week. He told me that he had found envelopes in a drawer belonging to his father, *alav hashalom*. Envelopes with very strange contents. He said that you ordered him — in anger and tears — to return the envelopes to the drawer and never again to ask you for an explanation of the pictures he'd found in one of them.

"Avraham is a good boy. He won't ask his mother if she doesn't want him to. But I'm concerned for his health. The lack of knowledge is seriously affecting him." Rachel paused. "That's the story he told me. Is it true?"

For a minute, Mrs. Rosenbaum did not answer. Then, without warning, she burst into laughter. "Is that all? I was worried about who-knows-what! Avraham, are you really making such a fuss over such nonsense? That doesn't become you. It's nothing. I don't want to talk about it, but it's really nothing."

Again, Rachel and Avraham exchanged glances. Her eyes still asked him to carry through with their plan; she could not fathom why he was not responding to her hints.

"Imma, I hope you're not angry with me," she said finally. "But, from what Avraham tells me, I gather that you became quite excited and emotional when you saw him holding those envelopes."

Mrs. Rosenbaum made a dismissive gesture. "Excited? Emotional — because of that nonsense? Oh, really! It's true that I was in a difficult mood that morning. Maybe I was in an 'excitable' state of mind. It was not easy for me when we returned from the cemetery."

"Still," Rachel persisted, "Avraham is very depressed over all this."

His mother looked at him directly. "But why, Avraham?"

Rachel answered for her husband: "Because he senses that you're hiding something from him."

With another, more forceful gesture of dismissal, Mrs. Rosenbaum said, "Hiding, not hiding! What foolishness! You two will also hide things from your children. Not everyone has to know everything. It's just a story — an unimportant story."

Silence descended in the kitchen. Mrs. Rosenbaum tried to smile at her daughter-in-law, who was sitting with a drawn and sober face. As for Avraham, he longed for the moment when this fruitless discussion would end and they could go home.

Rachel said quietly, "No, Imma. Don't be angry — but this is not just another story. What are pictures of an Arab terrorist doing in the desk drawer of a chassid like Abba? He was a G-d-fearing Jew!"

Sadly, Mrs. Rosenbaum nodded. "True. *Oy*, how true that is!"

"I don't remember him ever wasting time," Rachel continued. "He was always to be found with a *sefer* in his hand."

"True," Mrs. Rosenbaum sighed. "Now, the *sefarim* are orphaned. Who will use them now?"

"And suddenly, in the desk of such a man, his only son finds pictures of Arab terrorists! His mother then grows angry at him, in such a powerful way that Avraham is convinced she's hiding something from him. Is that 'nonsense'?"

Mrs. Rosenbaum lifted her head and said in surprise, "An envelope with Arabs? That's really nonsense! What Arabs are you talking about?" She turned to her son. "Avraham! Did you see Arabs in those envelopes?"

Avraham hesitated. He did not want to contradict his mother. But she had asked him a direct question. He had no choice.

"Yes, Imma. Don't be angry! I saw. I even asked you who this Abu Daoud al-Razak was."

Rachel hastened to add fuel to the fire: "Avraham told me that he saw, under the photograph, a story about the terrorist's death. And under that, in your husband's handwriting, the words, '*Baruch Hashem.*' What was all that about?"

Now Mrs. Rosenbaum was beginning to be angry. "Avraham, don't be upset if I tell you that you're dreaming. Forget about these things. You need to recover and go on with your life. You have sweet little daughters at home. Do me a favor and don't ask me anymore."

Avraham defended himself. "I didn't ask you now, either. Rachel brought up the topic, and the conversation just evolved. It was you who asked me a question. Forgive me, Imma, but I had no choice but to answer."

Now Rachel addressed her husband directly. "Put the envelopes on the table so Imma can see if you're dreaming."

Avraham did not put his hand into his pocket. Instead, he whispered, "The drawer was empty. The file folder was gone."

Rachel was stunned. With an effort, Mrs. Rosenbaum concealed the smile that persisted in lurking at the corners of her mouth. She said, "And perhaps there were no envelopes at all? Perhaps you simply imagined them, Avraham?"

Rachel used the last avenue open to her. She began to cry.

Burying her face in her hands, she said through the muffled sobs, "I'm afraid for Avraham. Why won't you understand me? Is it so hard to tell your only son the truth? Why? *Why?* What are you so afraid of?"

Tension closed in on the small kitchen like a stranglehold. Avraham looked down. The situation was extremely difficult for him. It was painful to breathe.

With an almost involuntary movement, Mrs. Rosenbaum picked up the bread knife and began to drum a light rhythm on the table with the handle. Her daughter-in-law had backed her into a corner.

Then, with sudden resolve, the older woman put down the knife and said, "All right. Let's talk."

Rachel's sobs gradually lessened in intensity until they faded away completely. With a last few shuddering sighs, she removed her hands from her damp face.

"She was really crying," Avraham thought. "It wasn't just an act. She's taking this whole thing very much to heart."

The elder Mrs. Rosenbaum looked downcast. Still sniffling, Rachel turned to her apologetically. "Don't be angry at me," she said. "I — I don't know why that happened to me just now." She tried, unsuccessfully, to smile.

"Never mind," Mrs. Rosenbaum whispered. Her eyes, Avraham saw, held a trace of suspicion; his mother did not give full credence to Rachel's tears. He stood quickly and went over to the kitchen counter. Picking up a glass there, he rinsed it at the sink, went to the refrigerator, and filled the glass with cold milk. A few deep swallows calmed him somewhat. From where he stood, he saw his mother begin to clear the table and carry dishes to the sink. She moved like an automaton, silent and stiff. Avraham and Rachel watched her every move, waiting for her to speak.

But *would* she speak? Was she prepared to divulge the secret?

Mrs. Rosenbaum returned to her seat at the table. With a frozen smile, she said, "Well, what do you want to know? I am prepared to go to great lengths for the sake of Avraham's health."

Rachel breathed deeply. "You know what we want to know."

"Shall we have some coffee first?" Mrs. Rosenbaum asked.

Avraham and Rachel exchanged a quick glance. The glance said, *Imma wants to postpone the moment of truth.*

"All right," Avraham agreed. His mother stood again, filled a kettle, and placed it on the stove. With her back to her son and daughter-in-law, she said, "Before I start, is it possible for me to ask you a question?"

Rachel and Avraham waited.

"Tell me the truth. Why does this whole thing interest you so much? Is it just curiosity?"

Slowly, Rachel said, "I don't think so."

"What don't you think?"

"I don't think it's simply curiosity. That is — yes. We are curious to know the secret of those envelopes, especially the one with the Arab terrorist. Because — Because —" Rachel groped for words. "Because we sense that there is something here. Something that — how can I put it —?" Her eyes implored Avraham's help.

Avraham looked at his mother. "We sense, somehow, that there is something here that has significance for us. For me, for Rachel, and even for the girls."

Rachel agreed quickly, "Yes. Yes, that's it exactly."

In silence, Mrs. Rosenbaum set cups of coffee before them on the table. "Would you like a piece of cake with that?"

"No, no thanks." It was glaringly obvious that Mrs. Rosenbaum was finding the upcoming ordeal a very difficult one, and was doing her best to put off the moment when she must begin.

She sat down once more, leaned her cheek on the palm of her hand, and regarded them steadily. After a long moment, she asked suddenly, "What kind of significance?"

"I don't know, exactly," Avraham replied. "It's just a feeling that there is some secret here that touches us."

"Why do you think that?"

"Do you want the truth, Imma?"

"Only the truth, Avraham."

"It's because of your anger at me, when I was holding the envelope. The powerful emotion that took over when I asked you for an explanation. Afterwards, when I came to the kitchen to eat with you, you didn't say a word to me the whole time. You were sunk in your own thoughts, very distant from me. And then, Imma, you got up from the table, said goodbye — and I heard you a few minutes later, crying in your bedroom. Do you think I don't understand that there is something here? Something difficult?"

He paused, finding it suddenly hard to speak. With an effort, he continued.

"It disturbs me. It disturbs me very much. It makes me believe that something must have happened in our family — something shameful, or tragic. I don't know what to think." He looked at his mother directly. "That's why I need to know."

The expression in his mother's eyes was anguished. She closed them for a moment. When she opened them again, it was to say with some force, "Really, Avraham! And if you had never come across that stupid envelope, what would have happened? You wouldn't have known a thing, and that would have been just fine!"

"True," he said quietly. "But now that I've found it, something has changed in my life."

She made her characteristic dismissive gesture with her hand. "So your life has changed overnight, because of some envelope? *Your life has changed because your father is no longer with us, Avraham!* Not because of an envelope."

Another silence fell, one that none of them knew how to break. Both Avraham and Rachel were beginning to feel that their chance to learn the answer to the riddle was slipping through their fingers. There had been too many other words spoken in the interim.

Avraham tried to recapture the moment. "Imma?"

"Yes, Avraham."

"You said you would tell us."

"Yes, I did — and I will. But I'm not to blame if you feel disappointed by the story."

"Of course not." Both Avraham and Rachel lowered their eyes discreetly as they sipped their hot coffee, as though to spare her any added pain in baring her heart.

"All right, children. I'll tell you." Mrs. Rosenbaum's voice was low. "It's a simple enough story. A painful story, and it is linked to the Holocaust."

The tension in the kitchen leaped to a new high. Mrs. Rosenbaum sighed deeply. "Abba was in Auschwitz. Did you know that?"

Avraham nodded. He had known.

"I don't have to explain the meaning of those words: 'He was in Auschwitz.' For several months, Abba was in the Sonderkommando. His job was to sort the clothes that had belonged to the Jews murdered in the gas chambers. He and his co-workers did their work in a shed known as 'Canada.' Day after day, he saw hundreds, and thousands, and tens of thousands of Jews carried off to the gas chambers. Old men, children, women. And every day he had to remove the clothes from their dead bodies — clothes they had worn just minutes before while being crammed into the chambers of death. He sorted and packed them into bundles, to be shipped to Germany.

"In the beginning, he used to tell me, he would cry as he held the trousers of a Jew whom, an hour before, Abba had seen alive and well. But, with the passage of time, his tears dried up. He and his friends could no longer cry. The tears died in their hearts, the way all other feeling had died."

She paused for a moment, then continued with another sigh.

"*Oy*, children, you cannot imagine such a hell! Who knows? Perhaps those Jews who died immediately on their arrival at that monstrous camp were better off. They went straight to Gan Eden without having to endure unspeakable suffering in this world. But the men of the Sonderkommando, who day after day dealt with the enormous number of dead, had to pass each day through the seven levels of hell. It was a suffering that you and I cannot even begin to imagine! And that was your father's fate. Do you understand?"

Avraham nodded again, without speaking. A golfball-sized lump had formed in his throat. Rachel looked equally stricken. The coffee sat forgotten before them.

His mother shook her head. "No. You do not understand."

She paused again, for so long this time that Avraham began to stir restlessly in his seat. At last, his mother continued sadly, "Yes, many of the men of the Sonderkommando did not remain completely normal human beings. Not that they became completely insane. But something was damaged inside."

She took a quick sip of coffee, which had cooled by this time. Neither Rachel nor Avraham dared make the slightest move to disturb the dense silence. In the quiet, they clearly heard the steady *drip, drip* of the kitchen faucet.

"It's not nice to say," Mrs. Rosenbaum said in a trembling voice, "but Abba was also damaged. Not in a way that was obvious in his daily life — but he was damaged. He adopted a habit that never left him — and that was to collect things. There, in that accursed Auschwitz, he would rummage through the victims' pockets as he worked. He would take small souvenirs for himself. In one man's suit pocket he once found an envelope. The envelope contained pictures of the poor man's family. Another day, he found another envelope with family photos. The *Kapo* caught him and beat him to within an inch of his life. It was only through a miracle that Abba was not sent to the gas chambers for his crime. A true miracle."

She lifted her eyes, and they were swimming in tears.

"Do you understand? They, the Nazis, may their names be blotted out, took those envelopes with the pictures. And from that day, your father felt compelled to collect envelopes. Any time he held an envelope in his hand, it seemed to him that it was *that* envelope. I once asked a doctor about this compulsion. He told me not to pay it any mind. He said that the behavior might actually be beneficial. In this single habit of collecting envelopes, Abba concentrated all the `craziness' he had acquired in Auschwitz. Everyone has some quirk, the learned doctor told me. With Abba, it was envelopes."

She leaned forward. "Do you have any idea how this hurt me? Abba was a wonderful person in every way, wasn't he, Avraham? And then, suddenly, this abnormal behavior. He hid envelopes everywhere. You found the ones he kept in his desk drawer. I had hoped to hide the compulsion so that no one would ever find out. That's why I cried and reacted the way I did when you found those envelopes."

Mrs. Rosenbaum stopped speaking. Avraham ventured, "But why were there articles on that specific Arab and no one else?"

The eyes his mother turned to him were filled with anguish. "*Nu*, do we ask questions about a compulsion? It pains me so deeply to have to speak this way about your father, *alav hashalom*." She leaned back in her chair, spent. "Well, do you feel better knowing all this? Do you think this has honored your father?" When they did not respond immediately, she asked again, insistently, "Tell me, do you feel better — or worse? Why did you force me to talk about something I had no wish to speak of?"

They did not answer. Mrs. Rosenbaum sat at the table a few minutes longer, trembling gently. Then, slowly, she stood up. In a broken voice, she said, "Good night," and bolted for her bedroom.

Avraham was at a loss as to how to react. Rachel was feeling the same way. Presently she stood up and began wordlessly to wash the dishes that were piled in the sink. Her husband waited while she restored the kitchen to its pristine state. Then they called loudly, "Good night, Imma," and waited a moment for her reply. There was none.

They exchanged scarcely a word on the drive home. But as they walked into their apartment, Rachel said suddenly, "Do you believe that story?"

His brows shot up. "Are you implying that my mother lied?"

"No. Of course not."

"Then what *are* you implying?"

Rachel walked over to an armchair and sank heavily into it. "I don't know, exactly. I had the feeling that she was trying to protect your father and the real story. And you know that, in such a case, one is permitted to alter the truth."

Avraham remained standing. "But why have you made up your mind that the story she told us is not the true one?"

She shrugged. "I don't know. It's just a hunch."

Sharply, Avraham retorted, "That's not enough to go on. It's not enough to make me believe that Imma didn't tell us the truth."

But Rachel would not be budged. "Don't *you* sense something fishy here?"

"No. Reality outdoes the imagination. The strangest things happen in real life. And in this case, it is certainly possible that what she told us is what actually happened."

Rachel set her handbag on the floor at her feet. "Let me understand this. In your opinion, Avraham, the case is closed?"

He hesitated. "I think so. And even if it isn't, I don't see how we can proceed from here."

"All right. If you feel comfortable with the explanation your mother gave, that's fine. But I am not so comfortable. And the fact that I have a feeling your mother tried to hide the truth from us makes me suspect that the real story's not that simple. I may be wrong, but that's the way I feel right now."

Avraham sat down facing her. "But what can we do?"

"Nothing specific. I never said that something ought to be done. My intuition tells me that what your mother told us tonight is not the full truth. In other words, I presume that the compulsion she described, where your father collects envelopes, is true. But it's not the whole truth."

Unexpectedly, Avraham's mouth opened in an enormous yawn. He grinned sheepishly. "You know what? I've had enough for one night."

Rachel's smile was pensive. She was still thinking about the evening they had just spent at her mother-in-law's. "Good night, then."

"Good night."

It was not until the next day that the disturbing telephone conversation took place.

Avraham arrived at his office the next day, in the Mad-Kal firm at the corner of Herzl and Achad Ha'am Streets in Tel Aviv. In the few days since he had returned to work, his colleagues sensed a certain reticence in him. Avraham was quieter than before, more preoccupied. Making small talk held no interest for him, and he smiled less frequently.

This morning, however, he was slightly better. He felt less oppressed by the weight of his concerns. In contrast to his wife, Avraham was inclined to accept his mother's explanation of the strange envelopes. Whether he was prepared to accept it because he genuinely believed it to be the whole truth, or just to bring the matter to a close in his own mind, was a question he was not prepared, right now, to explore. Either way, he enjoyed a newfound sense of peace.

Not all of his questions had been answered. Nevertheless, he was ready to be satisfied with the explanation, if only out of respect for his father's memory. He had no desire to continue digging. Survivors of Auschwitz, Avraham believed with all his heart, were above all criticism

— and certainly above the criticism of anyone who had not experienced that particular taste of hell. It seemed to Avraham that he was finally ready to resume a normal life.

Then, at 11 o'clock that morning, as he was trying to sort out the customs papers of a shipment of medicines from Switzerland, his phone rang. He picked it up with one hand, while the other still sorted papers.

"Hello, Avraham?"

Avraham put down the page he had been holding and leaned back in his leather chair. He did not immediately recognize the voice at the other end, though it sounded vaguely familiar. His own response was businesslike. "Yes?"

"Hello? Am I speaking with Avraham Rosenbaum?"

"Yes. Who is this, please?"

There was a momentary hesitation. Then the caller said, "You don't recognize my voice?"

Politely, Avraham hedged, "Maybe. I'm not sure."

The voice registered mild complaint. "It's me, your uncle Nachum. Nachum Holtzer."

Nachum Holtzer! How in the world could Avraham have been expected to recognize the voice? They had never before spoken on the telephone. Relations between the two men were extremely cold, despite the fact that Holtzer was his mother's brother. Avraham straightened abruptly. Curiosity swept over him — as well as a certain tension. Why was his uncle Nachum calling?

He said quickly, "Oh, really? I'm so sorry! Forgive me for not recognizing your voice. What's new? How are you?"

Nachum Holtzer lived in Haifa. He was a good number of years older than Avraham's mother. The distance between their homes, as well as the age gap and the consequent differences in their way of thinking, all contributed to the coolness that existed between Nachum and his sister. Apart from this, the fact that Nachum was not as religious as they were was more than a little troubling to Mrs. Rosenbaum.

"Everything is fine, *baruch Hashem*," the uncle replied. "And how are you, Avraham?"

"*Baruch Hashem.* Nothing new." He paused. "Has something happened?"

"No. I just wanted to see how you are."

Avraham opted to be cautious. There was something fishy about this unexpected conversation. After years of no contact, this sudden call in the middle of the day, merely to ask how Avraham was? It sounded suspicious to him.

Nachum Holtzer said, "Have you gotten over the tragedy?"

"It's hard. It's only been two weeks."

"Yes. I understand."

An almost irresistible urge rose up in Avraham to ask his uncle directly what he wanted to know. He managed to suppress the urge. Instead, he said quietly, "It's much harder for my mother."

"I know," his uncle said. "I just spoke with her."

The tension in Avraham rose a decided notch. What had Nachum and his sister spoken of to bring about this unexpected call? Had his mother told Nachum about their talk last night?

"Sure," Avraham said, shifting the receiver from his right hand to his left and leaning forward against his desk. "Why not? She's your sister, isn't she?"

"Yes, you're right. She's my sister, and now she's a widow. That has to strengthen the bond between us."

"It was good of you to call her, Uncle Nachum."

"You've got it wrong. *She* called *me.*"

"Why? What happened?" Avraham closed his eyes. The sense of peace that had accompanied him to the office was dissipating rapidly. It disintegrated further when he heard his uncle say, "She wanted to talk to me about you."

Avraham stopped breathing. "Interesting," he said with a forced nonchalance. "I've suddenly become a V.I.P. I hope she said only good things about me?"

When the answer did not come immediately, Avraham continued in a jocular tone, "Well? What high praise did she have to say of me?"

"Actually — It's a little difficult to say that we praised you at all."

The Envelope / 49

"Oh? Have I done something wrong?"

His uncle shot straight from the hip. "Tell me, Avraham — what's your interest in those envelopes?"

It was all clear now. A new calmness descended on Avraham. Quietly, he asked, "She told you about them?"

"Yes, she told me. Listen to me, Avraham. Forget that whole business. Stop asking questions about it."

"Why? I find it fascinating!"

"Don't be cynical. Don't you see that it's infuriating your mother?"

"Not really," Avraham said. "I only noticed that it hurts her."

"She doesn't want you to continue digging."

Avraham leaned back in his chair again and said thoughtfully, "She never actually said that. She only said not to ask *her* any more questions. If she'd told me to leave the whole thing alone, you know I would have obeyed. After all, I've got to honor my mother's wishes. But she never asked me to do that."

His uncle sounded impatient. "You're splitting hairs, Avraham. What difference does it make how she put it? It's her intention that counts!"

"Exactly," Avraham replied. "And I'm not at all sure that she doesn't want me to learn the secret of those envelopes." He had made up his mind not to reveal to his uncle that his mother had already told him the story of his father and the envelopes.

"Your approach is a little twisted, Avraham," his uncle Nachum snapped. "I'd strongly recommend that you leave those envelopes alone."

"Why?" Avraham asked sharply. "What's going on?"

"Nothing. It's simply not worth your while."

"Why not? Do I stand to lose some money over this?"

"Not money," Nachum said. "You stand to lose much more important things. Digging into this matter is liable to damage you — yes, damage you a great deal. You, and your children. So why do it?"

"This is really becoming interesting. The question is, why should I agree after hearing only a few veiled words from you? Can you elaborate — provide some details?"

"I could," his uncle said slowly, "but I won't. Forget about those envelopes, Avraham."

"And if I don't?"

"I'll be fighting you every step of the way. Let that be very clear."

Avraham forced a light laugh. "Now I'm even more curious! So you have a personal interest in the envelopes?"

"If I do, that's none of your business. It's an old story and one that's well worth leaving in the past, where it belongs."

"An old story? What are you talking about?" When there was no answer, Avraham pressed, "Uncle Nachum, tell me — *What are you talking about?*"

Without realizing it, Avraham had shot out of his chair and was standing at his desk, gripping the receiver so hard that his knuckles were turning white.

"Yes," Nachum said. "An old story."

"From when?"

"Avraham, why are you shouting at me?"

"Excuse me." Avraham forced himself to speak more naturally. "I didn't mean to shout. But when did the story take place?"

"It took place at a time when your father was not so religious."

Stunned, Avraham groped for his chair and sank into it. His limbs were suddenly rubbery, devoid of strength. His throat felt strangled.

At last, he found his tongue. "Again. What did you say? My father wasn't religious? I don't believe it!"

His uncle realized he had said too much. "What, didn't you know?"

"No. I didn't know. And I don't know *now*, either. I'm not inclined to believe this."

From the other end of the line came a lengthy silence. Then Nachum said, "All right, so I didn't say anything. Forget it. Leave the whole business alone. I don't want you to interrogate me. I tell you, I'll sabotage any move you make in that direction."

"Uncle Nachum," Avraham said between his teeth, "it's much too late to take back anything now. What you said, you said. The words are out of your mouth. You must know the saying, 'Birds are trapped by their feet, and people by their tongues.'"

His uncle chuckled. "I'm not familiar with the saying, but I am very familiar with the reality."

"But what did you mean when you said that my father was not always observant? This is shocking news to me! Tell me!"

But Nachum was adamant in his refusal. "I will not discuss this topic anymore. Do you understand?"

"Do you know what you've just done to me?" Avraham persisted. It was all he could do not to shout at the top of his lungs.

"I can imagine." His uncle sounded truly sympathetic. "I'm sorry."

"I'll tell you. Last evening, after my mother's explanation about my father and the envelopes, I felt calm. Reassured. Now, you've opened a whole new can of worms about my father, may his memory be blessed!" Avraham paused, then said again, urgently, "What do you mean when you say he was once not so religious?"

"What?" Nachum almost shouted. "She told you the story of the envelope with the Arab?" It was clear that he was shaken to the core.

"Yes, she told us. So?"

"What, exactly," his uncle asked, recovering his wits, "did she say?"

Here was a chance to check whether his mother was telling them the whole truth, or if Rachel was right in believing that there had been some sort of concealment. Avraham said, "She told us about my father's compulsion to collect envelopes, because of what he went through in the war. You must know the story. Now, maybe you can explain to me how that can possibly harm me."

With the receiver pressed tightly to his ear, Avraham tried with all his might to gauge his uncle's reaction. His straining ear caught a light sigh of relief. But his uncle did not speak right away. The seconds ticked past as the connection held between Haifa and Tel Aviv. Finally, Avraham's patience was gone. He demanded, "Why won't you answer?"

Nachum cleared his throat. "I'm not answering you because — because — Well, all right. If that's what your mother told you, then —"

"Then what?"

"Then — Then she's told you the story. You know it all now."

Avraham was far from satisfied. "When did you and my mother talk?"

"Just now. Half an hour ago."

"I don't understand. She said *today* she was upset by Rachel's and my interest in the envelopes?"

"Yes. At least, that's the way it struck me."

"Did she say so explicitly, or did it only strike you that way?"

"Avraham, a little courtesy, please — I told you, we spoke in a general way. I don't recall every word. But that was the gist of the conversation."

Avraham would not relinquish his quest for clarity. "I want to understand. She asked you to say something to me?"

"Not in so many words. But from what she did say, I could tell that she was worried."

"Worried? Why?" Avraham was bewildered. "She herself had just told us the whole story!"

Another long silence ensued. Avraham could hear the rise and fall of his uncle's breathing.

"I don't understand!" Nachum burst out at last.

"Uncle Nachum?"

"Yes. I'm listening."

"Did — Did she really tell me the truth?"

Silence.

"Why aren't you answering me?"

Nachum Holtzer asked, "If your mother said something, do you doubt that it is the truth?"

"Tell me," Avraham pressed. "Are you prepared to confirm that what my mother told us was the true story of the envelopes?"

He could hear the constraint in his uncle's voice. "I repeat: If your mother told you the story, do you have any doubt as to its truth?"

"My dear uncle," Avraham said softly, "you are avoiding my questions. You are hiding something from me, and that makes me suspicious."

"I'm telling you again: Forget those envelopes — for your own good! And don't get me mixed up in all this."

"And should I also forget the disturbing news that my father was not always observant?" Avraham was bitter.

"Yes. I'm sorry that I let that out of my mouth. I pity you if you so much as drop a hint about that to your mother. I made a mistake. To my distress, I can't undo what I've done. Your father was a *tzaddik*. You should know that."

"But, according to you, not always."

"Hashem is the One Who judges people in the end."

"Uncle Nachum?"

"Yes?"

"You have totally confused me."

"Listen to me," Nachum Holtzer said forcefully. "The way out of this confusion is to forget the whole business. Let the events of the past lie peacefully in the past. Do you understand what I'm saying, Avraham? *For your own good!*"

Avraham did not answer. His head was beginning to ache. *My father was not religious? How can that be?* The words pounded like hammers at his brain.

Through the fog, he heard his uncle say, "Well, goodbye. *L'hitraot.*"

"Goodbye," he answered weakly.

A quarter of an hour later, Avraham stood up, quietly handed the file he had been working on to a colleague and, without a word to anyone, left the office and went home.

In their spacious kitchen at home, Avraham and Rachel sat in silence after forcing down a hasty meal. Rachel was stunned at the story her husband had relayed on his return from the office. Silence, for the moment, seemed the only response of which either of them was capable.

Stepping into the house after work in the late afternoon, Rachel had been surprised and worried to find Avraham home before her. Her two daughters were standing just inside the door as she walked in. As soon as they saw her, they whispered, "Shhh — Abba's asleep."

Anxiety had leaped into her heart all at once. "Since when?"

"He came home in the morning, even before Margalit left."

Margalit, their cleaning help, doubled as a babysitter on the days that Rachel went to work. Dropping her handbag on the sofa, Rachel asked, "And she left you alone?"

"What do you mean, 'alone'?" the girls asked. "Abba's here! Abba told her to go. He said he would look after us."

"And did he?"

The Envelope / 55

Giggling, her daughters said, "A little. He didn't feel like playing with us. And in the end, he said he was going to take a nap. He told us to play by ourselves and to be good girls and not make too much noise. So we didn't!"

The worry in Rachel's heart grew to gargantuan proportions. She went to the bedroom and quietly opened the door a crack. Her husband was lying on his bed, eyes wide open. Rachel's anxiety turned into real fear. Pushing the door open so that she could stand framed in the doorway, she demanded, "Avraham, what happened?"

"Nothing happened," he said, staring at a spot on the ceiling above his head.

"Don't you feel well?"

"I feel very well."

Rachel tried to control the disorderly flight of her thoughts. To get the information she desperately wanted, she opted for a direct question. "Well, then, why are you at home instead of at the office?"

"I wasn't in the mood for work. It happens, no?"

She stared at her husband. Through clenched teeth, she said, "Avraham!"

"What?"

"Please, tell me what happened. Talk to me!"

Avraham did not reply at once.

"Why won't you answer me?" Rachel asked. "What's going on? Why are you home?"

"I'll tell you everything. Just give me a little more time to rest."

Rachel hesitated, then decided to respect his wishes. She left the room, closing the door behind her. For a time, she immersed herself in housework and child care, but all the while her mind was spinning with different possibilities to explain her husband's odd behavior. Had he quarreled with his boss? With a co-worker? Or was he simply in low spirits because of the exasperating affair of the envelopes?

The phone rang just as Avraham was preparing to leave his room. Through the door, he heard his wife call, "Avraham, it's for you!"

"Who is it?"

"Your uncle Nachum, from Haifa."

Anger swept over Avraham. What did his uncle want now, after so casually destroying his peace just hours earlier? He leaped out of bed and walked rapidly into the living room. Rachel watched closely as he brought his mouth close to the receiver and snapped, "Yes?"

"Avraham, it's me. Uncle Nachum."

In the same impatient tone, Avraham said, "I'm listening."

"Look, Avraham, I know you're angry at me."

"That's certainly possible."

"I wanted to apologize — and also to warn you one more time."

"I'm listening," Avraham said again.

"No," insisted his uncle. "I don't think you *are* listening. Please, put aside your anger for a minute and listen to me. I made a mistake this morning, and I apologize for it. I hope you'll forgive me.

"So much for the apology. Now, for the warning.

"This morning, I mistakenly mentioned the fact that your father was not always as religious as he later became. You should know that he was never completely unobservant, heaven forbid. It's all tied in with those envelopes."

"How?" Avraham asked quickly.

"I'm warning you: Any investigation you make into their contents will only harm you. Be satisfied with what you already know, and leave the rest alone. I say this for your own good, Avraham. I felt a need to tell you one more time, because I don't know if I emphasized it enough this morning."

Avraham breathed deeply. After a moment, when he felt able to speak, he burst out, "Apology accepted. But, as for the warning — No."

Without a "goodbye" or a pause for his uncle to react, he replaced the receiver gently in its cradle.

Rachel came quickly over to his side. She had been intently following the conversation. "Was it because of your uncle that you came home early?"

"Yes!" Avraham threw the word over his shoulder as he made his way to the kitchen.

Rachel followed. "What's going on?"

Avraham waited to tell her the story until after they had eaten. The meal was short and silent, as each sat sunk in his or her own thoughts.

The Envelope / 57

Now, after hearing her husband's account of the two conversations with his uncle, Rachel was confused.

For that matter, so was Avraham. He had not yet gotten over the shock wave that had engulfed him at his uncle's unguarded remark about his father, and it seemed to him that Rachel shared his feelings. Presently, she stood up and began to prepare coffee. In silence, she waited for the water to come to a boil in the electric kettle, then poured it into two mugs.

"I want to understand," she said. "What did he mean by saying that your father was once not religious? I simply don't understand."

"Believe me, I want to understand, too. Nothing seems the same to me anymore. I never knew a more pious man than my father. And now — this bombshell!"

"It's no contradiction," Rachel pointed out, as she sat down with her mug between her hands. "In the past, he wasn't so religious. Later on, he returned to Torah. There are lots of *ba'alei teshuvah* these days." She paused. "But maybe Nachum was just talking. Maybe it's not even true?"

"Impossible," Avraham said flatly. "You should have heard my uncle when he realized that I didn't already know what he'd just told me. He wouldn't have called back to apologize, either, if it wasn't true."

"So how do you explain it?"

He shrugged. "I told you: I have no explanation."

"Especially the fact that the story is connected somehow to the envelopes," Rachel continued, intent on her own train of thought. "What's the connection?"

"How do I know?" Avraham asked bitterly. "Before I discover the connection to the envelopes, I first want to learn what the whole thing means. Naturally, I won't ask my mother. She'd be insulted." He turned to face his wife. "Rachel, I don't want you to ask her either."

Rachel nodded. She understood on her own that she was forbidden to interrogate her mother-in-law. Sipping her coffee, she murmured, "A cloak-and-dagger business!"

Avraham said nothing. Raising his mug to his lips, he found it empty. He rose to fix himself another cup.

"Avraham?"

"What?"

"Let's put aside, for the moment, the bombshell about your father's religiousness in the past. Do you remember my telling you last night that I suspected your mother wasn't telling us the whole truth about those envelopes?"

"Do I remember? And how!"

"Good. Because now I know what made me suspicious."

"What?"

"You told me that you saw your father's handwriting on one of the newspaper clippings — the one describing the terrorist's death, I can't remember his name —"

"Abu Daou —"

"Never mind. 'The names of the wicked shall rot,' even if I don't remember them. Anyway, you told me that you found the words '*Baruch Hashem*' written there, in your father's handwriting. That means that he was personally rejoicing in the terrorist's downfall. Why? What possible link could there have been between the two men?"

Avraham made a dismissive gesture. "My father was in Auschwitz. He would rejoice at the death of any evil person."

Rachel shook her head in disagreement. "No matter how hard your mother tried to convince us that the whole business was tied up with some quirk of your father's because of his experiences in Auschwitz, that still doesn't explain why he focused specifically on that terrorist. That's strange, isn't it?"

Privately, Avraham admitted that his wife had pinpointed the source of his own doubt. He added, "And now, these phone calls from my uncle. They only add to the confusion. How do we find our way out of this maze?"

Rachel made an abrupt and unexpected turnaround. "Avraham, I'm getting fed up with this whole business. Maybe we should leave it alone, as your uncle suggested? Maybe he's right, and it really will hurt us? I wish you'd never found that envelope!"

"After my uncle's call," Avraham replied firmly, "I am not about to leave anything alone! It was Heaven's will that I find those envelopes."

"Why?"

"That," he said, "is something we'll find out only at the end."

They recited *Birchas HaMazon*. Rachel washed the dishes, while Avraham strode into the living room. He looked out the large window facing the street, which lay dark and quiet at this late hour of the evening. A single car moved slowly up the street. Its headlights momentarily lit the trees that lined both sides of the street. When it was gone, darkness returned. For some reason, the street lamps were not working tonight.

But Avraham saw none of it — not the passing car, nor the fleeting light, nor the returning darkness. What he was viewing in his mind's eye was the image of his father. His chassidic father, a soft-spoken man who tried to confine the lion's share of his talk to Torah topics. Though he had not been a brilliant scholar, a *sefer* was never far from his hand. All the conversations he had with Avraham, his only son, had been liberally laced with Torah insights and fear of Heaven. He would speak with Avraham warmly, patiently, telling him tales of his childhood in Poland and of the *rebbes* his own father had taken him to visit.

Sometimes, though, his father had been remote, lost in reflections of his own. At those times, it had seemed to Avraham that a black cloud hung over his father's head. He had attributed these dark moods of his father's to the memory of the terrible times in Auschwitz. But perhaps there had been something else behind his father's silences? Something mysterious? Avraham pressed his forehead to the cold windowpane. His breath fogged the glass so that he could not see through it.

He stood there long moments, in restless reverie. *My father was not a chassidishe Jew in the past? He was hardly religious at all? And it's all tied up with those envelopes? How can this be possible?*

All at once, a new thought struck with the force and speed of summer lightning. Avraham whirled away from the window. He stood frozen, turning the idea over in his mind. How had he not noticed this detail before? He might just have found the door that would lead him to some important truths. Jubilantly, he snapped his fingers.

Avraham walked back into the living room, calling aloud excitedly as he went, "I've got it!"

Rachel raced out of the kitchen. At the sight of her husband's sparkling eyes, she stopped short. "What happened?"

Avraham began to pace the living room, one hand kneading his forehead as he went. She heard him mutter, "Where is my common sense? How could I not have thought about this before?"

Curiosity made Rachel impatient. "Tell me already! What's going on?"

Avraham stopped in front of an easy chair near the small coffee table, and flung himself into it. Absently, his fingers moved a bowl of fruit first to the right and then to the left. He glanced up at Rachel. "Sit down."

She sat in the facing armchair.

"Listen," he said earnestly.

"I'm all ears," she assured him, tension making her feel coiled as a spring. "Well?"

Avraham extended one hand as though about to explain a difficult concept in *Gemara*. "Do you remember when I sat *shivah* a couple of weeks ago?"

"How could I forget?"

"During that time, people came to call, right?"

She nodded, at a loss. "Okay, so when are you going to tell me something I *don't* know?"

"You came to my parents' home in the evenings, when the men were *davening Minchah* and *Ma'ariv*, right?"

Her patience was stretched to the snapping point. "Yes, yes, true! What's this all about? Tell me already!"

"On Tuesday of that week, did you happen to notice the men who came to see my mother and me?"

She was silent for a moment. Squinting at the ceiling in an effort to remember, she said slowly, "I think so."

"Who was there?"

Surprised, she asked, "What's this? Are you testing me?"

Urgently, he leaned forward. "Who was there?" he repeated. "The solution is right in the palm of our hand! Wasn't there something unusual in their appearance?"

She breathed deeply, a certain nervousness creeping into her voice. "Avraham, I don't understand what you want from me. How were they strange? Was there a third eye in the middle of their forehead? Did they walk on their hands? Tell me what you're trying to say!"

But Avraham was going to go about this in his own way.

"You knew my father, right?"

She gripped her fingers tightly together, as though to control herself. "Yes. A little."

"Those men, the ones who came that Tuesday night — they weren't exactly my father's type of friends, were they?"

Wonder spread over Rachel's face. "How do I know your father's friends? Avraham, I don't understand your riddles!"

Without warning, Avraham sprang to his feet and began pacing again. Rachel's uncomprehending gaze followed him around the room.

"You're right about that. But, if you recall, after we *davened Ma'ariv* that night, a few people remained to sit with my mother. They spoke very animatedly to her."

"Okay, if you say so."

"You still don't get it? Didn't you notice that nearly every one of those people was either completely secular, or nearly so?"

Rachel relaxed slightly. "Yes, I noticed. So what?" Her manner made it clear that she was inwardly wondering, "Is this all?"

Avraham strode closer, taut as a soldier poised for combat. He continued his pacing a short distance from Rachel's chair, speaking rapidly. "What do you mean, 'So what'? Don't you see a problem here? How did those people know my father? How do they know my mother so well? They were speaking with her as though she were an old friend. And don't you remember that, as they were leaving, they whispered to me, 'You had a good father — a real personality!'"

He whirled around to face his wife. "I ask you — how did they know him? From the Palmach? From shul? From the beach? My father, who from my earliest memory hardly ever set foot out of Bnei Brak, and for whom even going into Tel Aviv to attend to important matters was a real burden. My father, who for many years — up until his death — went to work every morning, then returned home directly from there to eat and rest a little before going out to the *shtiebel* for his *daf yomi shiur* and *Ma'ariv*. That's the way it was, day in and day out! So, where, pray tell, did he come into contact with those people? How did they meet? And may I repeat that my mother seemed to know them quite well, too?"

Avraham stopped to catch his breath. His speech concluded, he waved his arms and asked dramatically, "Well, what do you say to that? How do you explain it?"

Rachel had noticed that the visitors Avraham had just mentioned, both men and women, had been irreligious. They certainly had not fit the mold of the other Bnei Brak visitors who came to comfort the grieving widow and her son. At the time, she had filed away the impression without thinking about it. And Avraham, it appeared, had done the same thing — until now.

She stirred in her armchair and asked, with feigned nonchalance, "You ask what I say? I say nothing. And do you know why? The thought has just occurred to me that perhaps those people were colleagues of your father's from work!" She shrugged.

Avraham waved away her suggestion. "I know my father's co-workers well. These people were not them!"

"All right, Avraham. Let's get to the point. What have you found?"

Slowly, Avraham sat down once more. He was suddenly spent. Quietly, and with emphasis on every word, he said, "I think that, with all the pain, the solution to the riddle lies in what Uncle Nachum said."

"Meaning?"

"I think Uncle Nachum is right. As much as I'd like to believe otherwise, I've come to the conclusion that those men and women were friends of my parents from an earlier time in their lives. From the time when they were apparently not so observant. It's hard for me to digest this knowledge. I can't imagine my parents living in such a different way. But it seems they did. There's no other explanation."

Rachel was disappointed. "That's your big revelation?"

"No! That's not it. That only leads up to what I've discovered. Why won't you understand?"

"I really don't, Avraham."

"Then let me explain. Those people are the key to the problem of the envelopes. I told you that Uncle Nachum said the envelopes are related to an earlier time, when my father was not so religious. Therefore, maybe those people know something that can help us unravel this mess that's been dumped in our laps."

"Very nice!" Rachel nodded approvingly. "Now I see. Logically, it seems sound enough. But can I ask a question?"

"Of course! What is it?"

"How, exactly, do you plan to track them down? Will you ask your mother for their names and addresses?"

A practical question — and a provocative one. Avraham was at a loss. "Of course not," he replied. "That's all I'd need."

"Then what will you do?"

With a gesture of helplessness, he answered, "I agree, it's a problem."

Rachel laughed. "In other words, you haven't found a thing."

"Of course I have! I found a direction for our investigation."

"I heard that already. So, we have a direction. What I want to know is: How do the Rosenbaum detectives continue their investigation?"

Avraham fell silent. After a moment, Rachel stood up and returned to the kitchen to finish her cleaning. Presently, Avraham rose, too. He resumed his pacing through the living room, lost in thought. Yes, Rachel was correct. She had brought him down to earth with a thud. He had found a lead, but not the way to capitalize on it. How to reach those people? What were their names? Where did they live? Where, exactly, had they known his parents? Had it been abroad? In the war, or the D.P. camps? And who could put him in contact with them? He knew with a certainty that his mother would not perform that kind deed. Uncle Nachum, then? Should he call Haifa and ask? But even as the thought crossed his mind, Avraham had to chuckle dryly: His dear uncle help him in this matter? Foolish hope!

He paused at one corner of the room, where he found himself facing a framed portrait of the Chazon Ish. *Were he still alive, I'd ask him what to do,* Avraham mused. *The Chazon Ish had sound advice in every area. Would he have advised me to drop the whole thing?*

Avraham clenched his fists. What should he do?

He walked into the kitchen and sat down without a word. Rachel continued to wash the dishes. Avraham listened to the soothing flow of water into the sink, and the clink of cutlery. The savory smell of soup cooking filled his nostrils. He tried to clear his mind, yet no answer to his problem presented itself.

"Well," he said, rousing himself at length. "What do you think, Rachel? What do we do?"

"I don't know. Maybe we can somehow get your mother to tell us who those people were?"

Alarmed, Avraham said, "I already told you — not a word to my mother! I'm not at all sure we behaved properly in pressuring her the other night."

Rachel turned off the flame under the soup and began to methodically dry and put away the clean dishes. "I didn't mean to suggest that we ask her directly. I meant a casual conversation, drifting from one topic to another, in the hope that the information we want will emerge naturally, on

The Envelope / 65

its own. After all, we have to go visit her, don't we? I offered to help her prepare the meal in honor of the *siyum mishnayos* on the *shloshim* for the men in your father's shul. That's in two weeks. I'll be spending many hours in her company then. Maybe she'll tell me something."

"Two weeks? That's a long time!"

Rachel smiled. "What are you afraid of — that the Arab terrorist will escape from his envelope? Remember, he's already dead."

Reluctantly, Avraham nodded. He saw the force of her argument. Suddenly, his eyes lit up. "Rachel, you're going to laugh at me when I say 'I've got it!' again. But I've got it!"

"Well? What is it now?"

"You're the one who solved the problem for me. You showed me the direction to take — without even meaning to!"

She took a deep, calming breath. "Avraham, I have no more strength tonight for long, pointless talks. Just tell me what's on your mind."

"You mentioned the *siyum mishnayos* in my father's memory."

"Well?"

"Two of the men who came to the apartment that Tuesday night, though dressed in a very modern fashion, also wore yarmulkas. I'm not sure whether or not they're religious, but I did hear them undertake to learn a *maseches* of *mishnayos* for the elevation of Abba's soul. They wrote their names, addresses, and telephone numbers on a paper that was placed on the table by the front door. I remember one of them saying to me, with a half-smile, 'We still remember how to read those small letters. In your father's honor, we will learn.' I'll go to Bnei Brak, get those names and addresses, and go see those men!"

"Do you think your mother will like that?"

"What do you mean? I have to call each person on that list to find out whether he's fulfilled his learning commitment, don't I? There!" He sat back, beaming. "The solution!"

Rachel considered, then nodded. "It sounds good."

"The best ideas come without trying."

Avraham stood up, put on his jacket, and headed for the kitchen door.

"Where are you going?" Rachel called.

"If you don't mind, I'll go see my mother now."

"But we were planning to visit her tomorrow night!"

"True — but I'm too impatient to wait. I want to check that list today. My mother will be happy to see me. She won't suspect a thing."

"Wishful thinking."

He grinned ruefully. "I know. But I'm really too restless to wait. This whole business is beginning to wear me down. Goodbye!"

Minutes later, he was in his car, heading to Bnei Brak.

"**H**ell-o-o-o! What a surprise!"

A broad smile broke on Mrs. Rosenbaum's face — a smile not untinged with speculation. She opened the door wide and Avraham stepped inside.

"I hope, Imma, that the surprise is a pleasant one?"

"What a question!" she responded instantly. "But you were supposed to come tomorrow evening, weren't you?"

"True. But that doesn't mean that I couldn't drop in for a quick visit tonight as well."

The expression on the mother's face changed to one of concern. "Has something happened to bring you here?" She gazed penetratingly into his eyes, as though to ferret out some secret lurking there.

Avraham remained calm. "No! Everything's fine, *baruch Hashem*. I came because I wanted to come."

Hesitantly, she asked, "Maybe you came because you had another question about those envelopes?"

"You'll be happy to know that, on that topic, I have no further questions to ask you. You already told us the story." He grinned. "Don't be so suspicious, Imma."

Mrs. Rosenbaum *was* suspicious. To keep her son from sensing this, she averted her gaze. After Avraham and Rachel had left her apartment, she had not felt at ease. Despite the spur-of-the-moment explanation she had concocted to satisfy their curiosity, she was left with the sense that her son and daughter-in-law were not satisfied. While she had not lied to them, a little voice told her that they did not believe she had told the whole truth. In that case, they would certainly not desist in their investigations.

She walked to the living room, smacking herself lightly on the forehead as she went. "Why am I like this?" she asked aloud. "What a bad mother I am! My only son comes to visit, and I ask him annoying questions. Please, Avraham, sit down. A cup of coffee or tea?"

Avraham sat at the table, hands folded before him. "You are certainly not a bad mother. You're allowed to ask me anything you want, Imma. I even understand your suspicions, after our conversation yesterday. In fact, I'd like to apologize — on my own behalf and on Rachel's. She feels uncomfortable after what happened. It was because she cried that you told us the story. I hope we're forgiven?"

Mrs. Rosenbaum walked slowly to the table and sat down opposite her son. "Is that why you came tonight?"

"No — Well, maybe that, too."

"What nonsense! Do you think I don't understand what happened? It's simple! After you told Rachel about that envelope with the Arab, it was clear that something like this would happen. I don't know exactly how you told her, but once she informed me that it was affecting your health, I had to tell you the story behind that envelope." She leaned forward. "Now, tell the truth, Avraham: Don't you feel better knowing that there's nothing to it? Nothing at all? When I caught you with the envelopes that day, I simply wanted to protect your father's memory. That was all!"

She breathed deeply, casting an apologetic look at him. "I don't think it was necessary for you to tell Rachel about the envelopes. And what have you gained from knowing the truth? Nothing!"

Avraham did not reply. All through their dialogue, all he could think about was his uncle Nachum's revelation about his father's past. It gnawed at his brain, demanding further information. But how to get that information? Asking his mother directly was out of the question. He sensed the vehemence with which she was trying to drive home the explanation she had already offered for the presence of the envelopes. Apparently, in her heart, she knew that he and Rachel did not fully believe her.

After a short silence, Mrs. Rosenbaum tilted her head and smiled. "Well, will you drink something with me? Let's have some coffee."

Avraham waited as she prepared their drinks. They sipped the hot brew in silence. It was some minutes before she spoke again.

"Avraham."

"Yes?"

"You just said that you have no further questions to ask *me* about the envelopes. Does that mean that it's only me you plan to stop asking, or that you have no more questions on the subject at all?"

Avraham set down his coffee cup. His mother's unease flowed to him across the table in strong waves. At all cost, he must restore her peace of mind.

"*Oy*, Imma, how you jump on every word I say! I said I have no more questions. Period."

She smiled. "That's not exactly what you said. But you're right, it's not important. Let's not talk about it anymore."

With a quiet nod, Avraham said, "All right."

They raised their cups once more. On the surface, the quiet was companionable. But every so often, as they drank, their eyes would lift and meet for a confused instant before scurrying away again. The silence grew slightly oppressive.

Suddenly, Avraham broke into a grin. Irresistibly, without knowing quite why, he said, "Look, Imma. I do have another question. It just occurred to me. May I ask it?"

His mother was taken aback. Recovering with remarkable haste, she said, "Certainly. What's the question?"

Avraham cleared his throat. "You explained the envelope thing to us, but I'm still a little curious about that couple in the photographs — in the other envelope. A couple that looks fairly irreligious. Who are they?"

Shock passed through Mrs. Rosenbaum, strong as an electric current sweeping through her body. For a moment she sat stricken, as though paralyzed. She had not been prepared for this question. Instinctively, she lifted her hand and clutched at her heart.

Avraham could see the powerful emotion that coursed through his mother. In an effort to spare her, he continued quickly, "Is it Abba's brother, who was killed in the Holocaust? Abba told me about him once."

The words acted like a tonic to revive his mother. "Yes, yes, yes — it's his brother, Yankel! Yes, you're right!"

Avraham stared at her in astonishment. There was something here he did not like. His mother's reaction seemed to him to be overdone and artificial.

And then, without warning, a frightening thought popped into his head. *Maybe that couple in the pictures were my own parents, in their past life? According to Uncle Nachum, there was a time when both of them were not very observant.* Now it was his turn to suffer a sense of shock. He longed to take up the photographs and study them carefully, to search the young, secular faces of the man and woman for traces of a resemblance to his own elderly father and mother. But he didn't dare ask his mother to let him see the snapshots again.

He began to have second thoughts. *Impossible!* he said to himself. *Those people can't be my parents. There was a little girl in the pictures, and I have no sister. So maybe it actually is my uncle, killed in the war? But then, why did Imma react so strangely when I asked her?*

"Avraham?"

"Yes."

"What are you thinking about?"

"Nothing. Foolishness."

"Tell me anyway."

"They're just aimless thoughts, nothing special."

She eyed him thoughtfully. Then, unexpectedly, she said, "You know what? Your uncle Nachum, from Haifa, was here today."

Avraham stopped breathing. His mother continued, "He told me he had a talk with you."

The blood was pounding in Avraham's veins with the force of hammer blows. Carefully, he set down his empty cup and asked, "Did you ask him to speak to me?"

"No. I only told him what happened here last night."

It seemed to him that his mother was enjoying his confusion. Or perhaps that was only the impression of his distorted imagination. He no longer trusted his own thoughts.

"What did he actually talk to you about?" Mrs. Rosenbaum asked.

"Oh, this and that. I'm an orphan now, remember?"

She sighed. "I understand." Without another word, she picked up the two coffee cups and carried them into the kitchen. Avraham followed her, seating himself on one of the kitchen stools.

"Well, then," his mother said, her back to him as she stood at the sink. "Why *did* you come tonight?"

"Abba's *shloshim* is coming up in two weeks."

"Have you come to remind me of the date? You can be sure that I remember it very well on my own."

"I didn't come to remind you about anything. I came because I want to remind other people about something — to remind those who made commitments to learn *mishnayos* in Abba's memory to actually do the learning. I want to phone them, and I need the list where they wrote their names and numbers. That's all."

"And you?" Mrs. Rosenbaum asked. "Are you learning?"

"What do you think?" he asked, insulted.

"And this couldn't wait until tomorrow?"

"I suppose it could have. I don't know, I just decided to pop over now." He waited, but she said nothing. After a moment, he asked, "Can I have the list?"

"No."

"Why not?" He was surprised.

"Because Uncle Nachum said that he would make the calls. He took the list with him to Haifa."

It took all of Avraham's inner resources to keep his face expressionless. Inside, however, he remained in turmoil. *Heaven itself is fighting me!* he thought in anguish. His uncle, he knew, would not divulge the information contained in that list. And who knew whether he had not taken it deliberately, in order to keep the secret of the envelopes.

Through his pain, he heard his mother say, "Why should you care if he makes the calls?"

"Who said I care? Let him do it."

Had his mother sensed his distress? And, even more worrisome — how was he going to go about trying to solve the riddle of the envelopes now?

The ringing phone at his elbow suddenly shattered the stillness. Wearily, Avraham reached out his hand to answer.

vraham brought the receiver to his ear and whispered a quiet hello. His mother watched him.

"Hello," a voice answered. "Is this the Rosenbaum residence?"

"Yes."

Mrs. Rosenbaum stirred uneasily in her chair. For an instant, she seemed about to snatch the receiver from her son's hand. Then she settled back, watching Avraham's face intently.

"Who is this speaking?" the man at the other end asked.

"This is Avraham. Avraham Rosenbaum. Do you want my mother?"

Mrs. Rosenbaum held out a hand for the phone, her impatience evident.

"Ah! Avraham!" the voice exclaimed. "I remember you as a baby. You were a cute child."

Embarrassed, Avraham grinned. The voice was not familiar. "Thank you," he said. "Who is this, please?"

His mother stood up and gripped his arm.

"This is Yaakov Eiloni, from Ramat Gan."

The name, too, was unfamiliar. "Do you want my mother?"

"Yes," Eiloni said. Then he added, "Actually, maybe you can help me. Afterwards, give the phone to your mother and I'll say hello."

"All right."

"Look, I was one of the people who came to the house when you were sitting *shivah*. Do you remember?"

"Give me the phone!" Mrs. Rosenbaum whispered. Her grip on Avraham's arm tightened.

Avraham neither heard nor felt her. Every particle of his attention was riveted on the man's voice. "I don't remember you," he said carefully. "I don't know to whom I am speaking."

There was a brief silence. Then the man said, "You're right. How could you know? The point is, I undertook to learn *mishnayos* in your father's memory. But I have a problem: I don't remember which *maseches* I said I would learn. Maybe you can recall who I am; I spoke to you just before I left the house, and signed my name on the list. I said that I still remembered something of those small letters — meaning, *mishnayos*. Do you remember?"

Avraham remembered. "Yes. Now I can visualize your face. I know who you are." It was the man with the secular appearance, the one he had mentioned to Rachel. Avraham had seen him signing his name on the *mishnayos* list, and the other man must have noticed the expression of surprise on his face. That was why he had whispered those words in Avraham's ear. "*I still remember how to read those small letters.*"

"I'm sorry to disappoint you, Mr. Eiloni," Avraham said now, "but the list isn't here. I will let you speak to my mother. Goodbye now."

He handed the phone hurriedly to his mother. His eyes were closed; he did not want her to witness the gleam of triumph they held. Inside, his heart was doing a merry jig — even merrier after the stab of disappointment when he had heard that his uncle had taken away the list. Yaakov Eiloni from Ramat Gan! He engraved the name in his memory. It held the key to everything he sought to know.

And the name had come to him so unexpectedly, he mused, without any planning or forethought on his part. To teach him — to teach him what, exactly? He recalled reading a book once that dealt with the subject of trust in Hashem. The book had said that Hashem's salvation always comes from an unexpected source and not through man's efforts, in order to teach us that everything comes about through Divine intervention. What more blatant example than what had just happened, during his impulsive and unplanned visit to his mother's home?

Avraham broke free of the web of emotion that held him transfixed, and began paying attention to his mother's end of the telephone dialogue with Mr. Eiloni. From the tenor of the conversation, he gathered that they were old acquaintances. Where and when had they met?

His mother replaced the receiver in its cradle. She forced a smile. "Well, Avraham, do you see? People are taking their learning commitments seriously on behalf of your father. *Baruch Hashem*!" Despite the cheerful words, a faint sigh escaped her lips.

"*Baruch Hashem*," Avraham echoed quietly.

He left shortly thereafter, wishing her a good night and reminding her that he would return for a visit the following evening, perhaps with the children this time. Then he was on the road, driving through the night in the direction of his home in Petach Tikvah.

※

"Were you successful?" Rachel demanded as he walked through the front door.

His eyes sparkled. "Yes. A miracle happened!"

Bewildered, she asked, "Reading some names on a list — that's a miracle?"

"The list wasn't in the apartment at all."

Rachel, he saw with satisfaction, was taken aback. He had succeeded in surprising her.

"What? Has she hidden the list along with the envelopes?"

"No, she didn't hide it." Avraham took pity on her confusion. "Uncle Nachum came to see her this morning — and took the list of those who promised to learn *mishnayos* to Haifa."

Rachel groped for a chair. Things were taking too quick a turn, and each one was more disturbing than the last. "I don't believe it! I simply don't believe it. What's going on here? That man, your uncle, seems to have made up his mind to fight you on every front when it comes to investigating this mystery. It's — it's frightening!"

"Not necessarily," Avraham objected. "It's entirely possible that my uncle took the list without any intent to stop me at all. Maybe he simply decided to help my mother by phoning the men on the list and reminding them of their commitments. It's hard to believe that he deduced ahead of time that I'd come for that list to find someone from the past who will talk to me." He shrugged. "It seems highly unlikely."

"And I," Rachel said with a vigorous shake of her head, "think that he deliberately took that possibility into account! When you declare war on someone, you take everything into account, even the remotest possibilities. You have to consider everything." She paused for air. "I tell you, I'm sure he considered the fact that the list is a source of information for you. In my opinion, he is *very* interested in stopping you cold. He's no fool, your uncle."

"I know." Avraham thought about what she had said. After a few moments' reflection, he said, "Maybe you're right." His spirits grew slightly less ebullient.

"Of course I'm right! And do you know what? I'm going to jump one step ahead. I'm going to propose that he has the envelopes, too!"

Avraham removed his hat from his head and slung his jacket over the back of a chair. His hand lifted in a dismissive gesture, reminiscent of his mother's. "Come on. That's going too far."

Rachel argued, "You have to start suspecting everyone and everything. Didn't he more or less issue a declaration of war?"

"True."

"He told you explicitly that he was going to do everything in his power to keep the information you want away from you?"

"Yes!"

"And this happened after your mother told him what happened when you found the envelopes?"

Avraham hesitated. "It seems so."

"Then think a minute, and you'll come to the same conclusions that I have."

Avraham considered, then shook his head. "You're exaggerating, Rachel. We're not talking about a world war here. You're adding a lot of drama and color to a simple incident. After all is said and done, they have no way of knowing how I feel inside because of these little secrets. They can't possibly see the envelopes in the same light as I do. So, please, calm down a little."

She laughed. It was skeptical rather than merry laughter. It faded away as she said suddenly, "But tell me this: If you never managed to see the list, then what did you accomplish tonight? You said a miracle happened."

"Yes — it was a miracle! Divine intervention, at the very moment when I needed it most."

"Tell me already!" Rachel's patience was running out.

"Just when I was feeling completely discouraged, the phone rang. It was some man from Ramat Gan. His name is Yaakov Eiloni."

Avraham told his wife about the conversation he had had with Mr. Eiloni. She listened attentively. Then she smiled, and said, "Heaven is helping you."

***

The next morning, before Avraham left for his office, Rachel asked, "What happens next?"

Avraham kissed the mezuzah and pressed the button to summon the elevator.

"What do you mean?" he asked. "The first thing I'm going to do when I get to the office is call him and let him know that I want to speak with him right after work, face-to-face. I don't like to discuss sensitive issues over the phone."

"Very nice! You don't think you're already too late?"

"What do you mean?"

"I mean that your uncle Nachum is going to get to him ahead of you. I'm instinctively a suspicious woman, and I believe that your mother must surely have called your uncle by now, to tell him that you came for the list and that Eiloni called and gave you a lead about where to find him. Do you really think that Uncle Nachum won't warn Eiloni off? Avraham, you've got to at least consider the possibility."

The elevator arrived. Avraham did not enter it. He stood lost in thought, unmoving. Privately, he had to admit that, in his enthusiasm, he had not entertained his wife's suspicion. It was a valid one. He felt a pang of irrational anger at her for bursting his bubble. The cold water of her doubt was dampening his ardor for pursuing the investigation.

The elevator waited another minute. When no one entered, its doors closed and it moved on to a different floor. Walking slowly, Avraham turned and reentered his own apartment.

"What's the matter?" Rachel asked in alarm.

"Nothing's the matter. You're right. I'll call Mr. Eiloni right now, from home. It's 7 o'clock in the morning; I hope he's awake."

Rachel smiled. "He's probably up and learning the *mishnayos* he promised."

Without answering, Avraham began riffling through the phone book to find the number he wanted. He dialed. At the other end, the phone began to ring.

"Mr. Eiloni?"

The voice that answered was gravelly and hoarse. "Yes. What do you want?"

"This is Avraham Rosenbaum. Did I wake you?"

"I'll answer with the punch line of a well-known joke: You didn't wake me, I had to get up to answer the telephone, anyway."

"Oh, I'm sorry. Please forgive me."

"Your apologies won't help me now. What brings you to call so early in the morning?"

"I wanted to come see you in Ramat Gan. May I?"

The man cleared his throat, and some of the hoarseness left it. "Now?"

"No, of course not! I thought of coming later this afternoon, at about 5 o'clock — after work. Is that possible?"

After a slight hesitation, Eiloni answered, "All right. What did you want to talk to me about? I'm curious."

"That's for later, not over the phone. I'll come and talk with you in person." Avraham paused. "By the way, did you find out what *mishnayos* to learn?"

"Yes. Nachum told me. It's *Maseches Makkos*. We had a long talk last night."

Avraham's heart sank. Keeping his voice deliberately light, he asked, "Did you talk about me at all?"

"What does that matter?"

A moment later, they said goodbye and hung up. Rachel studied her husband's face. "What happened?"

"They had a long talk last night, the two of them."

"Who?"

"Uncle Nachum and Mr. Eiloni."

"About what?"

"I don't know. 'A long talk' was all he would say."

"What," asked Rachel, "do they have to talk about for so long?"

"That's exactly what I want to know," Avraham said with feeling.

11

The hands of the clock stood at precisely 4 p.m. when Avraham walked out of his office on Achad Ha'am Street in Tel Aviv. He did not, as was his habit after leaving work, head directly for the nearest bus stop. Instead, he made for the Palatin taxi stand on the same street.

He stepped into a taxi which had been waiting at the curb, and seated himself behind the driver. As the taxi pulled out to merge with passing traffic, Avraham became aware of a definite tension building up inside him. The tension was making it difficult for him to breathe. Now that he was about to meet Yaakov Eiloni face-to-face, he found himself unaccountably nervous. What would emerge from their conversation? What would he learn, at last, about his father?

Various scenarios flitted through his mind. They ranged from Eiloni's full cooperation, to his refusal — overt or subtle — to pass on so much as a crumb of information that might help Avraham advance toward his objective. At one point, Rachel's image intruded on these thoughts. Just before he left for work that morning, she had said, "Listen. I have an idea."

The Envelope / 83

With one foot literally out the door, Avraham had little patience. "Well? What is it?"

"I have the day off today. How about if I go to the Beit Ariella Library in Tel Aviv?"

"To do what?"

"To study old newspapers. I'll look for some connection to that Arab terrorist — what was his name? Abdul something?"

Afraid that he would miss his bus, Avraham had almost snapped, "Abu Daoud al-Razak!"

"I'm terrible with names."

Avraham's fingers went to the elevator button. "What do you think you'll find out about him?"

"How do I know? Maybe one of the papers 'eulogized' him after his death. Maybe the articles include some biographical details that will help us understand how he merited the honor of being included in your father's envelope." Rachel shrugged. "What have I got to lose?"

"Your day off!" Avraham answered flippantly as he stepped into the elevator. Just as the doors closed, however, he called, "But you know what? Go ahead and try. You're right. Maybe you will find something."

Now, sitting in the moving taxi, he remembered the morning's brief dialogue. He glanced at his watch. It was 4:20; Rachel was undoubtedly home by now. Had she unearthed any treasure in her library search? His curiosity over his wife's efforts mingled with curiosity over his own upcoming talk with Eiloni. Together, they combined to form a web that clogged the furiously spinning wheels of his mind.

The driver lifted his eyes to the rear-view mirror to see his passenger. "Look here, we've been driving for five minutes. There's the 'Bimah,' on our right. Where do you want me to take you? I asked you three times already, but you haven't answered!"

Avraham started. "You're right. I've been thinking about something and didn't hear you. We're going to Ramat Gan."

"Thank you," the driver replied sarcastically. "But *where* in Ramat Gan?"

"Ah, yes." Avraham was angry with himself for being so scatterbrained, when he needed right now to focus all his mental energies. He glanced quickly at a page in his pad where he had jotted down the address. "Here it is. Ramat Gan, 74 HaRoeh Street. Excuse me, I'm a little confused at the moment."

"Okay, okay, I understand. You're the lucky one; you can be confused if you want. If a driver gets confused, he's apt to cause an accident." Avraham offered no response to this. After a short pause, the driver added in the philosophical vein beloved of cabbies worldwide: "Actually, everyone is the driver of his own life, no? And confusion and distraction can cause accidents in life itself, can't they?"

Avraham was not listening.

"Am I right, or not?" the driver demanded in a louder voice.

Aroused from his thoughts, Avraham said hastily, "Ah, yes, sure. You're absolutely right. One hundred percent!"

"Did you even hear what I just said?" Without waiting for an answer, the driver did him the favor of repeating his words of wisdom. "I said that every person is the driver of his life, and that distraction and confusion are liable to cause accidents in his life. Do you get it now?"

Avraham finally absorbed the words he was hearing. "Aha! Is that what you said? You are definitely right. You have no idea just how right."

Avraham stood on the doorstep, collecting himself. For a fleeting instant, he reviewed the events since his father's death that had brought him to this particular doorstep in Ramat Gan. There was so much he needed to learn if his life was ever to feel normal again. Resolutely, he lifted a finger and jabbed it at Eiloni's doorbell.

He was intensely aware of his own ragged breathing, very different from its usual measured rhythm. Soon the door was opened. Yaakov Eiloni stood in the doorway.

Avraham recognized him now from his week of mourning. He thrust out a hand. "Shalom."

"Shalom, shalom," Eiloni said, shaking it. "Come in, please."

Avraham's heart sank. Eiloni's grip was cool and his smile lackluster. There was certainly no welcoming warmth there that Avraham could see

The Envelope / 85

— none of the friendliness that Eiloni had exhibited at the house of mourning a few weeks earlier, when he undertook to learn *mishnayos* for the sake of the departed.

It must be because of the talk he had with Uncle Nachum, Avraham thought with a touch of panic.

Eiloni led the way to a small living room cluttered with old, heavy furniture. The sofa was plush but musty, the cushions faded with age. A large rug, frayed at the edges, was spread at their feet. Eiloni was wearing a yarmulka on his balding head, obviously in honor of his guest. The yarmulka constantly moved around on his head and Eiloni, with fumbling gestures, kept trying to anchor it more firmly.

Avraham cast a swift, curious glance around the room. On the wall were portraits of Theodore Herzl, Chaim Weizmann, Ben-Gurion, and other figures from the early years of the State. Not far from the television set was a small bookcase. Avraham did not see the *Rambam* anywhere on its shelves, or a *Chumash*, or any sign of a *Shas*.

This was a friend of my father's? he thought incredulously, and with real pain. The incongruity was almost impossible for him to accept, either with his mind or his heart.

"Please, sit down," Eiloni invited, gesturing at an armchair.

"Thank you." Avraham sank into the soft cushions. *This,* he thought, *is not going to be easy.*

Eiloni sat down in an armchair facing Avraham's, and finally allowed a small smile to touch his lips. "Well, what does the son of R' Elimelech Rosenbaum, *alav hashalom,* whom we all loved, want today?"

Avraham straightened his back. "That's exactly what I want to know. Who is 'we all'?"

Eiloni straightened as well. Surprised, he said, "What does that matter? All of us!"

"Look, Mr. Eiloni. My father died suddenly. As his only son, I want to learn everything I can about him. I am simply curious to — to know him better."

He paused. Then, inhaling a lungful of air, he continued, "Everyone tells me, 'Your father was a *tzaddik!* Your father who we all loved!' I know that he was a *tzaddik* and well loved. But I want to hear more. May I?"

Nodding, Eiloni said, "Certainly, certainly." He seemed to be thinking of something else.

"It would give me great joy," Avraham said softly, "if you'd tell me about my father."

Eiloni was not quick to respond. His eyes were glued to a spot on the rug that covered the living room floor almost wall to wall. Avraham's own gaze was riveted to Yaakov Eiloni.

In a low voice, Eiloni said, "I don't know anything special to tell you." There was a brief silence, as though he was considering his own words. Then he said, more firmly this time, "No. Really, I don't remember anything special."

He lifted his eyes to meet Avraham's, spreading his hands in a gesture of futility.

The atmosphere in the small living room was strained. *This is all Uncle Nachum's doing,* Avraham fumed inwardly. He was convinced that it was Eiloni's talk with Avraham's uncle, the night before, that had caused this sudden backing away. Eiloni had been so friendly on the phone. To come so close, only to be thwarted again!

Avraham persisted, "Tell me something, anyway! Where did the two of you meet?"

"We met! What difference does it make where?"

"Was it before World War II?"

"No. No, it was here, in Israel."

In despair, Avraham saw his chances of gleaning some information from Eiloni dwindling to zero. Uncle Nachum, true to his word, was setting every obstacle in the way of his finding out what he wanted to learn. Avraham decided to gamble everything on a single throw of the dice.

"They tell me that my father was once irreligious. Is this true?"

Eiloni almost jumped out of his chair. He threw his guest a furious glance. "I don't understand you! What are you trying to say — that your father was not a *tzaddik?* Huh?"

"Heaven forbid, Mr. Eiloni. I just wanted to know whether my information is correct."

Eiloni dismissed this. "Correct, incorrect! What does any of that matter after a person is gone? Are there no *ba'alei teshuvah* in this country? So your father was irreligious in the past, or nearly so. So he lived in Ramat Gan and not in Bnei Brak. So what?"

Avraham's heart stood still. Very carefully, he asked, "My parents lived in Ramat Gan?"

From the expression on Avraham's face, Eiloni realized that he had slipped up. "What? You didn't know?" Avraham shook his head. "Well, you didn't hear it from me. Remember that!"

"What did I hear from you?"

"Nothing!" Eiloni shrugged with frustration. "*Ach*, I don't want to discuss this with you anymore. Your uncle was right."

"Right — how?"

"Right about this."

"What's 'this'?"

Eiloni struggled out of the armchair with amazing agility for a man his age. "Don't ask me any more. I won't answer you. I'm sorry that I told you something you didn't already know."

"And I thank you for that. I know that my uncle Nachum has turned you against me. What did the two of you talk about?"

"Why does that matter to you?"

Avraham stood also. He had a thousand additional questions, but it was clear that this fruitless interview was at an end.

Avraham's self-control was nearly gone, too. In a stiff voice he thanked Eiloni for his time. He wanted to leave the apartment before something really unpleasant happened.

※

Rachel was at his side almost before Avraham was inside his front door.

"Well? What happened in Ramat Gan?"

Avraham walked in slowly. "I need a little time to calm down. Tell me first about your day. Did you learn anything at the library?"

"Why do you need to calm down?" She examined her husband carefully. Patience had never been Rachel's strong point.

Avraham's answer was tinged with annoyance. "Do me a favor. I asked for a little time. Why the interrogation?"

"All right," Rachel capitulated with good grace. "I'll tell you first. Your terrorist was a junior officer in the Fatah organization. No one special. Small fry, as they say. He lived in Shechem, where he managed a mediocre hotel. His Fatah assignment was to draft men for various local terrorist activities. Stealing weapons from Israeli soldiers, damaging Israeli vehicles passing through Shechem, things like that. Nothing spectacular. He was killed — you already know how. You read that in your father's article."

Avraham was disappointed. "That's all?"

"Yes. That's all, more or less. It took me ages to find a newspaper that had anything about him at all." She threw him an assessing look. "And you? Have you calmed down yet?"

"I suppose so."

"What did you find out?"

"Nothing! I went to see Eiloni, and our conversation was very unpleasant. Uncle Nachum apparently got himself involved. I learned only one new fact. My parents did not always live in Bnei Brak. They used to live in Ramat Gan."

Rachel listened to this information without any immediate reaction. Then, all at once, she jumped up and cried, "I forgot. I completely forgot!"

Avraham was startled. "What did you forget?"

"A fact that seemed unimportant — until now. A fact that just may be the missing link we're looking for!"

"What is it?" Avraham demanded.

"I forgot to tell you that, after the Six Day War, Abu Daoud al-Razak was a waiter in a Ramat Gan restaurant."

"In *Ramat Gan*?"

"Yes. And your father also lived in Ramat Gan."

Avraham willed himself not to get too excited. In a maddeningly calm voice, he asked, "So what? Lots of people live in Ramat Gan."

The Envelope / 89

"But maybe something happened between them. Maybe there's a link here?"

Abandoning his pretense at nonchalance, Avraham met Rachel's eyes in wild surmise. Scenes and possibilities, both probable and madly improbable, seized their imaginations. They fell into a deep silence that lasted the rest of that night. Both husband and wife were entertaining thoughts too profound, and too confusing, to be articulated.

It was 4 a.m. when Rachel awoke suddenly. One of the children was crying. Even in the dark, as she groped for her slippers, she sensed Avraham tossing and turning in the next bed, sleepless.

When she returned a few minutes later, she asked softly, "Can't you sleep?"

"No."

"Is something bothering you?"

"Yes."

"What is it?"

"What you told me about the terrorist — Abu Daoud."

Rachel was puzzled. "What was it? I don't recall."

"You must remember what you said. That Abu Daoud was a waiter in Ramat Gan."

"Ah, true. And your father lived in Ramat Gan at the same time."

"Yes. That's why I can't sleep."

The Envelope / 91

"But what is it, exactly, that's troubling you?"

Avraham was silent for a long moment. Rachel waited patiently.

"Look, I've been racking my brains," he said finally, "trying to come up with an answer to the question: Is there a connection between those two facts?"

Slowly, Rachel answered, "I see. It's painful for you to think of your father, the pious man you knew, eating in just any restaurant. But let's do a reality check. It seems clear that, at some point in the past, you father was not the G-d-fearing Jew that he was in the last decades of his life. Isn't this a real possibility?"

It was some time before her husband answered. "My father was a good man, down to his core. Even if he was secular, or nearly so, I don't think he would rejoice over another person's death simply because the man didn't provide him with good service at a restaurant. It just doesn't sit right with me."

"But isn't it true that fact is often stranger than fiction?" Rachel argued. "You have to admit that it *is* possible."

Avraham sat up and turned on his bedside lamp. "Then how do you explain the fact that my father became religious and moved to Bnei Brak? How do you see the two things connecting?"

"Who said there's a connection?"

"It's just a feeling I have."

"Based on — what, exactly?"

Silence.

"Avraham?"

"Yes."

"What is the possibility of our moving forward in this investigation?"

He shrugged. "I don't know."

"Let's figure out what we have right now."

"Very little," Avraham grimaced.

"Very little!" Rachel exclaimed. "I don't believe what I'm hearing! It's not 'very little' at all! Until very recently, you had no idea that your father was not always Torah observant, or that he had lived in Ramat Gan.

We've also discovered that Abu Daoud lived in the same city, and during the very same period. That's a lot, Avraham! It seems obvious to me that there has to be some link with the material in your father's mysterious envelope, the one dealing specifically with Abu Daoud al-Razak." She paused, fixing him with a challenging stare. "Tell me why, of all the Arab terrorist murderers, your father picked Abu Daoud. I'm sure they knew each other." She concluded on a note of triumph.

"Maybe," Avraham conceded. "The important question now is: Where do we go from here?"

Rachel was stumped. "I don't know."

With a tired smile, Avraham said, "Now you see why I can't sleep. I just don't know what to do next."

Two weeks passed. They were uneventful weeks. Rachel and Avraham did not discuss the topic that was uppermost in their minds. They appeared to have reached a dead end.

In their possession were a few crumbs of information, a smattering of fact amid a welter of speculation. They had no idea what to do with those crumbs. As he went about his peaceful daily routine — work, home, shul, *daf yomi shiur* — Avraham felt a gathering darkness in his heart. A black cloud of uncertainty hovered over him, accompanying him everywhere he went. It was extremely difficult for him to picture his father wearing anything other than his usual chassidic garb, the way he had during all the years Avraham had known him. It was next to impossible to imagine him as anything other than a G-d-fearing Jew. The conflicting images jarred and clashed in Avraham's brain, causing his head to pound.

Though he tried to act naturally at the office, his colleagues were quick to notice his preoccupation. "What's the matter with you, Avraham?" they asked. In reply, he merely shrugged and smiled. How could he tell them the truth?

In legends and fairy tales — but even more in real life — the unexpected always occurs, throwing open doors where none could previously be found. There was no reason why this law of nature should not apply to the young Rosenbaum family.

～•～

Friends and close acquaintances came flocking to the Bnei Brak shul on the thirtieth day after Elimelech Rosenbaum's passing. Avraham contemplated the assembled throng with new eyes.

Now, for the first time, he realized the unusual combination of religious and secular who had come to honor his father. There were two men with whom he exchanged only a cold "Shalom," the bare minimum required by politeness: his uncle Nachum, who had traveled from Haifa for the occasion, and Yaakov Eiloni from Ramat Gan. The two, he noticed, spent a considerable time in close conversation.

A respected Bnei Brak rabbi rose to speak. The meal, which the widowed Mrs. Rosenbaum had prepared with a good deal of help from Rachel, was elaborate. During the long hours they spent cooking together, neither of the women had broached the topic of the envelopes. It was as though the entire matter had been erased from their memories. Avraham, too, had maintained a strict silence on the subject, both with his mother and his uncle.

At length, the guests dispersed to their own homes. The family stayed behind to clean up. They finished the job amid desultory conversation. Avraham brought his mother a chair, and sat down beside her. Mrs. Rosenbaum looked at him and sighed.

"Tonight, during the *siyum*, I finally realized the extent of the tragedy that's happened to us. I thought I'd absorbed it. I no longer expect the door to open and see Abba walk in. And yet, I don't have the inner strength to go to the Ministry of the Interior to fill out the form for a death certificate. I just can't say the words. Do you understand? I just don't have the strength. I keep putting it off, day after day." She paused, her gaze beseeching. "Please, Avraham, take care of it for me."

Accordingly, on the following morning, Avraham went into Ramat Gan to visit the Interior Ministry branch on Jabotinsky Street. He waited quietly on the long line. When his turn came to speak to the clerk, he stated his need. The clerk brought his father's name up on the computer, asking Avraham for various identifying details. Then, unexpectedly, Avraham blurted a question of his own. "Excuse me. Can I have information on my father's former places of residence?"

Surprised, the clerk lifted her eyes from the computer screen. "What? You don't know where your father lived in the past?"

"I was an infant," Avraham explained, "when my parents moved to Bnei Brak. I was never particularly interested before."

"So what happened to change that now, when your father is no longer alive?"

Avraham shrugged. "I'm just curious, that's all. Also, I'd like to let his former neighbors know that he's passed away."

"You think they'll be interested after so many years?" The clerk sounded skeptical, but she ran her eye down the screen. "I see here that your parents moved to Bnei Brak over twenty years ago."

"I think their old neighbors *will* be interested," Avraham said stubbornly.

"Then why hasn't your mother told them?"

The question took Avraham by surprise. He had no ready answer. Anger began to smolder in him, and he had to struggle to maintain his equanimity.

"Miss, you don't have to tell me what I want to know. I asked you to do me a favor. You don't want to do it? So — don't!"

Now it was the clerk's turn to shrug. Her fingers continued to play over the keyboard. A few minutes later, she handed Avraham the death certificate. As he was about to turn away, she added, "Your parents' last address before their move to Bnei Brak was right here in Ramat Gan. They lived at 48 Bialik Street."

It was an effort for Avraham to conceal the emotion he felt at hearing this. Smiling broadly, he thanked the clerk. He left the building, but instead of heading directly to his office, he went toward Bialik Street.

In short order, he was standing across from the apartment building at the address he had been given, his eyes combing it from top to bottom. In his imagination, he tried to place his parents on one of the floors. It was a long time before he finally left the spot in search of a local restaurant.

The Envelope / 95

He walked up and down the block until, at last, he spotted a small, inconspicuous eatery tucked into a niche between two larger buildings across the street. It was possible that the restaurant served tasty food, but its owner clearly did not have very good taste in decor. It was an inexpensive place, a place that left no particular impression. In Avraham's opinion, it did not have the look of a kosher restaurant. It was hard for him to believe that his father could have eaten there.

He crossed the street. With a pounding heart, he approached the restaurant's entrance. A brief hesitation, and he was inside.

The owner, an elderly man whose hair was no longer black, was slicing bread with a large knife. He looked up at Avraham's entrance. "Hello, sir. We'll be serving lunch in two hours."

The man's voice was not particularly friendly. To Avraham's ears, there was even a tinge of suspicion there. He said quickly, "I haven't come to eat."

"What do you want here, then?" the owner asked impatiently.

"I wanted to find out whether you once employed a waiter by the name of Abu Daoud al-Razak."

Slowly, the restaurateur set down his knife. His dark eyes narrowed, then darted at his wife, who was standing to one side chopping cucumbers and tomatoes for a salad. Finally, he answered with an irritated, "Yes, yes, he worked here. Why do you want to know?"

Avraham shot out his next question. "And did you know a Jew by the name of Elimelech Rosenbaum?"

Another quick exchange of glances passed between husband and wife. The man said, "Yes, we knew him. Why do you care?"

Avraham felt distinctly uneasy. Still, he plowed on, "Was there any connection between the two of them?"

The glances that the restaurateur and his wife now exchanged were both startled and suspicious. The woman silently signaled her husband not to answer. Life experience had taught her it was better not to volunteer information where not strictly necessary. She turned to Avraham and stated flatly, "We don't know."

But her husband, at the same moment, said, "Yes, there was a connection. But who are you to ask about it?"

"I am his son!"

The other man's eyes opened wide in disbelief. There was apparently some genuine shock in his reaction. A painful thought darted through Avraham's mind: "What did my father do to make him react this way?"

The owner eyed him curiously. "I take it that you don't know anything, if you've come here to ask me." It was a question.

"I don't know a thing," Avraham confirmed. "My father died a month ago and he never told me."

Suddenly furious, the restaurateur shouted, "Don't know a thing! Then how did you know enough to come here to make inquiries? And you want *me* to tell you the story, after the damages I incurred? You get out of here — the faster, the better!"

He seized the long bread knife and waved it threateningly in Avraham's direction, walking toward him all the while. With a hasty backwards step, Avraham passed through the door to the sidewalk.

"The nerve!" the man sputtered to his wife. "Coming here to remind me about what happened when those two met! You know what? I'm sorry I chased him away. He ought to pay for those damages that his father caused here that night!"

His wife made a face, and turned back to her salad. "Let it be," she advised. "I don't want to remember all that. There are better things to think about, no?"

Still fuming, the man resumed his bread cutting, the knife flashing swiftly through the air with every slice.

Avraham stood frozen outside the restaurant. After a minute, he realized that he was trembling. He closed his eyes in an effort to banish the dizziness that suddenly assailed him. The scene in the restaurant played over and over in his memory, leaving his head aching. He groped for the wall with both hands and stood leaning against it, breathing rapidly.

When he had recovered enough to trust himself to walk, he began to wander aimlessly along Bialik Street. He noticed nothing of the elegant stores or the hurrying passersby. These, on the other hand, eyed him curiously before continuing on their way with a shrug. Like a menacing shadow, the image of his father kept intruding: bareheaded, or possibly wearing a tiny yarmulka, and behaving in some wild fashion in that tasteless restaurant.

Impossible! his mind screamed. *Not my father!* His heart felt as though it were breaking.

The traffic at the corner of Jabotinsky Street forced him to stop walking. He gazed at the traffic moving in the direction of Bnei Brak and

Petach Tikvah, and in the opposite direction toward Tel Aviv. The noise of their passage was deafening — to all ears except his, which were listening to other voices, strange and incomprehensible.

On impulse, he turned his back on the broad avenue and made his way back the way he had come, toward the restaurant. He stood on the opposite side of the street, staring at it. From that secure vantage point, he studied the place carefully.

It was a restaurant that attracted neither the eye nor the fastidious diner's interest. The front window was not especially clean, but it showed enough of the restaurant's interior: the small, square tables, the cheap wooden chairs, and the few customers eating there either out of habit or from some nostalgic connection to the Ramat Gan that once was.

And my father — the thought cut cruelly into his tired mind — *my father came here. For what? My father, so gentle, so fine, on whose nose a fly could feel secure because my father would never harm a living creature — my father caused this restaurant owner damages? How? Why? What happened here?* He stopped, struck by a new possibility. *Maybe it's all lies? It's just impossible!*

He did not know how long he had been standing there, anguished eyes glued to the dirty window. Ten minutes? Fifteen? Half an hour? Perhaps even an hour — he didn't know. And in all that time, the door had remained firmly closed, with no one either entering or leaving. "And my father had to come here and cause damages? Why? What happened to him that day? What caused it?"

Suddenly, the door opened and the owner stepped out. Avraham hurried away before the man could spot him. Walking to the bus stop was like stepping from the past into the present. Reaching the main thoroughfare, he caught the 51 bus to his home in Petach Tikvah.

It was only when he had descended at the stop near his apartment that he realized, in some confusion, that he was supposed to be at his office in Tel Aviv. The hour was just after noon.

He found a public phone. "Hello? This is Avraham Rosenbaum. Who's this? Leah? Good morning."

"Good afternoon, I presume you mean?"

"Yes," Avraham replied hastily. "You're right. Please give me Yair." Yair was the office manager, and Avraham's boss.

"Yair? Hello."

"Hello. How are you, Avraham?"

"Not so well, actually. That's why I called. I don't feel well, and I stayed home."

"Hmmm — did you make that decision just now, or this morning? Why didn't you call at the start of the day? It's 12 o'clock now, in case you don't have a clock nearby to inform you of that fact."

Humbly, Avraham said, "You're right. Really right. I must have dozed off and forgotten to call. I don't even know why. I'll be in tomorrow, please G-d."

"All right."

"Thanks. Goodbye."

"'Bye now. Feel better."

"Thanks," Avraham said again. He hung up.

His boss's "All right" had not sounded very promising to him. There was something in the way Yair had pronounced the words that troubled him.

With dragging steps, Avraham went home.

He was met at the door by the special peace of an empty house. Rachel was not yet home from work, and the girls were out for a walk with their babysitter. The place, for the moment, was his own.

Normally, this was something that Avraham relished. The peace and quiet allowed him to collect his thoughts, undisturbed. Today, however, he longed for someone — anyone — to walk through the door. He wanted someone to talk to, or even just to be around, in order to distract him from the painful and troubling thoughts that were making his head pound and bringing on feelings of depression. A month had passed since his father had left this world, and in that short time the image of his beloved parent had begun to change dramatically. Where would it all end?

On his way to the bedroom, Avraham passed the telephone. It lay innocently on its table in a corner of the living room. Avraham stopped short, staring at it. After a moment's hesitation, he reached out for the receiver.

For the space of perhaps fifteen seconds, he grasped the receiver in his hand, making no move to dial a number. Then, gently, he replaced it and went to his room.

He lay down on his bed. After a while, he realized that his pillow was damp. Tears, silent and slow, were trickling from his eyes. Avraham leaped out of bed as though he'd been bitten by a snake. Through clenched teeth he whispered, "I *will* call him!"

He grabbed the phone as though it were a wild animal ready to attack him. With shaking fingers, he dialed.

"Hello — Uncle Nachum?"

"Yes?"

"Uncle, it's Avraham!"

"Ah! How are you? Feeling better, are you?"

"No. I'm not feeling better at all."

His uncle's voice dropped. "What do you mean?"

"I mean that none of you wants to tell me about my father. And what I already know is making me absolutely miserable. Do you understand?"

"Maybe. But what do you want from me?"

"I want you to tell me everything that happened, everything you've been hiding from me! I don't want to remain with what I know today, because it's leaving me with a negative image of my father. My father wasn't like that!"

"That," Nachum said, "is why I told you to leave the whole matter alone. Now look what you've done to yourself!"

"I'm not at all sure that it was I who did it to myself. Maybe it was you who did it, when you decided to keep the secret from me."

His uncle fell silent. A tense silence sang along the telephone wire between Haifa and Petach Tikvah. At last, Nachum asked slowly, "Tell me, Avraham, what have you learned that has upset you so much?"

"I learned from you that my father was once irreligious."

"No, I didn't say that. I just said that he was much less religious. Please be precise."

"All right. Apart from that, I found out that he once lived in Ramat Gan."

"I know."

"Of course you know! You told Mr. Eiloni not to talk to me."

"Well —"

"And I know that my parents lived at 48 Bialik Street."

"How did you discover that?"

"That's not important," Avraham said impatiently. "And I also found out that Abu Daoud al Razak used to work at a nearby restaurant, and that my father, *alav hashalom*, caused some damage there."

Deeply shaken, Uncle Nachum tried to make light of the information that his nephew had uncovered. "Avraham, you're incredible. You ought to take a course in police detection and go professional! It's a pity to let such talent go to waste."

"Incredible?" Avraham almost shouted. "You're calling me incredible, when I'm all broken up! What else am I supposed to feel when my father, whom I loved and respected, turns out to be a wild guy who rampaged through restaurants?"

"No. Heaven forbid! Calm yourself, Avraham. I want you to remember him the way you've always known him. He was a *tzaddik* — a noble man. That was his true identity."

"Yes, but you've got to tell me what happened. I must know! My life is no life if I don't know the truth. Why can't you understand that?"

Nachum sighed. "Avraham, you're wasting your energy. I'm not going to tell you a thing. And I urge you again to cease your investigations — for your health's sake. I told you once before that it's not worth your while to delve into the past. I told you that it would only hurt you — and it has. Leave it alone."

"But half the truth is worse than knowing all of it."

"Maybe. But you're not going to hear anything from me."

Avraham breathed deeply through angrily dilated nostrils. The hand that was holding the receiver tightened until it hurt. "Then what do I do?" he asked with controlled softness. "Go on with half the truth dangling in front of my eyes for the rest of my life?"

"Forgive me, Avraham," his uncle said. "I'm afraid that's your problem. But I will tell you this, to make you feel a little better: The story ended by making your father a greater person."

Avraham implored, "Then please tell me about it, and we can put the whole thing behind us!"

"No! It's not good for you — period!"

Abruptly, the connection broke off.

Avraham stared at the receiver in his hand. Then he let it slip slowly from his fingers, until it dangled and twisted at the end of its cord like a man put to death by hanging.

Rachel returned home at 2 o'clock in the afternoon, to find her husband reclining in an armchair, totally spent.

"What happened?" she asked in alarm.

He looked up at her. "That's it. I'm finished."

"Finished? With what?"

"I'm dropping this thing. I can't go on any longer."

She sat at the edge of another armchair, facing him, and placed her handbag on the floor. "But what happened?"

He told her everything — about seeing his parents' former home in Ramat Gan, about the restaurant and the reception he had received there. He told her about the infuriating phone conversation with his uncle Nachum. "I can't go on any longer," he ended. "I'm finished!"

Rachel was quiet for several minutes. Then, decisively, she announced, "We *are* going on, Avraham. An unresolved issue is worse than one that is resolved, even if resolving it brings some negative consequences. The doubts that are eating away at your heart are much worse."

"But how," Avraham asked in despair, "do we go on?"

"I don't know. Maybe we'll hire a private detective." Rachel lifted her head in sudden decision. "And I'm going to talk to that restaurant owner. What was the exact address?"

Mrs. Rosenbaum picked up the phone on the third ring. "Good evening."

"Good evening. It's Nachum. How are you?"

"Ah, is it you? I'm feeling all right, *baruch Hashem*." A pause. "You can surely imagine how I'm feeling."

Hearing the deep sigh that accompanied the words, Nachum was silent.

Mrs. Rosenbaum continued, "So why are you calling? We spoke just this morning, didn't we?"

"Yes, we did. But I think we need to talk some more."

Mrs. Rosenbaum was taken aback. She had been in the kitchen when the phone rang, rinsing her plate and cup before retiring for the night. She sat down. "Has something happened?"

"No. *Baruch Hashem*, everything's all right. That is," he amended, "something *has* happened."

"Tell me."

"I beg you to stay calm when you hear what I have to say."

"*Tell me!*" She sounded half-hysterical.

"Do me a favor, Adina," her brother requested. "Try to calm yourself. Then I'll tell you."

Mrs. Rosenbaum felt as though she were about to lose her mind. Her imagination had already painted garish and frightening pictures across the walls of her mind. She groped for something, some clue, to help her guess what her brother had called to tell her. Finally, she managed to whisper, "All right. I'll be calm."

"Avraham is working. Working hard."

She was at a loss. "So that's good. Why shouldn't he work?"

"I'm not talking about his work at the office. I'm talking about his investigation into — you know what — what he discovered in the envelope."

"*Oy!*"

Weakness overcame her all at once. The receiver nearly fell from her hand. She gripped it with both hands, which were shaking noticeably. "What are you saying? What are you trying to tell me? What has he been doing?"

"What he's doing, I don't know. But he already knows too much."

"What does he know?" The question emerged in a moan.

"He knows that you lived in Ramat Gan."

Mrs. Rosenbaum breathed deeply, trying to calm her jangling nerves. She felt as though she had just been punched in the face.

"Adina? Do you hear me?"

"Yes," she answered feebly.

"He also knows the exact address of your home in Ramat Gan. From what he told me, I gather he's already seen the place."

Mrs. Rosenbaum's head was beginning to ache. The pain started at her temples and moved, powerfully and rapidly, to her forehead.

"Do you hear?"

"Yes." She closed her eyes, fighting the pain.

"He also knows that sometime in the past you were not so religious. At least, he knows you were not as religious as you've been all his life. Do you hear me, Adina?"

"I hear every word," she answered in a strangled voice.

"And he also knows what happened at the restaurant. He visited there."

"*No!* Don't tell me that!" The words burst out of her throat in a scream.

"I told you, that's what Avraham said. Yes, my dear sister — he knows."

A long silence weighed down the telephone wire. Mrs. Rosenbaum felt that she had come to the end of her endurance. "He — knows everything?" she stammered. "He knows what happened there?"

"I can't tell you that. He didn't give me details. But he knows."

Another silence. Mrs. Rosenbaum finally ended it by whispering, in a resigned way, "So what can I do?"

Her brother raised his voice angrily. "Are you aware that you are to blame?"

"*I'm* to blame?"

"Yes — you!"

She shifted her weight uneasily in the kitchen chair. "Why me? Why do you say that?"

"I keep telling Avraham to stop investigating. I tell him it's not in his best interest to keep digging into the past. That he's hurting his mother, hurting himself, and can hurt his children by trying to discover everything that happened. And do you know what his answer to me was?"

"What?"

"That you never asked him to stop being interested in this painful subject."

"So I'm to blame?"

"He says that you only told him not to ask *you* any questions on the topic. So he decided not to ask you, but to try to obtain the information through other means." Nachum paused, then added forcefully, "Do you know who I blame for being behind all this? The one who's pushing Avraham into this whole pathetic adventure is your American daughter-in-law — his wife!"

When Mrs. Rosenbaum didn't answer, Nachum pressed on. "You have to tell him plainly that you want him to stop investigating this matter, period."

"I can't!"

"Then why," her brother demanded, "are you making Avraham run around with his nose to the ground? Why not just tell him the whole story and be done with it?"

She responded with an incredulous, "*What?*" After a short silence, she added, "I can't do that. Why won't you understand?"

"I understand you very well. I just don't understand why you don't put your foot down with your son."

"I don't know."

"Well?" Nachum asked impatiently. "What *do* you know?"

"Nothing," she sighed. "I know nothing. Leave me alone for now."

The conversation ended there. Mrs. Rosenbaum hung up the phone, and then buried her face in her hands and wept.

Rachel traveled to Ramat Gan, where she located the restaurant easily enough from Avraham's description. Hesitantly, she pushed open the door and peered within at the decrepit place. The diners at the small wooden tables, few in number, turned to regard her with interest. It was very rare that an ultra-Orthodox woman was seen in that area of Ramat Gan — and certainly not in a restaurant whose *kashrus* was questionable.

Ignoring the curious stares, Rachel made straight for the cashier's desk. The person who manned it was clearly the one Avraham had told her about — the restaurant's owner. She walked up to him and said, "Hello. Are you Mr. Itamar Brinker, owner of this place?"

Suspiciously, he answered, "Yes. What do you want?"

"I'd like to repay a debt."

He wiped his hands on the dirty apron, once white, that circled his ample waist. Then, placing both hands on the counter and leaning slightly forward, he regarded Rachel narrowly. "You owe me money? You once ate here?"

"No," Rachel answered quickly. "This is my first time here."

"Then what's this debt that you're referring to?"

"It's my debt, and it's my father-in-law's."

The owner grew nervous. "Lady, I don't know what you're talking about. Tell me what you're trying to say."

At all cost, Rachel wanted to preserve an amiable atmosphere. Otherwise, he would certainly not be forthcoming with answers to her questions. Smiling, she said sweetly, "My husband came in here yesterday. He asked about one Abu Daoud al Razak, who worked as a waiter in this restaurant, and about his father, Mr. Rosenbaum. Do you remember?"

From his expression, it was clear that Brinker remembered all too well.

Quickly, Rachel continued. "From what he told me afterwards, I understand that his father, Mr. Rosenbaum, caused you some damage. Is that true?"

"It's true enough. He caused me damage."

Now Rachel's smile turned apologetic. "My husband's father is no longer alive. He died just one month ago. Did you know him?"

"Yes, I knew him. Get to the point!"

"My husband and I would like to pay those damages."

The owner's surly expression changed with dramatic suddenness. He broke into astonished laughter, saying, "Really, it happened years ago. Nonsense —"

"But —"

"You're not obligated to pay. Leave it alone."

"But I want to —"

"I told you, I'm not going to take your money! It's in the past. I've forgotten the whole thing."

"Please, let me explain something to you."

Grudgingly, the owner subsided. Rachel said, "First of all, you have *not* forgotten it — or you would not have gotten so angry at my husband yesterday. Apart from that —"

Brinker broke in brusquely. "Excuse me. Your husband came in and reminded me of that whole episode, so I got angry at him. Tell him I'm sorry, I didn't mean it."

"All right. Thank you, I'll tell him. But I want you to understand something. Religious people do not want to leave behind debts in this world.

We want my husband's father, my father-in-law, to be as pure and noble in the next world as his life was in this one. Do you understand?"

Rachel watched Itamar Brinker's face closely, waiting for his reaction. She wanted to discern, by his expression, whether or not he agreed with how she had categorized her father-in-law. This would tell her how he was regarded before he moved to Bnei Brak and so radically altered his lifestyle.

Brinker's face remained impassive. His eyes betrayed neither agreement nor opposition as he said, "Did you mention that your father-in-law has died? May his memory be blessed. Let's not talk about him, all right?"

Innocently, Rachel asked, "Was something wrong with him?"

Brinker's face was equally innocent. "Did I say that? Is that what you understood me to say?"

"No, no." Rachel beat a hasty retreat. "Forgive me, I must have misunderstood you. I hope I haven't insulted you."

"No, that's all right. I'm not insulted."

"I really just wanted to ask whether there was something wrong with my father-in-law when you knew him."

"Why would you think that? He was a good man."

It seemed to Rachel that these last words were forced. They did not seem to emerge naturally from Brinker. She took a deep breath; the moment of truth had arrived.

"Look, Mr. Brinker," she said. "I came here in order to pay you for the damages your restaurant sustained. What were those damages, exactly?"

Brinker rubbed his forehead with a calloused hand, a hand that had chopped innumerable salads and dismembered countless fowl. He chose his words carefully.

"He broke a chair. He also pulled a tablecloth off one of the tables and a number of glasses shattered." Brinker offered a faint smile. "That's all."

Briskly, Rachel took out her checkbook. "How much?"

"I told you that I'm willing to waive payment, but you keep insisting. You tell me that its important to you — a mitzvah — to pay your father-in-law's debts. All right. So you can pay — let's see — you can pay — one hundred shekels, say. Approximately."

Brinker's gaze glued itself to the check as Rachel filled it out. He noted with satisfaction that she made it out for 150 shekels. As Rachel handed him the check, he pretended to notice the amount for the first time.

"Thank you very much. I think you overdid it, but thank you."

Rachel put away the checkbook, then looked up at the restaurateur and said bluntly, "You agreed with me that he was a good man."

Busy folding the check and depositing it in one of his pockets, Brinker nodded. "Yes, certainly he was a good man."

"And a good man," Rachel whispered, "comes into a restaurant, breaks a chair and sweeps a tablecloth off a table, breaking some glasses in the process?"

Brinker stared at her. "I don't understand."

"It's a simple question. Why would this good man cause such damage?"

"He got into an argument with my Arab waiter. They argued hotly, and then Mr. Rosenbaum lost control and threw a chair at him. The waiter ran away and never came back here. In the end, he was killed in the Shomron hills. He was a member of Fatah."

"I know."

"That's what happened. And it can happen to a good man, too. No?"

"It depends what the reasons were behind it. What were they fighting about?"

Brinker's eyes widened. Suddenly, he felt as though he was undergoing an interrogation. He realized that this woman had come to milk him for all the information he could give her — just as her husband had tried to do the day before.

He asked, "You're Mr. Rosenbaum's daughter-in-law?"

"Yes. Why do you ask?"

"How long did you know your father-in-law?"

"I married his son four years ago. Why do you ask?"

"And in all that time, you never heard about the fight or the reasons behind it?"

"No. We found out only by coincidence, after his death."

"And his wife, the widow, didn't tell you?"

"No. She doesn't want to talk about it."

Brinker leaned forward. In a low voice, he asked, "And do you think it is ethical to investigate, after his death, something that your father-in-law wanted to keep hidden from you? If you don't want to honor his memory, that's your business. But I won't dishonor it by gossiping about him. Goodbye."

And Brinker strode resolutely away to tend to the two or three customers seated at his tables.

Rachel bit her lip. Without another word, she left the restaurant. When she stepped out into the street, she saw that evening had already fallen. Lights played in the store windows as she hurried away.

Avraham arrived at his office on time the next morning. The secretary called out to him as he passed, "Good morning, Avraham."

He stopped walking. "Good morning. What's up?"

"Everything's okay. The boss asked me to catch you the minute you walk in. He wants to see you right away."

Avraham was surprised. Wondering, he went to the manager's office and knocked on the door.

"Come in," Yair Peled called.

With a hesitant step, Avraham entered the room.

15

What could the boss want? As he entered Yair Peled's office, Avraham racked his brain for the reason behind this unusual summons. Peled did not, as a rule, interact with his employees. Most of his orders were issued by way of his personal secretary. Why, then, this unexpected request to see Avraham Rosenbaum first thing in the morning?

"Good morning, Avraham!" Peled sounded suspiciously hearty.

"Good morning," Avraham answered cautiously. He hoped he had managed to conceal the strain in his voice.

"Please, come in."

In the two years that Avraham had been employed at Mad-Kal, he had faced his boss in this way perhaps two or three times. Yair Peled, in charge of a multimillion dollar medical-supplies export business, knew how to maintain a proper distance between manager and employees. His office was lavishly furnished, with the intent of instilling respect in all who crossed its threshold. A brick-red carpet covered the floor from wall to wall, and the wood-paneled walls boasted vibrant Chagall reproductions. Most imposing of all were the room's dimensions: It was a long room, with an enormous desk strategically placed at the far end. Yair Peled sat behind this, unmoving, watching Avraham's approach. Anyone summoned to the manager's office would already be feeling slightly nervous; the endless walk across the room, under Peled's eye, was calculated to wilt even the most confident visitor.

At any rate, that was the effect it had on Avraham that morning.

"Please sit down," Peled said pleasantly. Avraham sat. Peled waited silently for a long moment, studying the young man seated opposite him. Avraham was obviously uneasy. His shoulders were slightly hunched as he waited for the other man to speak. Despite the fact that Avraham Rosenbaum was a religious person and he, Peled, was the product of a secular kibbutz, Peled liked him. He was a kibbutz boy who had fallen in love with the big city and the capitalist system of doing business.

The person responsible for this summons was Sigalit, Avraham's secretary. It was she who had told Peled about the feeling throughout the office that something was troubling Avraham. In fact, all his co-workers had noticed his preoccupation during these past few weeks. Avraham said little to anyone these days. He involved himself in his work, emerging at times to speak briefly before again withdrawing into himself. His eyes seemed distracted, and not all his answers — even those pertaining to the business at hand — seemed quite to the point.

No one had asked him for reasons. It all seemed to hinge on his father's unexpected death. Still, his reaction appeared exaggerated despite the fact that his father had not been very old. Was it natural to be *so* mournful, *so* broken?

Peled had listened to his employees, while discounting their worries. Time, he was sure, would gradually heal the wound. Avraham was doing his job adequately, despite his private pain. But when he learned that Avraham had simply failed to appear at work the day before, a red flag had begun waving in the wind. Peled's sense was that, far from improving, Avraham's condition was worsening. He did not know what stresses were taking place within Avraham's family circle, but as his employer he felt obligated to call him in for a talk.

Peled's aim, in this talk, was twofold. On one hand, he intended to ask Avraham, gently, what was troubling him. As the boss, it was his duty to show his employees that he was concerned about them. At the same time, however, he would drop a few well-chosen words to rouse Avraham to a renewed sense of his own responsibility to his workplace.

But watching Avraham seated opposite him, downcast and worried, Peled found himself speaking completely different words than those he had planned. He said, "Tell me, Avraham. Do you want to take a week off — or even two?"

Avraham lifted his eyes in astonishment. "But — why?"

Peled was taken aback. He cleared his throat and swept his eyes across his vast desk, as though seeking the right words for the young man facing him across it.

"I don't know, I thought I'd offer you a brief vacation. You look tired."

"No, no. I'm not tired at all."

"But you've been giving that impression. Apparently, your father's death has been difficult for you."

Avraham shook his head. "I don't think that the death of my father has impacted me any worse than other people are impacted by their parents' passing." He thought about it for a moment, then shook his head again. "No, I don't think so."

Peled leaned forward and asked bluntly, "Then what's going on?"

Avraham gave a small, nervous jump. "Who says anything is going on?"

"You!"

"Me? Has anyone heard me say a word?"

"That," said Peled, "is the problem in a nutshell. No one has heard you say anything. You've always been a friendly, lively, talkative fellow, but now you've become more and more quiet and withdrawn. Do you think people haven't noticed?"

In the silence that fell after he asked his question, Peled took out a pack of cigarettes and offered one to Avraham. Avraham made a gesture of refusal; he did not smoke. Peled took one for himself, lit it, and took a few puffs. Then he said, "I suggest a vacation. And not just any vacation — a trip to America. You'll be able to rest for a few days, and also represent our firm at the big pharmaceutical convention coming up soon. It's being held by the company that's come up with a new medicine to help Alzheimer's victims. Are you interested?"

"Thank you," Avraham said, inclining his head, "but I can't leave the country just now. Thanks, really. I just have to stay."

Yair Peled chewed on his lower lip. Avraham's refusal displeased him. He was not accustomed to having his suggestions brushed off in this fashion. It further annoyed him that he had no clue as to what was behind the refusal, and why his young employee felt he had to stay in Israel. He decided that the direct approach might be best.

"Tell me, Avraham. Why didn't you come to work yesterday? Why did you remember to call the office only at noon? Do you think that doesn't seem suspicious?"

Avraham was startled. No, it was more: He felt cornered. Yair Peled was waiting for an answer, and his expression told Avraham that there would be no evading him this time.

"I forgot," he said. "I simply forgot."

Peled crossed his arms across his chest. "That doesn't sound exactly normal to me, Avraham."

"I agree. I don't know. I — I'm going through a rough time."

"Because of your father's death?"

"No."

"Are you having problems at home?"

"Thank G-d, no!"

"Then what is it?"

Avraham straightened in his chair, took a deep breath, and looked directly at his boss. "If I thought you could help me, I'd tell you. But I doubt that. So I don't choose to talk about the matter."

He was surprised at his own temerity. At the same time, he felt a certain release. It was so confining to have to watch his words with his superiors all the time. How nice it felt to speak candidly for once!

Yair Peled fixed him with a steely glance. "Are you aware of how insulting you just sounded?"

"No. No, I'm not aware. But if I've insulted you, I take it back."

Peled drummed his fingers on the desk, and said, "Perhaps I *can* help you. How do you know I can't?"

"Okay," said Avraham. "Then, without asking me too many details, please let me know all the information known about a Palestinian terrorist by the name of Abu Daoud al-Razak, who was killed in the hills of Shechem a number of years ago."

Peled might have turned to stone. For a moment, he seriously entertained the possibility that the young man seated before him had lost his mind. What possible connection could Avraham have with a terrorist? Lunacy!

Avraham laughed. "Do you think I've lost my senses? No, I'm not crazy. I've just stumbled upon a crazy story and I don't know how to extricate myself."

"What's an Arab terrorist doing in your crazy story?"

With another bitter chuckle, Avraham said, "That's exactly the point that's been troubling me. I'd like to know that myself."

Peled tapped another cigarette out of the pack as he sought a way to end a conversation that seemed to have moved beyond his control. "I don't know anything about your story," he said at last. "But might I suggest that maybe — just maybe — the whole thing exists only in your imagination?"

"My wife is involved, too — as are my mother and my uncle. Ask them. I don't think they're all suffering from distorted imaginations."

Peled thought a moment. "You know what, Avraham? I'll find out whatever you want to know about him. Will that calm you?"

"I don't know. I'm not sure you can really help me find out what I need to know."

"Trust me!"

Avraham did not trust him. Prudently, however, he refrained from expressing this out loud. He suddenly recalled that he was facing his boss, toward whom he must behave in a polite and even humble manner. If Peled wanted Avraham to trust him, then Avraham must, at least outwardly, demonstrate that he appreciated that trust. Smiling, he said, "All right. I'll trust you."

Avraham had no idea how Peled might be able to help him. But his boss was kibbutz born and bred, he had served in the army, and he was wealthy. He must have connections. Who knew what might come of his efforts?

They parted warmly. No further mention was made of Avraham's taking a vacation. Peled was determined to free his faithful employee from the obsession that seemed to have taken over his life.

Every morning thereafter, Avraham made it his business to arrive at the office early. Each day, he hoped to hear his boss's voice calling from his office. Peled would be standing at his door, and he would motion for Avraham to come inside to hear the information he had been promised.

It did not happen for a full week after their talk. Avraham, on his part, never approached his boss with a direct question. He might have asked just how long he was supposed to rely on Peled to help him, but he did not — for the simple reason that he did not actually rely on him at all.

On Tuesday of the second week, the secretary, Sigalit, walked over to Avraham's desk and said, "I have a message from Yair."

Avraham looked up. "Yes?"

"He says that you should be in the lobby of the Hilton Hotel on Yarkon Street tomorrow at 5 p.m. You should be holding a copy of that religious newspaper — what's it called again?"

"*Hamodia*? *Yated Ne'eman*?"

"Yes, yes — *Hamodia*."

"Well, what's going to happen then?"

"Someone will approach you." Sigalit paused for emphasis, her eyes alive with curiosity. "I understand that he will be someone from one of Israel's security agencies."

16

Avraham arrived at the Tel Aviv Hilton at precisely 4:30 in the afternoon, one half-hour before the appointed time. He had been too restless to stay in the office another moment.

Curiosity gnawed at him: What would this meeting bring to light? In the past weeks, he had noticed that every fresh encounter provided him with some new information — while keeping the greater part of the puzzle concealed. He nervously awaited to see what new facts would emerge from his impending discussion with the stranger he had agreed to meet.

He walked into the hotel lobby, eyes already sweeping the place for a glimpse of a man who might be the one he was expecting. Most of the people were foreigners, tourists from abroad who were guests of the hotel. Uniformed doormen opened taxi doors for new arrivals: occasionally, some personage puffed up with his own importance, but more often a fresh group of tourists weary from their flight to Israel and looking forward to following the bellhops carrying their luggage up to their rooms. No one fit his preconceived image of the man he was slated to meet here.

Slowly, he crossed the ornate lobby. Prominently displayed under his arm was the copy of *Hamodia* that he had purchased before setting out for the hotel. After a few moments, he decided to hold it against his chest in an even more obvious way, in case the man was not able to identify him. While it was true that his religious garb set him apart from most of the others in the lobby, it did not do so in any definite way. There were others dressed as he was, though their foreignness was as clearly stamped on their faces as his own Israeliness was on his.

It was already 5:15. The man was fifteen minutes late. Avraham stopped patrolling the lobby and took up a stance by the broad front window overlooking the beautiful Mediterranean. The view did not soothe him at all. He crossed back to the hotel's front entrance, then began to cut back through the length of the lobby once more. His eyes, darting restlessly from face to face, betrayed the strain he was under.

Then, as he was walking past a grouping of armchairs, a middle-aged man folded the newspaper he was reading, stood up so that he blocked Avraham's passage, and very quietly asked, "Mr. Avraham Rosenbaum?"

Avraham swallowed. "Yes. It's me."

The two men shook hands. The man said, "Can we sit a little?"

"Certainly. You're the one who —"

"Yes. I'm the one."

"Can I know your name?"

"That's not important. I'm here because my friend, Yair Peled — your boss — asked me to speak with you. He explained what was troubling you, and after receiving the green light from my superiors, I agreed to come. That's all."

"Yes, yes," Avraham said impatiently. "But who are you?"

The man lifted a hand in a gesture of refusal. "Ah, it doesn't matter. For conversation's sake, you can call me Binyamin. I am from the G.S.S."

Though he had known this, hearing it from the man's lips made Avraham's pulse begin to race. "I understand," he said.

They sat down. For a long moment, they sized each other up. Avraham saw that the man who called himself Binyamin was holding a brown cardboard file. Irresistibly, the image of that other cardboard file, the one holding his father's envelopes, flashed though his mind. It was that file that had brought him here, to this moment, facing the G.S.S. man.

With a smile, Binyamin spoke first.

"Well, why are you so interested in a dead terrorist?"

"Strange as it may sound," Avraham said, "his life and death have had an impact on my own life."

"That *is* strange. What sort of impact?"

"I wish I knew. That's really what I was hoping to hear from *you*."

The other man looked taken aback. "From me? How's that?"

"I don't know," Avraham shrugged. "If you'll agree to give me a biographical sketch of his life, maybe I'll be able to pinpoint the detail that is connected to me."

Binyamin's lips were pursed in open astonishment. From Yair Peled he had heard that there was some unusual story here, possibly something truly out of the ordinary, that somehow involved the man seated opposite him. The G.S.S. man had agreed to meet with Avraham in the hopes of gleaning some new information which the G.S.S. could act upon.

Pleasantly, Binyamin said, "Look, Avraham. You must know that the G.S.S. doesn't give out information to just anyone who asks. I want to know if there is something specific that you wish to learn about Abu Daoud al-Razak."

"Yes!"

"What is it?"

"I am specifically interested in the period of time during he worked as a waiter in Ramat Gan."

Binyamin pursed his lips again, and murmured, "Hmmm — Interesting."

"What's interesting?" Avraham pounced on the word.

"Just — interesting!" Binyamin repeated with a smile. He did not elaborate.

The G.S.S. man opened his cardboard file and began to rummage through a batch of yellowing letters inside. Avraham's eyes followed his every move. At his elbow, a waiter materialized and asked, "Something to drink, gentlemen?"

"Water, please," Avraham said, not turning his head.

A few moments passed, filled with silence on Binyamin's part and escalating apprehension on Avraham's. Then Binyamin lifted his eyes to meet Avraham's, and said, "You're right. Al-Razak did work in a restaurant on Bialik Street in Ramat Gan, immediately after the Six Day War. Actually, it was at the end of 1967; that is, six months after the war."

Avraham made a rapid calculation in his head. "That would be twenty-two and a half years ago?"

"Yes, that's right. Twenty-two and a half years ago."

"How long did he work there?"

"As far as I know, just a few months."

Both men sipped mineral water from glasses the waiter set down before them.

"And did he really live in Shechem, the way I read in the newspapers after he was killed?"

"Yes. I see that you've done your homework on this subject. True, he was a resident of Shechem, where he managed a small hotel — his wife runs it now — as a cover for his Fatah activities." He paused. "Al-Razak's hotel business actually helped us with goals of our own." Binyamin did not explain this enigmatic statement, and Avraham did not ask.

"Was he already a member of Fatah back then, when he worked in Ramat Gan?"

Surprised, Binyamin demanded, "Why should that detail interest you? If you want to know, he was not a terrorist then. But why should that matter to you, either way?"

"Look, Mr. —"

"Binyamin."

"Binyamin. I'm groping in the dark. I'm trying every avenue I can find to solve a mystery. Why did he leave Ramat Gan?"

"Let's check."

Once again, the G.S.S. man looked through the papers in his file, which rested open on the small table before them. He glanced through page after page before suddenly nodding. "Yes, he left abruptly. One morning he simply did not show up for work at the restaurant, and never came back."

Avraham was finding it hard to breathe. The words emerged slowly, "Do you happen to know why? Why he left his job — and Ramat Gan?"

Binyamin observed the overwhelming stress in the younger man's features. An inner voice whispered that herein lay the crux of the whole matter. His intuition bade him to choose his words with care.

"It says here that he had a fight with one of the neighbors, who attacked him."

Avraham stopped breathing. He felt as though something had encircled his neck and was strangling him. *So the story is true!* he thought. *That restaurant owner did not lie to me or Rachel!*

Finally, with a visible effort, he asked, "What was the neighbor's name?"

"It says that his name was Elimelech Rosenbaum. Oh!" Binyamin sat up, amazed. "What a surprise! It's the same name as yours. That must be the reason the story interests you so much."

Frozen faced, Avraham managed to utter, "It was my father, *zichrono livrachah.*"

The astonished smile vanished from Binyamin's face, which grew instantly somber. "I see."

Some sort of block was preventing Avraham from framing the question that he most urgently wanted answered. Something within, some nameless fear, made him hold back from pursuing the answer. It was a long moment before he was able to force out the words.

"Maybe, maybe you also know what caused the quarrel between them?"

Binyamin glanced at his papers again. When he looked up at Avraham again, it was clear that he had stumbled across some information that carried a stunning impact.

"Your father never talked to you about this?" he asked.

"No. And if you do know, please have pity on me and tell me the secret — before I lose my mind!"

Avraham watched the other man, fearful that the scene with the restaurant owner was about to replay itself here in the plush beach-front lobby.

He was terrified that the G.S.S. man would refuse to reveal the facts that were weighing so heavily on Avraham's mind. His eyes implored Binyamin to answer.

Calmly, Binyamin sipped his water. He was not sure what to do. His file contained a secret, apparently, that this young man longed to know. He understood very well why Avraham's father had chosen not to tell it to him. The question was this: Was it proper to break the old man's silence, or not? Binyamin was not a religious man, but respect for the dead was an important value to him.

"Can you explain to me why your father never told you anything of this, all through his life?" he asked.

Avraham began to shift restlessly in his seat. Another moment, and he would explode. This man knew what had happened in the restaurant that day, and why. The questions that he was asking in place of providing the information were just a smoke screen.

"Please, I'm asking you, I'm begging you, don't do this to me! I don't know why my father didn't tell me. I just don't know! But now that I know part of the story, I must know the rest. *I must!* Do you hear me?"

People sitting nearby turned their heads at the sound of Avraham's raised voice, which ruffled the tranquil atmosphere of the elegant lobby. Avraham hung his head, ashamed of himself. At the same time, he was perilously close to tears in the expectation of seeing this man, too, get up and leave without telling him what he needed to know — why, in fact, his revered father had gone wild in a Ramat Gan restaurant.

A slight smile played over Binyamin's lips. "I never intended not telling you. I was simply interested in knowing how it happens that, until today, you've had no clue about this story."

"Don't know," Avraham answered tersely. It was impossible to be polite any longer.

"All right. According to the information we have, Mr. Rosenbaum demanded that al-Razak break off all contact with a certain young Israeli girl. When the Arab refused, the fight erupted between them."

Avrham reeled. This scenario had never entered his mind. Impatiently, he asked, "What was the girl's name?"

"Her name was Rivka. Rivka Rosenbaum. She was 19. Apparently, she was Elimelech Rosenbaum's daughter." Binyamin shot a swift glance through his papers, and added, "No, there's no 'apparently' about it. According to the information at my disposal, she was Mr. Rosenbaum's daughter. Is that what you wanted to know?"

Avraham's mouth hung open in shock. He felt as though the ornate ceiling had just collapsed in on him, brick after brick landing on his aching head. With uncomprehending eyes, he stared at the man who had released this thunderbolt.

"You — You mean — You mean to say that — she was a sister? *My* sister?"

Avraham's head suddenly drooped, as though his neck had lost its strength to hold it in place. Then, abruptly, he lifted it again and snapped furiously, "Impossible!"

Calmly, the G.S.S. man said, "If you are the son of Elimelech Rosenbaum, then we are talking about your sister. We are very precise about details, sir."

Avraham glanced wildly about the room. The lobby began to sway before his eyes, like a ship bobbing on an uneasy sea. First the tables moved, then the chairs, and then everything else! They danced in slow circles, with the people seated at them appearing first on top of him and then beneath him. And suddenly, the circles began to speed up —

In the first instant after they roused him from his brief faint, Avraham did not remember anything at all.

17

Binyamin stared into Avraham's ashen face in some consternation. With his unexpected revelation, he had shocked the younger man to the point of fainting.

While he believed that he had been correct in his decision to pass on the information, it occurred to him now that he might have broken the news a little more gently. He should have searched for other words with which to drop his bombshell. In fact, he should have proceeded with caution, pausing at every juncture to ask, "And what do you think about what happened in the restaurant? What could the quarrel have been about?" He might have used some of the psychological tools that help a person assimilate unexpected and traumatic information.

He peered at Avraham, who had begun to recover somewhat and had shakily resumed his seat. Unexpectedly, a doctor appeared at his side. Perhaps he had been sitting in the lobby, or else the management had urgently summoned him. Avraham threw him an embarrassed look. "Thank you, but I don't need medical help. I'm feeling better already." He smiled bashfully at the turmoil he had created and tried to gently wrest his wrist from the doctor's grasp. The doctor was trying, in vain, to take his pulse. "I'm really better," he whispered.

"What happened?" the doctor asked briskly. He wore a professionally impassive expression; it was not for him to show any reaction to the fact that a man had suddenly fainted in a crowded hotel lobby. "Are you diabetic? Do you suffer from low blood sugar?"

"No," Avraham said with a sad sigh. "I'm suffering from the opposite — from something quite bitter."

The doctor merely glanced at him with the same guarded expression and did not ask what he meant. Having ascertained that Avraham's pulse was in order, he released Avraham's hand. The brief examination was concluded with a terse, "Take care of yourself."

"Thank you, doctor," Avraham smiled. "*Baruch Hashem*, I feel all right."

The few gawkers who were still standing around realized that the show was over. They returned to their own seats, to their drinks and the conversations that the episode had interrupted.

Avraham turned to face the G.S.S. man who was sitting, ill at ease, in his own armchair. The smile Avraham gave him was that of a beaten man, a man resigned to his fate.

"Do you really feel okay?" Binyamin asked with concern.

"Do you expect me to feel fine, after the bomb you just unloaded on me?"

"I'm sorry. I didn't mean to upset you like that. But you did pressure me to tell you."

Avraham's voice softened. "It's all right. You don't owe me an apology. I wanted the information, and I appreciate your telling it to me."

"But look what it did to you!"

"True. Of course I feel strange. I'll have to come to terms with this new reality, which is bound to change my life in some ways. But without knowing, I think I would have gone out of my mind."

A profound stillness fell between them. Avraham picked up his half-full cup of mineral water and took small sips from it. His eyes closed of their own accord as the thoughts whirled and flapped through his agitated mind. He suddenly saw his parents in a different light. All at once, he understood the lengthy silences that had sometimes fallen in their presence, and remembered how much those silences had bothered him as a boy. He had always assumed that it was memories of the Holocaust that were causing those brooding spells. Now, at last, he knew that there were other, more recent, reasons for their pain. The war was behind them, but a daughter who had run away with an Arab was with them every single day. Now he understood why his mother had burst into hysterical tears at the sight of the envelope he had unearthed in his father's desk.

They were good parents, his departed father and his mother, may she live long. Very good parents. His father, may he rest in peace, had invested a great deal in his, Avraham's, upbringing. Perhaps even too much. Even after the age of 18, Avraham had been required to let his parents know exactly where he was going and with whom when he left the house. Now, at last, he understood why. Their failure with their daughter had brought about this anxious attitude with regard to their son.

A new thought struck him. Had it been that tragedy that had led them to do *teshuvah*? To flee Ramat Gan, where such a misfortune had occurred?

And what about her — Rivka? Avraham was seized with an inner trembling.

As these thoughts passed through his mind, he sat silently, eyes closed. Binyamin watched him closely. The G.S.S. man could well imagine the storm raging in the young man's heart. He knew when it was time to be still.

At length, Avraham stirred and opened his eyes. He looked confused for a moment, as though he no longer knew where he was. Seeing Binyamin, he regained his hold on reality.

"Can I ask you something?"

"Fire away."

"What happened next?"

"Next?"

"What I mean is, where is she today?"

"Who?"

"She. The one you told me about."

"Ah. You mean your sister."

Avraham hesitated. It was still difficult for him to say the word. "Yes."

"She? She followed him, to Shechem. Left home after the fight, and went with him."

"And today?"

"She married him. They lived in Shechem. What your parents' relationship was with her afterwards, I don't know."

Avraham said nothing. He could imagine what the relationship was, if his parents' complete silence on the subject of his sister was anything to go by. They had simply erased her from their lives. Had Avraham not happened to riffle through some of his father's papers that day, he would never have known, to the end of his life, that somewhere in the midst of the country's Arab population there lived a sister of his, daughter of R' Elimelech Rosenbaum, Radomsker chassid, Bnei Brak resident, who a few weeks earlier had departed this world with a sterling reputation.

It was terribly painful for him to assimilate the facts: that he had a sister, and that she had married an Arab. His imagination journeyed along Shechem's winding streets. She would be walking those streets, this woman who was his own flesh and blood, dressed perhaps in traditional Arab garb. And children? Had she had any children? Grandchildren of his father, the Radomsker chassid from Bnei Brak? She would speak to them in Arabic, no doubt, and let them be raised to hate Jews.

What was happening? He felt as though a foreign limb had been grafted onto his body. The room swam; he was near fainting again. A mighty rage welled up in him, threatening to burst from him with explosive power.

He raised a hand to his face, to hide the wave of emotion that left him feeling spent and helpless. Maybe Uncle Nachum had been right, after all. Should he have desisted while there was still time, instead of digging into the shadowed past so long concealed from him?

He loosed a bark of bitter laughter. "And my brother-in-law — Abu Daoud al-Razak?"

"You know that already," Binyamin said. "He became active in underground activities against IDF soldiers."

"My dear sister couldn't prevent him from doing this?"

"Look, he was relatively harmless. He was killed by accident, after escaping from jail. We didn't intend to kill him."

"You're apologizing to me, as if I cared. As if he were really my brother-in-law."

"No," said Binyamin. "I'm not apologizing. I'm only giving you the facts." He paused, then added, "Though, in his public speeches against the 'Zionist oppressor,' he was extremely poisonous."

Avraham considered this. "Maybe his quarrel with my father influenced that."

"Very possibly," Binyamin conceded with a nod.

The minutes ticked past as they sat again in silence. Avraham ordered fresh-brewed coffee and apple cake, in the hope of lifting his mood. Then, turning back to Binyamin, he asked, "And my dear honorable sister? Where is she today?"

"She? She's managing her husband's hotel."

"Does she also help the Fatah?"

Binyamin said slowly, "I don't know. You're encroaching on areas now where I can't answer you."

"Security reasons?"

"Yes. Security reasons."

"Am I to understand something from that?"

The G.S.S. man shrugged. "In my opinion — no. But you're a free man. Decide for yourself."

The two drank their coffee slowly. Binyamin, for one, was glad to bring their talk to a close. He had passed over the information that Avraham needed; Avraham must be satisfied with that. Any further digging was going too far. He began taking larger sips, to hasten the moment when he would take his leave.

Presently, he stood up and extended a hand. "Goodbye."

"Just a minute, Binyamin. There are still a few matters I want to clear up first."

With visible reluctance, the G.S.S. man sank back into his armchair. Speaking very clearly and decisively, Avraham said, "I want to meet her."

Binyamin stared at him in pure astonishment. "You don't know what you're talking about!"

"I think I was clear."

"Her hotel is swarming with terrorists. You'd be endangering your life."

"Then help me!"

"You're talking nonsense. We have more important matters to deal with."

"I believe that. But I must meet her. She's my sister."

"That's your business, sir. The security forces will not help you even get close to that hotel. It could end, Heaven forbid, in your death. Those terrorists are very suspicious. And besides," he hesitated, "besides, it would greatly disrupt our own clandestine activities in the region."

This time, Avraham was the first to find his feet. The two men shook hands. Avraham said, "I've made up my mind. I must see my sister, and speak to her, come what may! If I want to get in touch with her, how can I do it?"

"Not a chance," Binyamin said evenly. "We'll do our best to stop you." With that, he turned and left.

Avraham watched him go. Then, moving like a man in a dream, he went to the cashier's desk to pay for the coffee and cake.

Avraham and Rachel sat in the living room, facing each other in silence. Though the hour was approaching midnight, there was no lamp lit in the room. Only the streetlights, shining through the window, cast their faint yellow glow allowing Avraham to perceive the bewilderment on Rachel's face. He had just finished telling her what he had learned in the Hilton lobby that afternoon.

He had returned home within the past half-hour. After leaving the hotel, he had wandered aimlessly through the streets of Tel Aviv. With measured steps he had walked along HaYarkon Street, his ears never registering the hum of the passing cars. He walked without seeing the faces of passersby or the lavish hotels that dotted the sidewalk. At last, he stopped, and leaned against the boardwalk railing to gaze out at the Mediterranean, its waves bronze beneath the setting sun. Gradually, the bronze turned to indigo and then black, while Avraham spent over an hour standing there not thinking of anything, his mind a total blank. Emotionally, he was paralyzed.

Then, from the depths of his shaken soul, he heard a far-off wail of panic, rising and strengthening like an ambulance siren as it nears its goal. With a start, he disengaged from the railing and descended rapidly to Ben-Gurion Avenue. He wandered to no place in particular, until his feet carried him to the corner of Dizengoff. Night had fallen upon the bustling street, which responded with a dazzling neon display. Avraham continued his plodding walk to nowhere.

A single thought filled his mind, with the effect of a mental scream: *Life will never be the same again. Uncle Nachum had been right! I should not have attempted to unearth what had lain for so long buried and hidden.*

Then an answering fury rose to counter this thought and vanquish it. *No! Uncle Nachum was not right!*

"Mister, be careful! Can't you see that the light's turned red?"

Like a recently awakened sleepwalker, he instinctively leaped for the curb. A split second later, a speeding car zoomed past his face, close enough to touch. Other pedestrians were casting angry looks his way as they waited patiently for the light to turn green. Avraham glanced at his wristwatch and was astounded to find that it was 10 o'clock at night. What must his wife be thinking by this time? How many hours had he wandered aimlessly in the streets? At the nearest bus stop, he climbed aboard a 66 bus, headed for Petach Tikvah.

He opened his front door carefully, hoping against hope that Rachel would be asleep. That would let him put off sharing his news until the morning.

But she was awake, and waiting for him in the darkened living room. As soon as she heard the scrape of his key in the lock, she leaped to her feet.

"Where have you been?" she asked with near-hysteria. "I already called the police. I didn't know what to think!"

The hours of tortured anxiety were obvious in every syllable. She had known that her husband planned to meet with a G.S.S. man at 5 o'clock. Who knew what might have happened at that meeting? Such an encounter could very well have precipitated unforeseen results.

Avraham tried with all his might to smile, but his lips formed only a weird grimace. "It's all right," he whispered. "The important thing is, I'm here."

"It's definitely *not* all right! You should have called to tell me that you'd be delayed! I was going crazy with worry!"

She stood up to turn on a light.

"No," he said quickly, putting out a hand. "No, don't. It'll be easier for me in the dark. When you hear what I have to tell you, you'll really go crazy."

She sank back onto the couch. "Has something happened?"

"Let's sit and talk."

He talked, and she listened. And now, as the hands of the clock ticked away the seconds until midnight, they sat in a deep and impenetrable silence.

Avraham bore it as long as he could. Then, in a strained whisper, he asked, "Well, what do you think of the story?"

He heard her catch her breath. "What do you want me to say? What *is* there to say? It's a tragedy, plain and simple!"

But Avraham pressed, "Say something anyway."

"Say something? I have nothing to say. I'm thinking of how much your parents must have suffered. How awful!"

"I'm also thinking about her. About Rivka — my sister."

"Well, I don't know her. She doesn't disturb me as much."

He passed a trembling hand over his brow. "To think that I have a sister in Shechem —"

"Yes," Rachel nodded solemnly. "I know."

Silence fell again. Avraham rose and went to the kitchen, where he turned on the light and the electric kettle. What he desperately needed right now was a strong cup of coffee. Returning to the living room, he asked in the same whisper, "What do we do now?"

She whispered, too. "We forget the whole thing."

Avraham was taken aback. Bewildered and threatened, he cried, "What do you mean?"

"Quietly, please. The girls are asleep — I told you. It seems to me that we've reached the end of the road."

Again, he asked, "What do you mean?"

"It's very simple. Your curiosity has been satisfied. We now know what they were trying to keep from us. Right now, I think it a pity that we found out what we weren't supposed to know."

Shaken and confused by his wife's turnaround, Avraham felt himself on the brink of tears. "But why?" he demanded.

"Avraham, please calm down. I'll tell you exactly what I mean. I'm sure you'll agree with me. You're forgetting the society we live in!"

"A religious, healthy, and normal society, *baruch Hashem*."

"True, *baruch Hashem*. But you'll agree with me that this story is a stigma on our family. A stigma that your parents tried in every way they knew to keep hidden, erased, forgotten. True?"

"True, true. So?"

"Don't you see? Can't you understand on your own that if someone has a sister living in Shechem, who was married to an Arab and a terrorist, and whose children, if she has any, are growing up as Arabs — can't you see that this will harm our daughters' chances for making a respectable *shidduch*?"

Avraham felt as though a great weight had rolled from his shoulders. He had to suppress the urge to burst into laughter. It was only his wife's serious mien that prevented the laughter from escaping.

"You're worrying now about *shidduchim* for our daughters, in some eighteen or twenty years? That seems a little exaggerated to me, my dear."

"Exaggerated? As if you don't know how far people dig into the past, sometimes in a very ugly way, when a match is suggested for their child. Sometimes, through their research, they come up with things that happened decades before. Where have you been living, Avraham? Why aren't you afraid? I don't need this!"

"And if we hadn't learned the story ourselves? Would our future *mechutanim* not have done the usual digging?"

"Then at least I wouldn't have known! But now? The worry will be with me all through the years. I'll always be afraid that someone will find out about this tragedy and that it will prevent them from allying themselves with our family."

Avraham had never thought of this angle. Looking at Rachel, he asked, "Had you known that I have a sister in Shechem when they suggested me for you, would you have gone through with the *shidduch*?"

Very seriously, his wife answered, "Don't be so sure the answer is 'yes'."

Avraham sat back, nonplused. Their talk had taken a turn he had not anticipated. All the way home, he had been weaving plans for meeting his lost sister, of trying to bring her back to her Jewish roots and to her widowed mother. He had been so sure that his wife would join him in this extraordinary adventure. And now — this. "What happens now?" he wondered aloud.

Rachel never took her eyes from him. By the light of the street lamps she witnessed his inner turmoil. Still, she said nothing. The ball was now in his court. She had said her piece. It was up to him to face the challenge she had raised. To forget the whole matter, to leave it behind and agree with her that their own small family was more important than the terrible and painful history that had just been unfolded to them. In the secret places of her heart, she hoped that Avraham would make no further trouble, that they could return at last to their old life, their old routine. Would he understand this?

Abruptly, Avraham rose and turned on a lamp. They squinted as the living room flooded with light. He stood facing his wife, his face strangely peaceful. His smile was that of a confident man.

"Rachel, you know very well that there are no coincidences in this world. Everything hinges on *hashgachah*, on Divine Providence."

Rachel was silent.

"Was it a coincidence that I found that envelope?"

She did not answer.

"Was it a coincidence that my mother behaved the way she did, making me so curious? Answer me!"

"No."

"No, what?"

"No! It was not a coincidence."

"Was it coincidence that I was helped, in such a relatively short time, to discover this terrible secret?"

"Certainly not."

"Then isn't it clear that Heaven wants something from me?"

She hesitated. "Maybe."

Avraham sat down again. He had forgotten all about the cup of coffee he had intended to make. "Why 'maybe'?" he asked. "My heart tells me that I am obligated to meet my sister."

Rachel had no desire to argue with her husband. It was nearly 2 a.m. now, and she felt utterly drained.

"How do you plan to go about doing that?" she whispered.

"How? I don't know that yet. But I have high expectations that you will help me."

She did not answer. Struggling wearily to her feet, she said a low-voiced, "Good night," and headed for the bedroom.

Avraham went to bed that night thinking that life had dropped on his unwary head all the surprises it was holding in store for him. But another one awaited Avraham when, on some impulse he could not explain to himself, he picked up a phone the next morning and dialed his uncle Nachum's number in Haifa.

19

Avraham woke up in a strange mood. Restlessly he prowled the living room, nerves jangling and lips pursed in a tight line. His wife's reaction the night before had both stunned and angered him.

It made no sense to him that she would be content to put an end to their activities at this critical juncture. Why was she doing this to him? He understood that having a sister who had run away from home to live among the Arabs constituted a serious blot on his family's name. Still, Rachel's fear for their daughters' *shidduchim* seemed ridiculous to him. Why worry about something so far in the future? She was using that anxiety to avoid confronting the fact that they were talking about her husband's own sister! His only sister, the daughter of parents who had survived the Holocaust!

True, his sister had betrayed her parents and her people. It was also true that as a consequence she had been effectively banished from her parents' life. They had cut off all contact with her. But after all these years, was it forbidden for her only brother to try to reach her — to try, perhaps, to bring her home again? Even with a sharp sword resting on a person's neck, he must never despair of Heaven's help!

And maybe — just maybe — his sister, exiled in Shechem, was hoping in her secret heart for a sign from her family? Had so many years elapsed without any thought of home, of longing for her mother and father? Impossible! And perhaps she had children. Those children, according to *halachah*, were Jews. And he was — their uncle! Something must be done. Now that the secret had finally been revealed to him, he was obligated to make some sort of effort. Why wouldn't, why couldn't Rachel understand that?

He paused for a moment, one foot suspended in air. Then the nervous pacing resumed. There was no peace for his storm-tossed soul. He must meet with his sister! And to do that, he needed his wife's help. Without her, his goal would remain out of reach. That much was clear. Then why was she refusing her help? Why was she doing this to him?

Rachel poked her head out of the girls' bedroom. She sounded concerned. "Aren't you going to work today? It's already late, Avraham!"

"I'm going, I'm going! Don't worry."

His tone alerted her to the fact that all was not well with her husband. She attributed the drastic change in him to the surprising revelation he had heard the day before. The story was not a simple one; it was enough to shatter anyone's equilibrium.

She thought she understood. Not for a moment did she suspect that Avraham's sudden nervous irritation arose from her own opposition to his plans to move forward.

"Yes," she said reasonably, "but why aren't you ready to leave yet?"

He did not stop restlessly pacing the length of the living room. Nor did he raise his eyes, which were lowered to the floor. All he did was snap, "It doesn't matter."

"Is it because of what you found out yesterday?"

"It doesn't matter!"

With a shrug, Rachel returned to her daughters' room to get them ready for play group and pre-school. Avraham followed her.

As his wife dressed the little girls and chatted with them, Avraham stood in the doorway, one shoulder leaning against the frame, and silently watched. Rachel threw him a glance from time to time. There was something about his gaze that disturbed her. It held distress — and anger.

Inside, an argument raged in Avraham's soul. *Shall I listen to my wife and drop the whole thing?* asked one voice.

And the other replied with a resounding, *No!*

He whirled abruptly away from the doorway and returned to the living room. *I'm going on, no matter what!* The fact that he had managed to discover, through special Providence, that he had a sister living somewhere between *Har Gerizim* and *Har Eival* was, for him, a clear sign from Heaven that he must search for her. He believed that profoundly. Perhaps he was wrong, but that was what he believed.

With a rapid step he went to the telephone. When Rachel came out into the living room, holding the little girls by their hands, she saw that her husband was holding the receiver. An overwhelming anxiety swept through her. "Who are you calling now? What's happened to you?"

He did not answer. All his being was intent on waiting for the party at the other end to pick up.

"Hello — Uncle Nachum? Good morning. This is your nephew, Avraham."

Rachel gaped at him uncomprehendingly. She whispered, "What do you want with him early in the morning, before going to work?"

Again, he did not reply. Into the receiver, he said in a rush, "Do you have a minute, Uncle Nachum?... You want to know if it's important that I speak to you right now, this minute? Yes, I think it's important. It's unbelievably important to me!"

"All right," his uncle said, resigned. "If it's that important to you, ask away."

"Look, Uncle Nachum. Maybe you have a photograph for me? A picture of my sister, Rivka, who lives in Shechem?"

Rachel could not stifle a low shriek. Her hand flew up to cover her mouth, as though to keep a second scream from escaping. Her eyes, however, screamed for her: *What are you doing?* Avraham ignored her.

Dead silence from the other end of the line. Avraham had achieved his goal: He had shocked his uncle to the core. This was the man who had chosen to conceal, at any cost, the information that Avraham so desperately sought. Well, now Uncle Nachum knew that he knew. A direct question, without any lead-in or introduction, had had the desired effect: It had stunned and shaken his uncle.

In a tone of polite inquiry, he asked, "Why so quiet? Do you have a photo?"

Very low, Nachum asked, "How did you find out?" His voice cracked on the last word.

But Avraham's anger at his uncle had not yet abated. Calmly, he said, "What difference does that make? The important thing is that I know. Please, do you have a picture of Rivka?"

Instead of answering, Nachum asked a question of his own. "Have you told your mother?"

"No."

His uncle's labored breathing resounded in Avraham's ears. It was difficult for Nachum to speak. But Avraham wanted to continue the discussion. Rachel was frantically signaling to him, but Avraham ignored her. He heard Uncle Nachum ask, in a choked voice, "Are you — planning — to tell her?"

"I don't know," Avraham said. "I haven't decided yet."

"You'll kill her! Be careful."

"You know what?"

"What?"

"I'm not at all convinced that you're right."

"What do you mean?"

Avraham switched the receiver from his right ear to his left. "I've given it a lot of thought. I think that she might want to hear this news from me."

Nachum shouted, "Be careful! I'm warning you, don't say a word to her. *Do you hear me?*"

Ominously and softly, Avraham said, "I will certainly take into consideration your bellowing just now, Uncle Nachum, before I decide whether or not to tell her."

"I warn you — be careful!"

Avraham merely asked, "Well, do you have a picture for me?"

"Why do you need a picture?"

"Can't I know what my own sister looks like? Apart from that, I imagine she hasn't changed all that much. I'm sure I'll be able to recognize her."

"What do you mean, 'recognize her'? Do you think she's likely to go strolling down Dizengoff?"

"No. I mean if I happen to go to Shechem at some point in my life."

The receiver trembled with renewed screams. "Are you trying to tell me that you're dreaming of going to Shechem? To try and meet with her?"

"Maybe," Avraham said calmly. "What's wrong with that?"

"Are you insane?"

Avraham held the receiver several inches from his ear. "Why not? She's my sister, isn't she?"

Nachum suddenly quieted down. His tone took on a pleading quality. "Yes, she's your sister. Your sister who betrayed her family and her people in the worst possible fashion. You should know how out of the ordinary her behavior was. I don't know if there are many other girls like her. She remained living with her Arab husband, even after he'd turned terrorist. Do you understand? Even after he became a terrorist! And she never once tried to establish any sort of contact with home. I tell you, she shortened your father's life! She must certainly have had some children — Jewish children — who are undoubtedly Jew-haters. And you want to go see her?"

"Yes."

"That's why I asked if you've gone insane!"

"What can I do, Uncle? People aren't perfect."

"You're joking around at my expense," his uncle snapped. "Aside from the fact that you shouldn't be speaking to such a sinful sister, it's also dangerous to enter that kind of hornets' nest. It could risk your very life! Only a Jew intent on suicide goes into Shechem these days, especially to the hotel your sister runs, which is a hotbed of terrorism. And you, no doubt, intend to stroll in and present yourself as her Jewish brother! It's abnormal to even consider such a move! Why are you planning to do it? You have a wife, young children, a mother!"

Avraham did not deign to reply. All he did was reiterate his first question. "Uncle Nachum, do you have a picture of Rivka? Yes or no?"

"And if I don't want to give it to you, what will you do?"

Avraham burst into laughter. "As you've seen for yourself, despite all your warnings and all your activity against me, I managed to find out what I needed to know. With Hashem's help, I'll get a picture without you, too."

"We'll see," Nachum said grimly.

Avraham had an inspiration. "If you won't give it to me, I'll just ask Imma."

"No! Don't do that! Don't hurt her. You mustn't hurt her like that."

"Then send me a photograph."

Silence. Nachum found himself in a quandary. On one hand, he had no desire to supply his nephew with a picture that would enable him to act on his harebrained scheme. On the other, there was the distinct possibility that Avraham would carry out his threat of asking his mother for what he wanted. Such a move, Nachum knew, would cause his sister unbearable pain.

Unable to see his way out of the dilemma, he said in sudden submission, "All right. I'll send you a picture."

"Thank you," said Avraham. His voice was calm, but inside he was smiling in triumph.

Three days later, the photo arrived in the mail.

Rachel brought the envelope upstairs, but did not open it. That, she knew, was Avraham's privilege. As soon as he came home, he seized the envelope and tore it open with trembling fingers and visible emotion. His hands shook even more as he pulled out the picture.

Looking over his shoulder, Rachel saw a young woman in her 20's who bore an uncanny resemblance to Avraham's mother. Avraham studied the photograph intently. Rachel dared not say a word, although something, she saw at once, was peculiar about the picture.

Finally, she ventured, "Do you see something strange here?"

"No."

"Look carefully," she said.

Rachel's voice finally penetrated the shell of Avraham's excitement. He tore his eyes away from the photograph to glance at his wife.

"I don't understand what you're referring to," he said. "I don't see anything."

She took the picture from him and said, "Look." With the index finger of her other hand she pointed to a ragged edge on one side of the photo. "Do you see? It's torn. Not cut neatly, with scissors, but just ripped off."

"So what? Is this the first torn picture you've ever seen?"

"Of course not. But I think it would be interesting to know who was in the picture with your dear sister. Whoever it was, your uncle found it necessary to tear the person out. If he did that, he must have had a good reason, don't you think?"

Avraham considered this. "Of course. It was that al-Razak."

With a shrug, Rachel murmured, "Maybe — and maybe not."

"It seems to me the most likely possibility."

The Envelope / 145

"To me, it seems the least likely. Think a minute: If you're right, how would a photo of the two of them come to be in your uncle Nachum's possession? Do you want to tell me that she sent him the picture after her wedding ceremony to an Arab terrorist? Did she think he would rejoice at seeing it?"

Avraham ran his fingers distractedly through his hair. "Then who could it be?"

"How do I know?"

Hesitantly, Avraham wondered aloud, "Do you think it would be worth our while to ask?"

"Probably. If only to satisfy our curiosity."

With a probing glance, he asked, "Only for curiosity's sake?"

Rachel shrugged again. "For me, at this stage of the game, it's only curiosity."

Avraham bit his lip in concentration. It was obvious to him that she was still of the same opinion she had expressed a few days earlier: She had no desire to continue forward toward a meeting with his sister. Moreover, she was opposed to it. But he took heart from three words she had just said: *at this stage*. That left the door slightly open to the hope that she would change her mind.

Avraham asked, "Shall I ask Uncle Nachum himself, directly?"

"Who else is there?"

Nodding, Avraham dialed his uncle's number. At this hour of the afternoon, his uncle should be home from work.

"Uncle Nachum, it's Avraham. Thank you very much for sending me the picture. I was very moved to see it. It also gave me a lot of anger, pain, and shame — But thank you, anyway."

Cynically, Nachum replied, "Yes, self-flagellation is an obvious outcome. You love pain, don't you? You're like a man picking at a wound that's already begun to heal. Do you understand what I mean? Picking at the scab, despite the pain, until the wound is exposed all over again. What did you need that for?"

Avraham ignored both the question and the cynicism. "Can I ask you something?"

"Please," his uncle said guardedly. "Ask to your heart's content."

"I noticed that the picture you sent me was torn. It looks as though someone ripped it in anger. Was it you?"

"Let's say it was. What difference does it make?"

"Maybe it doesn't matter. But what is important to me is knowing who was in the other part of the photograph. And why was that person torn out?"

Nachum, at the other end of the line, smiled thinly. Here was his opportunity. "And why," he asked, "should I answer you?"

Stung, Avraham countered, "Why shouldn't you?"

Nachum laughed lightly. "What's happened to you, Avraham? You need *me* in order to find out who was in the picture with your sister? You, a world-class detective? You've already managed to learn all kinds of details about your sister that I didn't want you to know. You did it without any help from me. You won — and you were happy in your victory. I heard it in your voice when you asked me for a picture of your sister." He paused meaningfully. "Am I right, or not?"

"Let's say you are. Is that why you won't answer me?"

"Exactly."

"Why?"

Nachum inhaled deeply. "Sweat a little! Let's see you find out for yourself who was in the picture and why it was torn. Come on, investigate! Dig around! Get to work!"

After a moment's silence, Avraham said through his teeth, "All right, Uncle Nachum. I'm beginning my investigations, starting right now. Did I perhaps have another sister, one I don't know about?"

"I know nothing, Avraham. Don't interrogate me. You are the detective. I wish you the best of luck. But I warn you — you're going to regret it. The more you find out, the more you'll suffer." The uncle's tone changed, grew remote. "Still, having free choice bears with it grave responsibility."

When Avraham did not answer, Nachum continued, "What's the matter? I'm only making life interesting for you. Life won't be boring when you have the goal of finding out who posed for the photograph together with your sister. But remember one thing: It will come as a big surprise." After a brief pause, Nachum added slowly, "And definitely an unpleasant one."

Avraham decided to take the offensive. "When I meet my sister Rivka, she will no doubt be able to supply the name of the missing person in the picture. Of course, I'm planning to ask her about it."

Uncle Nachum burst into laughter. "Maybe you'll meet your wonderful sister, and maybe not. Maybe you'll get to speak with her — and, again, maybe not. Maybe she'll tell you what you want to know, and maybe she won't. But one thing is certain: You'll never get to tell me about the conversation."

"And why is that?"

"Simple. Because you'll never leave that place alive."

Avraham gnashed his teeth, but managed to keep his voice emotionless. "How do you know that? Do you have contacts in Shechem? Maybe you were there yourself?"

His uncle's breathing stopped, then resumed again in labored fashion. "To my sorrow, I do know. How? Was I there? All that is not important right now."

Suddenly, his voice was strained. With a hasty, "Goodbye," he hung up the phone.

Avraham stood disconsolate in the middle of the living room. Rachel had been trying to follow the gist of his conversation with his uncle; now he related it to her in broad outlines.

"I thought," he said sadly, "that with the terrible fact that I have a sister in Shechem, I'd exposed the entire secret. Now, apparently, it seems that we're not finished yet. There's another secret hidden inside that one."

When Rachel did not say anything, Avraham turned to her. "What do we do?"

"Nothing."

"What do you mean, 'nothing'?"

"It's time to stop. You don't need to know everything."

Fury began to well up in Avraham. "You're asking me to abandon my sister, to give her up without a fight?"

"I'm sorry," Rachel said, compassionate but firm. "The situation is actually the opposite. *She* gave *you* up."

"So —"

"So, nothing! Your dear sister chose her path. Our job is to focus on our young family, on our two daughters, to raise them with Torah and *yiras Shamayim*. From our point of view, I think the story's finished." She waited a beat, to let her next words sink in more emphatically. "The truth, Avraham? I don't want the girls to know they have an aunt like that."

Anger blazed from Avraham's eyes. But he didn't say a thing. Instead, without a word, he turned and left the apartment, headed for shul, his *shiur*, *Minchah*, and *Ma'ariv*.

⁂

The next day, he walked into his boss's office. Yair Peled sensed at once that Avraham was caught in the throes of some powerful emotion. Avraham said hesitantly, "Pardon me for disturbing you."

Contrary to his usual manner, Peled smiled at him. Perhaps it was the riveting story that Avraham had told him that made him attentive now, and patient. He wanted to hear the next installment.

"That's all right. What do you want now?"

"If it's not too much trouble, can you contact your friend in the G.S.S., the one who calls himself Binyamin?"

Peled leaned back in his vast leather chair. "What happened? Come, don't be afraid of me. You must know that I'm aware of the whole story."

It came as no real surprise to Avraham to learn that the enigmatic Binyamin had submitted a full report of their Hilton meeting to Yair Peled. He said, "I have something that I want to ask his opinion about. It's very important to me."

Without answering directly, Peled reached for the telephone. Avraham listened in suspense as his boss spoke quietly into the phone, and waited even more tensely during the interminable silence that followed. Finally, Peled nodded his head. Binyamin was prepared to meet with Avraham again.

"He'll be here, in the office, in one hour."

"Here?" Avraham was astounded. "Everyone will know that something's happened!"

Peled laughed at him. "And how would anyone know that our visitor is a secret service man? They look just like everyone else! This will be an ordinary business meeting. No one will suspect a thing. He told me that he's in the neighborhood and will drop by."

Avraham said nothing, but new lines of stress showed on his face. Peled, watching him, asked, "Do you want me to tell him not to come? You could meet in a few weeks instead. He's taking a trip abroad tomorrow night."

"No!" Avraham sat up as though electrified. "Let him come."

Approximately one hour later, Binyamin, the G.S.S. man, walked into the office. He was summoned to Yair Peled's inner sanctum immediately. A few minutes later, Avraham was asked to join them. The two men smiled in greeting and shook hands warmly. Then Avraham showed Binyamin the photograph he had received in the mail.

"This is a picture of my sister."

Binyamin took the photo and studied it carefully for several moments. Then he raised his head and asked, "Who tore the picture?"

Avraham's eyes lit up. "That's exactly what I wanted to ask you. I received the picture in this condition, and wanted to know who was standing beside my sister. And why did the person who gave it to me tear it like that?"

"Who gave it to you?"

"My uncle — my mother's brother. Nachum Holtzer, in Haifa."

Binyamin grunted. Quickly, Avraham asked, "Do you know him?"

"No. Should I?" Binyamin said in a surprised tone.

Avraham bit his lip. There was something in the other man's manner that made him doubt the veracity of that answer.

"Look, Avraham," the secret service man said. "Give me the picture. I will try to check it out in our own archives and get back to you. Today, if possible."

He reached out to take the photograph, but Avraham was in no hurry to hand it over. He was afraid he would never see it again. He wanted to guard it zealously as he planned, with Hashem's help, to find his sister in Shechem.

"I'm sorry, Binyamin. This picture is precious to me and I can't give it to you. Please try to help me without it."

With an enigmatic smile, the G.S.S. man said, "Okay. I'll call you tomorrow."

Binyamin was true to his word. On the following day, he phoned Avraham and got straight to the point.

"I checked it out. We have the complete picture in our files." He paused. "For security reasons, I cannot reveal the name of the person standing beside your sister in the photo."

Quickly, Avraham asked, "Was it a man or a woman?"

But, with a final little *click*, the connection went dead.

Slowly, wearily, Avraham put down the phone. His initial reaction was numbness. He felt drained of emotion, almost paralyzed, devoid of all thought.

Within a few minutes, however, his feelings surfaced. He was consumed with blazing anger. Furiously, he pushed away the phone as though it were somehow to blame for his disappointment. It skittered across his desk, upsetting several perfectly innocuous papers which rose in the air and then fluttered to the floor. Avraham made no move to retrieve them.

He stood, took a few steps away from his desk, and then returned to perch on its edge. He was angry at the indifference of those around him to the stunning revelation that had overturned his life, and to the pain that it was causing him. A strange isolation had begun to settle over him, setting him apart from the rest of the world inside a private cage of despair.

Everyone was against him. No one understood him. They could not have cared less about his anguish. One and all, they persisted in trying to wean him from his mad (in their opinion) plan to seek out his long-lost sister. And foremost among those who had disappointed him was his own wife. After a burst of initial enthusiasm, she now wanted him to desist, to back off, to leave the whole matter alone. To forget everything — including the fact that it had been Rachel herself who had encouraged him to investigate the mysterious envelope in the first place.

His uncle Nachum had been fighting him every step of the way. There could be no hope of help from him. Even more, by sending the torn photograph he had only added fuel to the all-consuming fire that was Avraham's speculation regarding the mystery surrounding his faithless sister. And now, Binyamin, the G.S.S. man, had also refused to help him! Had the three of them formed a secret pact to keep him from his sister?

But he must get to her! He must! There would be no peace for him until he had plumbed the story to its depths — until he had spoken with Rivka in person. And maybe, just maybe, he would succeed in bringing her back into the fold.

What was the meaning of the torn photo? What was the security reason behind the G.S.S.'s refusal to let him know who had been photographed with her? What was going on?

Suddenly, Avraham's eyes widened. His breath caught, then grew deep and excited. A new idea had sprung up out of nowhere.

Should he go see his mother, and tell her everything? Would she, realizing that he had discovered the truth, be the one to support him?

He jumped up from the desk as though it had caught fire. On second thought, it was clear to him that he could not speak to his mother. It was too soon. The shock was still too fresh. Only after he had been to Shechem — *If I ever do get there,* his doubting heart whispered — could he slowly reveal to her that he had learned the secret. It all depended on the outcome of that visit.

He walked to the window and threw it wide open. A blast of Tel Aviv heat greeted him, along with the never-ending roar of traffic. Both pounded mercilessly at his face.

Avraham had no idea how long he stood at that open window. He only knew, afterwards, that he found himself seated in his armchair once more, head back and heart brimming with tears. The phone rang and rang, unheeded. From the other side of the thin wall he could hear the babble of the secretaries' voices as they dealt with the firm's customers. At that moment, he had no earthly interest in the business or in his responsibility to it. A single question gnawed at him: What to do now? To listen to what everyone was saying? To give in, and forget the whole incident?

How could he do that? Why didn't anyone understand that he simply could not drop it? Particularly his wife, by nature so enthusiastic and so ready to lend a hand. What had happened to her so suddenly? Why? Why?

The pressure of his thoughts, of his powerful emotion, welled up all at once to choke him. Sudden tears filled his eyes and overflowed. He heard his heart pour out a prayer: *Please, Master of the Universe, illuminate my path. Show me what to do. Please, Hashem, help me!*

For several seconds, he sat perfectly still. Then, abruptly, he opened his eyes and straightened his back. He rested his hands on the broad desk, his spirit still troubled but less so than before. Even as his thoughts continued their aimless march, Avraham relished a sense of release. The short prayer had helped. The total submission to his Creator had freed him from the shackles of circumstance. He was still unsure of his next step, but he felt a greater sense of inner calm than at any time in recent memory.

After a moment, he decided to call an old yeshivah friend who, unlike Avraham, had stayed on at the *kollel*. He had not thought of Yitzchak Harari for a long time. As yeshivah students, they had used their *bein hazemanim* breaks to hike the length and breadth of Israel. Yitzchak was still a dedicated traveler who took every opportunity to tour the land, either on foot or in his car. He was animated by a spirit of adventure and a dash of daring. Also, the challenge of sparing Jewish children from receiving a secular education, of introducing young boys to Torah study, was his primary aspiration.

Avraham decided to recruit him in his own private war. Here was a challenge that should be right up his old friend's alley: adventure, and a call to save a strayed Jewish soul.

It was 4 p.m. Yitzchak, as far as Avraham knew, learned at home with a study partner in the afternoons. He dialed the number and waited in suspense for someone to answer. Yitzchak's name had come to him unexpectedly, culled from the depths of his memory. It was Heaven sent! Was his prayer being answered?

"Good afternoon, Yitzchak," he said. "This is Avraham. Avraham Rosenbaum."

"Oh, hello, Avraham! How are you? What made you call me all of a sudden?"

"I remembered that you love a good trip. I was recalling those good times we had traveling together when we were young — and I wanted to offer you another opportunity now. What do you say?"

Cautiously, Yitzchak answered, "You're talking about the upcoming *bein hazemanim*, I presume?"

"When else? You couldn't go before then."

He sensed his old friend's astonishment at this completely unexpected offer. "And where," Yitzchak asked, "would you be interested in traveling?" He had already made plans for the break, but was prepared to listen politely.

With an effort at nonchalance, Avraham said, "Not far from here. It's quite close, actually."

"Where?"

"Shechem."

Yitzchak did not react. He tried to remember whether his former traveling companion had come up with such bizarre notions back in their youth. He could not recall anything in particular.

"You understand," he said carefully, "that not only does your call come as a surprise, but your invitation is also very strange. Can you offer some sort of explanation to go along with it?"

Avraham explained. He told Yitzchak the whole story, beginning with his discovery of the envelope in his father's desk and ending with the startling revelation that he had a sister living in Shechem. Yitzchak listened in total silence. When Avraham was done, he, too, fell silent, and waited for his old friend's response.

After a long moment, Yitzchak asked quietly, "And now what?"

"I told you, I want to see her, to talk to her, to see what can be done."

"But it's dangerous!"

"I know. But what else can I do?"

"What do you mean? If it endangers your life, you're exempt from going."

"And my sister's spiritual life is not in danger?"

"*What?* You're dreaming that you can bring her back, convince her to do *teshuvah*?"

"I didn't say that. On the other hand, who knows? It's possible."

"What, exactly, do you want to accomplish by seeing her?"

"I don't know," Avraham confessed. "I'm hoping that a visit with her brother — her own flesh and blood — will influence her, at the very least, not to support her husband's terrorist friends. How do I know?"

"Do you really believe that? After so many years of being completely cut off from her family and the Jewish people?"

"Even if a sharp sword is dangling over a man's neck, he must never despair," Avraham quoted.

"But you're about to put a sharp sword on your own neck!"

"You misunderstood. It was my sister I was referring to, not myself. We can't give up on her."

"I see."

"Well?"

Yitzchak spoke directly. "I am certainly not obligated to risk my life. And I'd suggest that you consult a rabbi about your own course. Right now, you're laboring under strong emotion, not motivated by logic. You can't decide what's right or wrong. Avraham, consult *da'as Torah*! Then your conscience won't trouble you when you follow the path you are advised to pursue."

Avraham bit his lip so hard that it stung. The pain was sharp, but it prevented him from exploding. After a moment, he asked, "So you're not coming with me?"

"To go into Shechem these days is, in my opinion, suicidal. Especially to wander around among the people you're proposing to visit. And don't you go either — understand?"

"Then what's to become of my sister?"

"Heaven will have pity on her."

"In other words, do nothing!"

"I don't know," Yitzchak said candidly. "Ask a rabbi." After a short pause, he added, "Cheer up, Avraham. Let's find a consolation prize. We'll take some other trip during the break."

"I don't need a consolation prize," Avraham snapped.

"All right," Yitzchak said, losing patience. "Let's stop here, then. Ask a rabbi what to do next. I'll be glad to hear what he says, okay? I'm sorry if I've disappointed you."

With a curt "Goodbye," Avraham replaced the receiver and sank into a gloomy reverie.

Very shortly afterward, he stood up, painstakingly gathered his belongings, crammed them into his briefcase, and left the office. He was not upset with his old friend for rejecting his plea. It had, however, the opposite effect from what Yitzchak had intended. It only strengthened Avraham's resolve to get to Shechem, come what may. But he would do as Yitzchak had suggested. He would consult a rabbi first.

22

Avraham returned home from work nearly an hour later than his usual time. Rachel, perceiving that his frame of mind was uplifted — even a little belligerent — did not ask him why he was late. He seemed to be gearing up for some battle ahead. She could see that with the first "Hello" he uttered as he walked in.

The greeting seemed to echo through the living room, as though Avraham stood prepared to make some momentous announcement. What, Rachel wondered, had happened today in connection with the envelope — she had no doubt that this mood of her husband's had something to do with that — to make him appear this way? In silence, she waited to see what would happen next.

Avraham walked directly to the bookcase and removed a *Chumash Shemos* from one of its shelves. Curiously, Rachel followed his every move. After a few moments of flipping through the pages, Avraham began to read the words with concentration. With his free hand he groped behind him for a chair. Rachel tiptoed closer and, without his noticing, looked over his shoulder at what he was studying so intently. It was unusual for him to reach for a *sefer* immediately upon his coming home from work; his first act was always to prepare himself a cup of scalding coffee.

At last, unable to contain herself, she blurted, "Has something happened?"

Avraham lifted his head. "No. Why do you ask? Do I look upset?"

With a laugh, she said, "No. You actually look rather pleased with yourself."

His finger was poised over a certain verse. With a triumphant smile, he said, "Come see what I was looking at."

She bent over the *Chumash*. Her gaze went to the place where he was pointing.

"You see?" he asked.

"I think so. '*Vayavo kol ish asher n'sa'o libo*' ['Every man whose heart inspired him came.']. That's what I see."

"See — and also understand?"

"I think so," she said. "I learn *Chumash*, too, you know."

"Of course. What I'm asking is whether you understand why I'm pointing to this particular *pasuk* at this particular time."

She grinned. "And even before your inevitable cup of coffee!"

"True," he smiled back. "Even before my coffee. Well, do you understand?"

She thought for a moment before answering, straining to think about what he might mean. Finally, she admitted, "No, I don't get it. The *pasuk*, from what I remember, is speaking of the *Bnei Yisrael* in the Wilderness, who came to Moshe ready to build the *Mishkan*. But what does that have to do with you today?"

"Shall I explain?"

She shrugged. "If you like." Then she amended that to, "Yes, please explain."

"I'll read you the Ramban's commentary on the *pasuk*. That's the explanation." Lifting the *Chumash* to see the fine print, he read aloud, "And the reason it says '*asher n'sa'o libo*' ['whose heart inspired him'] to do the work [of the *Mishkan*] was because there were none who had learned the skills from a teacher or whose hands had practiced [these labors] at all; but each found in his own nature the necessary knowledge to do the work, and his heart was inspired in the ways of Hashem to come to Moshe and say, 'I will do it.'"

Avraham raised his eyes and asked confidently, "Do you see now?"

"Don't be annoyed with me — but I still don't get what you're trying to tell me here."

He closed the *Chumash*. Unnaturally calm, his eyes quietly glittered. He asked his wife, "Please, sit down and I'll explain everything."

She sat on the sofa and fixed him with an expectant gaze.

"Look," he began, "I'm still in shock. I'm reeling from what I've discovered. I don't sleep well at night, and I spend much of the day dreaming and distracted. You know why. You know whom I'm thinking about."

"Your sister Rivka."

"Yes. But along with those thoughts is another one, a very frustrating one that leaves me feeling completely helpless."

"What do you mean?"

"I suddenly felt — " he hesitated, "How do I say this? I felt how alone I am in this whole business. Alone, alone, alone —"

Her stare was penetrating. "Are you trying to tell me something?"

Avraham was quiet for a moment, discomfited by the bluntness of the question. Clearing his throat, he said diffidently, "Yes. Among others, I was thinking of you."

Rachel smiled, not as much at her ease as she would have liked to appear. "That's what I thought. But I think I spoke very sensibly when I asked you to put this matter aside."

"Very true, Rachel. You spoke sensibly and logically — but with very little compassion for the sister I suddenly find that I have. That is, toward your unknown sister-in-law. But I — what can I do? — feel a sense of responsibility toward her. That's why I was angry, to the point of despair, by your indifferent attitude. All of you. I can't talk to my mother. You know the situation with my uncle Nachum. The G.S.S. man, of course, owes me nothing. He, too, showed complete indifference to the pain I'm experiencing over all this. This morning, he informed me that, for security reasons, he can't tell me who was standing next to my sister in the torn photograph. He knew, but he wouldn't tell."

He fell silent. Drawing a deep breath, he smiled and spread his hands in a gesture of futility. "What can I do? I find it impossible to move on from my sister in Shechem to the ordinary business of the day."

Rachel sensed her husband's inner turmoil. She grasped, too, that the bulk of his criticism — though admittedly expressed politely and with tremendous self-control — was aimed directly at her. At the same time, as a practical woman whose feet were planted firmly on the solid ground of reality, it was up to her to prevent him from dangerous doings prompted by his powerful family feeling. Her husband's desire to meet his sister was a highly dangerous and impossible goal. In her opinion, she had done right to oppose his continued involvement in the whole affair.

It disturbed her that Avraham seemed to be oblivious to the complications implied by the torn picture. Who knew what lay behind it, if security reasons forbade even discussing it?

Folding her hands in her lap, she asked, "And why did you arrive at the Ramban?"

Avraham glanced slowly at the *Chumash*, then at his wife. "I was sitting in my office, discouraged. I decided to call my old friend. Though he spends his time learning, he still has a spirit of adventure from our younger days, and enjoys unusual trips. I hoped that he might be prepared to take a trip with me, for the sake of a mitzvah. Perhpas he would go with me to Shechem." He sighed. "But my friend let me down. He sided with the rest of you: 'Dangerous, dangerous, dangerous.' He advised me to consult with a rabbi."

"A good idea," Rachel said at once.

"Yes, it is. But as I put down the phone after that frustrating conversation, through my despair a *tefillah* burst out of me. A prayer to Hashem to help me. I don't know why. I don't know how. I don't even know exactly how that help should come. The main thing is for Him to help me out of the place I'm in right now."

"And what happened then?"

"I left the office, calmer. 'Throw your burden onto Hashem,' it says. So I threw my problem to Him. To *HaKadosh Baruch Hu.*"

"Did it help?"

"It always helps. That's the essence of *tefillah*. And then, on the way home, I suddenly thought of the *pasuk* I just read you. It popped into my brain and wouldn't go away. I remembered what I'd once read, I think it was in the name of R' Simcha Bunim of Peshischa, who stated, 'The *pasuk* says, "Many thoughts are in a man's mind, but Hashem's plan will endure."' In other words, included among the many thoughts racing through a person's mind are Hashem's plans, which will persevere in the end. So I seized on the *pasuk* that had entered my mind and wouldn't let go. Understand?"

"Yes. I think I do."

"I came home," Avraham continued, "and opened a *Chumash* to study the *pasuk* and its commentaries. And I found the Ramban. What is he saying? That a person who *'n'sa'o libo'* — who is inspired — is capable of doing whatever he must do, even without any special talent or skill. The Jews in the Wilderness did not study architecture; in Egypt they had not involved themselves with those skills. Yet they had faith that, if it was Hashem's will, they could accomplish their task. Faith, as the saying goes, can move mountains." Avraham looked at Rachel. "Do you understand me?"

Her spirits plummeted. She saw with utter clarity that her husband was poised for adventure — a dangerous adventure whose outcome was anyone's guess. She was deathly afraid, and she had no idea in the world how to dissuade him.

"And what about the rabbi?" she whispered.

"That's why I was late coming home. I went to see R' Aryeh, my former *mashgiach* in yeshivah. He's a wise man, and one with whom it is possible to really talk. He understands me."

Rachel skipped a heartbeat. In wrenching suspense, she waited to hear the rabbi's advice. A sudden weariness spread through her as she steeled herself for what she was about to hear.

"And what," she asked, "did R' Aryeh say?"

"R' Aryeh listened to me. He felt with me. I told him that people make such strenuous efforts to save Jews all over the world. Am I to be the only one forbidden to make the same kind of effort to save my own sister? Then he spoke, and justly so, of the great danger involved — which, R' Aryeh said, definitely falls into the category of *pikuach nefesh* [endangerment of life]. And one cannot save one person's life at the risk of another's."

Relief swept over Rachel in a mighty wave. In the thumping of her heart she could hear a fervent, "*Baruch Hashem!*"

Avraham was not finished. "On the other hand, there is also a question of saving lives, though admittedly, that is only a possibility. R' Aryeh empathized with my desire to do something for my captive sister. Therefore, he said that, if I can find a way to get to her with a minimum of danger, I was permitted to try."

He rubbed the palms of his hands in an unconsciously victorious gesture. Looking at his crestfallen wife, he declared, "So that's that! I'm going to try. Are you coming with me?"

Rachel gazed at Avraham expressionlessly. He waited for her answer. When none was forthcoming, he asked again, "Well? Are you coming with me?"

She stood up. "Let's go into the kitchen. First have your coffee. You need to calm down a little."

"Okay, okay. But you haven't answered my question." As he spoke, he rose and followed his wife into the kitchen. "You don't seem to get it. This is a done deal with me. I'm going ahead with this."

To hide her distress, she busied herself preparing coffee. Contrary to what Avraham seemed to think, she understood very well. Before, she had believed that his talk was only that, a hot-air balloon of good intentions emanating from a sudden enthusiasm. Now, she saw that he was dead serious. Her fear grew. Opening a cupboard over the sink, she took down two sets of porcelain mugs and saucers. From another she removed the jar of instant coffee. Then she filled the electric kettle and switched it on.

"All right," she said at last, turning to face him. "I understand what you're saying. And I don't mind telling you that I'm not at all happy about it. But tell me the truth: Do you know exactly what you're getting yourself into? Are you really clear on what you're planning to do?"

An impatient nod was his answer, along with a brief, "With Hashem's help, it will be all right. Don't worry."

His words only served to double and triple the worry she was already feeling. The fire that gripped her husband had only grown stronger, now that he had found a verse in the Torah to reinforce it. Rachel found this an alarming sign. As a rule, such runaway enthusiasm betokened a departure from logic and cautious good sense. The change in Avraham terrified her.

"You're overly confident," she warned. "That's not good."

"Excuse me, Rachel," he countered. "I'm confident that Hashem wants me to save my sister. I trust in *Him*. That's a different thing altogether."

Tilting her head, she threw him a look that was slightly mocking — a look that said, *Here's another guy who thinks he knows exactly what Hashem wants from him!*

She poured out two mugs of coffee, then sat down opposite Avraham at the kitchen table. "What name does your sister use these days?" she asked, almost casually.

"I don't know. But I'll find out."

"If you don't even know her name, how will you find her?"

Avraham set down his mug and answered rapidly, "I understand your purpose in asking these questions. And they are legitimate ones. But, unlike you, I won't allow myself to get stuck on a question. I'm going to look for answers. I want to see my sister, period."

She took small sips as she considered how to reply. Finally, in a low voice, she asked, "And how will you know which hotel in Shechem is hers?"

"Another excellent question!" he grinned, mocking in his turn. "With Hashem's help, I'll find the answer to that one, too. Please don't riddle me with weakness and doubt. My sister's blood is crying out to me from Shechem."

But Rachel was determined to make him face the reality of what he was proposing to do. She wanted to dampen his ardor, to throw cold water over his blind enthusiasm.

"Do you have any idea how heavily she is guarded by her husband's terrorist friends? Can you imagine how suspicious those terrorists will be toward a stranger who tries to get too close? As everyone knows, their fingers are very fast on the trigger."

"True," he nodded.

"So how do you intend to go to Shechem without doing your homework? How do you propose to organize this venture? I'm afraid that you're about to do some very foolish and dangerous things!"

Avraham smiled. "Now do you see why I want you in with me on this? I want you there in order to prevent me from doing something foolish. You're right: In my enthusiasm, I'm liable to forget myself. That's your job — to look after me." He stopped, then asked again: "So, are you coming with me?"

Silently, she gathered the empty coffee cups and put them in the sink. She turned to face her husband. "Good night," she said. "I'm going to sleep."

※

Avraham left for work the next morning without any answer from his wife. The moment he arrived at the office, he strode over to Yair Peled's door. In seconds, he was admitted and stating his request.

"I want to meet with the G.S.S. fellow again. Tell him that I have an offer he can't refuse."

Yair Peled leaned back in his leather chair and regarded Avraham across the expanse of his desk. "Meaning — what?"

With a mysterious smile, Avraham said, "From a security standpoint, this will be well worth his while. Forgive me if I can't go into detail."

Peled considered him another long moment, then nodded. "All right. I'll ask him to get in touch with you."

One hour later, the man who called himself Binyamin phoned Avraham directly. "Where do we meet?"

"You decide," Avraham said.

"The Techelet café, on the corner of Shenkin and Achad Ha'am. Is that okay with you?"

The Envelope / 167

"Why shouldn't it be?"

"Well, you look ultra-Orthodox. You might feel uncomfortable in a coffee shop facing the street."

Avraham thought a moment. "Let it be the Techelet. What time?"

"At 5 o'clock."

"Fine. Goodbye."

"Goodbye."

They met at 5 o'clock, at the café. Avraham ordered mineral water and Binyamin drank grapefruit juice. With subdued voices, Avraham outlined his proposal and Binyamin asked questions. Avraham answered each one in turn, using the same conspiratorial whisper.

An hour later, they parted ways. Binyamin promised to pass Avraham's message to his superiors, and obtain an answer for him.

Avraham waited a long month before that answer finally came. It was in the affirmative.

"When will you be ready to leave?" Binyamin asked him.

"Immediately."

"Is your passport in order?"

"I'll check at home."

"Before your departure, we'll meet for a briefing."

"All right. By the way," Avraham said, "I forgot to ask you something."

"What?"

"If my wife wants to come along, can she? She's an American, with an American passport."

"In that case, it's actually preferable that she come. But I'll double check with my higher-ups."

"Thanks!"

Avraham returned home from work in the highest of spirits. Rachel, seated at the table, said, "Well, what have you done with yourself today?"

Avraham took off his jacket and hat. "We're going to Canada."

Her smile vanished as though by magic. "What do you mean, 'we'?"

"You and I, of course."

"First of all, I'm not sure I'm going anywhere yet. But — why Canada?"

"The way to Shechem," he told her with a broad grin, "is through Canada. Didn't you know?"

Startled, Rachel leaped to her feet. So abrupt was the motion that her chair tipped over and fell with a crash. She did not bother to pick it up. Avraham watched her in some surprise, but held onto his equanimity.

In a voice shaking with astonishment and anxiety, she said, "We get to Shechem through Canada? I don't know what you're talking about! What's the connection?"

Avraham was, if truth be told, rather pleased at the impact his words had made. He had not only succeeded in surprising her, but also in bewildering her. He was not, Heaven forbid, out to hurt her. The surprise was calculated to bring her to see that, with a little creativity and a bit of a departure from routine thought, virtually any problem can be solved — including that of reaching Shechem in the most secure possible way. He wanted her to understand the words, *"asher n'sa'o libo"* as a power that brought out one's life force and elicited unusual solutions.

He fervently hoped that she would support the plan he was about to unfold. It was an elaborate plan, and a serious one — and, in his opinion, an irreversible one. Rachel had to realize that for him, her husband, there was no turning back. Maybe that understanding would induce her to join him for the ride.

The difficulty lay in the fact that he was not permitted to reveal many details — not yet. Binyamin had expressly forbidden Avraham from sharing too much information with his wife before they reached Toronto. Even on the airplane — even outside Israeli airspace — he had been adjured against speaking with her on the subject. "For security reasons, you understand," Binyamin had explained.

Maybe. In Avraham's opinion, the real reason for his enforced silence was that, should Rachel become privy to the actual plan, she would change her mind and veto it out of hand. And her presence was vital to its success.

And so, in a mysterious whisper, Avraham merely said, "You'll understand soon enough."

"You can't say more right now? I thought you wanted me to come with you!"

"I do. Nevertheless, at the moment I am not allowed to tell you what you're so eager to know."

Avraham saw her agitation. It was on the tip of his tongue to ask her to calm herself; quiet reflection and assessment were what he needed right then. But he quickly realized that a mere request on his part would do little or nothing to pacify her.

Rachel asked, "Why? Is it some military secret?"

"Exactly! Now you've got it."

She stopped. Suspiciously, she said, "Maybe you want to tell me that you've met with the intelligence people?"

Avraham leaned back in his chair and looked up at her. This, he knew, was the moment of decision. This was when she would either decide to join him, or stay behind. He put every effort into speaking in a pleasant and calm tone, to ease some of her distress. With the glimmer of a smile, he said, "There's no 'maybe' about it. I did meet with them."

Now Rachel's surprise was absolute. Slowly, she righted her overturned chair. Even more slowly, she sat down. Weakness assailed her. Her body seemed to be betraying her; the weariness she felt belonged to an old, old woman. Beads of cold sweat formed on her forehead, but she made no effort to wipe them away. Her husband had entered a dangerous and frightening new world, the world of undercover operations, and it all stemmed from his obsession with meeting his sister. What was going to happen now? What was going to happen?

With difficulty, she managed to speak one word. "And —"

In a low voice, Avraham continued. "And he listened to me very carefully. And he paid attention to my proposal. And that's all!"

Rachel was silent for a long moment. Then, despairingly, she asked, "When did you meet him?"

"One month ago."

"And he only gave you his answer now?"

"Yes. He just gave me the go-ahead, along with a plan of operation."

She smiled a bitter smile. "And I, fool that I am, thought that a month that passed quietly, without your saying anything on the subject, was a sign that you'd also realized the lunacy of going to Shechem." The smile changed into a wry grimace as she added, "I thought you'd forgotten about it."

"I apologize but one doesn't forget a sister. You know something? I haven't managed to forget her even for a minute. Everything in me is burning to return her to *Yiddishkeit*. I'm dumbfounded that you still expect me to forget her."

Ignoring this, Rachel reverted to an earlier issue. "And the intelligence person told you not to reveal the plan?"

"That's right."

"Not even to your wife?"

"Not even to you."

"What caution! What a responsibility!"

"Yes. That's exactly the way I see it."

Rachel did not answer. She sat immersed within herself, trying to digest the new state of affairs. Finally, with a weary sigh, she went to the kitchen to prepare supper.

He followed her. The kitchen was soon filled with the savory aroma of an omelette in progress, with the sizzling oil providing an appetizing backdrop. Quietly, he asked, "So you're letting me go alone?"

She didn't answer. In her heart of hearts, she knew that she would not let him go alone; but she was in the kind of mood that did not permit her to admit as much. She would go, if only to harness his foolhardy impulses. In his zeal to accomplish what he viewed as his mission, who knew what kind of danger he might court?

Avraham, she knew, was far from adventurous by nature. If anything, he was the opposite: quiet and steady. And now — what a personality change! Something had happened to her husband. The fact that he had met secretly with the intelligence service, and that they were involved in organizing his trip, frightened her terribly. What type of mission had he undertaken on their behalf, simply to get to his sister? The fear was paralyzing.

There was no use, she realized sorrowfully, in trying to dissuade him from taking the trip. Still, she was not yet prepared to agree openly to accompany him on a journey whose beginning was known but whose end was shrouded in mystery. She found the whole prospect extremely difficult to process. How had this happened to her, to them, to their sane life together?

Avraham, meanwhile, had perched himself on one of the kitchen stools. He asked suddenly, "You don't care that I'll be traveling alone?"

"I don't care? Of course I care!" she flashed. "I care a lot! If only you didn't have to go at all!"

He looked at her. "You do realize that that's a lost cause, don't you, Rachel? I want you to come with me. Binyamin said it's actually preferable."

"Oh, did he? Do I have a part to play in this mad scheme that I don't even know about?"

"Yes."

Standing at the stove with her back to him, she twisted her head to see him for a brief instant. "You don't think that's going a little too far?"

"No. I'll explain again: We're talking about my sister. So it's not going too far. Period."

They ate their meal in silence.

Rachel could not sleep that night.

Disturbing thoughts whirled around and around in her mind, hour after endless hour. The apartment was dark and shrouded in silence, which made the time drag on even more slowly. She had already made her decision — but it was a bitter one.

When morning light finally seeped through the bedroom windows, she rose before Avraham did and did not see him until he was nearly ready to leave for work. Then, as he walked to the door, she gathered her courage and called softly, "Avraham."

He turned. "Yes?"

She drew in a long breath. "Please. Come back here for a minute."

Surprised, he asked, "What happened? Is something wrong?"

She had something important to tell him; he could see that much from her expression. Just what that something was, he could not say. Would she join him in his adventure — or not? His throat tightened with tension. Resigned, he returned to the living room.

"Please, sit down."

He rebelled. "Rachel, it's late! I have to leave for the office. We can talk this evening. In a few minutes, I'll miss my bus. Or else tell me right now, quickly."

In a near-whisper, she said, "I've decided."

His heart began to thump furiously. Though his pulse was racing, he maintained his outward impassivity. "What have you decided?" he asked.

"I've decided —" Speech suddenly became difficult for her. "I've decided — that I'm coming with you."

An enormous relief nearly swept him off his feet. He knew just what it had cost her to say those words. Rachel was naturally obstinate. For her to reverse herself regarding a strongly held view was, in her own words, like splitting the Red Sea. Avraham knew the import of the gesture she had just made, and his smile expressed his infinite gratitude.

"Thank you," he said, inclining his head. "That's wonderful. This is to your everlasting credit." He paused. "Can I ask why you've decided to come along?"

The Envelope / 175

The tears stood bright in her eyes. "Because — because, after all is said and done, a woman has to stand by her husband."

"Just as a man has to stand by his wife," Avraham said quietly.

That was when the tears in her eyes spilled over.

Two weeks later, they were on their way to Canada.

Avraham had requested the vacation that his boss Yair Peled had offered him three months earlier, when he had been in the throes of the crisis over his discovery of his father's envelopes. A pair of Air Canada tickets were provided for them. Their daughters were entrusted to the care of Rachel's sister, Rina, who, like them, made her home in Petach Tikvah.

"I'm traveling with Avraham to the United States and Canada," Rachel had explained. "For just two weeks, approximately. His office is sending him. This will be his first time abroad, you understand."

"You look so tense," Rina had noticed.

"And no wonder! I'm excited about the trip. Also, I've never left the girls for two whole weeks." After an infinitesimal pause, she added, "— at least."

"Well," Rina had smiled. "The main thing is for the two of you to have a good trip. See you when you get back!"

The elder Mrs. Rosenbaum had accepted the news with equanimity. Though their going meant that she would miss having their company for two weeks, she did not inquire as to their motive for the trip. She believed it to be business related, and that her daughter-in-law had decided, for reasons of her own, to join Avraham.

Binyamin came to see them off at the airport. He drew Avraham aside and they conversed in an undertone for several minutes.

"There will be someone to meet you at the Toronto airport, don't worry. I wish you a safe journey — and the best of luck."

"Thank you," Avraham said gratefully.

Air Canada Flight 432 was ready to board. Rachel gripped her handbag and tried to still the painful pounding of her heart. Side by side, she and Avraham moved forward on the first leg of their adventure.

Long hours in the air brought them, at last, to Toronto International Airport. They emerged into the terminal, retrieved their luggage, and blinked at the throng of people waiting to greet their loved ones.

Among the crowd, they saw a tall young man holding a sign above his head.

The sign held a single word: "Rosenbaum."

They approached the tall man, their steps spritely despite some tiredness from the long flight. With a shy smile, Avraham extended a hand. "Avraham Rosenbaum."

Rachel nodded politely at the Canadian.

The tall man returned a courteous smile and said in a low voice, "My name is Howard Lincoln."

Avraham, of course, did not believe for a moment that this was the Canadian's real name. Despite the man's Anglo-Saxon features, Avraham was not at all sure that he wasn't Jewish. Why, he was probably part of Israel's worldwide secret service network. But Avraham did not waste much time on speculation. Nor did he ask any questions, merely waiting patiently for the other man to continue.

The Canadian gestured with one hand, as though to say, *Follow me*. In silence the Rosenbaums trailed him into the crowded parking lot outside the airport terminal. The man walked over to a black '85 Ford and opened the back door for them. He slipped behind the wheel and turned on the ignition. In short order, they were moving down Highway 401, whose sixteen lanes led into the heart of Toronto. Tension kept Avraham tongue-tied; no words were exchanged between the Canadian and the Rosenbaums during the drive.

Avraham and Rachel looked with curiosity out the windows at the city sights. When Avraham made some comment to his wife in Hebrew, he sensed that the driver understood what he was saying. He lapsed into a renewed silence that lasted for the rest of the trip.

The tall man deposited them at the four-star Diplomat Hotel. To their surprise, the couple found *kosher l'mehadrin* food waiting in their room — obviously ordered ahead of time, specifically for them.

The Canadian told them that he would be in touch in the morning. Then, with a quiet "Good night," he left.

Avraham *davened Ma'ariv*, after which he and Rachel sat down to eat. It was only near the end of the meal that Rachel asked, "What happens now?"

He gave her a look that was meant to be reassuring. "It'll be all right."

"I know that. But what's going to happen?"

"Tomorrow, I understand, they'll begin preparing us for the trip into Shechem."

Rachel was indignant. "Aren't I allowed to know *anything* yet?"

"Sure you can," Avraham said soothingly. "The trouble is, I'm not sure that I know anything myself, yet."

She did not answer, merely assessing him with her eyes. It seemed to her that Avraham genuinely did not know with certainty which direction their adventure would take. Once again, she prayed silently and fervently that all would go well.

✻

The phone rang at 8 a.m. Avraham picked it up. "Hello?"

"Shalom," a voice said in Hebrew. The voice was familiar to Avraham, but he could not place it.

"May I come up to your room?" the caller continued.

"Please."

Presently, there came a knock at the door. Avraham opened it — and exclaimed in open astonishment, "Binyamin! What are you doing here?"

Binyamin grinned. "I was in the neighborhood — well, in Europe, actually — and decided to drop in for a visit. To see how you're doing."

He entered and took a seat in one of the room's inviting armchairs. Smiling at the Rosenbaums, he said, "Seriously, now. I am in charge of your case. I'm here to prepare you for your upcoming visit to Shechem."

Slowly, he opened the black plastic file he carried under one arm. After a brief search, he produced two Canadian passports, which he placed on a small coffee table. Avraham and Rachel looked at them with interest.

"Starting now," Binyamin said, "you are — temporarily — good Canadian citizens. Open your passports and take a look at yourselves."

Avraham stood, picked up the passports, and handed one of them to his wife. Opening the one he still held, he saw that it was Rachel's. The passport photo was genuine. From his wife's reaction, he divined that his passport, too, had an authentic photo of himself.

Binyamin was very pleased with himself. "Good work, isn't it? Did you think I was asleep during the month you waited for my answer, Avraham?"

"Who gave you our pictures?"

"Never mind, we got them. What's the problem?"

"And the passports?"

"Oh, that was actually not difficult at all. Canada is a paradise for forged passports. It did take considerable effort, but you've promised to try to disengage your sister from terror activities in Shechem, if you can succeed in meeting with her. We decided to make the effort on your behalf."

"Thanks. And now," Avraham asked, "can you tell me what's going to happen next?"

"It's very simple. You, Avraham, are now Bill Fairhaven, and your wife is Pamela Fairhaven. You live in Vancouver — that's in western Canada. You're both radical leftists who support the P.L.O. in its operations against Israel." He paused. "By the way, this is all true. Your passports belong to two people who actually are leftists."

Avraham and Rachel sat bolt upright. "What? How —? Who —?"

Binyamin lifted a hand to stem the tidal wave of questions. "Just a minute," he said firmly. "I'll explain everything. You are a couple of newspaper reporters. In case you didn't know that until now, remember it from now on. As pro-P.L.O. reporters, you are currently planning a trip to the Middle East in order to write a series of articles for a magazine called the *New Commitment*."

"Which?"

"*New Commitment*."

"Where is it published?"

"Right here in Toronto. We'll be visiting the place soon, to get the editor's blessing before you leave."

Avraham said warily, "This is a pro-P.L.O. publication?"

"Yes. It's very radical. And the two of you work for it — you and your wife."

Avraham and Rachel exchanged a worried glance.

"Don't worry, there's no danger," Binyamin said, with an amused smile. "The magazine's own editors won't be able to tell the forgery from the real thing."

He stood up, stretched, and said, "Well, it's time to go meet your editors." With a sidelong glance at Avraham, he added, "Well, what did you think? Our own people established this pro-P.L.O. publication years ago, to serve as a cover for various operations such as this trip of yours. We'll go there now. Remember: Don't you dare speak a word of Hebrew! The people who work for *New Commitment* have no idea that they are actually serving us — serving Israel. The articles carry a definite anti-Israel bias. I hope that you'll write the same kind of stuff."

Avraham managed a smile; for the life of her, Rachel could not muster one. Her fears surrounded and all but throttled her. The unknown loomed just ahead, infinitely threatening. It took every ounce of self-possession for her to maintain a serene outward appearance as she followed her husband and the G.S.S. man from the hotel.

The black Ford was waiting for them at the entrance, with the same tall Canadian at the wheel. Binyamin sat in the front passenger seat while the Rosenbaums took the back. The car started forward. During the half-hour drive Avraham caught glimpses of blue, it was Lake Ontario peeking through the curving road hugging Toronto's shores.

Finally, on a street near the center of town, the car pulled up at the curb in front of a large building. *New Commitment* magazine, Binyamin informed them, had its offices on the fifth floor.

In silence, they rode up in the elevator, rang the bell, and waited for the door to open.

With feelings of trepidation, Avraham and Rachel followed Binyamin into the office. There was something cold and impersonal about the atmosphere; the receptionist almost glared at them in open suspicion as they walked in. Photographs plastered the walls, many of them featuring the familiar features of Yasser Arafat. This alone was enough to give the Israelis the feeling that they had stumbled into the wrong place.

Other enlarged photos depicted children of the *intifada* hurling stones at Israeli soldiers. In one, a uniformed Jewish soldier appeared to be cruelly beating an Arab youth. Anti-Semitic slogans filled the spaces between the pictures. Avraham and Rachel felt as though they had stepped squarely into enemy territory.

Binyamin whispered something to the receptionist. She lifted the receiver of the phone at her elbow and whispered something into it. Then, lowering the phone, she announced, "You can go in. Turn right, then the first left."

They passed rows of computers, each manned by a man or woman working in eerie silence. The only sound to be heard was the incessant clicking of the computer keyboards. Several pairs of eyes lifted curiously as the trio walked past, and the eyes followed them to the editor's office. Rachel, especially, felt choked by the atmosphere.

Irresistibly, her mind flew back to Israel, and all the suffering that her people had known at the hands of the *intifada*. A longing for her home swept over her with powerful intensity. How had she come to be walking through an anti-Israeli news office in a foreign city so far from home? Just yesterday, she had been safe in her own apartment in Petach Tikvah. What were her little girls doing right now?

"This is Mr. Calvin Bridge," Binyamin introduced. The editor of *New Commitment*, a man of 60, nodded politely. "And these are the Fairhavens. Bill and Pamela Fairhaven."

"Please, sit down," the editor invited. The others did so. Avraham noticed that Binyamin had not bothered to introduce himself.

"These are the newspaper reporter couple I told you about," Binyamin told Bridge. "I think they suit your purposes very well. They're pro-P.L.O., and burning with fervor for human rights in general. They are willing to undertake your mission. The Middle East fascinates them."

Rachel and Avraham exchanged a quick glance. The editor chuckled, "Glad to hear it."

He took out a fragrant Havana cigar from a box on his desk, rolled it reverently between his fingers for a moment, and then reached for a gold lighter. Avraham and Rachel waited with mounting tension for Bridge to speak. It was only after a thin plume of smoke was rising from the cigar that he turned to them and said, "First of all, thanks for coming. Are you familiar with our magazine?"

Confused, Avraham blurted, "No." The word, however, was swallowed up in Rachel's firmer, "Yes."

Bridge smiled. "Never mind. It doesn't matter. Granted, we're not *The New York Times*. Nevertheless, we number among our subscribers thousands of decision-makers in the political and business arenas, here in Canada, in the United States, and in other English-speaking countries. We are not a periodical for the masses. It's no shame if you don't know of us."

He paused to smile again at his guests before continuing. "After we talk, I'll see to it that you get hold of a few back issues, so that you can see what we're all about. I'm sure you'll enjoy them."

The Rosenbaums nodded, hoping that the Arab-loving editor could not see what was in their hearts.

"Anyway, we've decided to dedicate the forthcoming issues to the struggle of the Palestinian woman against Israeli occupation. We thought we'd interview several women Palestinian freedom fighters. This is the best way to bring the Palestinian woman's plight to the consciousness of the world. We've sent a reporter to Lebanon to interview Leila Chaled, the courageous airplane hijacker. She was one of the first brave women to fight side by side with her menfolk against the Zionists and their aggressive policies." He trained his glance keenly on the couple. "You two have agreed, or so I understand, to travel into the occupied territories — Hebron, Nablus, and other towns. I'm glad. You'll receive a list of people we'd like you to interview. Most of the names on it belong to women. Naturally, while in the field you will certainly come across other interesting angles worth writing about and capable of advancing our agenda. Any questions?"

There were none. Calvin Bridge lifted the receiver of his phone and whispered into it. A young clerk entered almost immediately, and stood waiting respectfully for the editor's orders.

"Bring me the blue file. It says 'Nablus' on the front."

As the clerk left, Bridge addressed the Rosenbaums again: "I want imaginative articles. A glimpse into the suffering Arab woman in occupied Palestine. The mother whose son has been killed by the conquering Zionists, or locked up in an Israeli prison. Do you follow me? I want our readers to know how Arab children are being raised in the occupied territories, how these families are subject to searches by Israeli soldiers on any night, and the trauma this causes the children. The hunger, the fear, the constant danger. How does the Arab woman cope? We are interested in the personal touch. Some illuminating dialogues with the man in the street can only help our purposes. Get it?"

Avraham and Rachel nodded. They understood all too well.

The young clerk brought in the folder Bridge had requested. The editor pulled out a list of Arab women.

"These woman have already agreed to be interviewed," he told Avraham, handing over the list. Avraham glanced at the names: Nadia al-Amin, Erin Yunis, Sarin Didawi, Samira Tukan, Hulud Hamud. He read them again, more attentively. Which of these names belonged to his sister?

Calvin Bridge continued, "You'll be well received there. We've already made all the arrangements. We're in constant contact with members of the opposition in the occupied territories."

Another rapid exchange of glances passed between the Rosenbaums. In his wife's eyes, Avraham read the question as clearly as if she had spoken aloud: *What did I need all this trouble for?* They looked away quickly, hoping that the editor seated opposite had not noticed. It would not do for him to grow suspicious that they were not the people they were purported to be.

"A liaison man from the Fatah will be waiting for you, and will accompany you during your stay. A local news photographer will also be at your service, to take advantage of any incidents or personalities you may come across."

The conversation continued a few minutes longer. The clerk, meanwhile, appeared a second time with a pair of airline tickets and several back issues of the periodical. Bridge wished them "Good luck" and, with handshakes and warm wishes all around, they parted. Rachel, for one, was impatient for the moment she would set foot out of the building and breathe fresh air. She felt suffocated by this very-close encounter with haters of Israel.

Binyamin took them to their hotel in his car. Scarcely a word passed between the three during the drive, as each of the Rosenbaums sat submerged in reverie. Binyamin was quiet, too, in deference to his companions' tension over the just completed meeting and their upcoming trip.

Back in their room, Avraham wondered aloud, "Who on this list could be my sister? None of the others interest me at all on this insane trip."

"It *is* insane," Rachel said promptly, from the armchair in which she was ensconced. "We may live to regret it. The flight is tomorrow morning; we still have time to back out. Your stubbornness really amazes me, Avraham." She paused, shaking her head with a combination of wonder and frustration. "You seem so certain that we haven't walked right into a trap. I tell you, I don't understand anything!"

Avraham had no answer. Had he known Binyamin's number, he would have phoned him then. At a loss, he murmured, "What next?"

Angrily, she snapped, "You're asking that now? I've been asking that question from the first minute: 'What next?' If you'd listened to me then, we wouldn't be sitting in a Toronto hotel asking 'What next?' Maybe you'll want to tell me again, '*Asher n'sa'o libo*'?"

Now it was Avraham's turn to grow angry. "Yes — exactly! That's just what I'll tell you. Let me remind you once again: Had Hashem not wanted me to be here, He would not have had me find those envelopes. Isn't that obvious? So — I'm going on! Even if I don't understand everything yet, I'm sure this is not a trap."

After that, they sat in a silence that stretched interminably. Darkness settled over Toronto, but neither made a move to turn on a light.

Then — just when it seemed that they would sit there in the gloom forever — the phone rang. It was Binyamin.

"Get down here, fast."

Avraham's breath caught in his throat. "What happened?"

"Nothing's happened. But we have to meet with someone, in order to plan your real trip."

As they descended in the elevator, Avraham said to Rachel, with a touch of triumph, "You see? It's not a trap!"

"It's too early to decide that yet," she retorted.

Binyamin was waiting for them in a taxi instead of his own car. Though Avraham wondered at this, he asked no questions. They rode for close to half an hour along Lake Ontario, its black waters reflecting Toronto's glittering lights. At last, they came to a complex of tall apartment buildings. Binyamin rang a bell and was buzzed in. The three rode up the elevator to the fourteenth floor. Unhesitatingly, Binyamin rang another bell — this one beside the door of one of the apartments.

The door opened. Right there, on the doorstep, a surprise awaited them: Calvin Bridge, smiling broadly as he whispered in fluent Hebrew, "How are you?"

The Rosenbaums stood transfixed on the doorstep. They might have stood there indefinitely, but Binyamin did not give them the chance to linger. With a quick gesture he shepherded them inside, saying urgently, "Go on in, please. We don't have much time."

The four quickly took their places around the dining room table. The editor of the *New Commitment* was clearly enjoying the shock on the two "reporters'" faces. Accurately interpreting the unasked questions stamped there, he said, "Binyamin is right. We don't have a lot of time. This is when we explain your real mission in Shechem — how to act, and what to be careful of. But, just so you'll understand, let me say that we bought that anti-Semitic magazine a few years back."

"Who's 'we'?" Avraham asked curiously.

It was Binyamin who answered. "You are intelligent enough to know the answer to that."

Calvin Bridge took up the thread again. To Binyamin, he said, "Thank you for coming from Israel to help us." Then, to the Rosenbaums, "Purchasing the magazine gave us access to a great deal of information in the Arab world and in the Palestinian one, through the material they send me and a great many meetings with their reporters. You might be interested in learning that most of our employees at the paper are non-Jews who really support the P.L.O."

"And you? Who are you?"

Bridge didn't answer. With a meaningful smile, he said, "Let's get down to brass tacks. Your sister's name appears on the list I gave you. She's called Samira Tukan. After her husband's death, she decided to change her name; we don't know why. In any case, she manages a small hotel called the Al-Quds. It hosts genuine tourists as well as our agents who manage to infiltrate from time to time. The hotel is a center for terrorist activity. Your sister, I'm pained to say, became very active after her husband was killed by our forces. This is a shocking phenomenon, perhaps the only one of its kind in the whole history of the Jewish-Arab struggle." He shrugged. "But those are the facts, friend. You've got to live with them."

"I'm going to drag her out of there!" Avraham declared energetically. From the corner of his eye he noted the slightly mocking look with which his wife greeted this pronouncement.

Binyamin said, "That's why we're helping you. If you succeed, it will be a significant achievement.. The G.S.S. will be grateful."

Calvin Bridge — who declined to reveal his true name — spoke rapidly: "We have no time. I can't stay in this apartment for long. Let's wind this up.

"You're going to Nablus, where you are to speak only English, even when you are alone. From what I've heard, you're both fluent in the language. Your American accent," he told Rachel, "is useful. Perhaps you should do most of the talking for the two of you. Both of you must keep your eyes peeled at all times. The Palestinians are extremely suspicious — and their suspicions can lead to violent reactions. Act quietly. Never use the word 'Israel'; always say, 'the Zionist oppressor.' During the flight, I'd suggest you look through the material I gave you, to familiarize yourselves with the international language of the pro-Arab left. I'm going to rely on your intelligence. Have a safe trip, and good luck."

They parted warmly, though the tension in the air could easily have been cut by a knife.

The next day, the Rosenbaums boarded an Air Canada flight and transferred to a connecting flight in London. Their plane landed before dawn in a small airport in Amman, Jordan. They were met by a young Palestinian who spoke a careful, if somewhat flowery, English. They arrived in Shechem late that night, and were taken directly to the Al-Quds Hotel.

27

Avraham and Rachel stepped out of the car into the chilly Shechem night and took a long look around them.

At 10 p.m., Shechem was asleep. A few dim streetlights illuminated the narrow street, fighting a losing battle against the starless night. The hotel entrance, which the couple stood facing with pounding hearts, was not particularly well lit, either. The darkness, and the utter silence surrounding them, only served to heighten their already keen feeling of trepidation. Their eyes darted from side to side, until they finally came to rest on the plain, two-story buildings standing shoulder to shoulder on the quiet street.

Only a very few windows in these residential buildings still showed light. The silence was oppressive, broken only by a dog's mournful wail in the distance. Rachel and Avraham stood locked in the grip of a fear that coiled and writhed inside them like a deadly serpent, as they stood together in the dark land of the enemy.

At last, Avraham forced himself to look directly at his goal: the hotel. Who would ever have believed he would actually make it here? This whole situation seemed to him, at that moment, unreal — even crazy. He lived in Petach Tikvah, an hour's drive from the spot on which he now stood, but it may as well have been a world away. This was another country — an alien and frightening one.

"*N'sa'o libo*" flitted rapidly through his mind. He could not tear his mesmerized stare from the faintly glowing sign hanging on the hotel in Arabic and English: "Al-Quds." It was a small, undistinguished-looking place. Like the other buildings, it consisted of two stories made of stone. A stone path led crookedly up to the lobby entrance.

Then, like lightning, the realization struck him: *My sister is in there, not a two-minute walk away!* He glanced quickly at his wife, but her eyes were still moving restlessly from side to side. *She's nervous*, he thought. He could well understand the feeling.

Mahmoud, the young Palestinian who had met them at the airport, opened the gate into the hotel courtyard and whispered, "Please."

Reluctantly, they began to move. With hesitant steps they followed the youth through the gate and along the path, walking carefully in the dark. An uncultivated undergrowth covered the ground on either side. They reached the front door, which was made of glass and appeared locked for the night. As he waited for Mahmoud to open the door for them, Avraham felt his breathing becoming more and more labored. Would his heart withstand this adventure?

Mahmoud held the door ajar. Avraham and Rachel stepped inside and followed him into the tiny lobby.

A single yellow bulb, surely not brighter than 40 watts, lit the place at night. Inside, in a dark corner of the lobby, sat two men who began to rise the moment the newcomers entered. Avraham glanced at them once, quickly, and then looked away. A definite sense of menace emanated from the pair.

The Rosenbaums approached the front desk, trying with every ounce of strength to conceal their inner turmoil. Behind the desk dozed a gray-haired woman. Avraham suddenly caught his breath: Was this *her*? Was it his sister? He waited impatiently for her to raise her head.

He hoped — he *knew* — that he would recognize her immediately. During the long trip from Canada he had spent hours gazing at the torn photograph, trying to imagine the way his sister might look now, more than twenty years later.

The woman dozed on, oblivious. Mahmoud shook her slightly. "Fatima, we have guests. Wake up! Welcome them properly."

The woman awoke with a start. Her head jerked up and her fingers rubbed the cobwebs of sleep from her eyes. Avraham's heart was hammering like a piston. The woman turned on the light, and for the first time he could see her face clearly.

His heart skipped a beat. No! It was not Rivka. The woman was too old, for one thing. There was also no resemblance at all to the features of the face in his photograph. The tension left him all at once, leaving a pounding headache in its wake.

Instinctively, he glanced at the corner of the lobby where the two men sat. Both were dark haired; both boasted thick mustaches on their upper lips. Both were also scrutinizing the arrivals with a cold, assessing look. It seemed to Avraham that he could glimpse the bulge of a holster under one arm. Fear began to envelop him.

Fatima took the Canadian passports the Rosenbaums held out. Drowsily, she opened them and began repeatedly checking the photos with the man and woman standing before her. Over and over came the same series of movements: Head lowered to check the passport photo; head lifted to scan the Rosenbaums' faces; head lowered to the passports once more — all with an infuriating slowness that wreaked havoc on Avraham and Rachel's nerves. At length, she limply offered the passports back, and added a room key: Room 204, on the second floor.

Mahmoud courteously escorted them to their door. "I am very familiar with this hotel," he explained in his careful English. "In the dark, you might take a wrong turn and have trouble finding your room."

Trailing after Mahmoud, Avraham and Rachel walked through the dimly lit corridors. Avraham wondered — but did not ask — why there were no adequate lightbulbs in place. They reached the foot of the stairs leading up to the second floor, and had begun to go up when a door from one of the rooms off the lobby suddenly opened and a woman came out. Strong light poured for a moment into the lobby from that room. In the circle of that light, Avraham looked down and thought, *It's her!*

He stopped abruptly. Almost at once, he realized his mistake. He had caught the woman's attention. Curiously, she lifted her head to look at him. Behind her stood two men, hands at their hips. Avraham needed no explanation to tell him what that meant: They were ready for a quick draw.

He resumed his climb at once, as though nothing had happened. Inside, however, his heart was beating like a drum. The woman came up to the foot of the stairs and watched his progress with interest. From where she stood, Avraham could have been no more than a silhouette in the gloom.

"*Min hada?* (Who's there?)" she called, in a low and quick voice.

Avraham did not answer. A strangling fear took over. Mahmoud called down, "They're reporters from Canada. We've just arrived from Amman."

"*Tiv (good),*" she said, relaxing, and turned back into the lobby. The two men followed.

Avraham's head was spinning like a top. That was his sister — he was sure of it! There was no calming the turmoil he felt. The dimness in the corridor shielded his agitation from Mahmoud, for which he was grateful. Rachel, walking along beside him, did sense something, but she was too wrapped in her own fear and tension to ask her husband any questions. In silence she strode along, wondering with every step how in the world she had ever landed in this place.

The ever-courteous Mahmoud left them at last at the door of Room 204. With a trembling hand, Avraham opened the door. It was only after he had shut it firmly behind him that he was able to find some relief from all the feelings that had been pressing on him during the past half-hour. He went directly to the window and threw back the curtains. Ignoring the cool wind that raked his face, he stood gazing out at the town without seeing a thing. A single image dominated his mind: the woman who had called up to him at the foot of the stairs five minutes before.

Finally, he turned to face Rachel, who was silently preparing for bed. In a choked voice, he whispered, "That was her! Rivka!"

She stopped what she was doing. "Are you sure?"

"One hundred percent!"

Her lips tightened. "Well, even so, don't rush into anything."

"Who's rushing?"

She said nothing in response to that. Nothing she might possibly say would have any effect. He was committed to this rash course, and she had promised to go along for the ride. If only they would come out of it alive —

Exhaustion finally embraced them like a heavy blanket, vanquishing both her fear and his excitement. They were in bed and drifting off when there came a sudden tapping at their door. Avraham shot up as though he had been bitten by a scorpion. Rachel, meanwhile, sprinted over to the window and drew open the curtains. Who knew if they would need an escape route?

The tapping had been faint at first. Now the knocks grew more urgent.

Clearing his throat, Avraham called out, in English, "Who is it?"

"Open the door."

Shaking from head to toe, Avraham obeyed.

He found himself facing one of the mustached men from the lobby. The man was wooden faced; not a trace of a smile in sight. Thrusting a brown handbag at Avraham, he barked, "You lost it!"

Avraham took the bag. With a distinct quaver in his voice, he said, "Thank you very much."

It was his wife's bag, inadvertently left behind at the reception desk. Without answering, the man left, closing the door behind him. The echo of his footsteps resounded for a long moment afterwards, gradually receding.

Avraham leaned weakly against his side of the door, breathing heavily. Midnight knocks on the door of a Shechem hotel that was swarming with terrorists — it was enough to leave him limp with fear. An impelling question welled up in him about just why he had been so determined to embark on this adventure. Rachel's voice cracked as she asked, as though reading his mind: "What do we need this for?"

Instead of answering, Avraham slid wearily back into his bed and tried to sleep.

But sleep did not come.

Hours passed. Outside, Shechem's dogs were beginning to bark their greeting to the new day, the first cars were beginning to move in the distance, and a neighboring rooster crowed. He heard a whisper in the gray light: "Avraham?"

"Yes."

"Were you sleeping?"

"No. I couldn't fall asleep."

"I can understand that. Neither could I."

Silence returned.

"Avraham?"

"What?"

"Are you afraid?"

"No."

"Well, I am. I couldn't fall asleep because I am so afraid. I'm shaking like a leaf. Avraham, I'm afraid that we won't come out of this adventure alive."

"Nonsense. A little trust in Hashem wouldn't hurt."

"If you're so confident, why couldn't you sleep?"

Slowly, he sat up. "I was too excited, that's why!" He drew a long, shaky breath. "This morning, I'm going to meet my sister."

28

At precisely 8 a.m., the phone in their room rang. It was Mahmoud calling. In his ever-polite manner, he said, "Good morning. I hope I didn't wake you."

"Ah, good morning!" Avraham responded. "No, no, you didn't wake us at all — well, maybe a little. We're still tired from the trip. We'd like to rest a little longer, okay?"

"Okay."

"Call again in an hour or two."

"Okay."

Avraham dressed hurriedly. Placing his suitcase on the table, he pulled out the false bottom that had been prepared for him in Toronto, and removed the *tefillin* hidden there. If Binyamin had had his way, the *tefillin* would have been left behind as a security precaution. The slightest suspicion could lead to a search of the Rosenbaums' luggage, with unpredictable and possibly fearsome results. But Avraham had dug in his heels. Without his *tefillin*, he was not going.

He put them on and recited the morning prayers. Every word he said was focused on the single goal that filled his mind and heart: a successful meeting with his sister. Rachel was *davening*, too, but her mind constantly wandered to Petach Tikvah, and her daughters. The silent prayer that filled *her* heart was that they might merit a safe return home from this adventure.

Afterwards, they ate some biscuits and vegetables brought from Toronto, and had a speedy, silent meal.

Rachel was first to speak. "Avraham?"

"What?"

"I'm worried about the girls. I so much want to know how they're doing."

Avraham suppressed a twinge of impatience. This was no time for thoughts that would weaken their resolve. "I'm sure they're fine," he said. "They're better off than we are, at any rate. You can be sure of that, Rachel."

Sighing, Rachel said, "That's exactly the problem. I keep wondering if we'll ever see them again. If anything happened to us — the girls would not have it easy, *chas v'chalilah*."

Avraham turned to her in anger. "Why do you speak that way? This is not something I'm going to worry about. You're forgetting that we were sent here, and that our own people — even without our knowing who they are — are nearby. Maybe even in this very hotel. Understand?"

"I understand. I guess I don't really believe it, that's all."

They were whispering in English. The possibility that someone was listening placed a great strain on normal conversation. Halfway through their talk, Avraham turned on the radio. A quick check of the available stations led him to the BBC, broadcasting from London. The room was filled with the morning news, in English.

"That's your problem, Rachel!" Avraham hissed. "Your lack of faith in what I was led here to do."

"Maybe," she admitted. "But I did come this far with you —"

In an attempt to lighten the atmosphere, Avraham chuckled slightly. "To fulfill what the *pasuk* says: 'You followed Me into the Wilderness, into an uncultivated land —'"

"Whatever. But maybe you can finally fill me in on your plans for your sister? How do you intend to introduce yourself to her? Will you just walk over and say, 'I'm your brother'?"

The sound of approaching footsteps in the corridor froze them into silence. When the steps reached their door, the couple held their breaths. Then the steps continued on, past the door and down the passage. Slowly, they grew faint, muffled by the rug that covered the length of the hall.

Avraham started breathing again. He turned to his wife. "What were you saying?"

"I asked how you plan to present yourself to your sister."

"Just the way you suggested. 'I am your brother.'"

"Come on. Really!" she protested.

He shrugged. "The truth? I haven't a clue. But I believe that, if Hashem wills it, when the moment comes, it will just happen." He grinned. "What's happened to you, Rachel? Suddenly, our roles are reversed. I'm the brave one, and you're the coward!"

Rachel parried that sally with a bitter smile. "I guess my courage is dependent upon my location. Petach Tikvah — yes. Shechem — no."

Avraham went to the mirror, where he donned a sports jacket and adjusted his tie. "Rachel, I really need your help right now. Please be brave, even here in Shechem. If you behave timidly, it might arouse unwanted suspicions. With Hashem's help, we'll be home tomorrow."

"You're so certain that you'll succeed?" she asked quizzically.

"No. Not at all. But either way, tomorrow we go home. Binyamin's men will get us out of here. We agreed on that back in Toronto."

"I didn't know that."

"There are some other things that you don't know. There are also things that I don't know. A little courage, that's all."

She went to the suitcase and locked it securely. Avraham and Rachel glanced around the room to make certain that all was in order. Then they went down to the lobby without waiting for their escort, Mahmoud.

As they stepped out into the dim corridor, Avraham whispered once again, "Stand by me, Rachel. Help me."

The Envelope

She smiled sadly. "I'll try."

"The moment of truth is here. Today's the day!"

"I'm well aware of that," she returned dryly.

They walked slowly down the steps leading to the ground floor. Avraham's eyes went immediately to the door adjacent to the lobby — the door through which the woman whom he believed to be his sister had emerged. It stood slightly ajar. Nothing could be seen of the room's interior through the crack, nor could any voices be heard from within. He presumed that the room was an office rather than a bedroom.

They went into the lobby. Avraham felt the weight of the new Canon camera bought in Toronto dangling heavily from his shoulder. The "tourist/reporter" couple chose a pair of matching armchairs in a corner of the lobby, from which vantage point they could observe both the lobby's entrance and the front desk. It was nearly 10 o'clock; Mahmoud should be making an appearance at any moment.

A sallow, emaciated-looking waiter approached and asked, in well-rehearsed English, whether they would care for some breakfast.

"Thank you, no," Rachel answered quickly. "Just two glasses of mineral water, please."

The waiter bobbed his head and hurried off. Both Avraham and Rachel noticed the speculative look he gave them before he left, and neither of them felt comfortable.

He returned shortly with their order. The Rosenbaums sat back and sipped the refreshing water, very conscious of their surroundings. Gradually, the lobby began to fill with life. The guests at this hotel were not the kind of people calculated to arouse either admiration or liking in Avraham and Rachel. For the most part, they were tall young men, clearly armed, and many boasted magnificent mustaches. Their suspicious eyes raked the small lobby, moving from person to person. Binyamin had warned them that the hotel was a hotbed of terrorists. Avraham was not especially afraid. His newspaper-reporter identity provided adequate camouflage.

But where was his sister?

People entered the lobby, people left the lobby, people crisscrossed the lobby, and in all this bustle of humanity only Rivka seemed to be missing.

Avraham wanted to study her as much as possible before gathering the courage to introduce himself. But she did not appear.

He glanced at his wristwatch. It was 10:30. Mahmoud was a half-hour late. This pleased Avraham. Sitting at his ease in this lobby served his purposes far better than following Mahmoud through the city streets, which held no interest for him at all. There was only one thing he would have liked to do on this visit to Shechem: to recite a few chapters of *Tehillim* over the grave of Yosef *HaTzaddik*. But this, he knew, was impossible in his present situation.

Then, suddenly, she was there.

The unexpectedness of her appearance threw Avraham into uncontrollable confusion. He had no idea from where she had sprung; she was just there, standing by the front desk. Incautiously, his face alive with emotion, he whispered to Rachel, "I think that's her!"

The woman turned. Had she heard him? Perhaps, in his excitement, he had not whispered at all, but had spoken aloud, drawing her attention yet again?

The woman regarded them — or, more particularly, regarded Avraham. Despite the changes that the years had wrought, her face was that in the photograph in his pocket. He found it impossible to maintain an impassive countenance, and he knew that she was aware of his excitement. In an attempt to calm himself, he grasped his nearly empty glass of mineral water and raised it with a trembling hand to his lips. The woman gave him a long, frightening look. Avraham was downcast; had he failed already?

Rachel, on the other hand, was amazingly self-possessed. She sensed the storm of emotion that was battering her husband, and knew that it was up to her to salvage the situation.

"Come on, let's go!" she said aloud to Avraham. Standing serenely, she began to walk with supreme nonchalance toward the reception desk where the woman who was probably Rivka stood. The woman did not move her eyes from Rachel.

Ignoring the penetrating stare, Rachel went to the woman who had received them the night before and tranquilly handed over her room key. She was standing very close to the person who was, in all probability, her sister-in-law. She could hear the other woman's rapid, shallow breathing.

Her own and Avraham's presence had apparently aroused some suspicion in the hotel proprietress.

For an instant, their eyes met. Rachel's were open and guileless, with a friendly warmth. Politely, she said to the woman, in her clear American English, "May I ask you something?"

"Yes," the woman answered hesitantly.

"Are you Mrs. Samira Tukan, owner of this hotel?"

The suspicion in the other's eyes mounted. "Why do you ask? Do you have complaints about the service?"

"No, no," Rachel laughed. "We've only been here one night. We slept beautifully, thank you."

"In that case, what is the problem?"

Rachel opened her eyes very wide. "They didn't tell you that we were coming?"

"No. Who are you?"

"My husband and I are Bill and Pamela Fairhaven, reporters for the *New Commitment* in Toronto. We've come, among other things, to interview you."

Samira Tukan considered this, then smiled. "Ah, yes. I didn't know that was you."

Rachel smiled back. She waved at her husband. "Bill! Hello, Bill, over here!"

Avraham stood up and walked slowly over to where the two women were talking.

"See, Bill? This is Samira Tukan, owner of the hotel, whom we're supposed to interview today."

Avraham nodded his head courteously. "Pleased to meet you."

His voice sounded strangled in his own ears. Samira stared at him, uneasy for some reason. Rachel saw that it was up to her to keep the situation under control.

"We're so excited to be here," Rachel gushed. "This opportunity to visit and write a series of articles on the situation in Nablus under Israeli occupation is one that interested us very much. We support the Palestinian struggle for independence, and pray for an end to the oppression."

Samira listened impassively while Avraham stood by in silence, moved by his wife's take-charge behavior. *Baruch Hashem*, Rachel had returned to her usual self.

Samira murmured halfheartedly, "Welcome."

"When can we sit and talk?" Rachel asked. "Actually — interview you?"

Taking a step back, Samira asked, "Why do you want to interview me, especially?"

With her characteristic enthusiasm, Rachel said, "They told us that you're active in the opposition to the Zionist conquest. And, apart from that —" She let her words trail off, the sentence unfinished.

"Apart from that?" Samira pressed.

"Well," Rachel said hesitantly, "they also told us that your husband was killed by the Israelis, and was recently declared a *shahid* (holy man). I'm so sorry. We share your pain."

Samira drew a deep breath, as though to keep the sigh from bubbling up from her heart. "Yes. Thank you for empathizing with us."

"So when can we interview you?"

Samira paused for a long moment before answering. "In the late afternoon, the hotel will be quieter. Do you have any plans for today?"

"Nothing special." This time, it was Avraham who answered. His voice was still slightly choked, and he spoke rapidly. It was a rather pathetic attempt on his part to join in the conversation, to prove that he was all right. But the suspicion did not leave Samira's eyes.

"In that case, I suggest that you take a tour of the city. Talk to people, try to hear from them how they feel under the Zionist boot. That will give you background material for our interview. All right?"

Before they could answer, Samira glanced over their shoulders and said, "Ah, here is Mahmoud. He will accompany you."

They parted, the "Canadians" to go with Mahmoud, and Samira to return to her office. The moment she saw the guests leave the hotel premises, she hurried to her private phone.

"Abu Joda, come see me immediately."

The Envelope / 205

Abu Joda — a tall man of thirty summers; black eyed, black haired, and heavily armed — arrived at Samira's door within minutes. He saw at once that, though the hotel proprietress presented a cool exterior, she was actually extremely agitated.

"Sit down," she said curtly.

He sat down in an armchair not far from the desk at which Samira sat, and folded his hands expectantly.

"Did you notice that pair of reporters who arrived from Canada last night?"

"I noticed."

"Where did you see them?"

"I saw them enter the hotel. I was on guard in the lobby."

"Good. What did you make of them?"

Abu Joda shrugged. "I don't know. They made no special impression on me. Another foreign couple! They'll write some supportive articles about us in the world press, and that's about it. You and I both know that all the articles in the world won't get the Israelis out of our city."

His answer, he saw, did not satisfy Samira. Curiously, he asked, "Has something happened?"

"I don't know," she answered frankly. "For some reason, I'm not at ease."

Abu Joda was Samira's lieutenant in her struggle against an IDF presence in the neighborhood. He gave pep talks intended to incite groups of young Arabs in the valleys surrounding Nablus, reinforcing their faith that the day of liberation from the Israelis was coming. He also provided these youths with basic weapons training. Their zeal was kept at a constant simmer by way of impressive parades through the streets of Nablus, to the accompaniment of hypnotic drumbeats and chants such as "In blood and fire will we redeem you, Palestine!" These marches always kindled in the young men a vengeful fire against the hated Israeli conqueror.

Of course, these public showings were only the revealed side of the other, more clandestine agenda: performing acts of terrorism, inflicting damage on Israeli vehicles, setting fires, throwing stones, a great deal of theft — even uprooting trees in the *Yahud* settlements nearby. It was Samira who set the tone for these activities: She was always cool, calm, and calculating.

In contrast, it was clear that something was frightening her now. Abu Joda leaned forward, eyes alight with curiosity.

"Why?" he asked.

She waved a hand. "I wish I knew."

"Did you notice something about the reporters that aroused your suspicion?"

She lowered her face, for a moment, into the palms of her hands. When she lifted it again, Abu Joda noted the signs of fatigue showing suddenly around her eyes. Slowly, she said, "I don't know why, but that young man seems somehow suspicious to me."

"Why?"

Samira spoke as though she were thinking out loud. "He behaves strangely — especially around me. Maybe it's just my imagination, but I don't think I'm wrong. His eyes keep following me. Why? I don't know. He seems nervous, excitable. That's suspicious."

Abu Joda asked, "GSS? Mossad?"

She laughed. "No, no. Those men know how to control themselves only too well. They're not so stupid, those Israelis, as to send out an agent like that inexperienced young man who shows every emotion so clearly on his face. They wouldn't send someone like that reporter — if, that is, he really *is* a reporter. He does not display knowledge of the basics of espionage and spying." She ended with an impatient gesture. "But — who knows?"

"Then what do you think? Or rather, what are you afraid of?"

"I wish I knew," she said again. "I don't know what to think. But you know that we have to be wary of the Israelis."

They fell silent. Abu Joda lit a cigarette, then offered one to Samira, who waved it away.

The silence stretched some minutes longer. Abruptly, Samira spoke. "Listen, Abu Joda. Just to calm my nerves, I want you to make some very thorough inquiries in Toronto, Canada, about those two. Find out if a magazine called *New Commitment* even exists. If it does, who owns it? And who, exactly, are the two reporters they sent here? All right?"

"All right." Abu Joda was already on his feet and on his way to the door.

"And do you know what else?"

Abu Joda stopped and looked back. "What?"

"Arrange for a small but thorough search of their room on the second floor."

Abu Joda nodded and left the room. Samira knew that Abu Joda — the man in Nablus most loyal to her — would carry out her orders without thought or hesitation. Much of Samira's strength and authority emanated from Abu Joda's loyalty. He was not reticent about displaying muscle to anyone who was unwilling to help her, who, after her husband's death, had become one of the leaders of the opposition to the Israeli occupation of Nablus.

Samira remained behind in her office, alone. With every ounce of concentration she could muster, she tried to logically analyze just what it was about that young reporter from Canada that so disturbed her. Why was he paying so much attention to her? Though she had dismissed, to Abu Joda, the notion that he might be an Israeli agent come to expose her hotel's secrets, she had definitely not discounted that possibility entirely. While it was true that he behaved like a novice in that field, there was no way of knowing whether he possessed some sort of hidden "sting," the kind the G.S.S. were so skillful in accomplishing.

What really surprised her was the fact that the couple had reserved their room for only two nights. That meant that they would be leaving tomorrow morning. According to the itinerary they had left at the front desk, they were due to fly from Amman to Riyadh, Saudi Arabia, tomorrow. In that case, what exactly was going on here? Her fears must be groundless. They must emanate from an overly suspicious mind, which she had cultivated after the Israeli border police hunted down and killed her husband, Abu Daoud al-Razak, in the hills of Nablus. Was that the answer?

The phone rang. She picked it up, to find Abu Joda on the line.

"I spoke with Canada. Everything's in order."

"What's in order?"

"There is a magazine by that name. It is a great supporter of the Palestinian struggle."

"And the reporters?"

"They're also legitimate. There's nothing to worry about."

"You understand, Abu Joda, that I will hold you responsible for what you're saying."

"I understand that very well."

How he understood! Samira was merciless with anyone who failed in carrying out an order, or who later was found to have supplied incorrect information.

"And what about their room?" she asked.

"There? Almost everything is in order."

She pounced on the word. "What do you mean, 'almost'?"

"We didn't find anything out of the ordinary. But we did come across one item that might lead to various conclusions."

"What is it?" Her voice rose to a near-scream, and she was immediately angry with herself for the momentary lapse of self-control.

"A package of biscuits, that's all."

Samira was at the end of her patience. Icily, she snapped, "Are you prepared to explain? Have you never seen biscuits before?"

Laughing, Abu Joda said, "Of course I have. But this package had Hebrew letters on it."

Samira was silent. They might actually be dealing with a disguised Israeli, one of "their" agents. But — no! That was not possible! This would make two mistakes the man had made so far. The first had been in watching her with such open interest; the second was bringing Jewish, perhaps even Israeli, products into her hotel. Something was not right.

Abu Joda waited patiently while Samira considered her reaction. At last, she asked, "The biscuits — are they Israeli?"

"Hm — they don't look like it. It looks like they came from New York."

"Bring them here, please. I want to see them."

And then, even before he had time to replace the receiver, she changed her mind. "No! I don't want to see them. Don't bring them."

Surprised, Abu Joda asked, "Why not?"

"I don't know. I just don't want to see them, that's all."

"All right," her henchman said quietly. "Whatever you say."

The call ended. Samira leaned back and closed her eyes. She had astonished herself. Why did she refuse to look at the suspicious biscuits? Was it because of — because of — the Hebrew letters? Letters that she had not intentionally looked at for — how many years? At least twenty, now. Was she so afraid of those letters?

And who was this mysterious couple who had brought those biscuits to her hotel? Did they not understand that they were endangering themselves? Perhaps that was precisely what they wanted, for reasons of their own, to accomplish. But what reason could they have for placing themselves deliberately at risk?

She made a resolution. During the interview she had promised the Canadian reporters in a few hours, she would do everything in her power to unravel the mystery surrounding the couple.

Avraham and Rachel concluded their tour of the city and returned to their room. They wanted to eat something and take a brief rest before their upcoming interview. Avraham turned the key, opened the door — and stopped short.

"What's the matter?" Rachel asked at his shoulder.

Avraham did not answer right away. Holding his breath, he let his eyes slowly roam the room.

"Why aren't you answering? What is it?"

Avraham whispered, "I'm not sure. But my instinct tells me that someone visited our room while we were away."

"Why do you think that?"

"I don't know how to explain it. It just seems to me that we left the room looking a little differently."

"What do you mean?"

"For example, I positively recall that I didn't leave my suitcase lying on the table the way it is now. Whoever searched it apparently wanted us to know he'd been here."

"How do you know?"

Avraham's gaze remained riveted on his suitcase. He walked slowly into the room and approached the table.

"See?" he said, very quietly. "The zipper was facing the window. Now it's facing the door."

"Maybe you don't remember for sure?" She seized on the hope the way a drowning man grasps at straws.

"I told you, I remember it positively. One hundred percent!"

All at once, Avraham hurled into action. He threw open the suitcase and his hands riffled through its contents until they reached the secret compartment at the bottom. Pulling that open with wild haste, he let out a long sigh of relief. The *tefillin* were in their place, just as he had left them. That meant that the intruder had not discovered them.

The overwhelming tension that had been gripping him dissipated, with dizzying abruptness. He felt limp, and he had broken out in a cold sweat. One thing was certain: He had a pounding headache.

Rachel suddenly put a finger to her lips. She gestured for Avraham not to say a word. Pulling a small notepad from the pocket of her skirt, she tore off a page, scribbled a few words on it, and passed it to him.

Avraham read: "If you think they're suspicious of us, then maybe they've planted a bug in the room?" He nodded: She could be right. Tearing off another page, Rachel wrote a second brief message: "Do you still think we should be involved in all this? Believe me, when we passed the central square on the main street and I saw the *Tzahal* jeep passing by, I felt such a longing for home that I wanted to run over to it, tell our soldiers everything, and beg them to take us out of here!"

He threw her an angry glance. Turning over the page to the blank side, he wrote, "You want to back out now, when we're nearly finished? Just before the final stage?"

She read what he had written and gave him a look of mingled pain and confusion. She wrote back, "I'm sorry. Really. Maybe I was too hasty just now. But think for a minute what would have happened if 'they' had found the *tefillin*. It makes me shake all over to think what our fate would have been in that case. How right Binyamin was when he said it was dangerous to bring them."

With quick, nervous strokes, Avraham penned his reply: "Did you really expect me to travel without my *tefillin*?! It says, 'One who observes a mitzvah will not know a bad thing.' Look at the bright side — they searched the suitcase and didn't find the *tefillin*. Heaven is protecting us. Please have a little faith in what we're taught: 'When Hashem approves of a man's path, even his enemies will make peace with him.' I'll thank you all my life for coming here on this crazy adventure with me. Let's *daven* to Hashem now, and ask that the last stage end safely, too."

She wrote: "When is it going to take place — the last stage?"

"Tonight!"

"How?"

"I don't know. I'm hoping for help from Above. It's tonight, or never!"

30

Mahmoud rang their room to let them know that Samira Tukan, the proprietress, was ready to meet with them.

"Come down to the lobby. I'll be waiting for you there."

Tension gripped Avraham and Rachel. The hour had come. As they prepared to leave the room, Avraham felt suddenly weak around the knees. He was trembling from head to toe. He turned on the radio to cover their voices.

"I can't do it," he whispered. "The excitement, and the emotion, are killing me."

Rachel was astounded. "But this is the moment you've been waiting for! You dragged me here just for this!"

With unsteady fingers, he knotted his tie. Almost inaudibly, he said, "You're right. But what can I do? This feeling is too strong for me, it's killing me. *Oy* —"

The Envelope / 215

"But you have to!" Rachel said, biting her lip. "If you start something, you have to see it through to the end. What was it you kept telling me? '*N'sa'o libo, n'sa'o libo.*' Let's see your '*n'sa'o libo*' now!"

Avraham groped his way to the bed and sat down heavily. He was deeply ashamed of the weakness that had overtaken him. "You know what, Rachel?"

She was already at the door. Impatiently, she said, "What?"

"You be the reporter, while I observe. Maybe I'll recover during the interview."

"What do you mean? That will only make them more suspicious. The fact that they've already searched our room is a bad sign."

"No, no. You don't understand," Avraham said, more clearly now. "They don't know for sure who is the reporter and who's not. Apart from that, it's more appropriate for a woman to interview another woman. Do me this favor."

She regarded him penetratingly. "I would not have believed this of you, after all the speeches you drummed into my ears during this whole trip."

He tried to draw a deep breath, then another. His heart was so full that his breathing came rapid and shallow instead. Rachel saw that her husband was indeed in the grip of a powerful emotion. At last, he spoke: "I would not have believed it, either. But that's that."

The phone rang again. Mahmoud was on the line. "Why aren't you coming down?"

"Yes, yes, we're on our way!"

Rachel said urgently, "Avraham, get up and come on. We have to go down. There's no way back."

"You do the talking, with your American English. My own English is Israeli. That might give me away."

"You only thought of that now?"

"No — But it's right now that I'm afraid it might do damage."

She nodded impatiently, and opened the door.

"All right, I'll interview her. What do I ask her?"

He followed her slowly to the door, passed through, and closed it behind him. Through the dim corridor they made their way to the stairs that would take them down to the lobby.

"Ask her whatever you want," Avraham replied. "I trust you."

Out of the side of her mouth, Rachel muttered, "How our roles have suddenly changed. Now I'm the leader again."

He had no choice but to acknowledge the truth of his wife's words.

They reached the lobby. It was very quiet. Only the two ever-present watchmen were there, in their dark corner, their eyes raking the newcomers. There was nobody else in sight. The silence felt oppressive to the already apprehensive Rosenbaums.

Mahmoud appeared, gesturing for them to follow him. They did so in silence. He led them to the room that was apparently Samira's office. It was the same room whose door Avraham had seen open the night before, as he climbed the stairs to the second floor. That was when he had first glimpsed Samira, and recognized that she was his sister.

They entered the room.

Samira sat behind her broad desk, which was bare of papers. Head high, her cold glance studied the Canadian couple. For an instant, her eyes met Avraham's, and he lowered his own quickly. This troubled her. What was it about her that so disturbed this young man? Merely meeting her eyes seemed to be painful for him.

Avraham noticed a large framed photograph on Samira's desk. The man in the picture was no doubt her late husband, Abu Daoud al-Razak. His face resembled the one in the newspaper clipping that Avraham had found in his father's desk at home.

Samira stood up, smiled coolly at her guests, and invited them to sit on the sofa. She took her own place in an armchair, facing them. The door opened, to admit two mustached men, who silently sat down in the two remaining armchairs in the room. A bowl of fresh fruit rested on the low table in the center of the seating arrangement.

Samira opened the conversation in adequate, though accented, English:

"I understand that you are reporters for *New Commitment*."

Avraham and Rachel inclined their heads in assent.

"I have been told that you've come to Palestine in order to witness, from up close, the struggle of the Palestinian woman against the Zionist oppressor?"

"Yes," Rachel replied. "It is a struggle that arouses admiration and support among us young radicals in the United States and Canada."

"And what do you want now?"

Avraham and Rachel exchanged a swift look. Rachel said, "We have come in order to experience that struggle directly, on its own territory. We'd like to speak with several of its heroes. We were given the names of a number of people to interview. Hanan Ashrawi, of course — But we want to talk with those who are active participants, so to speak, and not with the professional public relations folks."

Samira did not hurry to answer. Once again, her gaze went to Avraham, sitting so quietly that he might almost not have been present. Their eyes locked for another instant — and, again, it was Avraham who immediately looked away. It seemed to Samira that she detected a trace of fear in his glance. She did not understand. According to the report she had been given, he was the reporter who was supposed to interview her. Why was his wife doing all the talking?

To Rachel, she said, "I understand. And I am a woman whom you refer to as an 'active participant'?"

Rachel leaned forward. "We'd like to publicize the stories of some of the struggle's genuine heroes. From the facts we've been given, you are one of them."

Samira glanced at the two men seated at her side. Something here disturbed her. How had these Canadian reporters received such detailed information about her? Suspicion flared up in her again, renewed and reinvigorated. And this fellow, the husband — what was it about him that so infuriated her? He sat there exuding tension any time he looked at her. What was going on?

And she must not forget the biscuits! The biscuits with the Hebrew lettering on the package that Abu Joda had found in their room —

Controlling herself, Samira kept her face expressionless as she asked politely, "How did you get these facts about me? I work secretively, you know."

"I don't know," Rachel answered, with disarming frankness. "The editor of the paper described you as a brave and dedicated woman who spends a great deal of time working with other women in Nablus, in order to elevate their national pride. Am I mistaken?"

Samira laughed. "Maybe — anyway, it's true, I do work hard to help the women. To imbue them with pride that they are women — that they are Palestinian women."

Avraham sat as though mesmerized. He was straining mightily to picture this tough, almost fanatically dedicated woman as the daughter of his gentle mother and father. Had she been like this in Ramat Gan as a girl? Or had the abrasive qualities crept into her personality during the years since she had taken up residence in Shechem?

Rachel had her notepad out and was busily writing down every word Samira uttered. She worked as naturally as though she was a born and bred reporter accustomed to conducting interviews every day of her life. As she wrote, she racked her brain for additional questions to ask, to keep the conversation flowing.

"For the purposes of this article, may I ask a few personal questions?"

"Certainly," Samira asked smoothly. "What do you want to know?"

"Where were you born?"

Rachel was thunderstruck at the question that had just emerged from her lips. Why in the world had she asked that particular question just now? It struck Samira, too, as unusual. And, she saw suddenly, it had shaken the other reporter as well. Why? The suspicion grew very strong in her that he was not a reporter at all, but instead — instead — Who was he? And why this interest in her birthplace right at the onset of their talk? Or perhaps the woman had asked the question innocently?

Without blinking an eye, Samira answered tranquilly, "I was born in Al-Quds, Jerusalem. When I married, I moved to Nablus. But that's a separate topic."

Suddenly, she turned to Avraham. "Mister Fairhaven, weren't you supposed to be interviewing me?" She wanted to hear his voice, and to glean from his conversation who and what he might be.

To his own astonishment, Avraham found his vocal cords in working order. He was actually able to speak without betraying the enormous tension churning inside.

"My turn will come, don't worry," he said, with a fair semblance of a smile.

"Mrs. Tukan, let's proceed to another topic," Rachel said hurriedly. "What contribution has the Palestinian woman made to the struggle to liberate the land from the foreign oppressor?"

Samira sighed. "The Palestinian woman is the one who, essentially, bears the weight of the struggle on her shoulders. The public praise, in general, falls to the fighting men. You see them in the field, arrested by the Zionist army, thrown into prison, undergoing tortures, and sometimes sentenced to long jail terms. But who makes it possible for these men to dedicate themselves to chasing the enemy from our land? It is the women at home, who raise the children — tomorrow's heroes. Without notice or praise, they are the true creators of the struggle, the glory, and the honor."

Rachel wrote down every word, while Avraham sat listening intently. The mustached pair seated opposite were silent, but their eyes never left Avraham and Rachel. *Who are they?* Avraham thought. *Bodyguards? Henchmen?*

Outwardly, Samira was the only one who was genuinely relaxed. She answered Rachel's questions easily and fluently. The questions dealt with the Arabs' relations with the Israeli occupiers in Shechem and elsewhere. What was her opinion of an armed struggle? Were the Arab women also learning how to fight with arms? Samira spoke with pride of training young Palestinian women to handle weapons, so that they might protect themselves and their young when Israeli soldiers burst into their homes in the dead of night to search for terrorists.

"Do you support the actions of Hamas, namely kidnapping and killing Israeli soldiers and civilians?"

Samira hesitated before answering: "I oppose bloodshed. But the oppressor must leave our land, our cities, and our homes. Only Allah knows whether this can be accomplished without violence. But all supporters of our cause, worldwide, ought to know that our own violence comes generally as a defense against that of the foreign oppressor."

Samira went on to relate, with pride, the tale of her efforts to awaken Palestinian women to an awareness of their rights, both as women and as human beings. She spoke of her work in organizing the women to better their lives, of advances in education and economic reform within the Arab community. She touched on the difficulty in persuading the average Arab male to learn to respect his wife as his partner in the struggle for Palestinian liberation and the establishment of a Palestinian state — and how this respect must translate itself into full rights for women in the Arab community.

"The liberation of the Palestinian woman," Samira concluded, "must precede the liberation of Palestine. One is dependent on the other."

During all this talk, Avraham did not take his eyes off the speaker. The things his sister was saying were almost unbearable for him to hear. Listening to her enthusiasm for the Palestinian cause, it was impossible to believe that here sat the daughter of R' Elimelech Rosenbaum and his wife. Had he made a mistake? Had he come to the wrong address? Perhaps the Mossad and the G.S.S. had erred in their identification, and this entire trip to Shechem was a mistaken venture?

No! Though she had aged, of course, the woman seated opposite him closely resembled the face in the photograph that rested in his pocket right now, ready to be drawn out at the right moment to surprise her. But how could she have changed so drastically? The Israeli girl who came from a good home, albeit not such an observant one, had turned into her own polar opposite: an active supporter of the PLO! It made Avraham want to cry. He longed with dreadful intensity to speak out, right then and there, but was prevented by the troubling presence of the two men at the meeting. As long as they persisted in remaining at Samira's side, Avraham could not reveal himself to his sister.

Samira and Rachel continued their dialogue, speaking almost as though they were friends. Watching his wife, Avraham was amazed at her capacity to play her role of newspaper reporter to such perfection. Now she was asking Samira about her life as a widow. Samira spoke of her two sons, one an oil engineer and the other a student in the university at Bir Zeit with propensities in the direction of Hamas. (*And these,* Avraham thought in anguish, *are the grandsons of my revered father, a Radomsker chas-*

sid!) Then Samira asked about their life in Canada. Avraham listened in growing astonishment as his wife described that far-off country, where she had never lived a day in her life.

Rachel began to speak more slowly as a sudden thought struck her. It seemed to her that Samira was not really interested in her — she was interrogating her. Rachel recalled, with a start, the "visit" someone had paid to their room while she and Avraham were out. These seemingly innocent questions about their lives in Canada would be subject to scrutiny by PLO personnel. She tried discreetly to shift the talk into other channels.

At that moment, Samira rose with a smile. She was convinced that the couple was covering up something. She had no proof, but she had her unfailing instinct — the instinct for self-preservation that awakens whenever any living creature is in danger.

The two Arab men got to their feet. Avraham and Rachel took the hint: The interview was over. It was time to leave.

Avraham felt as though he were about to faint. The opportunity he had dreamed of, and for which he had taken such a drastic and even foolhardy step, was slipping through his fingers. In the depths of his heart, he had hoped that his courage would see him through and allow him, in the midst of the interview, to confront her with the truth. He had yearned to see her reaction when the photograph was placed before her on the table. But his opportunity was lost. Those two accursed Arabs who seemed glued to his sister's side had dashed his hopes. Had he come to Shechem in vain?

Avraham and Rachel parted from Samira with a forced heartiness, then walked into the lobby.

"Let's go outside, I need some fresh air," Avraham muttered.

They found the street dark, chilly, and empty at this night hour. "You were terrific," Avraham whispered to his wife. "But I lost the chance of a lifetime."

"As long as we're here, the chance still exists."

"But we're leaving in the morning."

"The night is long," Rachel said. "Come on, let's go in. I'm cold."

Disappointment continued to gnaw at Avraham's innards. He did not see how "The night is long" would provide him with another opportunity to make up for the one he had lost.

And then — it happened.

They were near the top of the stairs, en route to their room, when Samira passed by and wished them another polite "Good night." Avraham looked at her, hardly more than a shadow in the ill-lit hall, and a voice cried strongly within him, *Now!*

He called softly, in Hebrew, "Rivka? Rivka Rosenbaum?"

Samira made a blunder. Those words, unheard for twenty years and more, unnerved her. Caught by surprise, she wheeled around, walked quickly back to Avraham in the dimness, and asked with deadly quiet, "Who are you?"

Avraham felt the cold thrust of a gun against his ribs.

Avraham could not speak. His throat was choked with emotion, with surprise — and with fear. The feel of the gun against his ribs removed whatever shred of equanimity he might have hoped to retain. The gloom in the narrow passage contributed its share to the grim atmosphere.

Without warning, the pressure of the gun intensified. This was accompanied by the repeated question, barked out angrily and with infinite menace, "Who are you?"

Avraham looked around. The only illumination where they stood was a thin band of light shining from beneath one of the locked doors. Even in the dimness, however, he could discern his wife's face, rigid with shock. Then, from nowhere, Mahmoud appeared, along with two tall, armed men — the pair of watchdogs from the lobby whose job was to scrutinize every new arrival and investigate every suspicious movement. As the men closed in on them from behind, Avraham and Rachel stiffened further. The backs of their necks prickled. Some instinct made Rachel twist her head to look around. Her eyes met a pair of hard, black ones.

Samira asked her question a third time, in a shout. Despite his fear, Avraham recognized the note of hysteria in her voice. "It's because I called her by her Hebrew name," he thought. Or, perhaps not. Maybe it was simply because she felt herself hounded and spied upon by Israelis. He must overcome his terror and confusion, and answer her. In her present, superagitated state, who knew what Samira would do next?

"Me? You're asking who I am?" he said. His voice cracked, and he spoke in gasps because of the gun grinding into his ribs. Deliberately, he had chosen to speak in Hebrew.

Samira replied in English. "Yes! Who are you? I will not ask again. The next time, I will act!" The gun pressed even more deeply into his aching ribs. But Avraham was inwardly rejoicing. The Arab woman with the gun understood Hebrew! While she had chosen to answer in English, she had responded accurately to the question he had posed in his native tongue. Even in the midst of his turmoil, he was pleased with himself for having thought to speak in Hebrew.

Slowly, he said, "I am Avraham. Avraham Rosenbaum."

"What are you doing here?"

"I came to see you!"

Samira took a step backwards. Suddenly, the gun was no longer grinding into his ribs. Avraham gratefully took in a deep breath of air. The proprietress continued to retreat. And then, when he was least expecting it, she lifted the gun with both hands and aimed it straight at his face.

Samira was coiled tight as a spring. Too late, she realized her mistake in responding to the Hebrew question. She snarled, again in English, "I don't understand. Take care how you answer!"

Beside him, Rachel muttered in anguish, "What did we need this for? What will become of the girls?"

But Avraham's attention was completely riveted on the threatening figure standing opposite him. He, too, was beginning to regret this lunatic adventure. Was this what Uncle Nachum had meant when he foretold that Avraham's investigation would lead him into trouble?

He answered Samira, this time in English. "I came to see you!"

He had placed his cards on the table; now, with a powerful sense of fear and expectancy, he awaited her reaction. He sensed the men behind him advancing slowly, until he could feel their harsh breaths on the back of his neck.

Very quietly, Samira asked, "Why?"

The moment of truth had arrived. He had never, in his imaginings, pictured it as happening in quite this way. From the depths of his unconscious, a voice commanded, *N'sa'o libo! Now!*

His breathing became ragged. Emotion threatened to dissipate with his self-control, and it was only with difficulty that he was able to articulate the words, "Because you are my sister. My sister Rivka. Rivka Rosenbaum!"

A vast relief swept over him. He had done it! He had succeeded, after all his efforts and planning, to reveal himself to his sister. His vision had come true! The results of his action were in Heaven's hands now. Despite the gun pointed at him, despite the armed men standing behind him, he felt sure at that moment that he and his wife were safe. His sister would not harm him, come what may.

Samira said nothing. A weighty silence descended on the dark passageway. Then Samira snapped something in Arabic. At once the men stepped up from behind to seize their arms, which they held painfully in a tight grip.

Samira continued her backward progress, never removing her eyes from Avraham and Rachel, and never letting the gun drop. Down the stairs they went in this way, with the men prodding their backs to hurry them along. With her left hand, Samira groped for her office door and pushed it open, letting out a flood of light. Avraham and Rachel were shoved into the room and propelled to the sofa where they had previously been seated. With a gesture, Samira told the guards to leave the couple alone. The men took their places behind the sofa, clearly ready to execute any order she might issue.

Samira took her seat behind her desk. Avraham's eyes met his sister's, but this time he did not look away. For some reason, his fear had evaporated. It was Samira who averted her gaze after a second or two. She set the gun down on the desk. Avraham viewed both these actions as minor victories of a sort.

Samira lifted her head sharply and, with a cool, proud air, studied Avraham. He longed with all his heart to know what his sister was feeling at that moment. Though she had not, in so many words, admitted to the fact, she must know that she was seated opposite her own brother. But not by the quiver of a muscle did her face betray any such knowledge.

Her voice rang out suddenly. "And now, the truth!"

Quietly, but with confidence, Avraham said, "You just heard the truth."

"You are risking your life with these nonsensical lies, sir!"

Unexpectedly, Rachel broke in. "How do you know he's lying?"

Samira threw her a disdainful glance. "First of all, if he came here to search for his sister, he came to the wrong address. Secondly, your own turn to answer questions will come. Right now, keep quiet. The two of you don't seem to realize what trouble you've gotten yourselves into!"

She turned back to Avraham. "Are you a reporter?"

"No."

"Do you come from Canada?"

"No."

"Were you there?"

"Yes."

"Did *New Commitment* send you and your wife here?"

"Yes, they did!"

Without removing her eyes from him, she sat back silently for a long moment. Then she said, "You're a little too sure of your answers."

Avraham, who had decided that he was no longer afraid of his sister, answered politely, "I am trying to answer your questions to the best of my ability. I know that I've stumbled into trouble."

She returned to her interrogation. "Does the editor of *New Commitment* know that you fooled him?"

"Of course not."

"You're not from Canada?"

"No?"

"Where from, then?"

Avraham and Rachel exchanged a swift look. Together, in chorus, they answered, "Petach Tikvah."

She sprang up to her full height, and screamed, "Then you are Israelis! Why have you come here?"

Avraham tried to get to his feet as well, but heavy hands clamped down on his shoulders, restraining him on the sofa.

"I told you," he said evenly. "I came to meet my sister. A sister who, until just a few months ago, I didn't know existed."

He saw, with satisfaction, the involuntary way she bit her lip. It seemed a promising sign in this peculiarly intense verbal struggle. She had heard what he had to tell her.

Slowly, Samira sat down once again. Curiosity prompted her to ask, "Let's say, for argument's sake, that this is true. Did you not know that coming here would be dangerous for you?"

"Yes. I thought about that."

"Then why did you do it? It's insane!"

"Yes," he agreed. "Insane."

"Well, what's your explanation for doing such a thing? Which," she added parenthetically, "I don't believe for a minute."

"I admit that it's crazy. But blood is thicker than water! I couldn't help myself."

Samira was quiet again, considering this. Then she said, "All right, all the joking is over. Let's get down to business. If you do not confess the true reason for your being here, we will find ways to get it out of you. Even under Israeli occupation, we manage to have our methods of interrogation. Cooperate with us, and save your life. Who sent you? The truth, now! The G.S.S.? The Mossad? The C.I.A.?"

Rachel burst in again: "If any of those organizations had sent us, do you think you would have found us out so quickly?"

"You are insolent!" Samira said angrily. "You are trying to insult us! Believe me, we have found out more than one G.S.S. and Mossad agent!"

Softly, Rachel said, "I did not mean any insult. I only meant to say that those agents would certainly not behave as stupidly as we have. True?"

The Envelope / 229

"True," Samira snapped.

"And they would not have revealed themselves to you the way we did tonight. And what a silly story to concoct — to claim that the leader of Arab freedom fighters is actually my husband's Jewish sister. Am I right?"

Samira plunged into silence. Avraham and Rachel kept their eyes trained on her. Samira's face was still stone cold and expressionless.

Suddenly, she looked across at her two henchmen and motioned for them to leave the room.

Mahmoud, the Rosenbaums' Arab guide, started for the door, too. But, with an imperious gesture, Samira stopped him. "You — stay here!"

Before they closed the door behind them, the two guards glanced back with intense curiosity at their leader. Avraham could read the astonishment in their faces at having been asked to leave. This, apparently, was not the usual routine when Samira was conducting an interrogation. On the contrary, this pair doubtless took a very active part in such sessions, Avraham thought wryly. Mahmoud remained standing just where Samira had stopped him, near the door.

Samira stood up and walked over to the Israeli couple sitting mutely on the sofa. A fresh wave of apprehension swept over them. What was she planning to do now? Avraham noted, with relief, that she had left the gun on her desk. For the present moment, at least, she seemed to have no use for it.

Samira advanced until she was just steps away from the pair. She stood there, facing them, without speaking. Suddenly, Avraham stood up, too. Under the influence of a welter of emotions, all of them intensely powerful, he needed to stand eye to eye with his sister. Rachel remained seated, twisting her fingers around and around in her lap.

Samira took another step forward. Avraham stood his ground, still as a statue. His heart pounded loudly in his ears. It was hard to breathe.

As he watched, an expression of indescribable pain and anger crossed Samira's face. Slowly, she closed her eyes. He sensed that something was happening deep inside her. Difficult memories, buried for over twenty years, had surfaced at once, like a depth charge exploding in the sea. Painful scenes from the past swept up to engulf her. In particular, she relived the last, horrible scene with her parents — especially, her father. She was back in her childhood home in Ramat Gan, on the night she was thrown unceremoniously out of the house.

Everything she had worked for decades to suppress and forget came rushing back now, because of this young man who was saying that he was her brother. Why? Why? She had hoped that all those things were erased from her heart forever!

Her hand reached for the support of an armchair; she was suddenly reeling under the onslaught of her memories. With her eyes closed, she could clearly hear, again, the curses her father had heaped on her head because she had pursued the Arab waiter, Abu Daoud al-Razak, and refused to leave him. Her father's furious words echoed in her head now, with renewed force, the way they had in that last, terrible hour before she was thrown ignominiously out of her home and fled to Shechem.

Standing opposite Avraham, she felt again all the old anger and the piercing pain that had made her hate her parents that night. They had not understood her, and they would not help her just when she had so urgently needed their help.

"Leave this house!" She heard her father's wild cry again. He had taken off his shoe and hurled it at her. She ducked; the shoe did not touch her, but instead shattered the glass door behind her. The glass fell to the floor in a myriad of sparkling pieces, with shards flying in every direction. Rivka/Samira fled to a corner of the room. But she encountered her mother there, who greeted her with a ringing slap to the cheek.

How she remembered the way she had stood there, stunned and confused.

"G-d's curse be upon you!" her father had shrieked madly. "To become friends with an Arab? You — a Jewish girl? My daughter?" In the grip of a blinding rage, he had screamed uncontrollably, "I'll be happy to hear that you're no longer alive!" It was a poison-tipped arrow, aimed directly at her heart.

"But, Abba," she recalled shouting back, her eyes filled with tears, "it's you who are to blame! You! You! You!" She, who had always taken care to treat her parents with respect, had lost all vestige of self-control as well. "You let me go to nightclubs, to go out with the gang without even checking who my friends were! What do you want from me now? Now you're complaining? And another thing — you, yourself, are practically irreligious. You're always talking about loving people just for being people. So why does this bother you so much?"

Her father had not answered. With the same enraged glare in his eye, he had shouted, "I told you to leave my house!" Running toward her threateningly, he bellowed, "Immediately."

The bellow was loud enough to set the light fixture above their heads swaying with the force of the sound waves.

She stood there, in the center of her office in her Shechem hotel, eyes closed and perfectly motionless. The silence in the room was total. Neither Avraham, nor Rachel, nor Mahmoud by the door moved a muscle. They almost dared not breathe. Each of them sensed that they were a part of some unseen and inexplicable drama. Instinctively, they understood that they must not disturb her, not by the merest breath.

Avraham saw Samira chewing on her lower lip. Anxiously, he wondered what was going through her mind. A tornado of emotion seemed to be blowing through his sister. He felt a sudden stab of pity for her. It was the compassion of a brother for a sister in trouble, a deep bond that he had not expected to feel. It seemed to him that she had suffered, and was continuing to suffer, over her enforced exile from her true home. These surroundings were unreal to her. Twenty years in an alien environment — that had to be excruciatingly painful.

Avraham longed to throw her a lifeline. Maybe it was for this very thing that he had been led to Shechem. Involuntarily, he blurted the thought out loud: "Can I help you?"

Without opening her eyes, Samira issued a bloodcurdling scream. "Quiet! You don't have any idea of what's waiting for you!"

Shaken, Avraham stole a glance at his wife. But Rachel, on the sofa, was completely engrossed in watching Samira.

The movie reel was still unwinding in Samira's mind, replaying scenes and emotions from years gone by. Most of all, she kept coming back to that awful moment when she stood, lost and in shock, staring at her overwrought parents. She had tried to say something, she remembered, but the words were stuck in her throat. All at once, she understood the reality of her situation. Running to her bedroom, she grabbed some clothes and a few personal items and crammed them into an overnight bag. Then she went over to the crib where her baby brother, Avraham, lay sleeping. The wild shouting from the living room had not disturbed him in the least.

The child was the only thing she still loved in that house. She leaned over and kissed his little face, bathing it with her hot tears. When she whispered goodbye, she knew it would be forever. How she had hated her parents at that moment!

And now, that hatred was reignited — all because of this young man who claimed to be her little brother. Toward him, she felt only rejection, scorn, and even some of that same hatred.

Her eyes opened slowly. Avraham caught the gleam of suffering in their depths. Still, Samira had not said a word. She merely stared at Avraham as though seeing him for the first time. Was this truly her baby brother? She searched for something familiar in his face — features that resembled her father, whose image was etched indelibly in her memory. She did not find it. Was he speaking the truth? Or was this some G.S.S. trap?

Once again, she began to gnaw at her lower lip until it hurt. She decided: No. She would not admit her identity to him. She had severed all ties with her former family; she would not inflict upon herself the pain of a renewed connection with this man who might or might not be her brother. She lived here, in Nablus! Her two sons had grown up here. She would never leave this place.

She turned slowly and walked to her desk. Quietly, she said, "Mahmoud, bring me a glass of water."

Mahmoud left with alacrity, to return very shortly with the water she had requested. She sipped it in a leisurely fashion, spent from the mental and emotional storm she had just experienced. Without a word, Avraham returned to his seat on the sofa beside Rachel. The silence stretched until the tension was well-nigh unbearable.

It persisted for several minutes more. Then, without warning, Avraham heard Samira ask: "Why have you decided that I am your sister?"

"So they told me."

"Who did? The G.S.S.?"

Avraham did not answer.

"Tell me!"

"No. But they did help me."

"Can you explain?"

Avraham hesitated. Carefully, he said, "After I found out, I asked for their help."

With narrowed eyes, she asked, "After you found out? How did that happen?"

Avraham glanced at his wife, then back at Samira. "After I learned of your existence — that I had a sister somewhere in the world."

With those words, Samira felt as though an arrow had mortally pierced her heart. With rising rage, she realized the implication of what he had just said: Her parents had hidden her very existence from him! They had simply erased her from the book of their lives. For them, she did not exist! They preferred that their son, Avraham, grow up believing himself to be an only child. The dormant hatred she harbored against her parents surfaced with a fresh fury. She felt as though she were about to explode.

With a self-control that she had not known she possessed, she managed to maintain her outward composure. In a dry, almost indifferent tone, she said, "You mean that you learned of a sister you may have. This has nothing to do with me, young man. Stop referring to me as your sister. Understand?"

Avraham nodded. Inwardly, however, he longed to say something quite different. He wanted to say something like, "Stop playing this game! We both know the truth. You are my sister." But he held his tongue. Seeing that his nod did not placate her, he murmured, "I understand."

"We'll move on," she said, in the confident tone of an experienced interrogator. "Have you ever seen me before in your life, that you dare call me 'sister'?"

Sensing a trap, Avraham answered humbly, "But you said I mustn't call you 'sister'!"

Samira laughed, a harsh laugh that held no merriment. "True. But I know what you're thinking deep inside. And curiosity, I'll admit, impels me to learn how you came to such an odd conclusion — to the point that you were willing to risk your life for it. Life is full of surprises, mister. I'm sure it comes as a surprise to you that you have a case of mistaken identity on your hands. But how did you come to this strange conclusion? I want to know."

Avraham was at a total loss. Was it possible, he wondered, that he really had mistaken this woman's identity, and thrust himself and his wife into danger in vain? The awesome confidence of this woman, this terrorist leader, rattled his own confidence in his conclusions.

And yet, something in his heart violently rejected his mind's logical deductions. He stood helpless, with no clue in the world how to answer her.

Samira seemed almost amused. She sensed his ambivalence very clearly. Through her teeth, she hissed, "I believe I asked you something?"

Rachel spoke up then, jumping into the fray to rescue her husband. "We identified you from a photograph that we received."

For an instant, Samira's face softened with natural, human curiosity, and the artificial hardness melted away. "A photograph? Of me? What are you talking about?"

Avraham revived a little. "Yes, I have a picture of you."

Samira considered this, then asked quietly, with a tremor of real feeling in her voice, "Can I see it?"

Avraham pulled the torn photo from his pocket and began to walk up to the desk behind which Samira sat.

"Stay where you are! Don't come near me!" she ordered harshly.

Confused, Avraham froze. The wild beast that lived inside this woman, he thought bleakly, had suddenly come alive again. He had no way of knowing that Samira dreaded having her brother come too close, lest she lose herself completely and throw herself weeping on his neck.

She turned to Mahmoud.

"Mahmoud, bring me the photograph that this Israeli spy is holding."

Mahmoud did as he was told. He plucked the picture from Avraham's unresisting fingers and carried it across the room to Samira. Her hand trembled as she took it. She stared at the photograph. It was one that she remembered well — as she remembered the pain and suffering that it had caused. Where had he found this? She certainly had never sent this picture to her "dear" parents. Had he received it from the Israeli intelligence archives? He had said that the G.S.S. had helped him to identify her.

"Hmmm — interesting. Really interesting. I see how you make your mistake, Mr. Petach Tikvah." A moment later, her cynical laugh rang out. "So where did you find this picture?"

Gathering his courage, Avraham shot back, "I got it from Uncle Nachum."

His heart leaped. His surprise remark had elicited a definite reaction; he could read it in Samira's face. As always, she got her features under control in a hurry, but he had seen something before the mask of indifference fell over them again.

"Why," she asked almost casually, "is the picture torn?"

She had not, Avraham noticed, asked who Uncle Nachum was, a question that would have been natural in such circumstances. She must know very well who Uncle Nachum was. The thought emboldened him further. He said, "I don't know. That's how I got it from Uncle Nachum. I decided that it would be one of the first questions I'd ask you, when we met: Who was standing beside you in the photograph?"

A quick look flashed into Samira's eyes: a look of open hatred. Then she threw her head back and burst into harsh and wicked laughter.

Avraham stood watching her, wondering what would happen next.

The Envelope / 237

T he laughter ended abruptly. Samira held the torn photograph in one hand, looked at it sideways, and then lifted her head and waved the picture at Avraham and Rachel.

Once again, her face wore its official cold, hard mask. A cynical smile lingered at the corners of her mouth as she said, "You people at the G.S.S. have done a good job, mister. You created a fine composite of my face. It must have looked like a reasonable facsimile to you, and you thought it would succeed in fooling someone. But not us, you'll be disappointed to hear. For us, it's merely laughable. It is clear beyond all doubt that something else lies behind this tired joke of yours. We are not as stupid as the Israelis believe."

She glanced once more at the picture. That was the way she had looked twenty years ago, younger and more graceful than today. There was, however, no smile on the face of the girl in the photo. That girl's eyes radiated sadness and stubbornness. The picture had been snapped at a point in time, she recalled, when the crisis in her home had been at its apex. She worked hard to conceal the feelings the picture aroused in her

— to school her face into an attitude of disdain. She knew that Avraham was closely following every changing expression.

Interesting, she told herself. *Why did Uncle Nachum tear the photo?*

Then, all at once, she remembered. An involuntary tremor seized her. *Of course I understand now! And how I understand!*

Slowly, she set the photo down on her desk. Steepling her fingers, she said coldly, "And now, I am going to ask you for the last time before the real interrogation begins — and I am sure you can imagine what *that* will be like, mister. I want to hear the truth this time! What did you really come to Nablus to find, and why this hotel? Please don't repeat the same silly story as before."

Breathing deeply, she added, "You'd better answer me quickly. My men, outside, are doubtless growing very impatient!"

Avraham was in a quandary. What to say? And why, indeed, had she sent those two armed thugs from the room? He was convinced that she had done so in order to avoid having them hear her confess her identity, *Just like Yosef with his brothers,* he thought, amid his fear and uncertainty. Hesitantly, in a voice that was far from steady, he said, "I know that my appearing here is out of the ordinary. My story sounds very strange. But it pains my heart that you don't believe me. I am speaking the truth!"

Samira sat unmoving and silent. She hardly even seemed to blink. She believed him. Oh, how she believed him! On some deep and very basic level, she knew that confessing her identity to him would make things easier for her in the long run — and this, despite the flood of pain and anger that such a confession would bring in its wake. But the vow she had made never to return to the Jewish people, and never to meet anyone from her family, had erected very tall and very strong walls around her heart. Those walls simply refused to crumble!

And yet, after years of complete exile, she was powerfully curious to learn what had become of her parents, and about her brother's life — her brother, whom she had left as a baby and who stood opposite her now, with his wife. It was a supremely difficult moment for her — as difficult as the day the Israelis had shot and killed her terrorist husband — and not at all unintentionally, as they subsequently claimed. What would her Arab family think of her? And what of the small army who were answerable to her — what would they think if they knew of her past?

And so, though she honestly did not know what the unfortunate couple before her could say, she said in a cold, menacing voice, "I'm still waiting."

Agitated, Rachel stood up. Everything that she held pent up inside wanted to burst out with hurricane force. For a moment, she forgot where she was, and in whose hands. She said, "I want to tell you something."

Samira likewise rose to her feet. She was blazing. She wanted to hear what her brother had to say, not have his wife speak for him. "I will ask you for silence. At once!"

Rachel was totally beside herself now. She headed toward Samira's desk, as though she had not heard the order at all. Samira signaled Mahmoud with her eyes, and the Arab shot forward to block Rachel's way. Were she not willing to return to the sofa at once, he was clearly prepared to drag her there by force. Quickly assessing the situation, Rachel returned to the sofa and, still on her feet, faced Samira. "I can't take this anymore!"

Samira stood shaking with fury at her insolence. "You can't take it anymore? You should have taken that into account when you decided to become Mossad agents, or G.S.S., or whatever you are." She paused. "Tell me the truth already. I promise to treat you with mercy if you do. The Arab is noble, and he keeps his word. But, if you don't do as I say" — her finger lifted threateningly — "you are in for some 'very special' treatment!"

The threat had no power to deter Rachel, who was beyond all control now. She seemed to have made peace with the fate that awaited her. She was weeping inwardly for her two young daughters, left behind in Petach Tikvah, and furious with herself for having been such a fool as to follow her husband here to Shechem. Right now, she had nothing to lose.

"I don't care about anything anymore," she declared. "I know what is awaiting me." Her voice cracked slightly as she made this pronouncement. "But I *have* to talk now. I've been sitting quietly for hours, and I don't understand what's going on here. I want to say, Rivka, that —"

Samira cut sharply into the flow of words. "Samira, if you please."

The Envelope / 241

"Samira, or Rivka — it really doesn't matter to me. I want to tell you that my husband has been obsessed about you for months! He has dreamed of only one thing. He wants to see his sister, to meet her face-to-face —"

Samira found herself deeply moved. With an effort, she broke in to say curtly, "What does any of that have to do with me?"

Rachel continued in a rush. "It's been months since he first began to dream of coming to Shechem. It began shortly after his father died, when he discovered —"

Samira choked back a gasp of surprise. "What? Father died?"

At once, she bit her tongue. A low moan succeeded in escaping before she clapped a hand over her mouth. With anguished eyes, she stared at the Jewish couple, knowing that she had made a horrific blunder. She had stumbled right into the trap. Her unthinking reaction had given her away. In a single instant's lapse in self-control, the secret she had so jealously guarded for so long had been exposed. Without meaning to, she had let her mask fall. What to do now?

A silent tension, dense and heavy as a thundercloud, filled the room. Every person in that room felt it — even Mahmoud, standing restless in his corner. He was very curious about the drama unfolding before his eyes. As they watched, Samira sat down and put her head down on her desk. Avraham leaned forward: Was she crying?

Rachel stood open mouthed, shocked at the results of her speech. Without intending to, she had achieved their goal. Samira had confessed to the truth. She had revealed that she was, indeed, their sister Rivka.

As for Avraham, he stood in the grip of a powerful current of emotion that made thought almost impossible. Almost, but not quite. Why, he wondered, had his sister so forcefully denied her true identity? Why had she played this cruel game with them, making him and Rachel fear that they had been terribly mistaken, and that they had fallen into the fearsome hands of Jew-hating Arabs? Why had she treated them so callously? Avraham could not begin to fathom why.

Without waiting for permission, he sat down on the sofa once more. The weakness had returned, sapping his strength. Lifting both hands, he buried his face in them. This was the moment he had dreamed of —

but not like this. It was the most difficult moment in his life. His sister, he sensed with dismal clarity, had not returned to him. She had merely been startled into admitting her past, nothing more. What next? What to do?

After a few minutes, he rose and began to walk toward the desk. In a flash, Mahmoud was there, blocking his way. "You can't!"

Avraham tried to push him out of his way. "I want to!"

Samira, alerted by the raised voices, lifted her head and signaled Mahmoud to step back. Rachel joined her husband. The couple stood a short distance from the desk. Avraham was still afraid of her, afraid of stretching his sister's taut and frazzled nerves to the breaking point.

They regarded one another. Now, Samira's eyes were telegraphing a different message than they had held ten minutes earlier. There was little affection or friendship in them; mostly, they registered surprise, hurt, and curiosity. It was crucial, Avraham felt, that they keep talking. This moment must not be allowed to die. He chose his words carefully.

"I see that, despite everything, you still care about your father."

She answered in a clear, ringing voice. "No."

Surprised, Avraham blurted, "Really?"

"Really!"

Now it was Samira who felt that she had nothing to lose. Some of her strength came flowing back. As for Avraham, he found it hard to believe that these were her reactions after more than twenty years. He fell silent.

Rachel, on the other hand, was prepared to continue. "Why?" she asked.

Samira glanced at her. "Did you know your father-in-law at all?"

"Of course. He was a good man, gentle and patient."

Rivka/Samira laughed bitterly. "Oh, really? Then you didn't know the same man I knew. He hit me! He humiliated me! He threw me out of his house! He said he was looking forward to the day I died! He erased me from his memory —"

Emotion overpowered her, choking off further words. Her breath came ragged and quick, and her entire body trembled uncontrollably. Closing her eyes, she willed herself to stop shaking. Finally, she was able to finish her thought. "So I also erased him from my heart and from my life! He doesn't exist for me! Understand?"

The last word emerged in a shriek. The door opened a crack, and a mustached face looked in. With a wave of her hand, Samira motioned for the door to be closed.

Quietly, Avraham said, "Yes. I understand."

Then he thought about it, and changed his mind. "Actually, I don't understand so well. According to Jewish law you are obligated to honor him, even if he did something bad to you. He is still your father. That's what it says."

She chortled, "Jewish law? That's what it says? What do you or my father have to do with Jewish law?"

"He had a lot to do with it, and so do I."

Instantly, she sobered. With open curiosity, she asked, "Are you trying to say that you are religious?"

"Yes. And so was our father, may he rest in peace."

A flame blazed up in Samira's eyes. "Ah, now I see. First he killed me off, then he turned religious. Very nice. And you want me to honor him!"

"Exactly!" Avraham said. "After what happened to you because of the kind of unrestricted upbringing he'd given you, he understood that it was time to return to his roots."

Her voice grew softer, and at the same time mocking. "Yes, I've heard of your *ba'alei teshuvah*. It amuses me. And you also chose this way of life?" After a moment, she added in a near-whisper, "Yes, it happens with us, too."

"With us?" Avraham asked.

Samira smiled. "All right, I get the message. This is a phenomenon we're seeing in the Arab world today, too. They're also returning to their religious roots. My own sons did."

"Your — sons?"

"Yes. My sons."

"You mean, our father's grandsons?"

"Yes, exactly so."

"That means they're Muslims! That's — that's shocking!" Avraham suddenly felt strangled.

"So be shocked," she shrugged. "It doesn't matter to me. But remember that it's all because of your father. He is to blame!"

"Why?"

"I told you. He erased me from his life." She leaned forward. "For example, when did you even learn that you had a sister?"

"One week after he passed away."

Triumphantly, Samira said, "You see, I'm right! I did not exist for him at all. He never even told you about me. True?" She stopped. "By the way, how *did* you find out?"

"I found an envelope."

"Envelope?" she repeated, bewildered.

"Yes. An envelope specifically concerning you."

Curiosity devoured her. "What was inside the envelope?"

"All kinds of newspaper clippings related to you and your..." He could not bring himself to say the word *husband*. "— and Abu Daoud al-Razak."

She pounced. "He was my husband, in case you didn't know."

Ignoring this, Avraham decided to add a lie, for the sake of peace. "There were also a few scraps of paper on which he had written how much he missed you."

Samira listened intently, but could not say a word. The turmoil in her heart grew so great that she was forced to close her eyes again. She felt as though she were caught in the fury of towering, storm-tossed waves that were doing their best to drown her. Her feeble cries for help were blown away by the wind, unheard. There was no one to toss her a lifeline. The waves were dragging her back, back —

Her eyes flew open. She stood up, trembling visibly, and spat out, "You are a miserable liar. I don't believe a word you've said! My father did not miss me, not for a single minute. Impossible. Impossible!"

She sank down — almost collapsed — onto her chair. She could not bear this any longer. Without warning, she turned to Mahmoud.

"Bring them in, please!"

Within seconds, the two armed terrorists were back in the room.

34

This is the end, Avraham thought in despair. His eyes darted from Samira to her two henchmen, who glared back with cold eyes. To Avraham they looked like a pair of wild gorillas which had escaped from the zoo.

What would happen now? Gruesome scenarios played themselves out in his mind, each following hard on the heels of the one before. Then he became aware of Rachel, standing beside him in a state of complete agitation.

"Calm down," he whispered. "Everything is from Above. Don't do or say anything to make her any angrier."

She answered in a murmur he could scarcely hear. "Avraham, there's nothing to lose. We're trapped! I want to say a few more things to her, so that she'll remember me for a long time. Something to make her conscience ache."

"Do me a favor, leave it alone. Don't fight with her and don't try to teach her. It's a waste of words. You can see there's no one to talk to."

Samira observed this interchange between her brother and his wife, but aside from a random word here and there she had not heard what they were discussing.

"What are you plotting now, when you've already been exposed?" she snapped.

Rachel lifted her head and answered quickly, "We're not plotting anything. You know that very well."

Samira bit her lip, as though to hold back a threatening explosion. "You are insolent and brazen, Mrs. Rosenbaum. You'd be wise to be very, very careful when you speak."

They noticed that this was the first time she had uttered the name "Rosenbaum." She said it as though she were reluctant to let it go. Rachel said proudly, "Samira, you know very well that we came to Shechem and to your hotel at great personal risk, solely because my husband hoped to meet you. He was so overwhelmingly excited when he saw you for the first time. His goal was to heal the breach with his sister, and to bring about a reconciliation in the family."

Samira lifted her hand in a dismissive gesture. "There's nothing to talk about."

Rachel sighed sadly. "Why do you insist on perpetuating the rift?"

"I said, there's nothing to talk about!" Samira almost shouted. "My men will take you back to Israel, and this will all be over."

She said something over her shoulder to the two "gorillas," who obediently began to approach the Rosenbaums. Rachel was in a quandary. Though she had been dead set against this trip into Shechem, she did not want to leave now without a victory. She hated losing. The Arabs were nearly upon them when Rachel took several steps back, calling out to Samira as she did so: "Just a minute! I want to tell you something. I know that you felt humiliated by your parents, and very deeply hurt by them. But your brother, Avraham, is not connected to any of that. He is not to blame! In that case, after so many years, isn't it time to make peace?"

"No!"

"Don't you even appreciate the great lengths to which he went to come here and see you, just because he longs to know you?"

Samira felt the white-hot arrow pierce her heart once again. It was impossible to remain impassive in the face of her very real emotion regarding her long-lost brother. She felt as though she were about to burst into tears that would never cease.

But her voice, when she spoke, was cool, controlled, and authoritative as ever.

"To come here was the act of a madman. I can hardly believe in its sincerity. By the way, tell me, madam — does our mother know about this little adventure?"

It was Avraham who answered. "No. She knows nothing."

A cynical smile played on Samira's lips. "So? You see?"

Avraham and Rachel exchanged a surprised glance. Avraham said, "See what?"

"That this was done on your own initiative, and that our mother opposes renewing any tie with me. It's a fact: You told her nothing about coming here."

"That's not exactly the way it happened," Avraham said excitedly. "You see, when I began to investigate the family's history, Imma cried a lot. She begged me not to talk to her about it any more. My instinct told me that she wanted me to uncover the truth, just not to involve her. The whole experience has been emotionally devastating for her — and, remember, she's a recent widow, who lost her husband unexpectedly."

Samira was quiet for a long moment. Without asking, Mahmoud brought her another glass of water. She thanked him with an abstracted smile and a nod, and took a sip. Avraham and Rachel, watching her, were suddenly aware of how parched they were after the ordeal they were going through.

Samira said, "All the same, there's something suspicious in the whole story. I don't know what it is."

Avraham said simply, "All right, Rivka. I know when I've lost. All this was for nothing. But know this: *I want my sister back. I miss her.*"

And suddenly, without the faintest idea that it was coming, he burst into tears.

He let the tears stream down his cheeks without making any attempt to wipe them away. When they reached his lips, he could taste the salt. And still, he cried.

Samira could not bear it. Her fingers gripped the edge of her desk until they ached. Whatever happened, she must control herself. There must be no sign of what was going on inside! She must not let emotion triumph over logic. Never!

Don't give in, don't give in, a tiny voice within ordered repeatedly.

Then she became aware that her brother's wife was sobbing, too. Her face darkened. What was happening here? This must stop — at once! The words with which she would order her men to take them away trembled on her tongue — but she didn't say them. She sat instead, dumb as a stone, eyes gazing helplessly at the spectacle before her.

In a broken voice, Avraham whispered again, "I want my sister back."

"Back?" Samira asked. "Back to where?"

"Back home! Back to Israel! Back to the Jewish people!"

She spread her hands in an almost gentle gesture. "Too late, young man."

"It's up to you!"

"And I — don't want to."

"But why?" he wailed passionately. "Why, Rivka, why don't you want to?"

"Samira, please," she snapped.

"No! Rivka!"

"I said: Samira!"

"And *I* said — Rivka!"

Samira stood up. "If this name game doesn't stop, I end this conversation now, and you two are out of here."

The thought flashed like lightning through Avraham's mind: *She wants to keep talking.* This was an encouraging sign. He pulled a handkerchief from his pocket and wiped his eyes. "All right, Rivka, I'll call you Samira from now on. Even though, to me, you'll always be Rivka."

"What I am to you makes no difference to me. Here at home, call me what I'm called."

He looked at her sadly. "Is your hatred for our father so deep, then?"

"I do not have to answer that. But I think you're intelligent enough to understand what they did to me."

"Rivka — uh, Samira. I know I've failed. But please, answer one more question for me."

"What is it?" Her head was held high as she waited.

"Do you feel good about the way you've betrayed your people?"

Her eyes lit with renewed fury. The words spilled from her in a frenzied torrent.

"I am not a traitor to my people. That's just a libel that you're trying to pin on me because I don't want to do what you want. I am no traitor! I do not kill Israelis. In fact, I work with all my might against the use of violence. But the Israelis are the ones who killed my husband. True, he was a freedom fighter, and he'd escaped from prison. But to shoot down a man who, like me, opposed violence and murder?"

She paused, regaining her breath and her equilibrium. Then, very low, she added, "And anyway, aren't you ashamed to accuse me of betrayal, when my parents were the ones who betrayed *me*? Well? Tell me that!"

Avraham's goal now was to keep the conversation flowing as long as possible. There was still a faint hope that maybe, just maybe, she would have a change of heart. Therefore, he dragged out his answer.

"I was a baby then," he said, quietly but emotionally. "I don't know the circumstances of your leaving. I don't even know, exactly, what happened. No one ever told me. They must have been ashamed. It must have been terribly hard for them to revive that whole tragic matter. Try to understand them, too!

"But I do know one thing: You're angry and frustrated over what happened, and, from your perspective, I understand that completely. But I'm positive that Abba, may he rest in peace, must have had a very different perspective. Don't ask me to be the arbitrator between the two of you. But — all right, we won't use the word 'betray' — for this you leave your own people?"

Rachel decided suddenly to contribute her share to the conversation. "How can a person stand against her family and her nation in such an extreme way? It's not natural! It's — it's not normal!"

Samira stood up and began to walk toward them. "Don't talk to me that way!" she snarled. "I owe you no explanation for my behavior. I don't even know you. You invaded my life without my consent. It's true that I share a sense of identification with the Palestinian struggle for national liberation, for a life they can govern alone without a foreign occupier standing over them, or an Israeli one. So what? That's why you see me as a traitor? There are plenty of Israelis who think exactly as I do!"

"True," Avraham said. "But they only talk. They don't take an active role against their own people. They don't help the Arabs in this struggle, the way you do. I can't bear the idea of your doing that. Come home — please!"

"I told you. It's too late."

"You're saying that you'd like to go back, but it's too late." He paused, shaking his head. "You're on the wrong side."

Samira grimaced, as though she had just heard something ugly. "What do you mean, 'the wrong side.'"

"Just that. Not on the winning side!"

"Do you mean to tell me that it's just to oppress people against their will?"

Avraham grew very excited. "Who's talking about justice? Who said anything about oppressing people? We're fighting here for control of this land — the land that belongs to us, not to the Arabs. They have no right to this land. Living here, as citizens, they have full rights. The Torah recognizes the rights of a foreigner living in the land."

Angrily, Samira said, "The Torah again. What happened to you? Are you really religious?"

"Yes."

This fact seemed to disturb Samira greatly. She could not deny to herself that she felt a certain sense of kinship toward her brother, but the fact that he was religious made her very uncomfortable.

What's the matter with you? she thought to herself. *You've been living with the Arabs for over twenty years now, and you care whether a Jew is religious or not?* For a brief moment, she had felt like an Israeli again.

"We'll leave the subject of religion for the moment," she decided aloud. "That's not the point. But I do want to understand. You talk of the Jews' rights to this land. But the Arabs were here before the Jews."

"That's exactly the point! *We* were here long before the Arabs came. All through the generations, we've been yearning for our Holy Land." He looked at her sorrowfully. "Have you moved so far from your people?"

Samira laughed. "You've become religious, so you view things differently than they are in reality. They never taught us that in Ramat Gan."

"True," Avraham said gravely. "That's the real tragedy."

She laughed again, longer and harder. "Now I understand. You came here to try to get me to repent — to become religious, too. Is that it?"

"No. I want you to return to your family."

Samira froze. After a long moment, she returned to her seat behind the desk. "Enough! As far as I am concerned, this show is over. Mahmoud, your faithful guide, will take you to your room, where you will pack your things. Then my men will accompany you to wherever you wish to go within the Green Line. The fact that you're coming out of this dangerous adventure of yours alive and well is my modest tribute to the fact that you're my brother."

She turned to the two Arabs and gave them their orders, in Arabic. Avraham and Rachel did not understand a word that passed between them. They had no way of knowing whether she was indeed releasing them, or setting the stage for some other fate. Her soothing words about letting them return to Israeli territory might have been calculated only to calm and distract them so that there would be no thought of resistance on their part.

The men came over to the Rosenbaums and grasped their forearms painfully. Any attempt to delay their departure from the room seemed futile. Over her shoulder, Rachel screamed, "I'm certain, Rivka, that your conscience is troubling you a lot. If something should happen to us, it will lie on your head and cause you sleepless nights."

Samira did not answer. The same cynical smile was evident on her face.

It seemed to Rachel, twisting her head for a final backward glance, that there was wickedness in that smile.

The Envelope

35

The armed men accompanied Avraham and Rachel to their room on the second floor. As he opened the door for them, Mahmoud hissed, "Hurry and pack your things. We're leaving Nablus before dawn."

Apprehensively, Avraham ventured, "Is it dangerous to travel at night?"

Perhaps, he thought, the reason they shunned daytime travel was to avoid an IDF patrol that might stumble upon them. But all he received in reply was a sharp, "Hurry!"

Without a word, Avraham and Rachel obeyed. They rushed into the room and, with the trio of Arabs waiting just outside the open door, began nervously to gather their belongings and toss them any which way into their suitcases.

Rachel whispered into her husband's ear, "Do you think they're really going to take us back into Israel? I'm terrified!" Her eyes darted to the door, wondering fearfully whether the Arabs had heard her.

"I don't know," Avraham whispered back, as he struggled to lock one of the full-to-bursting suitcases. "I believe they will. I don't think my dear sister would hurt me. I am, after all, her own flesh and blood." This last comment was muttered ironically.

"Really?" Rachel was sarcastic. "Did you notice her 'dear' behavior toward us? The coarse way she treated us, even after she knew the truth about who you are and why you'd come here? What do you know about what she may or may not choose to do now?"

A shudder of fear ran through Avraham. Hard on its heels came anger. Yanking on the strap of the suitcase so hard that it snapped in two, he said, "Of course I saw how she treated us! She broke my heart — and I'm convinced that she did it intentionally. Still, she's my sister, and she knows that I'm her brother."

Three minutes later, they were done. Avraham and Rachel carried their bags to the door. Their guards did not offer to take the heavy suitcases; they merely grasped the couple's forearms roughly and propelled them down the stairs at top speed. The rug muffled their footsteps until they were nearly inaudible. And yet, as they reached the lobby level and passed near Samira's office, the door opened with startling suddenness. Light from the room poured out onto Avraham and Rachel. They squinted at the abrupt transition from darkness to light.

Avraham tried to convince himself that Samira had opened the door for a last look at her brother before he was once again swallowed up in his land. She stood in the doorway, leaning silently against the frame. In her hands was a small package. The guards guided Avraham and Rachel past her on their way out to the car. Looking back over his shoulder, Avraham blurted, "Goodbye. Despite the pain, I am happy that my dream has come true. I met my sister."

She gazed back coldly, and said with open mockery, "I am overjoyed to have given you so much pleasure. But you — you caused *me* fresh pain, great anger, and a strong desire for revenge."

Avraham trembled. "Revenge against whom? Against me?"

Disdainfully, she said, "I don't know anymore. Revenge against all of you. Literally, all of you."

Before Avraham could answer, she went on. "I will satisfy myself with a small vengeance, however. Tell our mother everything, all right? Tell her how I look. Though I know that none of it will interest her after so many years of wiping me out of her mind, and never bothering to inquire about me and my lot."

Rachel called softly, "Rivka, is there no limit to your hate?"

"It's mutual. I don't think my mother hates *me* any less."

"It hurts me to see you make such a mistake about your parents. We explained to you — it's just not true! It's time for you to take us seriously."

With a flush of rage, Samira shrieked, "*Enough!*"

She strode up to Rachel and delivered two ringing slaps to her sister-in-law's cheeks.

"You forget where you are! You are under my control and you'd better stop being insolent! You are a new member of this family. Where do you find the nerve to talk about things that happened between my parents and me over twenty years ago? You will not tell me how my mother feels about me! Understand?"

Avraham was battling with his own fury. He wrested his arm away from his guard, but the other soon overpowered him again. All at once, Avraham felt calm returning. His assessment of the situation told him that it would be wiser, for now, to swallow this insult to his wife.

Samira took a step toward him. "And you, Avraham, the baby brother I loved so dearly," she said with a break in her voice, "you tell Imma everything, you hear? Tell her that I have two sons; they are her grandsons. Tell her that one of them is an oil engineer in Kuwait and the other, tell her, is called Saib. Yes, yes, Saib, and he's a student at the University at Bir Zeit. His views lean toward the Hamas, but I have not permitted him to join them. Hamas is too extreme for my taste. For now, he's active in the Fatah. What's the matter, doesn't she deserve a little *nachas* from her grandchildren?" The mockery was glaring.

Avraham felt the tears well up and spill out of his eyes. This was the second time he found himself weeping like a baby on this crazy night. "I can't l-listen to this —"

"Then don't listen. I also couldn't listen to what our parents threw at me!"

Avraham willed the tears to stop, inwardly vowing not to answer her again. He contented himself now with directing a wounded look at his sister. Rachel, for her part, had her eyes trained on the glass doors leading out of the lobby. She no longer cared about anything. All that mattered was getting away from this accursed and alien place. They had suffered enough humiliation for one night.

Samira nodded curtly at her men, who proceeded to drive the Rosenbaums out into the cold night. Unexpectedly, Samira called after them, "I ask your wife's pardon for what happened just now. I lost control."

Rachel said nothing. Still reeling from the shock of those ringing slaps, and consumed with a red-hot anger, she did not vouchsafe the other woman so much as a glance. They had passed through the glass doors when Samira suddenly called out again: "Ah, just a minute — I forgot something. Wait."

She repeated her words in Arabic. The men stopped. The entire small group waited patiently for Samira to approach, wondering at the delay.

She handed the small package to Avraham. Hesitantly, he accepted it.

"Open it, please!" It was half an order, half a plea.

He carefully tore open the wrapping — then stared in dismay at the parcel's contents. Samira smiled with pleasure. "Do you recognize this little thing?"

He recognized it — of course he did. He was at a complete loss. Samira asked, with quiet authority, "Whose crazy idea was it to come here posing as journalists from Canada, and to be caught with such a revealing thing as a package of biscuits with Hebrew letters? Eh?" She laughed.

"Do you mean to tell me that you had our room searched?" Irresistibly, Avraham remembered the *tefillin* hidden in the suitcase's false bottom. What would have happened had they been found? With an effort, he pushed aside these troubling thoughts. They were no help to him now.

Samira moved closer. "Of course we searched your room. Did you think that some heavenly angels brought me those biscuits? Where is your head? To come here with something that can so easily identify you!"

Avraham tried to turn the topic to his advantage. "Isn't this another sign that no one sent us here, and that we came of our own initiative?"

Samira smiled without answering. After a pause, she said, "Hearty appetite. And don't forget to say your blessings —" She laughed again, more animatedly this time.

At her signal, the Arab men continued their shepherding, moving the Rosenbaums firmly and quickly toward their waiting vehicle, an ancient Ford parked at the curb. Samira watched them go. Just before the group got into the car, she called, "Take better care of your two little girls. Treat them better!"

Mahmoud turned to one of the other Arabs. "Abdul, let me go instead of you. I won't have problems with the language; I understand English."

Abdul shot a questioning glance at Samira, who was still standing in the hotel entrance. With gestures, he helped her understand Mahmoud's request. As she nodded her acquiescence to the change, Abdul noticed that Samira appeared to be crying.

Noticing his curious look, she turned on her heel and disappeared at once into her private office, slamming the door behind her with a slam that shook the old building to its foundations.

❧

With a protesting whine, the engine of the 1975 Ford came to life and the car began to move down the street. Mahmoud sat in front beside Nawil, the driver; Avraham and Rachel sat silent and troubled in the back. Though they had been promised a safe return home, they nevertheless were fearful as they sped through the night in the Arab car. Inaudible chapters of *Tehillim* mingled with the roar of the engine. Up front, Nawil and Mahmoud did not exchange a word.

The streets of Shechem were left behind. For reasons of his own, Nawil chose a route along narrow, unpaved roads which circumvented Arab villages and Jewish settlements. The Rosenbaums' eyes were glued to the window in a vain effort to make out the passing scenery. Here and there, a light shone in a distant cottage or hilltop, but neither Avraham nor

Rachel could see enough to know where they were being taken. After a while, they gave up and sat back.

Faintly, Rachel heard her husband whisper, "Failure really hurts."

"You accomplished so much — more than any one person could be expected to do."

He sighed. "But — I failed. I'm all broken up about that."

"Don't let your conscience weigh you down," she urged. "Very few brothers would have gone to these lengths for a sister who had been lost."

"It's not a question of my conscience. It's the fact that I didn't succeed — that I failed to accomplish my goal."

Suddenly, they fell silent. Up front, an argument had erupted between Nawil and Mahmoud. Though neither of the Rosenbaums understood a word of Arabic, the tone of the debate sounded violent somehow. They felt vaguely apprehensive.

A moment later, the fright turned to pure terror. Nawil had whipped out a gun and placed it squarely against Mahmoud's head. Rachel's own head swam; she thought she would faint.

"You're coming with me, you hear?" Nawil screamed.

"All right, all right," Mahmoud said quickly. "Anyway, my life is worth more than two Zionist worms."

With an abrupt motion, Nawil cut the engine. Without hesitation he leaped out of the car, yanked open the rear door, and bellowed, "*Out!*"

The waving gun persuaded Avraham and Rachel to obey with alacrity. Not having understood what the men were saying, they had no idea what was going to happen next — though their hearts were laden with doom. They stood shivering on a desolate stretch of ground, buffeted by the cold wind that blew off the night-shrouded Shomron mountains. In the distance, the lights of a Jewish city winked at them. Was it Kfar Saba?

Hashem, what will happen to the children? From whence cometh my help? Fragmented thoughts and snatches of prayer pushed and jostled in Rachel's agitated mind.

With madness peeking out of his eyes, Nawil yelled, "Walk!" His finger pointed toward an olive tree, some hundred yards away. Weak kneed, Avraham and Rachel began to move toward it.

They were only ten paces away when, without warning, Nawil shouted, "Stop!"

Confused, they turned back to face him.

Two gunshots rang out in the pre dawn air. Their echo spread through the sleeping sky, toward Shechem on one side, and Petach Tikvah on the other.

36

Avraham and Rachel flung themselves onto the rock-strewn ground. When the last echo of the gunfire had died, they rolled cautiously behind a nearby hillock and lay there, barely breathing, and utterly at a loss to understand how they were still alive. The gun had been pointed right at them, spewing certain death — As they waited, they heard a sharp cry, followed by the thud of a falling body. After that — nothing. Silence.

Hearts pounding, they waited for the next shots to find their mark. Their faces were buried in the dirt as they lay as motionless as the stones around them, ears straining for the slightest noise that might warn them of an approaching attack. So profound was their fear that their frozen lips could not form the words of prayer, though supplication filled their hearts.

A minute passed, seemingly as long as eternity. Only the wind sighed through the barren land, and only the cold touched their shivering skin. Why were the terrorists holding back? Had they changed their minds about killing them after all? Had they fled? What was going to happen next?

Gathering his courage, Avraham lifted his head a fraction and ventured a peek. The darkness was still deep, despite the approaching dawn. His ears caught the sound of heavy breathing, and also the rasp of something being dragged along the ground. He made out the dim outline of a human figure. At once, he ducked his head into the ground again.

Several moments passed. Then Mahmoud's voice came softly to them out of the darkness: "Mr. and Mrs. Fairhaven! Get up and come here!"

They did not move. What new trap was this? Sooner or later, they knew, they would have to obey — they had no other options at this point — but their petrified limbs refused to budge. Footsteps approached. Their fear leaped to a new high. This was the end.

Hysterically, Rachel whispered, "Let's get up and run. Maybe one of us will manage to get away. They didn't succeed in killing us the first time. Maybe we'll be worthy of another miracle. Come on!"

Avraham did not move. He muttered, "I'm afraid."

"But to lie here is much worse! Avraham, please, come on!"

Mahmoud was nearly upon them now. Without lifting their heads, they heard him: "Mr. and Mrs. Fairhaven, get up! Don't be afraid! You are saved. It is I — Mahmoud."

Avraham was first to raise his head, very cautiously. He saw Mahmoud standing nearby, a gun in his hand. The plea burst from Avraham's lips, "Please don't kill us. We are not enemies of yours. We're not from the G.S.S. or the Mossad. We just wanted to see my sister."

"Get up already," Mahmoud said impatiently. "I have not come to kill you. Quickly, there is no time."

Even as he spoke, Mahmoud stooped to pull Avraham upright by force.

"Get up, Mr. Fairhaven. Nawil wanted to kill you — and so I killed him. That's all! He is dead! See for yourself. There he lies."

Avraham sat up. Following the direction of Mahmoud's pointing finger, he saw a figure huddled shapelessly on the ground. The figure did not move.

"Nawil is dead?" he croaked. "He didn't fire on us?"

"He did not have the chance to fire. I stood behind him and shot him twice. I saved your lives!"

Avraham took his first real breath since the gunshots had rung out. "But what happened? Why did he make us get out of the car?"

"Ah," Mahmoud said, shaking his head. "Nawil was hot headed. He turned to me in the car and said, 'Let's kill them. It's our chance; two less *Yahud* in the world. No one will ever know.'"

"'Are you crazy?' I asked. 'Samira will be furious.'

"'Samira will not be angry,' he said. 'She told me that if I have the chance, I should kill them.' I became angry. 'I did not hear her say that,' I told him. 'I do not believe you!'

"Then Nawil raised his voice. 'What am I, a liar? I tell you, that's what she told me!'

"'I will not take responsibility for this,' I said. 'If you do anything to harm them, I will tell Samira.'

"Nawil lost his temper. 'Why do you protect them like this?'

"I tried to calm him down. Quietly, I said, 'I am not protecting them. They were Samira's guests.' Nawil started to laugh. 'We saw what kind of guests — guests who get slapped on the face. Mahmoud, I am not going to wait any longer. In ten minutes, we reach Kfar Saba. I want to end this first.'

"And that," Mahmoud finished soberly, "is what happened. The rest, you saw for yourselves." A note of urgency crept into his voice. "And now, get up! We have to get out of here!"

"I am not returning to Nablus with you," Avraham said firmly. "Not under any circumstances."

Mahmoud was already striding toward the car. "What are you babbling about Nablus? They'll kill me there! Haven't you figured that out yet?"

Shakily, Avraham found his feet. Rachel followed suit. "So where do you intend to go?" Avraham asked.

"To Israel!"

"What do you mean? You're an Arab terrorist; they'll never let you in. They'll throw you in jail!"

"Even if they arrest me, it's better than dying in Nablus tomorrow."

Subduing their considerable doubts, the Rosenbaums climbed back into the car, which was soon rattling along the road at high speed.

✤

Saib Tukan, Samira's son, arrived at the Al-Quds Hotel at 9 a.m. He went at once to his mother's office, but found it locked. This surprised Saib; at this hour, his mother was generally in her office. It also worried him a little. Early that morning, at 7 o'clock, he had been awakened in his university bedroom by a phone call from a man who refused to identify himself.

"Saib?"

"Yes. Who is this?"

"It doesn't matter. The important thing is — go home immediately. Something happened here last night. I think it's important that you be near your mother."

"*What happened?*" Saib shouted into the phone. But the line was already dead.

Slowly, he had hung up. While he had no clue as to the caller's identity, it was clear that the fellow knew him and his mother, and also that the caller had been in the vicinity of whatever had occurred the evening before. What could have happened? Had there been a sudden invasion of Israeli troops? Did several Fatah freedom fighters have a shoot-out in the hotel, wounding Samira? Saib did not know what to think.

And so, by 9 o'clock that morning he was already at the entrance to his mother's office. But the door was locked.

He went to the elderly receptionist. She greeted him with a smile. "Ah, Saib, it's been a while since we've seen you here."

"True. I've been busy — my studies and various other things. You know."

"Ah," she nodded knowingly. "Of course."

Saib got straight to the point. "Where is my mother?"

"I think she's still sleeping."

"Did something happen to make her suddenly so tired?"

"Yes. There was some excitement here last night."

Instant tension filled Saib. "Tell me," he ordered.

She looked uneasy. Why should she be the one to tell him what had happened? Let him ask his mother. With a shrug, she said, "I don't know exactly. There was a strange couple staying here. They came from abroad — from America, I think. They spoke English with your mother. She knows English very well."

His mother's fluency in English did not interest Saib at the moment. He pressed, "You said they were 'strange.' How?"

She spread her hands. "I really don't know. But Nawil and Mahmoud escorted them from the hotel, and then your mother gave the woman two slaps on the face."

"Did you see it yourself?" he demanded.

She recoiled at the menace in his tone. "No. Fatima, who was manning the front desk last night, told me."

"Were they spies?"

"Saib, what do I know? Here comes your mother. Ask her! She'll provide the answers you want."

He turned quickly, to find his mother at her office door. He ran to her. Seeing him, Samira smiled broadly. "My Saib!" she cried. "What are you doing here suddenly, without even letting me know in advance?"

"Let's not stand by the door. Let's go inside and talk," Saib urged.

Samira gave him a penetrating glance. Her finely honed intuition told her that there was something going on here, something that warranted further study. She opened the door, then led the way to a comfortable arrangement of armchairs and a sofa designated for important guests. It had been in this very corner that she had hosted her brother and sister-in-law last night. She sank into one of the armchairs and watched her son take another, facing hers. For a long moment they regarded one another wordlessly, each trying to read something in the other's face.

Finally, Samira asked, "Has something happened to bring you here?"

"Yes. Something happened."

"What?"

"That's what I want *you* to tell *me*."

Samira straightened with a surprised jerk. "What do you mean?"

Crossing one ankle over the other knee, Saib said calmly, "I understand that there was some excitement here last night. Is it true?"

Samira gave him her cynical smile. "I gather that you've managed to hear some good gossip from Massouda at the front desk, eh?"

"Not at all. I just asked her what happened. Because at 7 o'clock this morning, someone called to tell me that something had happened here last night. Is it true?"

Controlling herself with an effort, Samira asked, "Who called?"

"I don't know. He didn't give me his name. He also disguised his voice so that I couldn't identify him."

Silence reigned for several seconds. At last, Saib stirred and said, "I came, Mother, because I was concerned about you. I thought that something had happened to you. Tell me about it — if only to remove the worry from my heart."

Her stony face softened at this. "Saib, it's very hard for me to tell you."

"Why?"

"From the day your father was killed until now, last night was the most difficult in my life."

Saib frowned. "That bad?"

"Yes. That bad."

"And don't you think that telling me would make you feel better?"

"Not yet. Give me a few minutes to recover. Please, bring me a glass of water."

Saib hurried to the kitchen. He returned shortly with a pitcher of cold water in which ice cubes floated in profusion. He poured out a glassful and handed it to his mother. Samira thanked him with a smile, and took a sip. This time, Saib chose a corner of the sofa, closer to her.

"I understand," he said, "that there were strange guests staying here, from the United States."

Samira inclined her head, privately amazed at the wealth of information her son had managed to garner in so short a time.

"And the situation reached a point where you actually slapped the woman on her face. She must have angered you somehow."

"And how!" Samira said with feeling.

"And who were those two guests, exactly?"

Samira sighed. Saib was puzzled by her strange reluctance to speak. Patiently, he waited, though he felt close to bursting with curiosity. Pulling a cigarette from his pocket, he lit up and began to smoke in silence.

For Samira, the silence was suffocating. "The guests," she blurted, "were Israelis, Saib."

With a last puff, Saib threw the rest of the cigarette into a nearby ashtray. "From Israel? Interesting. Mossad? G.S.S.?"

"I don't know. And it doesn't really matter. What *is* important."

She fell silent, studying her son. With his springy black hair and slightly sunken eyes, he had always looked like his father. Now, having sprouted a small mustache on his upper lip, the resemblance to Abu Daoud al-Razak was uncanny. For the first time in her life, Samira searched her son's face for signs of the father who had rejected her, or the brother she had sent away only hours ago. Why was her heart suddenly constricting so painfully?

Saib whispered, *"Who were they?"*

Samira had never, ever spoken to her children about her Jewish family. They knew that their mother was a Jewess, but that fact had never seemed to affect their lives in any special way. They had friends, Arabs like themselves, who were born to Jewish mothers. They all thought of themselves as proud Arabs and felt no connection with the Jewish nation. Samira's sons regarded their father as a hero and sought to emulate him. He had been their role model.

Now it was time to tell Saib things that she had kept hidden from him all his life. How to begin?

Uncle Nachum was growing anxious. For several days now, he had been trying to contact his nephew by phone, but there was never any answer at

Avraham's home in Petach Tikvah. He tried calling Avraham's place of work, and was informed that the Rosenbaums had taken a trip to Canada.

"For what purpose?" he demanded.

"I don't know," the secretary answered.

"Was it a sudden trip?"

"I think so."

"When are they due back?"

"I don't know. Please leave your number. As soon as Mr. Rosenbaum returns, I will let him know that you called. All right, sir?"

"No, thanks. That won't be necessary."

Uncle Nachum felt increasingly nervous. A little voice whispered to him that this was no ordinary trip, and that its ultimate destination was not Canada. His nephew had informed him that, sooner or later, he intended to visit Shechem. He had made it clear that his uncle's warnings would not be heeded. The fact that both Avraham and his wife had suddenly disappeared worried Nachum to no small extent.

Scenes from the past rose up in his mind's eye, difficult and painful scenes. *Why are they doing this?* he asked himself in dismay as he paced his living room like a caged tiger. Over and over, he slammed his right fist into his left palm in frustration, until both hands ached.

All at once, he spun on his heel and returned to the phone. He dialed his widowed sister's number in Bnei Brak.

The car sped along the dirt roads of the Shomron. In the back seat, the Rosenbaums hung on for all they were worth, trying — without much success — to avoid a painful buffeting as the car swung from side to side. Their bones ached.

Mahmoud paid no attention, either to their discomfort or to their pleas that he slow down. He was busy glancing in the rear-view mirror at frequent intervals, checking whether they were being followed. For fear of running into an IDF roadblock, he avoided the paved roads.

At some point, the car crossed the Green Line. Avraham and Rachel had no idea where they were, until at last they turned onto a road not far from Kfar Saba.

Mahmoud checked his watch and saw that it was already 7 o'clock. He stopped at the first gas station they came to and asked the *Yahud* owner for permission to make a call. The owner watched suspiciously as Mahmoud spoke briefly into the phone, in Arabic. He hung up and returned to the car.

Another hour's drive brought them to the outskirts of Petach Tikvah. At the sight of their own home, the Rosenbaums felt an almost overpowering sense of relief. Their eyes lit up as though they were seeing it for the first time. Smiling, they invited Mahmoud to come upstairs with them and have a cup of coffee.

As they sipped their coffee, Avraham was able to speak freely for the first time in days. He turned to Mahmoud and asked, "Who are you, and what do you intend to do now?"

Mahmoud tilted his chair back. "I saw you give Samira a torn photograph."

"True."

"Well, I am the son of the second woman," Mahmoud said gravely. "The one who was torn out of the picture."

Samira closed her eyes and leaned back in her armchair. Saib sensed that her breathing had become labored. For an instant, he contemplated repeating his question — then held his tongue. Even if she did not say another word, he resolved, he would not press her further. He would wait patiently for another opportunity to talk, when perhaps she would volunteer the information of her own accord.

At the same time, he was burning with curiosity. What was there about a couple of visitors from Israel to have thrown his mother into such turmoil? This was certainly not the first time Israeli visitors had appeared at the hotel. Samira always treated them very properly, though with marked indifference. So, what had happened last night? What was it about those two that had shaken her so?

Saib lit a second cigarette and puffed on it in silence. And suddenly, without the slightest warning, he sat bolt upright. It was as if a thunderbolt had struck his heart. That must be it! He thought he understood it all now. He was not sure, but he believed he had the answer.

The Envelope / 273

He leaped to his feet and began to prowl the room. Sensing a change in her son, Samira opened her eyes. "Saib, what's wrong?

Her voice was tinged with an anxiety that touched on hysteria.

"Nothing's wrong, Mother."

"Tell me anyway."

"It's nothing. I just think I understand who those visitors were."

Samira stopped breathing. "How could you possibly know?"

"Would I be mistaken in saying that those guests were your Israeli relatives?"

Her eyes closed again. It seemed to Saib that he saw a tear seep out of the corner of one of them as she whispered, "Yes — you are right!"

He returned to his seat, folding his arms across his chest. "Well, so what happened, Mother? What shook you up so much?"

Samira opened her eyes again and said in a trembling voice, "It was — " She breathed deeply. "It was my brother."

Saib waited patiently for her to go on.

"My — only brother. I left home when he was a baby. He was the only one who — I kissed goodbye when — I left. And now — he came here — with his wife."

Her distress was almost palpable. With a pang of something like fear, Saib realized that something had happened to change the tenor of their lives here in Nablus. Just what that change would be, he did not yet know.

He studied his mother, who despite her *Yahud* origins identified in a very practical sense with Arab nationalist aspirations. She had raised her two sons on the ideal of a Palestinian revolution. Never had she allowed her origins to influence either her attitudes or her decisions. And now, that same woman was sitting weak and helpless, as though beaten down.

Was this a symptom of some fundamental change, Saib wondered, or merely the passing effect of the emotions aroused by coming face-to-face with a brother she had not seen since he was a baby? Another thrill of fear passed through Saib. It had the effect of hardening his heart. He must squelch this tendency at the onset — at once!

"Are you going back to your former home?" he asked in a low voice.

Samira, eyes closed once again, murmured, "No! What makes you think that?"

"Your emotional state, your weakness. You're nearly in tears!"

She did not answer.

Saib leaned closer. "Did your brother awaken doubts?"

Still she said nothing. Moving in even closer, Saib pressed, "Perhaps he aroused *Yahud* feelings in you?"

And still, Samira would not talk. The only sound was that of her breathing, short and quick. They sat in this way for several minutes. Then Saib rose to his feet and headed for the door.

"Where are you going?" Samira asked.

"I'm leaving."

"Where, I asked?"

"Back to the university."

"Why? Why won't you stay here with me?"

"Because you don't want me to stay."

She lifted a hand, then let it fall back onto the arm of the chair, totally devoid of energy.

"Please stay," she said. "I will be all right soon."

With his hand on the doorknob, Saib hesitated. Then, slowly, he returned to the seat he had just vacated, facing his mother.

"You have to understand," Samira said. "Despite everything, 'blood is thicker than water.'"

Saib understood those dreadful words all too well. He sensed approaching danger. In a play for time, he asked, "What do you mean?"

"I mean what you said before."

"You miss it?"

She nodded her head and wiped away a tear.

"You miss being *Yahud*? You miss being part of a people who oppress your own children? You know very well why my older brother fled to Kuwait."

Her eyes mirrored her exhaustion. Smiling faintly, she said, "Are you afraid of something?"

"Yes."

"What is it?"

"I'm afraid of you, Mother."

"Why?"

"It looks like you're leaving and abandoning us."

"Leaving — to go where?"

"You know. To your first home. To betray us and our father." His voice hardened. "I must be open with you. We were always afraid that something like this would happen especially after Father was killed by those Israeli terrorists. We were afraid then that you would return to them. Because 'blood is thicker than water.'"

"True!"

"And my blood," he declared, "likewise is not made of water. It's Arab blood!"

"Mixed with —"

"True. Mixed with Jewish blood." He stood up and towered over her, adding quietly, "To my misfortune."

Those words pierced her heart like a sharpened sword. She tried to grasp her son's hand, but he whipped it behind his back. Her gaze was soft and pained, but his was stony — *His father's Arab blood*, the unbeckoned thought flitted through her mind. It had been years since she had thought in this vein. What her brother had brought about in a single night —

She sat up straighter and seemed to gather her strength. Confidence returned all at once. She stood up, facing her son.

"Saib, you are mistaken. I have linked my fate to this place. When they killed your father, I lost all feeling for or sense of connection to them. No! It's over! I am not leaving, Saib — you are speaking nonsense." She paused. "But —"

"But what?" he asked sharply.

She smiled sadly. "But — blood is thicker than water. Saib, blood is thicker than water. The sudden appearance of my brother, despite the fact that I treated him cruelly and he left here humiliated, has hurt me. It has aroused in me feelings that I thought no longer existed. But don't worry. I will be strong."

Suddenly, as though waking from a dream, Samira looked around. "What time is it?"

Saib glanced at his wristwatch. "It's nearly 10 o'clock."

She appeared agitated. "Why haven't Nawil and Mahmoud returned yet?"

"Where did they go?"

"They took my brother and his wife to Petach Tikvah. They should have arrived there long ago. I'm worried."

"Which route did they take?"

"The route we usually take when going into Israel, by way of Kfar Saba."

Saib nodded. He was familiar with those unpaved and winding roads.

With a rapid stride, Samira went to her desk and sat down behind it. Her anxiety over Nawil and Mahmoud succeeded in pushing aside the storm of emotion that had descended on her in the wake of her brother's visit. Saib said, "Shall I take the same route, see what happened?"

"What will you see? Perhaps they went to get a drink, or to catch a nap, or who knows what."

"I understand. All the same, I think I'll go and have a look around."

His mother did not answer. Saib took his own car and set out on the dirt roads that the terrorists favored.

He returned an hour and a half later, eyes bulging and breathing hard.

"They killed him!"

Samira leaped up. "Who?"

"Nawil!"

"What are you talking about? Where? Who killed him? I don't understand what you're talking about!" She sounded on the brink of hysteria.

"Mother, calm down. I tell you, I found him — Nawil, with two bullets in his back. I've brought him back."

"And Mahmoud?"

"Not a sign of him. Or of your *Yahud*!"

Samira began to pace the room in agitation. Saib heard her whisper to herself, "That despicable fiend. He must have been G.S.S. or Mossad, after all."

"Who?"

"My dear brother!" she flared. "He toyed with my feelings. Why did they kill him? Where is Mahmoud? Who knows where those people hid *his* body?"

Suddenly, she stopped and cried aloud, "I will have my revenge on them — my revenge for Nawil and Mahmoud!"

With satisfaction, Saib welcomed the return of her former manner. Her eyes sparkled with their former fire. Mother had come back, to him, to his people. Blood was, after all, not thicker than water. His heart soared.

Avraham and Rachel exchanged looks of astonishment and confusion. Their coffee rested on the table, untouched. Mahmoud's hands shook as he set down his own cup, careful not to spill a drop. The Arab was clearly feeling far from calm.

Rachel recovered first. "Can you explain? We're — we're stunned! Even without knowing why —"

Mahmoud managed a smile. "Yes, I can explain. I, too, am shocked to find that you, the Rosenbaums, have no idea who was in the second half of that photograph."

Avraham wiped his upper lip with a napkin and rested his forearms on the table, bringing his face close to Mahmoud's. His voice was warm, yet filled with curiosity.

"Believe me, Mahmoud, we have gone through a great deal these past few days — and yet, the secret of that picture continues to plague us." He paused, then added, "Do you know what? I even tried to find out about the picture from the Israeli intelligence people. They said that, for security reasons, they could not provide the answer I wanted. They couldn't tell me who it was in the photo, or even whether it was a man or woman. Naturally, that only escalated our curiosity."

Smiling fixedly, Mahmoud whispered, "It was a woman. I find it very interesting to hear that the G.S.S. would not reveal her identity. Very interesting indeed." His voice grew a trifle stronger. "Actually, they were right in not telling you *then*."

Rachel stood up. In an effort to master her consuming curiosity, she began to mechanically clear the table. Yet, as she worked, she could not help herself. "You're making me terribly curious! Tell us already! Why is it so difficult for you?"

Mahmoud took a long, deep breath. "You will understand why in a minute." There was a short pause while he collected his thoughts. Then, emotionally, he said, "The second woman in the picture was Samira's cousin."

With one voice, Avraham and Sarah exclaimed, "*What?* Which cousin? Where does a cousin come into the picture? What are you talking about?"

Shaken by his own revelation, and the effort it cost him to verbalize it, Mahmoud said, "Excuse me, but did you know, until recently, that you had a sister in Nablus? You did not know, correct? Then let me tell you something else: You also did not know that you had a cousin there as well!"

Rachel returned to the table. "What do you mean, 'had'? Is she no longer alive?"

"No." Mahmoud lowered his eyes. "No, she is not alive. My mother died — Actually, she was killed."

"*Killed?*"

"Yes."

"Who killed her? Israeli soldiers?"

"No."

"Then who?"

Mahmoud looked as though he were choking in his own effort to breathe. For years, he had kept the story locked away in his heart. Now it emerged from his subconscious to face the light of day, and he knew that he must let it out, difficult as that might be. The blood in his veins began to pound, and his heart felt jumpy as a frog. He tried to speak, but the words simply would not come. Limply, he said, "You're asking who killed her?"

"Yes, yes!" Avraham and Rachel cried impatiently.

Mahmoud hesitated just a few seconds longer before answering, in a whisper, "Her father. Her father killed her." His fingers started to drum a monotonous rhythm on the tabletop.

Silence struck the small kitchen like a fist. No one said a word. Mahmoud did not even venture to glance at his hosts; as for the Rosenbaums, they could not meet his eyes and sought refuge in the ceiling and the walls. What Mahmoud had just told them had no bearing on reality as they knew it.

Finally, Mahmoud lifted his head. An apologetic smile played about his lips and lurked in his drooping eyes.

"Yes, my newfound friends who owe me their lives. I expect help from you, as I can no longer return to Nablus."

Rachel instinctively made a placating motion with her hands. Her voice, too, was soothing: "Mahmoud, we are truly in your debt. But let's get to that in a little while. First, I know that I — and Avraham, too, I believe — am totally lost. We don't understand what you just told us."

Mahmoud inclined his head as a sign that he understood their confusion. Rachel went on, "So, please, let's go through this bit by bit. Okay?"

"Okay."

"Let's start at the beginning. You, Mahmoud, claim to be the son of the other woman who appeared in the photo that someone, for some reason, tore in half. Correct?"

"Correct," Mahmoud said in a low voice.

"And what is this woman's name?"

"*Was* her name, you mean."

"Yes, that's right. What was her name?"

"Latifa."

"And you say she was Jewish?"

"Yes. A Jewish woman who married an Arab."

"In that case, you are also Jewish. Correct?"

"No. I am half-Jewish. My father was an Arab."

"No. According to Jewish law, you are completely Jewish, through your mother."

Mahmoud laughed bitterly. "And according to Arab law, I am completely Arab. Now you understand what a strange creature I am."

Rachel decided to let this go. She pressed on with her questions. "And you say that Latifa, your mother, was a friend of Samira's, my husband's sister."

Mahmoud sat up a little straighter. It was important that they fully grasp what he was about to repeat to them. "No, I told you. Latifa, my mother, was Samira's *cousin*."

For the first time, Rachel and Avraham gathered the full import of his words. If Mahmoud was telling the truth, then he was Avraham's cousin! This, Avraham felt, was almost more than he could assimilate.

But which cousin was Mahmoud referring to? Rachel leaned forward. "Mahmoud, another question."

"Please."

"You said that her father killed her?"

"Yes. He killed her accidentally."

"I see. But who was she? We don't know of any such cousin. Does her father also live in Nablus?"

"No, who said he did? He lives in Israel. As far as I know, in Haifa."

Avraham and Rachel exchanged a startled glance. "Haifa?" Avraham exclaimed. "Are you talking about my uncle Nachum?"

At Avraham's vehemence, Mahmoud shrank back. "I really don't know. I don't know him. My mother told me that her father lived in Haifa, and that he had thrown her out of their home, just as Samira was thrown out of hers. And —"

Rachel broke in: "So it seems that your mother, Latifa, was the daughter of our uncle in Haifa, Uncle Nachum?"

Mahmoud nodded. "Yes. It seems that way."

"In that case, according to you, Uncle Nachum, whom we always believed to be childless, actually had a daughter — and *killed her*?" Her voice was shrill, almost hysterical.

Mahmoud did not answer. Rachel took his silence as acquiescence. "Mahmoud?"

"Yes?"

"I don't believe you!"

Mahmoud shrank back again. "But — Why not?"

"It sounds like a wild fantasy. It doesn't sound true at all!"

Angry now, Mahmoud said, "Do you think I invented the whole story?"

"I don't know. Maybe you heard all kinds of things from Samira and concocted this story to save your own skin. Let's see you prove it!"

❧

Mrs. Rosenbaum picked up the ringing phone. "Hello?"

"Good morning, Adina. It's Nachum."

She was surprised. "Good morning. What's going on? You just called an hour ago!"

Jokingly, Nachum said, "You don't want to hear my voice again? Okay, I'll hang up!"

"Oh, no, please don't! I'm sorry — were you insulted? I'm very happy when people call. I just asked."

There was the briefest hesitation. Then, cautiously, Nachum asked, "Avraham doesn't call much?"

"Now and then. But he visits me now more often than he used to. *Baruch Hashem*, I have no complaints."

"Did he call or visit this week?"

Mrs. Rosenbaum's heart skipped a beat. Her brother's question troubled her.

"No," she said slowly. "No, he hasn't called. He hasn't visited me, either. He's gone abroad."

"Where to?"

"To America, I think — or, no, maybe I'm mistaken. I think he went to Canada."

"Hm. Does he phone you from there?"

"Yes, he did call. Why do you ask? Something doesn't feel right to me."

Nachum emitted a short bark of laughter. "Nor to me."

His sister sank down onto a chair. Her fingers tightened on the receiver. "Nachum, can you tell me what you meant by that comment?" Before he could answer, she added on a rising note, "Tell me the truth! Has something happened?"

"No, no. Heaven forbid."

"Then why are you frightening me?"

Soothingly, he said, "Don't get scared. Nothing's happened to Avraham or Rachel. But —"

"But *what?*"

"Just a moment, Adina. I'll explain. This is hard for me to say to you, but — I am not at all sure that he actually traveled to Canada."

"What are you saying — that he lied to me? And, besides, where *did* they go? Is it somewhere I can't know about?"

"They think you can't know about it."

The tension in her grew until it was almost overpowering. "Tell me already!"

"I'm very much afraid that they may have gone to Shechem."

"*What?* What makes you think that?"

"I'm afraid they may know the truth."

Nachum fell silent. From the other end of the line came the same thing — a stunned, bewildered silence. For several days now he had been mulling over in his mind the notion of telling his sister that her son and his wife were busy investigating the old affair concerning Rikva. He had sought ways of letting her know that they knew everything.

He was angry with himself for not having done more to prevent their digging into painful family history. Immediately after he had sent his nephew the torn picture, he had regretted the act: a monumentally foolish one. He had dashed over to the central post office and tried with all his might to persuade the branch manager to have his clerks sift through thousands of letters to find his own, so that he might take it back. The manager had laughed in his face.

"You want me to halt the entire mail system to find your letter?"

"But it's critical!"

"Next time, then, think twice before you put it in the mailbox."

"There won't *be* any next time — not with this letter."

The branch manager had met his glance with expressionless eyes. "I'm sorry. Good luck to you, and goodbye."

At that moment, Nachum had known that his fate was sealed — his secret revealed. How could he not have suspected that the torn photograph would spur Avraham on to further investigation?

Suddenly, he remembered that he was holding the phone in his hand. Shaking himself free of his thoughts, he said into it, "Adina, are you all right? Why don't you answer?"

It seemed to him that there were tears in her voice as she asked, shakily, "How did they find out?"

"You're asking me? It all began with that envelope!"

"Yes," she sighed. "I understand. But who told them about the true contents of the envelope? It wasn't me!"

"How do I know? Your son made up his mind to dig down to the bottom."

"Then — then you mean to tell me that they really know everything?"

"I don't know if they know everything," he said, "but they certainly know a great deal. And you know something, Adina? You are to blame!"

Mrs Rosenberg raised her voice, "Me, why me all of a sudden?"

"I've told you this before: It's all your fault. Avraham mentioned to me several times that you did not forbid him to investigate the matter!"

"That's not true!" she cried. "Not true!"

"Adina, calm down. You only told him not to ask you any questions. You never stated, explicitly, that he should not ask anyone about it. Am I right or wrong?"

In a near-whisper, Mrs. Rosenbaum replied, "Yes. You're right."

The Envelope / 285

"You wanted him to find out that he has a sister living among the Arabs. Don't you understand how this will be detrimental for him, especially in your ultra-Orthodox circles?"

She sighed. "You're right."

"And didn't it cross your mind what might happen if your dear detective son continued to pick away at our numerous old wounds? You know very well what I am referring to."

Mrs. Rosenbaum knew very well. She closed her eyes and whispered again, "You're right."

"Then why did you do it? Why weren't you firmer with him?"

"I don't know."

Mrs. Rosenbaum truly had no clue. Perhaps, in the secret recesses of her heart, she wanted her son to know the truth, despite the emotion and social harm that might ensue. More than once through the years, Mrs. Rosenbaum had sorely missed her wayward daughter. She had not spoken of these feelings with her husband, who, she knew, was going through the exact same pain and she chose not to add to his troubles. He, her husband, had buried his sorrows in those envelopes of his, in his *Gemara*, in fleeing to the *shtiebel* — while she was left within the prison of her lonely thoughts, imagining her Rivka in the society of those wild and alien people in distant Shechem. Those hours had been indescribably painful for her.

Had she really wanted Avraham to learn the truth about his sister? She truly did not know. She said as much, quietly, into the phone now. "I don't know. I really don't."

With a sigh, Nachum said, "All right — what's done can't be undone. That's fate."

"Not fate. It's Divine Providence." She paused, then went on, "How do you know they went to Shechem?"

"First of all, just a bad feeling I have. A very bad feeling. One mustn't dismiss a hunch, you know. Apart from that, I checked at several places in Canada with which his office has dealings. No one there had either met with or heard of him. At one place, the editor of some magazine (and what possible connection could Avraham have with a magazine?) told me, 'Don't get involved and don't ask questions. He and she have traveled to the Middle East.' How many other clues do I need?"

"So — so you really think they went to Shechem? To — Rivka?"

"I don't only think it — I'm nearly sure of it!"

There was no answer. Nachum caught a sound like a toppling chair, and then a painful clatter in his ear as the phone fell to the floor. Sharply, he cried, "Adina, what happened? Answer me, Adina. *Answer me!*"

But no sound came from his sister's apartment in Bnei Brak.

Nachum hastily hung up, and then dialed the number of one of Mrs. Rosenbaum's neighbors.

S parks of fury flew from Samira's eyes. "This will not pass unnoticed!" she cried. With anger-fueled energy she paced the room, forgetting her son, Saib, who watched her with interest.

"What do you intend to do?" he asked at last.

Samira paused at the window, looking out at the light traffic in the street. She answered without turning around. "I don't know. But I will not forgive this."

Saib's mind began weaving various dark plots. Hesitantly, he asked, "Do you want me to kill him?"

At that, Samira did turn. She stared at her son in total incomprehension. "Kill who?"

Saib came closer, keeping his face expressionless as he studied his mother. He was not at all sure that she was over, emotionally, that brief encounter with her brother. Carefully, he chose his words: "Kill your brother — my uncle!"

In a flash, Samira leaped toward him and seized his shoulders with both her hands. Staring deeply into his eyes, she gasped, "Have you gone mad? Kill — kill — my brother?"

Saib was stunned. His mother, he saw now with heavy finality, would never be the same. *She isn't totally on our side anymore,* he thought sorrowfully. One week ago, this reaction would not have occurred. In a situation like this, she would have had no qualms about killing an Israeli.

But perhaps, he thought, he had been wrong all along. His mother had never opened her heart to him fully. Maybe she had always been this way. Maybe that was why she had not permitted him to join the Hamas, the Islamic Jihad — from fear that he would end up murdering Jews?

When he replied, he spoke calmly, very quietly, and with complete conviction.

"Yes! And why not? He murdered a friend of ours, a man loyal to you. And he may even have killed two men. He may have done away with Mahmoud, my cousin, Latifa's son. Yes! Why not kill him? Why not avenge the blood that was spilled?"

"No!"

Now Saib was angry, too. He hissed, "You are not here, Mother. You are not standing with us!"

She raised her voice, trembling all over. "I *am* here! And you know it! But to kill a man — and my own brother, too — Not that!"

Saib let his face show hurt. "You're not here with us!" he repeated.

Stamping her foot, she cried, "I am!"

And then, suddenly, quiet descended. After a moment's troubled thought, she said slowly, "Then again, maybe you are right. Maybe I belong to them, too."

"That miserable visit did this," Saib snapped.

Samira's eyes filled. With a single tear coursing down her cheek, she said, "I don't think it was the visit. That only exposed it — My dear, it is not easy to disconnect oneself completely and permanently. It is an indescribable suffering. You have no idea."

"And I don't *want* to know!"

"I don't think that will help you," she said softly. "Blood *is* thicker than water, in the end."

"Not for me, Mother. I am an Arab — and proud of it. An Arab who hates Jews, despite the fact that their blood flows in my veins. And in order to prove that once and for all, and also to save you, I want —" He closed his eyes for a long moment, the quickened tempo of his breathing testifying to an inner drama. "I want to kill my uncle your brother, *that* Jew — and you must consent!"

"Never," she said flatly. "And if you move in that direction, you will no longer be my son."

"Is a brother more important than a son?"

"It's not a question of making a choice. You are presenting this matter in a distorted way."

"Then what do you intend to do? How will you get your revenge?"

"I will frighten him. I'll make sure that he will live in fear for years — that he has a taste of what we suffer here. Such fear will be more painful than death. My brother, a murderer? He's killed off nearly every spark of feeling that meeting him had raised in me."

"Then you won't even let him be injured?"

"No. Absolutely not. But the terror will be — genuine terror."

Furious, Saib left the room without another word.

That night, he joined the Islamic Jihad.

᠅

Mahmoud sat frozen in his seat. Rachel's rejecting words — her expression of total disbelief in his story — both wounded and bewildered him. He did not understand why she could not believe him, and he felt insulted by it. He was at a loss as to how to answer.

Mahmoud noticed that Avraham seemed less certain than his wife. While Rachel was on her feet, shaking with anger and ready to do battle, Avraham sat with bowed head, eyes glued to the floor.

"Do you also think that I fabricated this story?" he asked Avraham bluntly.

Avraham raised his head. "I don't know what to think."

Slowly, Mahmoud stood up. His limbs felt heavy as lead, and a great fatigue washed over him. Sadly, he said, "I'm sorry that this is how you choose to relate to me. I — who saved you from certain death."

Rachel softened. "For that, Mahmoud, we are truly grateful. But it doesn't justify telling us fantasies."

"I understand my situation," Mahmoud said, going toward the front door. "I see that I have no choice but to return and face my fate." After a brief pause, he added quietly, "And you both know what that fate will be."

A quick glance passed between Avraham and Rachel. Avraham stood up and walked over to Mahmoud. "Wait! Don't go yet. I am asking you: Did you tell us the truth? Did the story really happen the way you said?"

"What do you want me to say?" Mahmoud replied with a shrug. "I told you my story, and you don't believe me."

"Can you prove it?"

Mahmoud was silent. What proof could he bring? His mother had died when he was young. All he knew of her had been gleaned from stories he had been told, particularly from Samira, his mother's cousin. He had been raised on these tales, never doubting their veracity. How could he now prove them true?

Suddenly, his eyes lit up. Crossing his arms over his chest, he said, "You say that your uncle lives in Haifa?"

"Yes," Avraham replied.

"Is he a healthy man?"

"Why do you ask?"

"Latifa's father — that is, my grandfather — was beaten almost to death. His condition was critical when some Israeli soldiers, passing through the area, came and rescued him. So, I ask again: Is he completely healthy?"

Avraham's answer was slow in coming. His uncle Nachum walked with a limp. He often used a cane to help him get around. Avraham had never thought of asking him how he had been injured. Also, Avraham knew that Uncle Nachum often visited the health clinic on Mount Carmel. Had the story really happened the way Mahmoud had described it?

Mahmoud was waiting.

"Look, Mahmoud," Avraham replied. "He's an older man, so if he were sickly that would be no proof of anything." He shrugged. "The truth? He's not completely healthy, no."

Frustration was stamped clearly on Mahmoud's face. The proof he had sought to bring home in triumph seemed to have petered out right from the start. "Maybe you can phone him," he suggested, "and ask him directly?"

Avraham and Rachel looked at one another, startled. Mahmoud seemed to have hit on a solution to which they could find no objection. He elaborated on his idea: "That will give you the best proof of all. If he denies the story — I return to Nablus."

The Rosenbaums could not explain to Mahmoud the complex nature of their relationship with Uncle Nachum. They had no desire to describe his determined campaign to keep them from learning the truth or from traveling to Shechem. They remembered all too well the warnings he had dinned into their ears. And maybe, thought Avraham, as the three stood in silence in the small Petach Tivkah kitchen, that was the real reason Uncle Nachum had been so reluctant to have them dig into the past — so that they would not uncover his own role in the story.

But could they simply pick up a phone and ask him, directly, for the truth?

No. They just could not do it.

Mahmoud broke the silence. "You know that I've cooperated with the G.S.S. They sent you from Canada to me, didn't they?"

"Yes. They did."

"I helped them a lot. I passed on a lot of information to them about your sister, Samira. I didn't do it for money! The only money I took was to cover my expenses, nothing else."

"Then why did you do it?" Avraham asked. "What did you gain?"

"I gained nothing!" Mahmoud answered angrily. "I did it because I know I'm half-Jewish. And, in fact, I'm searching for a way back to my Jewish roots."

"Very nice, Mahmoud," Rachel said. "If you want to return to the Jewish people, that's great! But why do it by telling us such crazy stories? Why?"

The Envelope / 293

Furious, Mahmoud snapped back, "You are insulting me again, without any reason! I think you owe me an apology."

"Why? You still haven't proved that you've been telling us the truth."

"I did! You just don't have the courage to follow up on my suggestion."

Rachel smiled disdainfully. "The last thing you can accuse me of is a lack of courage. Where did you meet us? In Nablus! I, a Jew and an Israeli, walked into that hotbed of Palestinian terrorists."

"Yes, that kind of courage is something you do possess. But you are not brave enough to admit that you've made a mistake. You don't have the courage to call your uncle in Haifa and find out whether or not I've spoken the truth."

The Rosenbaums had nothing to say. Logically, they knew that Mahmoud was right. They ought to phone Uncle Nachum. Emotionally, however, they found themselves unable to do it.

Avraham asked, "Maybe you can think of another way to prove it? It's hard for us to call my uncle."

"That's the best and the only proof there is." Mahmoud was shaking with rage. "You two are ungrateful. I saved your lives and you are sentencing me to death! I'm ashamed of you!"

He wheeled around and once again headed for the front door. Avraham and Rachel watched him anxiously, Avraham leaning against the table for support; he definitely was not feeling well. Mahmoud reached the door without looking back. His sense of betrayal had turned him into a raging beast. Everything he had heard against the Jews — things he had struggled with all his life — came to the fore now, fresh and strong.

His hand on the knob, he slowly opened the door to take the first step toward what was a certain sentence of death.

"Wait!"

It had been Rachel who called. "Please," she said urgently. "Close the door and come back."

Mahmoud hesitated. He had lost his faith in them or their power to find a solution to his problem. He was not in any hurry to obey any of their demands.

"I said 'please,'" Rachel said softly.

Mahmoud closed the door and returned slowly to the kitchen. The Rosenbaums, husband and wife, stood in exactly the same positions in which he had left them. "What do you want?" he asked ungraciously.

"I don't know," Rachel admitted frankly. "Right now, I just want you to stay. You saved our lives, and we are obligated to save yours."

"But —"

"No 'buts'."

"Call your uncle."

"We can't."

The phone rang.

Avraham jumped. As it rang a second time, he picked up the receiver, said, "Hello?" and listened to the voice at the other end. His face paled until it was white as chalk. His heart began to pound so wildly, he was afraid it might fly right out of his chest.

Stumbling, he felt his way over to a chair and sat down, holding the phone firmly with both hands.

40

A combination of surprise and apprehension constricted Avraham's throat, making it impossible for him to speak. Rachel, noticing his distress, asked anxiously, "What happened?"

He put a finger to his lips. The gesture made it clear that he did not want whoever was at the other end of the line to know that she was standing beside him.

"Hello?" he heard again. This time, the word was laced with a trace of worry. "Avraham, do you hear me?"

With resolute strength, he forced himself to reply. Calmly, he said, "Yes, I hear you."

"It's me — your uncle Nachum."

"Yes. I recognize your voice."

"Then why are you speaking so coldly? Is there something you're afraid of? That's the impression I get."

Not knowing where this unexpected conversation would lead, Avraham held onto his artificial cool. "I'm neither cold nor afraid. A little tired, maybe."

"Tired? That must be from the trip. Am I wrong?"

Suspicion leaped up in Avraham. "What trip? What are you talking about?"

His uncle chuckled. "Really, don't act so naive. In any event, don't think that *I'm* so naive!"

In an instinctive attempt to deal with his rapidly accelerating anxiety, Avraham switched the phone from his left hand to his right, moved closer to the wall, and leaned against it. Those few seconds afforded him an opportunity to gather the remaining shreds of his courage and calm.

At the other end of the line his uncle waited, while facing Avraham in the small kitchen — if Mahmoud's story could be believed — stood Uncle Nachum's grandson. Avraham wondered if he might find a way to clarify the strange and terrible tale that had resulted in his wife's outburst and Mahmoud's affront. *Was it true?*

"Avraham, are you there?"

"Yes, yes."

"Why are you so quiet?"

"I'm not quiet!"

"Then answer me. Where were you?"

"How do you know I went anywhere?"

"I even know," Uncle Nachum said triumphantly, "that you were in Canada. What do you have to say to that?"

Avraham did not answer. Astonishment had robbed him of speech.

"Just a few months ago, you were very happy to surprise me, weren't you? To show me that you were a top-notch detective who could uncover matters I did not want exposed. Well, I've done the same thing."

Avraham was at a loss to understand what his uncle was driving at. "So what do you want now?" he asked angrily.

He heard the deep intake of breath at the other end before Uncle Nachum spoke.

"Avraham," he asked bluntly, "were you in Shechem?"

The question, direct and forthright, caught Avraham by surprise. Rachel, who had been watching her husband's expressions closely, whispered, "Who are you talking to?"

Placing a hand over the mouthpiece, Avraham whispered, "Uncle Nachum!"

Her jaw dropped and a hand went to her throat. Mahmoud sat down without either of them noticing.

"Why aren't you answering?" Uncle Nachum asked. "Were you in Shechem?"

"And if I was? What then?"

"That would interest me. I didn't want you to go. But if you did, I'd like to hear what happened there — But I didn't actually call for that reason. I wanted to tell you that your mother's fine now!"

Avraham straightened with a jerk. Gripping the receiver firmly, he demanded, "What happened to her?"

"Don't get so excited. It was nothing terrible. She fainted."

"When? Why? What happened?"

Alerted by his tone, Rachel said, "Avraham, what happened? Tell me!"

"Please don't bother me now," he said urgently. "I'm trying to listen."

Uncle Nachum said, "Calm down. I just spoke to her half an hour ago. I'd been looking for you — and I mentioned to your mother that you might have gone to Shechem."

Avraham clutched his chest. "You *told* her? Why? How did she react?"

"I told you. She fainted, right there by the phone. But she's all right now. I called her neighbors, they entered the apartment — they have a key — and she regained consciousness. I called you now to suggest that you go see her."

Avraham was silent for a long moment. He looked at his wife, pacing restlessly around the kitchen in an effort to contain her anxiety and curiosity. Mahmoud was sitting motionless as a statue, unable to grasp the nature of the drama being enacted before his eyes because all the talk was in Hebrew.

"Uncle Nachum, I can't go right now! I have to think, long and hard, about what to tell her and what not to say."

The Envelope / 299

Mahmoud opened his eyes very wide. It seemed to him that Avraham was speaking to his uncle, in Haifa. At any rate, he had heard Avraham call the person at the other end "Nachum." Maybe this was his grandfather! Mahmoud stood in a way that would attract Avraham's attention. Emotionally, his eyes pleaded with Avraham to ask the burning question uppermost in their minds. The answer to that question would tell them whether or not he, Mahmoud, had spoken the truth.

But Avraham was oblivious to Mahmoud at that moment. It was the image of his widowed mother that he was seeing in his mind's eye.

"Apart from that," Avraham continued, "if I suddenly pop in to see her in the middle of the day, she'll be instantly suspicious! I have to visit her at the right time, when conditions are right, understand?"

There was no answer. Nachum wanted his nephew to travel to Bnei Brak at once, to deal promptly and directly with his mother regarding the painful topic. In that way, he hoped to glean some interesting details about Avraham's trip. But he ended the conversation on a neutral note.

"All right, do what you think is best. We will talk further about this. Goodbye."

The line went dead.

Slowly, Avraham replaced the receiver. Then he quickly related to his wife the gist of their talk. As she listened, Mahmoud moved closer to the couple. Belatedly recalling his presence, they looked at him questioningly.

"Were you just talking to your uncle in Haifa?"

Suddenly, Avraham remembered why Mahmoud was asking. He stammered, "Ye — yes. I was."

Anger flashed in Mahmoud's eyes. "That was your chance!"

"What chance?"

"What do you mean, 'what chance?' Your chance to ask him if the story I told you about my mother is true!"

"Did you really want us to ask him," Rachel inquired dryly, "whether he killed his daughter?"

Once again, Mahmoud felt insulted to the depths of his being. "You have no courage! It's much easier for you to call me a liar!" He shook with rage. "I worked for the G.S.S. I saved your life. Not only for your sake, but also for my own. I want to move closer to the Jewish people. And you —" his hand flew out, pointing an accusing finger at Avraham and Rachel. "you arrived home safely — and then rejected me! You're prepared to leave me to my fate."

He hid his face in his hands for a long moment. When he removed them, there was a strange glint in his eyes. He hissed, "Now I know! Now I understand! If my story is true, then I, Mahmoud, am your cousin's son. In other words, a relative of yours! And you don't want an Arab for a relative. That's why you're pushing me away from the Jewish side within me!"

At that moment, he felt utterly lost and forlorn, without a friend in the world. The old hatreds on which he had been raised, hatred against the Jews who desire only to oppress and humiliate Arabs, rose up in him with fresh insistence. He felt ready to explode. With a great effort, he managed to ask, "Why are you silent?"

It was Rachel who finally said, with difficulty, "It hurts that you think of us that way."

Mahmoud gave her a long, cold look. Then, without a word, he strode to the front door. Just before he left the apartment, he turned and spat, "I am not sorry that I saved you. You are my family. But I have come to understand much in these last few minutes. In fact, I understand everything."

He flung open the door — and froze.

Terror glued him to the spot. His eyes widened in shock. Pulling out his gun, he cried, "What are *you* doing here?"

Mrs. Rosenbaum sat huddled and preoccupied in a capacious armchair. Her good neighbors had lifted her from the floor and sprinkled cold water on her face to revive her. Their initial panic was gone now, leaving in its place an anxious solicitude.

"How do you feel?" one neighbor asked.

"Would you like to eat something?" another interjected, before Mrs. Rosenbaum could answer the first query. Yet a third question followed hard on the heels of the second: "Or maybe something to drink?"

The two women looked at the widow with compassion. "I think," one said, "that it would be a good idea to call a doctor."

"I agree," said the other. She turned to Mrs. Rosenbaum. "Have you taken your blood pressure pills today?"

At that moment, Mrs. Rosenbaum wanted nothing more than to be left alone. She lifted her head and smiled faintly at her good neighbors. "There's no need to call a doctor. I took my pills this morning. I don't want to eat or drink right now. Thank you very much. Really."

"Then what do you want?" they asked worriedly.

"I'd just like to be alone now. It's that simple. I am really grateful to you both — but right now, I want to be by myself. Everything is fine."

Her head rested on one hand, and her eyelids drooped.

The women exchanged a glance. Mrs. Rosenbaum's answer smacked a bit of ingratitude; she was rejecting their well-meant offers of help. They had dropped everything and hastened to her apartment when her brother from Haifa had called. Why was she now pushing them away?

With identical shrugs, they prepared to leave the small apartment. A final word over their shoulders: "If you need help, remember us. Feel good!"

"Thank you! Really, thank you very much!" she called after them in a low voice, waiting for the moment when the front door would close with a click. Then silence would return to her home, and the painful memories along with it, and she would give herself up to them entirely.

Weakly, she got to her feet. First she went to the front door and locked it securely. Then she walked slowly into the second bedroom, to the old cupboard that had stood for years in a corner there. With trembling hands she opened its doors and pulled out one drawer. Her fingers groped for a few seconds until she found the catch that opened a secret compartment in that drawer.

Slowly, she pulled out the small package hidden inside. It had been a long time since she had held it in her hands.

Two large tears spilled from her eyes and coursed down her cheeks. Turning shakily, she went back into the living room and sank again into the armchair. Her eyes closed and her head leaned tiredly back.

Then she roused herself, and began — with some difficulty at first — to open the package that rested in her lap.

Mahmoud gripped the gun in shaking hands. The suddenness of the encounter, and the tension it brought on, made his blood pound in a dizzying fashion. Through narrowed eyes, he stared at the man standing before him.

The man's name was Ahmed Shahada, and he was a Palestinian from Shechem who in recent years had been an active agent working for Samira and other terrorist leaders in the area. Mahmoud had personally witnessed the way Ahmed, with his own hands, squeezed the life out of an Arab who had collaborated with Israel. Many dark tales were whispered in the streets of Shechem about this man's murderous instincts and terrifying physical strength. It seemed crystal clear to Mahmoud now that Ahmed had come here today to murder someone: either himself, or Avraham and Rachel.

Ignoring the gun, Ahmed's towering figure moved slowly forward. Mahmoud retreated a step, screaming with all his might to mask his fear: "Stop right there, Ahmed! Stand still and keep your hands up! Or else — or else I'll empty this gun into you!"

Ahmed was more than a head taller than Mahmoud and capable of flattening him with a single blow of his hammerlike fist. A rapid assessment of the situation, however, told him that Mahmoud's threat had been made in all seriousness. By the time he could manage to strike out at Mahmoud, the gun would have succeeded in putting a couple of bullets into his stomach, something that would in all probability disturb the smooth and efficient functioning of his digestion. Ahmed stood still.

"Hands up, I said. And quick!" The last word emerged from Mahmoud in a shriek. He seemed about to lose all self-control. Hastily, Ahmed raised his hands above his head. There was a scornful smile on his lips and not a trace of fear in his eyes. "Dirty traitor!" he spat.

Mahmoud became even angrier, but he held his tongue. His eyes followed every move of the murderer from Shechem, who continued, "Samira thought that you were killed along with Nawil by that abominable couple sent by the G.S.S. She's convinced that she was the intended victim of their mission. And you led them to her! Dirty traitor!"

Mahmoud's palms were sweating. Tension was sapping his strength, but he maintained a battle stance, knees slightly bent and hands outstretched with the gun held tightly between them. He answered emotionally, "I am no traitor, Ahmed. I am a Jew on my mother's side — and you know it! I decided to return to where I feel I belong, to the place where my mother came from! Understand?"

The big man's black eyes shot sparks. Mahmoud's panic leaped to new levels. Ahmed said, "So that's why the three of you killed Nawil?"

"No! Nawil planned to kill the couple — Samira's brother and his wife — in direct contradiction to Samira's orders. I had no choice."

Ahmed Shahada glared. "Samira will have her revenge on you! We will get you — Never fear, traitor!"

"I'm not so sure," Mahmoud said. "I'm not so sure she'll take revenge. Remember, she is also a Jew. And you know that she is against murder, even of Israelis. What *is* certain, Ahmed, is that you won't get me. You'll see!" He gestured with his head. "Inside! Hands above your head the whole time. Walk to the wall and stand by the door. Don't move an inch."

Ahmed obeyed, his brain seething with half-formed ideas for revenge and escape from this trap into which he had unexpectedly walked. He moved slowly. Mahmoud noticed that Ahmed was holding an envelope in one hand.

"Drop the envelope to the floor!" he barked nervously.

Ahmed hesitated. "I'm supposed to hand it over to Rosenbaum. It's a letter from Samira to her dear, murdering brother."

"Don't talk to me about murder!" Mahmoud screamed. "Do you hear me?"

Avraham and Rachel stood transfixed in the kitchen doorway. The conversation between the two men from Shechem had been conducted entirely in Arabic, of which the Rosenbaums understood not a word. Suddenly, Avraham caught one word he did know: "Samira." Clenching his fists anxiously, he muttered, "What did I need this for? I'm beginning to regret this whole business —"

Rachel threw him a glance that was both stern and frightened. "You mean you don't feel that Hashem is guiding us?" she whispered sardonically. After a moment, she added with a shudder, "How lucky we didn't bring the girls home. They didn't need to see this."

Ahmed stopped by the wall, as instructed.

"Drop the envelope, I said!" Mahmoud ordered. As Ahmed continued to hesitate, Mahmoud screamed. "*Now!*"

Ahmed was afraid that Mahmoud would open fire. The envelope fluttered slowly to the floor.

"Now turn around and place your hands on the wall. High up!"

Ahmed obeyed.

Mahmoud turned to Avraham. "Call the police! Call them to arrest this man."

Ahmed made a sudden movement. Mahmoud fixed the gun on him, shouting, "Don't move — unless you want a trip to the cemetery!"

Avraham rushed to the phone and dialed the police. In words that stumbled over themselves, he described their situation.

"A patrol car is already on its way," a voice informed him.

"You'll pay for this!" Ahmed shrieked. Mahmoud did not answer. He felt ready to explode with tension. Behind him, by the kitchen door, the

The Envelope / 305

Rosenbaums stood silently and helplessly. They prayed with all their hearts that this terrifying episode would end soon — and end happily.

Suddenly, without any warning, Ahmed Shahada made a mighty lunge for the door. Surprised, Mahmoud fired several shots, but missed his target. Ahmed dashed into the stairwell and burst out into the street.

The police car had arrived on the scene at precisely that moment. Its officers leaped out and began to give chase. They did not waste precious minutes going up to the Rosenbaums' apartment to ascertain what, exactly, had occurred there.

The moment the terrorist was gone, Avraham ran to the envelope and picked it up.

"Wait! Don't touch it," Mahmoud warned. "I know my 'friends.' There's no way of knowing what's in that envelope."

Avraham glanced up. Rachel, too, tore her eyes from the envelope and looked at Mahmoud.

They both saw Mahmoud raise his gun and train it directly on Avraham's heart.

At the sight of the pointed gun, Avraham paled. An agitated moan — *oy!* — burst from Rachel's lips. Both shrank back in fear as they caught sight of Mahmoud's face. It was clear that he was held fast in the grip of some powerful emotion. His entire body was trembling and his eyes scurried to and fro like some cornered animal. There was menace in his expression.

Gathering her courage, Rachel asked, "What's happened to you, Mahmoud? What did we do to you this time?"

He ignored her. All his attention was riveted on Avraham, at whose heart the gun was pointed. "You are calling your uncle right now, you hear?"

Avraham did not move. Deep down he was relieved; Mahmoud was only interested in verifying the truth of his story. He was not a secret terrorist intent on killing them. Mahmoud shouted, "Hurry!"

"Okay, okay, I'll call," Avraham said placatingly. "Why the big rush all of a sudden?"

Slowly, Mahmoud advanced on Avraham, the gun never wavering. From some protective instinct, Rachel moved closer to her husband.

"You ask why the rush?" Mahmoud answered in a voice that, although loud, was none too steady. "I'll tell you why. I am simply fed up! I am fed up being a man without a place where he belongs. Neither Arab nor Jew; or rather, even worse, both Arab and Jew. I loved my mother, but she never stopped to consider the kind of anguish she would be bringing on me when she ran away with an Arab. How self-centered! She thought only of herself. What would happen afterwards, to her children, didn't interest her."

The flow of words stopped for a moment, as Mahmoud, still trembling, took several rapid, shallow breaths. His eyes darted continuously, from Avraham to Rachel and back again.

"Do you understand? I am suffering for it today! I don't know whom I belong to. And that hurts — In my heart, I have been drawn for years to my Jewish side. I don't know why, but that's the way it is. And I haven't come all this way to Petach Tikvah with you in order to have you refuse to help me! Call your uncle, and that's that. Understand?"

Avraham went slowly to the phone. As he dialed, he heard Mahmoud say, "Avraham, this is no joke. This is critical for me. Otherwise — I'm finished. I will be a man with no place on earth to call home —"

At the other end of the line, the phone in Uncle Nachum's house was ringing. Only three seconds passed before his uncle picked up, but they seemed endless to Avraham. The impending conversation filled him with an almost unbearable tension.

"Hello?"

Holding his breath, Avraham said, "Uncle Nachum, it's me."

"I hear very well that it's you. What happened to make you call? We just spoke an hour ago."

Avraham filled his lungs with air, then emptied them again. "Yes. I just wanted to tell you that you were right. I *was* in Shechem." He waited a beat. "I also know who the second woman was, in the picture you sent me."

At first, there was no response at all. It seemed to Avraham that he could almost hear his uncle's heartbeats in the silence. Finally, Uncle Nachum blurted, "Well —" and lapsed into silence once again.

"And I also understand," Avraham continued, "why you tore the picture."

When his uncle did not reply, Avraham said, "If I tell you who she was, will you deny it?"

"N-no —"

"Then — Look, Uncle Nachum, it's hard for me to say this. She was your daughter. Your daughter was the one standing beside Samira in the photo, right?"

"Go on."

Avraham leaned against the wall. "She's no longer alive, right?"

He waited. No answer came over the phone from Haifa. Cautiously, he asked, "Is what I said not true?"

Reluctantly, Nachum admitted, "Yes, it's true. But don't talk to me about it."

Avraham was unable to grant that favor. The gun pointing at his heart made sure of that. He pressed, "Why did she die? Or rather, how did she die?"

Suddenly, his uncle roared furiously into the phone. "Aha! I see now! Someone down there must have told you all sorts of stories about me. You must have heard that I beat her — and that I killed her. Tell me the truth, Avraham!"

Avraham answered indirectly, "But were you actually in Shechem?"

"Yes, I was there! Are you the only one who can chase your sister? Can't I go after my own daughter?"

"I never said you couldn't. Why are you so angry?"

"Because I know that they told you stories. Lies."

"But — the truth. Did you and she quarrel there?"

"Why do you care?"

"It's very, very important for me to know. I'll explain later. Did you quarrel?"

Silence returned. Finally, he heard his uncle speak, very low. Apparently — for the moment at least — Uncle Nachum had succeeded in containing his anger, in reining in the emotional storm that raged within.

"Yes," he said quietly. "We quarreled. I hit her. It's true that I hit her repeatedly, and hard. I admit it: I lost control. Looking back now, I'm sorry about that. I know I made a mistake. But to say that I killed her is a lie! She was hurt, and they took her to the hospital. But I think they killed her there, so that they could pin the blame on me. Don't you know Arab tactics by now?"

Avraham did not reply at once. He glanced at Mahmoud, to reassure him that the talk was proceeding well. Mahmoud seemed to relax slightly; the gun was now pointed at the floor instead of at Avraham. This made Avraham relax in turn. He heard his uncle ask: "Who told you the story? Your wonderful sister?"

"No. I didn't hear it from her."

"Then who?" Uncle Nachum asked, suddenly impatient.

"From Mahmoud."

"Who is that?"

"Mahmoud is Latifa's son. That was the Arab name your daughter used. What was her Hebrew name?"

"M-Mahmoud?" Uncle Nachum choked. "My daughter's son?"

"In other words, Uncle Nachum, I heard the story from Mahmoud — your grandson."

It seemed to Avraham that he could hear a quiet weeping coming down the line. "Look," he said, in an effort to be comforting. "Mahmoud is a good boy."

"A good Arab, you mean," his uncle said brokenly.

"No — a good boy. A good Jew, according to Jewish law. And the fascinating thing is that he wants to return and live as a Jew."

"How do you know?" Uncle Nachum demanded. He sounded better already.

"He told me so himself."

"Really? I can hardly believe that!"

"Then why don't you ask him directly? He's right here. He's standing beside me."

"Right there? *In your house?*"

"Yes. Do you want to talk to your grandson?"

The change in Uncle Nachum's mood was as dramatic as it was sudden. "NO!" he bellowed — and slammed the receiver down, hard.

Avraham reeled. After a moment, he gently replaced the receiver. Mahmoud's eyes were filled with questions, begging him to tell everything about the conversation with his uncle — Mahmoud's grandfather. Avraham told him.

Mahmoud listened intently, then said, "At least now you know that I didn't lie to you, as you thought."

He closed his eyes. Avraham and Rachel watched him, trying — unsuccessfully — to guess what was passing through his mind.

Avraham's thoughts returned to the envelope on the floor. Cautiously, he asked Mahmoud, who had replaced his gun in his belt, "Now, can I read my sister's letter?"

"Wait. Let me check to see exactly what the envelope contains. I'm a bit of an expert in these things. Did you hear the sound the envelope made as Ahmed dropped it?"

"Yes. There was a sort of metallic ring."

"That's right. You'd better let me check it out first."

Slowly, Mahmoud moved toward the envelope.

Mahmoud approached the envelope cautiously and bent to inspect it closely where it lay on the floor. Without touching it, he studied the envelope from every angle and with full concentration. The metallic ring he had heard as the envelope fell to the floor made him suspect the possibility of a letter bomb. Avraham and Rachel watched his every move with a mixture of curiosity and trepidation.

Mahmoud moved closer to the envelope. With the barrel of his gun, he touched it lightly, ready to spring back at the slightest sign of danger. He knew that his chances, should the envelope explode, were next to zero; still, he was willing to take the gamble.

Suddenly, he stood up. To Avraham and Rachel he said, "Please go into the kitchen. Quickly, now."

They obeyed instantly. Mahmoud drew back his leg and kicked the envelope into a corner of the room, then dove behind the sofa.

Nothing happened. The envelope did not explode.

He stood up. Walking over to the envelope, he picked it up. Avraham and Rachel peeked out of the kitchen just as he was opening it.

A bullet dropped out of the envelope and clattered onto the floor.

Mahmoud paled. He understood the message of that bullet all too clearly. Samira was prepared to go to any lengths — in order to kill her brother.

"You can come out now," he called.

The bullet was accompanied by a long letter, written in Hebrew.

As Avraham emerged from the kitchen, Mahmoud handed him the letter. "This," he said, "does not contain good news. I don't know what it says, because I don't read Hebrew. But this bullet is meant to convey a threat. Samira sent Ahmed here in order to show that she knows exactly where you live, and that her people can ambush you at any time. I am afraid you've got a problem."

Avraham and Rachel exchanged a quick, anxious glance.

"What do we do now?" Rachel asked.

Mahmoud was surprised. "You are asking *me* that? Do I know what you must do? I haven't a clue. You are living among your own kind. *What am I supposed to do?*"

His words reminded the Rosenbaums, with the suddenness of a blow, exactly who was standing in their apartment with them. A long, tense silence ensued, broken at last by Avraham: "We will see what can be done. Hashem will help."

He began to read the letter.

After a moment, he looked up, walked into the living room, and sat down in the first chair he came to. Rachel hurried after and stood beside him, reading in his face his reaction to the words he was absorbing. Mahmoud, too, followed, though he stood at a little distance from the others.

> *To my "dear" brother, whose visit has cost me very dearly — both in emotional anguish, and even more, in the loss of two of my men through your treachery.*

You came to see me. The iron wall that stood between us did not fall in a hurry. I did not believe that you came in innocence, merely to meet your sister, to become acquainted with her and to love her. I suspected that this was just one of the tricks perpetrated by the G.S.S., and that you were searching with all your might to find some angle, some way to arrest me and close my hotel — my inheritance from my husband, whom your people murdered.

I will admit, however, that I did not succeed in keeping my emotional distance for long. Blood is thicker than water; what could I do? Your presence aroused powerful feelings in me — feelings that I needed a great deal of strength and energy to conceal from you. You could say that you managed to tear down, in a single night, a structure that I've spent half my life building. I admit also that you aroused longings in me that I had hoped were long dead. Through our meeting, to my great surprise, I discovered that they were merely buried, hiding in the depths of my subconscious, waiting for the chance to surface to the light of day and rob me of my peace of mind — an artificial peace, apparently.

By the time you left, I was no longer the same Samira — or, as you insist on calling me, the same Rivka that I had been the day before. I was very angry at you for bursting so unexpectedly into my life and shaking it up so. At the same time, however, I felt a desire to draw near, to ask you how our mother is and about your lifestyle in the world that I had forsaken more than twenty years ago. I decided to leave all that for the next time, perhaps for another meeting that would take place when I had succeeded in soothing my stormy spirit.

I stood outside before dawn yesterday, and my heart ached despite its outward appearance of callousness — ached to see you and your wife driving away in the car I put at your disposal. Suddenly, I believed you. I believed in you, Avraham, and I cried for a good few hours afterwards. My son, an Arab through and through, was very angry at me — and even angrier at you, when he saw the state I was in.

But, Avraham! It is all over! Your treachery and betrayal serves to highlight what we knew about the conscienceless nature of my fellow Jews. Either alone or with the help of other Israeli agents, you killed two of my men, one of whom, Mahmoud, happened to be your cousin! I will not tell you his story now. It is no longer important, now that he has been killed and even his body has disappeared.

I hate you now as I have never hated anyone before in my life. It is a deep hatred, a bottomless hatred, after the way you toyed with my emotions, with my natural yearnings and the desire for family ties buried so long — and all in order to spy on me and to bring me to my knees! I will never forgive that. Never. You are no longer my brother!

My vengeance will reach you, wherever you may be. Revenge for the murder of my two men, who faithfully set out to deliver you to your home, secure in my personal orders. Shame on you, despised brother. I curse the day you appeared in my hotel.

Guard the bullet well; your day of reckoning is yet to come.

Samira

Avraham finished reading the letter and looked up at his wife. She saw the deep turmoil reflected in his eyes. The hands that were clutching the letter were trembling.

"Tell me," she said.

"Read it for yourself," he whispered. "I can't."

He handed her the letter, then leaned his head back in his chair as though unbearably tired.

Mahmoud, standing to one side, knew exactly what was happening. The bullet told its own tale; he had no need of a long letter to understand its meaning. Avraham was in mortal danger.

"Listen, Avraham," he said urgently. "You must immediately contact those who sent you to Nablus! Tell them exactly what has happened. They will figure out what needs to be done. Do it quickly!" He paused, then added, "And remind them about my situation as well."

Avraham did not answer. A storm of feeling precluded speech. He did not know what hurt more — his fear of his sister's threats, or the fact that the thin thread of connection that had formed between them last night had been brutally severed. Severed in an instant, because of a terrorist who had decided to kill them and who himself, by G-d's mercy, lost his life as a result. Avraham felt on the brink of a breakdown.

Rachel put the letter down on the table and burst into tears. Her voice emerged muffled through the hands that covered her face. "We've only been home a few hours, and look at what's happened already. Oh, *Ribbono Shel Olam,* what's going to happen next?"

Avraham turned suddenly to Mahmoud. "Do you think the danger from Samira is imminent?"

Mahmoud considered before replying, "I don't think so. Still, it's impossible to be sure."

"Do you think it would be a good idea for my wife and daughters to go to her parents in the United States?"

Rachel whirled on him. "And you intend to stay here? It's you who are in the greatest danger!"

Avraham addressed Mahmoud again. "What do you think? Should they go? Alone, I will be better able to protect myself from her." This was his indirect answer to Rachel.

Mahmoud was flattered at his sudden transformation into a security expert. "May I sit?" he asked. Permission graciously granted, he sat down and began to assess the situation from a Palestinian perspective.

"Look, Samira is no murderer. She is against the taking of life. All her activity has been in opposition to your occupation of Arab land."

Avraham smiled slightly. "Don't you mean *our* occupation?"

At first, Mahmoud did not grasp his meaning. Then he nodded. "Ah, yes, *our*. I understand. Yesterday's *your* has turned into today's *our*. All right, all right." He smiled, and continued. "I know Samira fairly well, and I believe that she is only making threats to frighten you. On the other hand, it's never possible to know for sure —"

Rachel rose abruptly and went to the kitchen, calling out, "Does anyone want tea or coffee?"

"This time," Avraham said, "for a change, I'll have some tea. Thanks."

"And you, Mahmoud? We need to find you a Jewish name already! What will you drink?"

"Tea for me also, thanks!"

Rachel had gone into the kitchen in an effort to calm herself, but the two men could hear her whisking about like a whirlwind. In the living

The Envelope / 317

room, Avraham said, "If you had read this awful letter, you would not think it an empty threat."

"Maybe not. And that's why I urge you again: Contact your G.S.S. agent now — and remind him about me as well."

Avraham realized that this was the only appropriate possibility at this time. He stood up and dialed his workplace. After a brief talk with his boss, Yair Peled assured him that he would try to track down Binyamin.

A short while later, the phone rang in the Rosenbaum apartment. It was Binyamin, Avraham's man in the G.S.S.

Mrs. Rosenbaum thumbed through the pile of envelopes. From each one in turn she pulled out a small note that lay inside. She held each note with shaking hands, and with a reverence that was close to awe. Lips moving soundlessly, she read what was written on those scraps of paper, sometimes repeating a phrase or a sentence. The tears flowed continuously.

Finally, she began to slowly return the notes, and also the larger pages she had found inside, to their envelopes. With a loving hand she caressed each one. It was difficult for her to part from them. Her husband had passed away only a short time before. It had been years since she had held this box — many long years. But her brother, Nachum, with a willpower over which she has no control, had forced her into it.

Gently, she closed the box and placed it on the table. She sat unmoving for several minutes, feeling the weakness spread through her, from limb to limb. She lifted a hand to wipe away her tears, then tried to stand.

But, though her hands pressed down hard on the armrests of her chair, she did not succeed in standing erect. Instead, she leaned back, as devoid of strength as though she were carrying a superheavy burden. Indeed, it was a very heavy burden.

Avraham was due back in Israel today, she thought. *Why hasn't he called? Has something happened to him?*

She stretched her right hand to the phone. It rested on the receiver, but she did not lift it. Did she really want to see him now? Would her aching heart be strong enough to bear the tales he would bring from — there?

She lifted the receiver. Before dialing, however, she considered the matter again. Perhaps Avraham had not come to see her because he believed her to be ignorant of the fact that he had visited Rivka in Shechem. Telling him otherwise would throw him into confusion. "Better wait until things happen on their own. If he doesn't come today, he'll surely come tomorrow, or the next day." She replaced the receiver. No. She would not call.

But how could she wait? Now that she knew the secret behind Avraham's disappearance, the wait was onerous. She just couldn't bear it.

Once again, she picked up the receiver. She dialed the familiar number slowly, her very fingers aching with fatigue. She heard the phone ring at the other end — and hurriedly replaced the receiver. At the last second, her courage had simply failed her.

She sat weeping silently for a long time, not bothering to wipe away the tears.

❦

Saib sent a telegram to his older brother, Nashashivi, in Kuwait:

"Come home quickly! Mother in danger."

The next morning, Nashashivi boarded a plane to Amman, Jordan. From there, he drove directly to Shechem.

44

"What happened?" Nashashivi was tense. He tried, from his brother's eyes, to fathom the nature of the danger that had brought him here so hastily. The two were meeting in a small, unused room in their mother's hotel.

"You have to speak to her right away," Saib said urgently. "I tried, but she wouldn't listen."

"But what are you talking about? What happened?"

Saib placed a hand on his brother's shoulder and began pacing the room with him. "Her brother came to see her."

Nashashivi stopped. *"Her brother?"*

"Yes, yes, her *Yahud* brother, curse him!"

"And what happened?"

"I don't know exactly. I do know that she experienced a deep emotional trauma when he was here — feelings that confused her. And — who knows? — she may also have begun to think about her former home." He turned to look directly at his older brother. "We've got a problem, Nashashivi."

"What might that be?"

"She is showing signs of compassion for the *Yahud*, starting to understand him. And that's not good."

Nashashivi fell silent, trying to digest this new information and to weigh their options. Saib began his pacing again, pulling his brother along with him.

"And don't think the story ends there. Mother sent him home, accompanied by Nawil and Mahmoud, our cousin. Neither one returned home."

"What? They ran to the *Yahud*?"

"No. They were murdered. We found Nawil's body in the hills."

"And Mahmoud?"

"His body seems to have disappeared. We didn't find it."

"Who killed them?"

"You tell me who killed them. Our *Yahud* uncle, that's who! Mother suspects — really, she's sure — that he's a Mossad or G.S.S. agent."

Nashashivi lowered his voice to a whisper. "And what happened next? How did Mother react?"

"Here," sighed Saib, "is where we get to the hard part."

"What do you mean?"

"Mother was furious. She cursed her brother — but would not give me permission to hurt him — to pay him what he deserves for what he did."

"Do you intend to kill him?" Nashashivi asked bluntly.

"Yes. Why not? Understand this, brother: As long as he lives, Mother is in danger."

"Did he threaten her?"

"No. But I'm afraid that she will be drawn back *there*, to her people — and we are Arabs, right? We are Palestinians, right? If he is dead, there will be nothing to draw her back."

"True. You're right."

"So something must be done. Something to prevent her from fleeing. Something that will have her continue in our struggle for independence."

Nashashivi considered the situation. He had been in Kuwait for over a year now, earning a respectable living as a chemical engineer, and the distance from home had muted, in him, the rebellious flame that burned so brightly in his younger brother. From the perspective of quiet, prosperous Kuwait, things looked very different.

Nevertheless, Saib's fear infected him as well. Abruptly, he went to the door. "Come on, let's go see Mother."

Samira's face lit up in surprise and happiness at the sight of her first-born son.

"My Nashashivi! What are you doing here? What a surprise!" She embraced him warmly.

Then she held him at arm's length and studied him, suspicion in her eyes.

"What happened to make you come like this, without sending word?"

The direct question did not leave him much room for vacillating. He said, equally directly, "I came because I felt the need to speak with you personally."

With her cynical smile, Samira said, "Has your brother been talking to you?"

"Yes. What's wrong with that? He wants to save his mother. Isn't that commendable on his part?"

Samira slowly went to her chair and sat down. "To save me? Am I in prison? In some Israeli jail? What are you talking about? I don't like this!" She looked angry.

"I don't like it either," he said. "Your brother, I am told, has been here, and has influenced you. We are afraid that you will return to the *Yahud*, Mother."

Furious now, Samira leaped to her feet. "I — influenced by him? Who told you such lies?"

Quietly, Nashashivi said, "Saib told me about his conversation with you yesterday."

She threw a disgusted glance at her younger son. "What did I say to frighten your excitable younger brother?"

The Envelope / 323

"I don't know. But Saib is not stupid, Mother. He sensed what you've been going through, and wants to support you."

"What I'm going through?" Samira repeated.

"Mother, don't deny it. Your brother's visit shook you up. Maybe he's awakened a nostalgia for your past. That worries us."

For some moments, Samira stood silent, lips compressed. Then she snapped, "And just why, Saib, did you come to that conclusion?"

Saib, leaning against the window frame, had been following their dialogue. Now he came forward to stand near his mother and brother. "Because you wouldn't let me see to it that your brother dies for his treachery. He killed people close to you, though they did nothing to him."

"True. I don't want you to kill him."

"This is exactly what we're afraid of!" Saib cried. "You've already gone back to them!"

Both young men stared at her, blatant anger in their dark eyes. For the first time, Samira felt a pang of fear.

"I am here," she said simply. "You know that. I will not betray the memory of my murdered husband."

Saib seized his mother's arm. "You told me that blood is thicker than water."

"Yes. But that says nothing."

His grip tightened painfully. "Then agree to let me kill your traitor of a brother!"

"*No!* Never!" she cried.

Nashashivi found all his former ardor for the Palestinian cause flowing back to him. The quiet years in Kuwait might never have been. He grasped his mother's other arm and said with quiet menace, "You will give us permission to kill him. Do you hear?"

Samira's arms ached from the double pressure of her sons' angry and insolent grips. "What's happened to you?" she demanded. "Let go of me at once!" Her tone was slightly hysterical.

Her sons did not respond, nor did they relinquish their hold. Icy eyes bore into her own. They loved their mother, but felt compelled to treat her cruelly now. Together, they demanded, "Give us permission! Otherwise, we'll do it without your consent!"

Samira's thoughts suddenly wandered to her father. She was gazing with pain and sorrow at her sons, who were staring back with hateful looks and hurting her — physically hurting her. It was almost unbearable. And suddenly, for the first time, she understood the full extent of the pain she had caused her father on the day she left home. A great ball of pain welled up inside her, climbing until it reached her throat and choked her.

"Answer us!" her sons insisted. The words came to her as if from a fog.

"I gave you my answer," she said. With a mighty wrench, she freed her arms. She retreated to the sofa, screaming with all her strength, "OUT!" Her index finger pointed to the door.

The young men were startled. For a moment they stood transfixed, undecided. But they were not equal to their mother's fury. Slowly, very slowly, they moved backwards to the door, and left the room.

Samira stood shaking. Her sons' behavior had destroyed her equilibrium. Wild thoughts bombarded her brain, making her head ache. After standing frozen for ten long minutes, she walked across the room to the liquor cabinet and slowly opened it. One by one, she removed the bottles from the shelves, depositing them on her desk. She went to her office door and locked it securely, but soundlessly, taking the key with her. Then she returned to the cabinet.

It was empty now. Very carefully, she lifted a layer of formica that had lain untouched for long years. With trembling hands she reached inside the space and pulled out an envelope.

※

In the Rosenbaum apartment, the phone rang. Rachel picked it up.

"Hello? Avraham Rosenbaum, please."

She passed the phone to her husband, whispering, "I think it's Binyamin."

It was.

"How are you, Avraham?" the G.S.S. man asked.

"Thank G-d, I'm all right. I returned from Shechem without succeeding in my goal. And, as if that weren't enough, my sister is now threatening me."

Avraham spilled the whole story of the last few days to Binyamin — including the fact that Mahmoud was sitting in his apartment at that moment.

Several seconds passed before Binyamin spoke. "Look, Avraham, don't worry. We'll take care of this matter. Your sister won't trouble you too much. As for your lack of success, we have yet to analyze what happened."

"Don't hurt her!" Avraham said quickly.

"Of course not. Don't worry."

Binyamin added, "Please put Mahmoud on the phone."

Binyamin and Mahmoud spoke in English. It was clear that they knew one another personally. Binyamin let Mahmoud know that he was shortly to be transferred into G.S.S. authority. They would care for all his needs.

Avraham came back on the line. "Until matters are cleared up with your sister," Binyamin cautioned, "it's best for you to be careful. Don't walk in dark or deserted places. Be cautious. In a few days, this whole thing will be behind you. Don't ask me how — or why."

Avraham did not ask. Still, he feared that something would happen to Rivka. Despite his sister's threats, he did not want any harm to come her way.

A short time later, a private car pulled up in front of Avraham's building in Petach Tikvah. Two young men emerged. They rode the elevator up to the Rosenbaums' apartment and introduced themselves as Binyamin's messengers. They had come to fetch Mahmoud. They saw Mahmoud on his way with goodbyes and good wishes.

Avraham and Rachel were alone. They felt a certain measure of relief; for all their desire to help the man who had saved their lives, his presence in their home had not been easy for them. They were glad that he was in good hands now, hands capable of dealing with such situations.

As for Mahmoud's grandfather, Uncle Nachum, Avraham and Rachel hoped that they would be able to sit down and discuss matters with him before too long. Blood, after all, was thicker than water.

Avraham went to see his mother the next day. He went alone, without his wife. He knew it would be a difficult visit, replete with stormy emotions and painful undercurrents. Better that it be an intimate meeting between mother and son.

Slowly, he climbed the stairs to her apartment. As he did, he tried in vain to picture the upcoming session. Now that all the secrets had been exposed — or had they? — when they met it would be as two different people than they had been before. He was certainly a different Avraham, an Avraham who had matured in these last weeks in the wake of a secret he had never dreamed of. And his mother, no doubt, would be changed as well, now that all stood revealed between them.

He rang the bell. His breathing, he noted, had become uneven. This was the first time in his memory that he had stood thus, so tense and jumpy, outside the door of his parents' home. He rang again. After another long moment that seemed fated never to end, the door opened. In the entrance stood his mother, a forced and very tired smile on her lips.

With hands that shook uncontrollably, Samira pulled out the envelope. She stared at it for a long time without making a move to open it.

It was an old envelope — over twenty years old. At the edges, the paper was yellowed. When was the last time she had held it in her hands? She could not remember. Only once before, perhaps.

It had been a stormy day in Shechem. The skies were gun-metal gray and rain had pounded on the streets. Someone, she could not remember who, had placed the letter on the reception desk. Samira could still see her name written on the front in Hebrew letters: Rivka Rosenbaum.

The letter was from her father. She received it about two months after leaving home to marry Abu Daoud al-Razak, in his aging parents' modest hotel in Shechem.

Moving in slow motion, Samira opened the envelope. She pulled out the letter. The lines were crowded together, the words rising and falling as though to the tune of some compelling emotional state. Her eyes ran down the page, lips moving slightly as she read what was written there.

> *Rivka, Rivka who has betrayed me and betrayed her people. Rivka, who no longer lives at home after murdering me in my innocence. The Nazis, may their names be blotted out, killed my parents and all my family. For a full year, serving in the Sonderkommand in Auschwitz, death was my constant companion. I lost all hope and lived only with despair under the dread blow that had fallen so suddenly upon our heads. It was a feeling that did not fully leave me, even long afterwards.*
>
> *You, Rivka, were the first spark of hope for me. Your birth restored my faith in life, in the future, and in the Jewish people. From the moment I first held you in my arms, I drew new strength from your presence in the world. Here, I thought, is the continuity. Hitler, despite everything, did not triumph.*
>
> *Now you have killed all that in me. You have murdered me, a man who passed through the purgatory of Auschwitz and dreamed of rebuilding his life as a Jew in Eretz Yisrael. You murdered me.*

Samira looked at the wall. The picture of her husband that hung there seemed distant and muddled, through the mist in her eyes. She lowered her eyes once again to the letter.

> *These are the last words I will say to your deaf ears, words that I do not believe will ever find their way into your blackened heart. I have heard rumors that Hitler, may his name be blotted out, and others in his dastardly circle, had Jewish blood in their veins. In their desire to wipe out this terrible "stain," they turned inhumanly cruel toward the Jewish people. You silly fool. Just a generation or two ago, some Jewish girl ran away with a German boy, or a Jewish boy with a German girl. They had faith in their bond, and believed that it would help to do away with the barriers that exist between the nations of the world. They bore offspring — who later turned into murderers of Jews. I don't know if the rumor is true or fabricated. But know this: The conclusions they reveal are correct. I hope you never have children. And if, Heaven forbid, you do, they will be the greatest killers of Jews. All in order to prove to their Arab friends that their Jewish blood has no influence on them. But — blood is thicker than water.*

The last sentence hit her like a bolt of lightning. Now she recalled where it had come from, to lodge so firmly in her own mind. *Blood is thicker than water.* And this was true in a negative sense, as well — the cruel, dark sense. Blood could propel a person to greater wickedness, just to prove that it was not thicker than water at all. Her own sons wished to murder her brother. They had even hurt her, just to prove that they were good Arabs.

She could not bear it any longer. Her hands were trembling violently now, and tears splashed unheeded onto the letter she had not succeeded in finishing. She could not bear to read all the terrible things her father had to say about her, and the bitter end he wished upon her, which had deepened her hatred toward him all those long years ago.

And — now? What now?

She sat on the floor beside the open liquor cabinet, and gave herself freely over to weeping.

"Hello," his mother said, her voice all but inaudible to his ears. "Come in."

Avraham entered the apartment with a firm step that belied his nervousness. Mrs. Rosenbaum shut the door behind him, then followed silently. At the entrance to the living room, Avraham looked around the familiar space as though seeing it for the first time. The powerful experiences he had undergone in Canada and Shechem — especially in Shechem — had created a different world in his mind. The room in which he had grown up with his parents looked different to him after his dramatic encounter with his sister, beyond the dark hills.

"Sit down," his mother whispered.

He chose an armchair; she sat down opposite him, on the sofa. They were as quiet as two strangers who had nothing to say to each other. Or perhaps they were silent because they had too much to say to each other.

Mrs. Rosenbaum looked wearily across at her son. Avraham's head was slightly bowed, his fingers drumming lightly on the arm of his chair as he cast about in his mind for the right opening words. Then he lifted his head and smiled — a little shyly, and a little sadly, too.

His mother's face was the same, but she appeared much older to Avraham. When had this happened? When had he last laid eyes on his mother? How many decades ago? Only two weeks, he thought with wonder. Two weeks that felt like an eternity.

"I know that you know," he said finally.

Mrs. Rosenbaum said nothing.

"Uncle Nachum told me."

Still no reaction. The thick silence felt suffocating.

Then he heard her voice, quivering with an emotion she was struggling to suppress: "Why did you do it?"

His fingers drummed their nervous rhythm. The question surprised him. "Did I have a choice?" he countered.

"You opened old wounds. Why?"

He leveled his gaze at her. "Were the wounds really healed, Imma?"

She did not respond. Avraham was genuinely surprised. The secret he uncovered had provided an explanation for the sad undercurrent that had pervaded his parents' home all through the years. He had always assumed it was because of the Holocaust, but now he knew that the Holocaust was not the only reason. And just as he believed that it was impossible for the wounds of that war to ever really heal, he also believed that the wound of losing a daughter in the way they had was equally impossible to heal. In that case, why had his mother just said what she did?

"Were old wounds opened up there, too?" she asked.

Avraham understood that "there" referred to Shechem, and that the "old wounds" were Rivka/Samira's.

"Yes," he said quietly. "There, too, I don't believe the wounds were ever really healed."

Mrs. Rosenbaum sighed deeply. "Really?"

The sigh, and the pathetic question, pained Avraham to his depths. "Yes — why not?" he demanded. "Do you think that everything's smooth and easy in *her* heart?"

Suddenly, he recalled the threatening letter he had received from his sister. At the memory, he felt a prickle of fear. But that same letter had also brought welcome news: news of how his visit had shaken her. Now it was up to him to convince his mother that a Jewish heart still beat in her daughter, weak and sporadic as those heartbeats might be.

"How did she look?" Mrs. Rosenbaum whispered.

Avraham rejoiced at the question. His mother was still, after all, a mother.

"She looks like you!" he said. "She reminded me of the way you looked years ago."

His answer appeared to upset her. She covered her face with her hands, in the grip of an emotion growing stronger with each passing second. And then, to his astonishment and dismay, she burst into tears.

"Tell me, Avraham," she cried, the words coming muffled and indistinct through her tears. "Tell me, how is she? How is she? Did you speak with her? Did she talk to you? Did she —?"

Once again, she buried her face in her palms, the tears flowing over and between her fingers. Avraham watched her, at a loss. He wanted to get up, to go to her, to hug and comfort her. But this, he decided, was not the moment. Over twenty years of pain were pouring out of her now with these tears. Over twenty years of a secret buried deep inside, of an ache that would not go away. Crying now was a positive thing; it was beneficial. It was good.

So he sat and watched her, and waited. If a few tears found their way down his own cheeks, he dabbed them quietly away with his handkerchief.

Mrs. Rosenbaum sobbed a long time. At last, she removed her hands from her tear-stained face, self-control slowly returning. "Did you get the impression from her that she regretted destroying her own and our lives?"

Avraham was not quick to reply.

"I understand," his mother said sadly. "I understand that she does not. Am I right?"

Avraham roused himself to say, "It's not exactly like that, Imma. The whole subject is more complicated than that. She certainly has regrets."

His mother's expression spoke volumes. She did not believe him.

"If she really regrets it," Mrs. Rosenbaum said, "then why is it so complicated? It seems very simple to me."

When Avraham did not speak, she lifted her head and gave him a penetrating stare. "Avraham, I'm waiting."

He positioned himself more comfortably in his armchair, buying time with a meaningless smile. In his mind's eye, Rivka/Samira stood as she had on that last night in Shechem. Had it been only the night before last? Avraham could palpably feel the waves of hatred radiating toward her parents' home.

"It's hard for me to talk about it, Imma. But —"

"But what?"

"She's carrying around a great deal of anger inside —"

"She's *still* angry?" Mrs. Rosenbaum raised her voice. It seemed to Avraham that she had turned the clock back by twenty-two years, and that all the fury of that bygone time had returned to her in full force. This was definitely not something he wished to arouse now. He had no choice, however, but to answer.

"Not just anger, Imma. Also a powerful hatred toward Abba. Why? I'd like to understand."

A tremor ran through his mother, her face reflecting inarticulate rage. Avraham hastily held up his hand to stave off the impending explosion. "Imma, please, all I'm asking is that you tell me what happened — and I'll tell you who I met in Shechem, and how I met her. Maybe, after twenty years, we'll look at things a little differently. Please."

To his amazement, his mother calmed down almost at once. With eyes still reddened with weeping, she asked, "Did you tell her that Abba — it's hard for me to say the words — that Abba passed away?"

"Yes."

"And —?"

"It came up in the middle of a difficult conversation. Rachel threw the news out almost by the way, in the middle of an emotional scene, saying that from the day Abba died and I discovered the secret, I'd been yearning to meet my sister."

"How did she react?" Mrs. Rosenbaum's eyes blazed with curiosity.

"She was very surprised, and expressed real pain. She asked, 'How is Imma?' I told her. Then she sat down and was quiet for a long time."

Mrs. Rosenbaum fell silent. Avraham tried — unsuccessfully — to read his mother's feelings in her face.

"And then," he continued, "I told her how I'd learned of her existence — about the envelope I found here in the apartment. I said that it was through that envelope that I reached her."

"What was her reaction to that?"

"She was stunned. 'What?' she asked. 'All these years, you didn't know that you had a sister somewhere?' And I answered clearly: 'No.' I sensed that the news really shook her up."

☙❧

Samira had no idea how much time passed while she sat on the floor. The square of glass at the window was suddenly dark, night having fallen without her noticing. And then she heard someone trying to open the locked door of her office.

She leaped to her feet and hurried to hide away the envelope. In a clear, loud voice, she called out, "Who's there?"

Without a word, Mrs. Rosenbaum got up and left the room. For several long minutes Avraham fretted and wondered alone in the living room, before she returned, an old wooden box in her hands. She placed the box on the coffee table. Avraham regarded it with interest. As far as he knew, he had never laid eyes on the box before.

"Open it!" she commanded softly.

With marked hesitation, Avraham did as he was told. He wore the air of a man who does not know what to expect. What he found was a pile of envelopes.

There were blue air-mail envelopes, and envelopes that had once been white but were now yellowed with age. He saw long envelopes and short ones; flat envelopes and puffy ones. He looked at them curiously, but did not reach out to handle them, waiting instead for a further cue from his mother.

"Do you know what those are?" she asked in that same soft tone.

The Envelope / 337

"No. But I'm willing to take a guess."

She smiled slightly. "Let's hear."

Avraham glanced again at the envelopes, and said slowly, "No. I don't think I will."

She pulled the box closer and began to thumb through the envelopes.

"I didn't lie to you," she said, "the day you discovered those envelopes of your father's. I didn't lie when I said it had become an obsession of his since Auschwitz, as I told you. We lived our lives in the shadow of his envelopes. Even I was not allowed to touch them. They were a secret kept from me as well. Sometimes I would discover one underneath his shirts, for example, or in the laundry hamper, or in any number of other strange and unexpected hiding places he used."

She paused to take a deep breath, which turned into a sigh and a half-smile, as though caught in some embarrassing act. Avraham kept his expression impassive to hide the tension mounting inside. He waited for her to go on.

"Do you understand, Avraham? When we returned from the funeral, I began to collect them. They are my souvenirs — strange and painful souvenirs, but something to remember him by. I collected them quietly so that others — you, especially — would not discover them."

"Why?" The question burst from Avraham unwillingly.

"Why? Because I knew that they were his secret. He must have known how odd it was, but the uncontrollable obsession was just another tragic legacy of Auschwitz. At least, that's the way I understood it."

"But you didn't collect them all." He waited a beat, more to control his own suspense than to add to hers, and continued, "You know which one I mean."

"That's it exactly, Avraham. When I saw you holding that envelope and asking me what a picture of that accursed Arab terrorist was doing in Abba's desk drawer, my world went dark. I hadn't succeeded in hiding from you, your father's only son, the truth about his strange behavior. And, in the process, you stumbled upon our most deeply hidden and devastating secret."

A tear slipped from the corner of her eye. "I couldn't bear it. I thought I was going to faint. Or — or even worse —"

"I sensed that," Avraham said quietly. "But I didn't understand."

"How could you?" She pushed the box close to her son and whispered, "Open the envelopes. Every one of them has something to do with your sister."

※

The knocking at her door did not stop. Once again, her heart in her throat, Samira called, "Who is it? Who's there?"

"Mother, open quickly. It's us."

Hurriedly, she wiped away the lingering tears. Praying that her sons would not notice her reddened eyes and learn of her secret and bitter bout of weeping, she went to the door. Her sons stood there, exuding something dark and powerful and dangerous.

"What happened?" she asked with the beginnings of panic.

They walked inside in unified step. Without answering, they sat on either side of the couch. After a moment Samira followed, sinking into one of the armchairs opposite.

"Look, Mother," Nashashibi said flatly. "Our decision is final."

"What decision?" Her heart was knocking hard against her rib cage. She felt an impending sense of doom.

Nashashibi and Saib exchanged a fleeting glance. It was Saib who said, "You know very well what we mean."

"No," she said, clutching the arm of her chair as if to prevent herself from toppling over. The room seemed to reel around her. "I don't know what you're talking about."

"Do we have to spell it out for you? All right, then. Here it is: the decision about your brother. It is clear to us that as long as he remains alive, we do not have our mother. And we love you. We want you to stay with us."

Like a wounded tiger, she shrieked, "What are you babbling about? *I'm right here!* I'm staying here with you. Stop talking such dangerous nonsense!"

"Maybe you're here physically, but your heart, your feelings, are somewhere else, Mother," Nashashibi said. "This has got to stop. Your brother must die. And we are going out today to take care of it."

Samira jumped up as though bitten by a snake. "NO! *Oh, no —*"

Her scream reverberated through the length and breadth of the hotel.

⁓⁓⁓

Avraham's hand trembled as he reached for the box. It pained him to realize that he was about to go through something that his father had wished to keep hidden.

"It's hard," he whispered.

"I know," she said. "But I've thought about it a great deal. Why did Heaven bring things about in such a way that you found the one envelope that could lead you directly to the most difficult and secret part of our lives? All the other envelopes that you see here, Avraham, deal with Rivka, too — but you would not have understood anything from them without knowing the secret first. And that secret was contained specifically in the envelope that I neglected to hide from you. Do you think that was a coincidence? Or maybe it was a sign from Heaven?"

Suddenly, for no reason, Avraham's tension dissipated. He felt liberated. With a laugh, he said, "That's exactly what Rachel kept saying! Heaven must want something here. She was the one who pushed me into this whole adventure."

Mrs. Rosenbaum leaned her head on the palm of one hand. Their eyes locked.

"And I," she said softly, "wanted you to find it."

Avraham was astonished. "But you became so angry at me when I found that envelope! You were furious when I asked questions about Abu Daoud al-Razak, who was in the newspaper clipping there."

"Yes. Yes, I was angry. Or, more accurately, I was stunned. I was stunned to see that the very envelope of whose existence I was unaware was the one you found."

"I don't understand. You ordered me never to talk to you about it."

"True, I did say that. Don't you see? A war was being waged inside me. On one side was your father's wish that Rivka's name never be mentioned again, after she betrayed us and the Jewish people and joined a band of Israel-haters. And, on the other, was a mother's natural desire to know what's become of her daughter!" Her voice softened. "Rivka was the one who rekindled my hope when we came to this country after the war, completely alone in the world. Don't you understand that? Don't you see what she was to me, how we both felt when she was born — and born in no less a place than *Eretz Yisrael*! The light returned to our hearts and to our eyes, Avraham. There was hope for the future again!"

She sank into a silence which Avraham was loath to disturb. At last, his mother stirred and began to speak again.

"Your father was not able to withstand the blow. He tried to erase her from his heart. Everything grew dark for him again — completely dark. In his heart, he had returned to Auschwitz; it was that simple. And I — followed him there. Did I have a choice? But my heart" — she thumped her chest with both hands — "my heart wanted something else."

She smiled again through another heavy sigh.

"That was why I told you not to speak to me about it again. But my heart —"

Avraham nodded to show that he understood. He withdrew into his own thoughts. As the minutes passed, his mother never took her eyes off his face. Patiently, she awaited his reaction.

"I'm happy, Imma," he said finally. "Happy that I was not wrong in my hunch that you really did want me to do what I did. Though, I'm sorry to say, I did not succeed in my goal of bringing her back home."

Mrs. Rosenbaum nodded sadly. "Read them," she said, pointing to the envelopes. "In the meantime, I'll make you something to drink."

"Why are you so interested in my reading these?" he asked curiously. "I don't really want to pry into Abba's secret."

His mother was smoothing the cloth that covered the table. "Read them. It's important. You'll find that, despite everything, your father did not manage to wipe Rivka from his heart. Read them, and see how far

The Envelope / 341

Abba was from hating her. He was a broken man to his last day on earth. Deep, deep down, he pined for his little girl. His mind refused to let him speak of her, but his heart spoke volumes, all the time. Oh, how it spoke."

※※※

Saib and Nashashivi stood up. *"Yes!"* they shouted back at their mother, to counter her still echoing, *"No!"*

"There's no choice, Mother," Nashashivi said. "We have made up our minds and you will not succeed in changing it. We want his address and phone number."

Nashashivi, who seemed overnight to have turned into the more radical of the brothers, added sarcastically, "He must have left you his address and phone number, didn't he? To stay in touch?"

A desperate weakness overcame Samira. All of her customary stamina, her natural authority, deserted her. She felt completely helpless.

"I don't have his address," she said, "nor his phone number. We parted angrily. Don't do what you're planning. Don't kill him. 'Blood is thicker than water.' He's my brother!"

They paid not the slightest heed to her pleas. "What is his address?" they pressed. "We need to know."

"I told you — I don't have it!"

"Mother, don't lie to us. This is critical. This is very, very serious. It's vital to our Palestinian revolution. Don't you understand!"

Samira did not answer. She felt like a trapped bird as her eyes darted wildly from one son to the other. Another minute of this, and she would explode.

Suddenly, she bent her knees and spread her hands in the classic attitude of supplication. "My dear sons!" she cried. "Have pity on me! I will not be able to continue living, if —" She could not finish.

They looked at her with frozen faces.

"Mother, stop that. Be strong. It's too late! We have decided, and that's that. If you won't give us the address, we'll find it by some other means."

They stormed out of the room, slamming the door behind them with a resounding bang.

Samira threw herself onto the couch, sobbing brokenheartedly. A picture flashed into her brain of a long-ago evening when she'd sobbed the same way. The night she decided to run away to Shechem with Abu Daoud al-Razak —

"G-d!" she screamed into the cushions. "Help me. Save my brother from my sons!"

All at once, she lifted her head.

"G-d?" she thought. This was the first time in her life that the word had escaped her in this fashion. Slowly, she settled back onto the couch, stunned.

Carefully, as though handling a holy object, Avraham drew the topmost envelope from the box. He studied it from every angle. As he did, a thought occurred to him: How long had it been since he had stumbled upon his father's hidden envelope, the one that had started him on this whole crazy adventure? A year? Two? No it had actually been slightly more than three months! Incredible.

So crowded had the days been, and so powerful the emotions packed into them, that it felt as though a much longer span of time had elapsed. And now, his mother had laid in his lap the full evidence of his father's strange secret. He opened the first envelope and pulled out a folded page.

It was a receipt from a store. On the back, his father had written something. Though the writing was clear, the lines rose and fell in uneven waves, betraying the writer's emotion. Avraham read the words silently, only his lips moving in intense concentration. But even through the intensity of his focus, he sensed his mother watching him, sensed the play of her own emotions as she watched.

> *Oy, my Rivka'le, jewel of my life! You were the shining light that obliterated the darkness that filled my heart, so badly scorched at Auschwitz. Why have you extinguished the light again? Rivka'le, come home to me.*

> *I will take you back with open arms, with compassion and blessings. All is forgiven from this moment, if only you return from the prison you chose of your own free will. Oy, my heart! Can it stand another day of this?*

Very slowly, Avraham refolded the paper and slipped it back into its envelope. With a weary gesture, he set it on the table and then pulled another from the box. In the total silence that filled the apartment, he could clearly hear the beating of his own heart.

There was no date on the paper he drew from the second envelope, so he could not know when it had been written. But many years had certainly passed since then:

> *Rivka'le, light of my life that was extinguished at its height. Talk to me, send some sign of life. Is there any hope that you will one day repent? I did. I did because of you! Has this suffering come upon me in order to lead me to repentance? In that case, please come home, return to us! I will accept you as you are. My heart goes out to you, my child.*

Avraham lifted his head, his eyes moist. They met his mother's, which were blinking away tears of their own. Who knew how many times she had read these poignant letters which her husband had written to his vanished daughter, far away over the hills?

"Yes, Imma," Avraham whispered. "It disturbed me very much to learn that you and Abba once lived in Ramat Gan as secular Jews."

His mother did not seem surprised that this information, information that she and her husband had kept from their son all these years, had also been uncovered. Avraham pressed, "Is it true? It's hard for me to picture Abba as a secular man."

Mrs. Rosenbaum smiled tiredly. "Yes. It's true. You can't picture it? But you saw the photograph of us in that envelope you first found. Abba was standing in it, younger and bareheaded. I was in the picture, too — and Rivka'le. Do you remember?"

Avraham remembered it well.

"So what happened? How did the two of you become observant? Was it really because of Rivka?"

"Yes."

"I'm curious."

"All right," she sighed. "It happened this way —"

The phone rang, cutting off her next words.

※ ※

In Petach Tikvah, Rachel had brought the children home the following day. Their mutual excitement and joy at the reunion were heart warming. She hugged her little daughters as she had never hugged them before. The tears flowed freely.

Now, as night fell and she left their room after tucking the girls tenderly into their beds, the phone rang. She hurried to answer.

"Mrs. Rosenbaum?" The words were spoken in clear English, though they bore an unmistakable Arabic accent.

"Yes. Who's calling?"

"Is your husband home?"

"No. Who is this, please?"

"We're Samira's sons. Samira, from Nablus, your husband's sister. You've met her, right? When will he be home?"

Her hand froze on the receiver. She felt paralyzed with fear. Her throat closed so that it was impossible to speak.

"Mrs. Rosenbaum? Are you there? Why aren't you answering? Mrs. Rosenbaum!"

Mrs. Rosenbaum picked up the phone. Her eyes lit up. "Oh, Nachum, is that you? How are you?"

Avraham could not hear his uncle's reply. A moment later, however, his mother handed him the phone. "He wants to talk to you, Avraham."

What was his uncle calling about? Avraham took the phone. "Good evening, Uncle Nachum."

"Good evening, Avraham. Tell me, where is that gem of a fellow who calls himself my grandson?"

Avraham resented his uncle's manner of speaking. Why must he abuse Mahmoud this way? What did he know of Mahmoud at all? He forced himself to reply calmly. "Why do you ask?"

"Because the G.S.S. called me about him. What does he want from me?"

Avraham's anger grew. "Ask them!" he snapped. "What do *you* want from *me*? Why are you so disdainful about him? What did he ever do to you?"

"Son of a wretched Arab," Uncle Nachum practically spat into the phone.

"Pardon me? He is the son of a full-fledged Jewess! According to Jewish law, he is a Jew!"

"Not in my book!" Uncle Nachum raged.

Irresistibly, Avraham blurted, "Is this hatred of yours really a camouflage for something else?"

This inflamed his uncle. His scream literally hurt Avraham's eardrums. "Don't start up with me! Do you hear? You insolent little — What do you mean when you imply that I'm hiding something? Hah? Tell me that!"

Avraham said nothing. His uncle's reaction only validated his belief in Mahmoud's story about his mother's life — and her death.

Uncle Nachum continued, "What does the G.S.S. want from me? To take him in? To adopt him? What are they thinking?"

"And why not?" Avraham asked, as mildly as he was able. He knew that anything he might say now would only serve as fuel to the inferno of his uncle's rage.

"*What?* What are you saying?" Uncle Nachum bellowed. "Are you out of your mind? What connection do I have with him?"

"A blood connection, Uncle. 'Blood is thicker than water.' You are in a position to save a life. He saved Rachel and me from being killed by terrorists. Mahmoud has had feelings like a Jew for some time now, not like an Arab."

His uncle cut him off. "What interest do I have in that?"

"If only my nephews, Rivka's sons, would follow Mahmoud's example. He wants to return to the fold — and you, his grandfather, would prevent that?"

"Return to the fold? Do *teshuvah*, the way your father did? You know that I'm not a religious man!"

"No, no. I don't mean that he's planning on becoming an observant Jew. He just wants to join up with the Jewish people. From Mahmoud's perspective, that's a form of repentance. He is a Jew, because his mother was Jewish. He does not have to undergo conversion."

A profound stillness traveled through the line. Avraham heard nothing, nor did he say anything to break the silence. A fierce inner battle, he presumed, was being waged in his uncle's heart.

Finally, the voice from Haifa floated to his ears: "I see," Uncle Nachum said curtly — and slammed down the phone.

Avraham glanced over at his mother, whose face was a mask of curiosity. With a grim smile, he related the gist of the conversation. He informed her of Mahmoud's existence, and of Uncle Nachum's refusal to acknowledge his grandson.

"In other words, Avraham," Mrs. Rosenbaum said, "you know the whole story?"

"Yes, Imma. I think I do. Is there something I don't know?"

She shrugged her shoulders.

For some minutes after hanging up the phone, Nachum paced his apartment in a frenzy. All the old anger came surging back: the anger he had not felt for many years, since the death of his wayward daughter in Shechem. All these years, he had struggled to forget her. Only thus might he protect himself from the deep anguish and suffering that had overwhelmed him when she ran away with an Arab. Added to that pain was the niggling question of whether his beating her had, indeed, been the cause of his daughter's death.

He thought the idea nonsensical. He knew that he had not delivered anything near death-blows, and that her Arab husband had merely used the opportunity to attack him and smear his name.

Then again, it was just possible —

For years, his heart had lain dormant. His daughter's memory was buried deep, so deep that its presence hardly rippled the even tenor of his days. It was for this reason that he had tried so valiantly to prevent Avraham from traveling to Shechem. He had been afraid of that trip, afraid of the flood of memories that could rise up and swamp him all over again.

"And now," he cried into the empty room, "now someone else, an Arab, has come along to intensify my pain — to make the pain live on for the rest of my life!"

He hurled himself onto the sofa. For a few moments, he sat there, shaken and spent. Then he began to cry.

The tears ceased as suddenly as they had begun. Nachum stood up, took up a stance in the center of the room, and shouted, "*No! Never!* He will not enter this house — not while I live. Even if he *is* my grandson!"

As though to underline the resolution, he made a fist and pounded with all his might on the coffee table. The thick glass that covered the table shuddered and cracked. His fingers ached — but not nearly as much as his heart, as the events he had tried so hard to forget came flooding back. The pain was as sharp now as it had been on that long-ago day when he had struck his daughter in the middle of a Shechem street.

Samira did not sit still for long. At the thought that her sons might actually carry out their threat, full-fledged panic rose up in her. She felt exactly like a wounded animal, trapped and unable to free itself. Her soul cried out for help, but she had no address for that heartfelt cry. She darted aimlessly around the room, mind awhirl with half-formed plans and strategies for restraining her sons before they could act.

Suddenly, she stopped short. A bolt of lightning flashed through her brain, hitting her like an electric current. In that instant, she understood — or rather, sensed — the terrible pain that she had caused her own parents. It was the pain she had just suffered at the hands of her own children. A small voice inside whispered forcefully, "You deserve it! You deserve it all!"

Tears filled her eyes once again.

She spun around and raced headlong for the door. Flinging it open, she dashed out of her office and across the small lobby. At the hotel entrance, she pulled open the outer door, darted into the street, and began running like a madwoman.

Rachel held the phone for a long moment, frozen in fear. She kept hearing the voices calling her at the other end of the line: the brutal accents of her sister-in-law's sons.

"Mrs. Rosenbaum, answer me! When will your husband be home? We're going to catch up with him, you can be sure of that. As you can see, we already have your phone number."

Rachel literally could not speak. At last, they hung up with a sharp, disgusted *click!* The sound of the dial tone buzzed in Rachel's ear. It sounded to her like a siren, screaming its warning: *Danger! Danger approaching!*

It was some time before she returned the receiver to its cradle, her hands shaking so hard that she could scarcely execute that simple maneuver. It was even longer before her mind began working again. The first person she thought of was Samira.

Inwardly, Rachel cursed her husband's sister, who, she was convinced, was behind this threat to their lives. Samira had sent her sons to make this call. It was a follow-up to the daunting letter she had sent Avraham, and the menacing bullet which had been enclosed.

Ribbono Shel Olam, where is all this going to end? she thought madly. *Is this our punishment for endangering ourselves by going to Shechem?*

Shakily, she rubbed her forehead in an effort to clear her mind. *What to do?* she wondered. Those two might really catch up with her husband in the end. Run to America, to her parents? What was best? And where was Avraham?

She remembered then: He had gone to visit his mother in Bnei Brak. She hurried to call him. Three times, she dialed the number incorrectly and had to start over. In her frustration, it took all of her self-discipline not to hurl the phone at the wall.

At last, she succeeded in making the connection. Her satisfaction, however, was short lived: The line was busy.

"Now?" she wailed. "Just this minute they have to be talking on the phone?"

She threw down the receiver and raced into her daughters' bedroom. They slept with the innocence of angels, tucked neatly under their blankets. Obsessively, Rachel covered them up anyway, smoothing the blankets again and again. On some instinctive level, the action made her feel that she was doing something to protect her children.

She ran back to the phone.

Avraham's life was in danger. She must warn him at once. She dialed her mother-in-law's number again; this time, the line was free. Impatiently, she waited for someone to pick up. But no one did.

———

With sudden resolve, Mrs. Rosenbaum picked up the phone.

"Who are you calling?" Avraham asked.

"Nachum."

Uneasily, Avraham shifted in his seat. "Do you expect to influence him? He's the world's most stubborn man!"

Chuckling, his mother said, "You're telling *me*? He's my brother!"

"Then why are you bothering to call?"

"I want to talk to him — to try to explain. To explain that now that the whole secret is out in the open, both his and our own, it's better for him to make peace with reality instead of fighting it."

Confused, Avraham asked, "What do you mean?"

"I mean that he should take his grandson into his heart, this grandson who has returned under such strange circumstances. He should reach out a little. Years and years have passed since the tragedy. I want to explain to Nachum that if he doesn't patch up the quarrel now, more and more people are going to learn what happened all those years ago — the very thing that he wants to conceal."

They stared at one another, both envisioning the patterns of past, present, and future in all their immense complexity. Into the silence, the phone began to ring in her hands. Neither Mrs. Rosenbaum nor Avraham made any move to answer it. It rang repeatedly for several minutes, then abruptly stopped.

"Well, what do you think?" she said. "If your father and I hadn't done *teshuvah* and left Ramat Gan for Bnei Brak — had we been secular or minimally observant Jews and remained where we were — everyone would know about our tragedy today. But we changed direction, and all was forgotten."

With a pained smile and a sigh, she added, "Until you found that envelope, that is."

The phone sprang back to life. It seemed to Avraham that its strident call sounded nervous. But he was more interested in this revealing talk with his mother. He tried to ignore the persistent ringing.

"You sound as though you wish I hadn't found out, Imma. Do you?"

She shrugged. "I don't know the answer to that, myself."

Softly, he said, "Help me understand why you and Abba decided to become so religious."

The ringing of the phone disturbed them. Mrs. Rosenbaum made as if to answer, but Avraham held up a hand.

"Imma, please — no. First tell me. This is a question that has been weighing on me from the moment I found out that my parents had once been irreligious. I simply cannot imagine Abba like that."

"But maybe it's an important call?" his mother fretted.

"Maybe. But it's more important for me to finish this — to close the subject, once and for all. Please, Imma."

She yielded. The nerve-racking ringing stopped.

"Why did we do *teshuvah*? I'll tell you, Avraham. I think we had always been bothered by the fact that we had moved away from the lifestyle of our parents in Poland. We remembered what Shabbos had been like there, and the Jewish way of life in general. What Rivka did taught us the tragedy inherent in leading a secular lifestyle — if, that is, one wishes to remain a Jew. And we did. The shock of her running away brought us home, to the Torah and the mitzvos."

The phone started ringing again. They tried to ignore it.

"And Bnei Brak?" Avraham asked. "Why did you move here?"

Closing her eyes, Mrs. Rosenbaum answered quietly, "We had to leave. The change in our lifestyle was drastic. But mostly, Avraham" — she opened her eyes and looked her son full in the face — "we were worried for your sake. What, we wondered, would happen to you if we continued to live in such an open and secular environment? Look at what had happened to Rivka. Her life in Ramat Gan was too free. She went everywhere — and look how it ended."

After a brief pause, she added, "We wanted you to grow up in a religious atmosphere. Or, more accurately, an ultra-Orthodox one." She smiled. "Have we succeeded with you? I think we have."

They both fell silent. Mrs. Rosenbaum asked, "And now, do I have your permission to answer the phone?"

He nodded. She picked up the receiver in mid-ring. The sound of screaming came clearly through the wire.

"Why didn't you answer? Why? Why? Our lives are in danger!" Rachel's voice was almost incoherent. "I've been trying to reach Avraham for over an hour now, and you haven't picked up! Why?"

Mrs. Rosenbaum turned pale. She had no idea what her hysterical daughter-in-law was talking about, but its import struck her as serious. Hastily, she handed the phone to Avraham, whispering, "It's for you. It's Rachel. I don't know what happened to her."

Avraham's heart stood still. "What happened?" he barked into the phone.

"Where are you? Why didn't you answer when I called and called? I've been going out of my mind! I can't take it anymore, Avraham! I'm going to America, to my mother!"

Avraham gripped the phone tightly. "Calm down, Rachel! Tell me what happened. I can't understand you like this."

"They called!"

"Who did?"

"Them. Samira's sons!"

"What did they want?"

"They were looking for you! They want to harm you, Avraham. Apparently, on their mother's orders — your dear sister!"

Avraham was silent for a moment, absorbing this. Then he asked, "When did they call?"

"Two hours ago."

"Why didn't you call me right away?"

Rachel turned hysterical again. "*I* didn't call? It was *you* who didn't answer!"

He lowered his voice in an effort to calm her. "Okay, okay. It's all right. What do we do now?"

"That's what I'm asking you. You decide. I'm frightened!"

Avraham made up his mind. "First of all, call your sister and brother-in-law and ask them to come get you and the girls immediately. Sleep at their house tonight. I'll stay with my mother. I hope the night will pass peacefully. Tomorrow morning, I'll contact Binyamin at the G.S.S. Please, take care of this quickly. Call me when you arrive at your sister's house. Good night!"

"What happened?" his mother asked, gazing at him with profound anxiety.

Avraham told her about the danger which had been brought about at the hands of Rivka and her terrorist sons.

"My daughter? My grandchildren? They want to kill you?" With a hand to her heart, she moaned pitifully, "I can't bear any more!"

48

Samira ran like a woman possessed. She ran aimlessly at first, caught in the grip of anguish and despair. The awful thing her sons intended to do had sapped the last of her emotional reserves. Vaguely, in the back of her mind, she wanted to stop them. She sobbed as she ran, crying in the middle of the street. At this hour of the evening, few pedestrians were out and about; but these glanced oddly at her as she passed. Those who recognized her were stunned at the strange sight, but none had the courage to ask the simple question, "Samira, what happened?" And those who did not know who she was merely categorized her as just another crazy person wandering their city's streets.

Gradually, her aimless running became purposeful. In the distance, the rumble of a heavy vehicle reached her ears. It was an IDF half-track, rolling slowly along Shechem's streets. What a change, she thought bitterly. Just a few days ago, she would have regarded that half-track as the enemy. It represented the Israeli occupation that was oppressing the Palestinians with whom she, Samira, had cast her lot. And now, here she was, standing in the middle of the street in the dark of night, waving for the Israeli army vehicle to stop.

It did not stop. The helmeted soldier-driver regarded her impassively, making no sign that he even saw her frantic signals.

"Stop!" she cried finally, in perfect, Israeli-accented Hebrew. The soldier, recognizing the word as being in her native tongue, glanced at her — and then immediately faced forward again. He had no way of ascertaining what lay behind her strange call and even stranger, distraught manner.

Samira was taken aback. The half-track continued inexorably on its way, ignoring her. After a moment, she began to run after it, screaming, "Wait! Stop! This is important! This could save a life!"

Several passersby, recognizing her, stopped in stupefaction. "Samira!" they called. "Samira, what's the matter? What happened?"

She did not answer them. In fact, she never even heard them. The steadily rolling half-track was frustrating her to the point of madness. She willed it to stop. She wanted those soldiers to prevent what was about to take place. She would even be willing to see her sons arrested, if only to spare her brother's life. But — the half-track did not stop.

Two men ran toward her. "Samira, what's wrong with you? Did the Jews harm you? What happened?"

She did not answer.

"Come, let us take you home," one of them offered solicitously.

"No!" she shrieked, until it seemed that the very leaves on the trees overhead quivered. "Take me to the governor!"

"The governor? You mean, the Israeli military governor?"

"Yes — and quickly!"

The two men exchanged bewildered glances. What had come over Samira? They moved closer, cautiously, the way they would have approached a raving animal. Grasping her forearms, they said, "Come on, we'll take you home. You look like you're under a lot of stress. You need some rest. What's been happening?"

With all her might, Samira struggled to free herself from her self-appointed jailers. But the men were many times stronger than she.

"Leave me alone!" she cried, thrashing wildly. "I don't want your help. Let me go where I want!"

Her screams rent the quiet night. Here and there, a window was flung open; a head peeked out, and then quickly withdrew once more. Why get involved?

The men did not release her. "Samira, it's all right. We're your friends. We're taking you back to the hotel."

Slowly, slowly, her resistance grew weaker. Helpless, she allowed herself to be led homeward.

❦

"Calm down, Imma. Nothing is going to happen," Avraham said soothingly.

"What do you mean?" she cried. "Everything's already happened!"

"I don't understand."

"What is there not to understand? My daughter and her sons — my own grandsons — want to kill you. Is that 'nothing' in your eyes?"

"But, Imma, they won't succeed! You'll see."

Sobbing bitterly, she said, "That's not what I'm crying about. I'm crying about the fact that she wants to kill you, her own brother." Through a throat clogged with tears, she added, "To have lost her way so badly —"

Avraham was at a loss. His mother was right. How could he possibly comfort her?

"Do you want a drink?" he asked lamely.

"No!"

Avraham experienced the sudden onset of an entirely new feeling which had unexpectedly taken root. It was a feeling of rejection, almost of hatred, toward his sister. Sitting beside his mother, skimming through his father's envelopes with their poignant messages, he had felt close to Rivka. He had dreamed of getting through to her somehow, of presenting her with the envelopes so that she might have a glimpse, at last, of what had truly been in her father's heart, so that she might finally understand how badly she had gone astray. Perhaps these heartfelt notes might soften her own heart, which had hardened like concrete over the years in the belief that she was hated and rejected.

He had entertained an even rosier dream, in which they sat together reading the contents of those envelopes. Reading them and weeping together, because their father had not lived to see his family reunited. He had not seen his wayward daughter return, understanding at last that his behavior toward her had stemmed not from cruelty, but from the necessity of the moment. In his heart, Elimelech Rosenbaum had remembered his daughter, had loved her, and had longed for the day when she would come back to him.

Mrs. Rosenbaum spoke again. "When you came here tonight, Avraham, I had a spark of hope. Maybe, I thought, just maybe, a miracle would happen, the miracle I've waited so many years to see. But I was mistaken. And do you know what that means for me?"

"What?" he whispered.

"It means suffering terribly again, the way I suffered back at the beginning, when she left home. All these years, we tried our best to push the painful topic away. Now, it's all come back. And like a tidal wave, it's crashing in my face and throwing me back — way back —"

Avraham looked at the box on the table. He thought of the envelopes that lay within. In his fury, he wanted to pick up the box and hurl it to the ground for the satisfaction of seeing it shatter into a thousand pieces. In his mind's eye, he entertained another, equally satisfying picture: He saw himself burning these envelopes, one by one. Enough! Burn the last bridge to Rivka. Let her remain an outcast forever, there beyond the dark foothills where she had willingly cast her lot.

His hand shot forward. At the last second, he stopped short of his goal. Perhaps it was the renewed ringing of the telephone that stopped him.

He was afraid, at first, to answer it. His mother glanced at him anxiously. Could it be that those — people have discovered her own phone number — their Jewish grandmother — and were calling even now with the news that they were on their way to get Avraham?

Avraham looked at his watch. It was 12:30 a.m. Midnight had come and gone without his realizing it.

The phone continued ringing. With a heavy sigh Avraham picked up the receiver and cleared his throat.

"Hello, Avraham?" It was Rachel.

His heart stood still. "Is everything all right?"

"Yes — Well, almost."

"What's that supposed to mean?"

"*Baruch Hashem*, Yitzchak came with the car, and the girls and I are at his and Rina's place now. That part is okay."

"So what's the problem?"

There was a moment of silence. "I don't know," Rachel said finally. "Maybe it's just my imagination. But there was a car parked downstairs, not far from the house. Its headlights were off, but I saw two men sitting inside. Maybe, like I said, I imagined trouble. For all I know, they might have been two innocent men sitting and chatting, without any connection to me. But — what can I say, Avraham? Fear is a hard thing to deal with."

Avraham did not answer immediately. His wife waited, then said, "Avraham?"

"What?"

"What did we need all of this for?"

He knew full well what "all of this" referred to. Rachel pressed, "Don't you regret the trip to Shechem now?"

"Good night," Avraham said tersely. "Tend to the girls and go to bed."

Slowly, he lowered the receiver. His mother asked no questions. From the snippets of conversation she had overheard, she drew her own conclusions.

<hr />

The next morning, Avraham relayed the new turn of events to Binyamin.

"When did they call?" the G.S.S. man wanted to know.

"Last night."

"What did they say, exactly?"

"They spoke with my wife. They said that they're looking for me, and that they plan to get me."

Silence. Then: "And you think your sister, Samira, is involved?"

"I can't imagine that she isn't. You remember the threatening letter and the bullet she sent me, while Mahmoud was in my house. By the way, how is he?"

"Mahmoud's all right. Right now, he's trying to choose a Hebrew name. He's planning to call you in the near future. But let's get back to this other matter. Your wife thought that they were Samira's sons?"

"They told her so explicitly. What do I do now? I sent my wife and the girls to sleep at her sister's house last night."

"Good move."

"But what now?"

"Now you leave the matter in our hands. We'll keep you posted."

⁂

Saib and Nashashivi sat in the living room of the small apartment they had rented on the outskirts of Shechem for the duration of Nashashivi's stay. They sat in silence, chain-smoking cigarette after cigarette. The ashtray and the floor around them were littered with the debris of the past hour.

"Are you sure we'll succeed?" Saib asked.

"No."

Saib leaned forward to light another cigarette from his brother's. "Why not?"

"We made a mistake yesterday."

"What was that?"

"The phone call."

"Which?"

"To our dear aunt, Rachel."

They exchanged a wicked glance and broke into brief but raucous laughter before assuming their former severe expressions. Saib asked, "What are you afraid of?"

"She will have talked. She must have warned her husband. She may have tipped off the G.S.S. Who knows?"

"So?"

"So — you know them. They know who we are."

"But how does the plan itself look to you?"

"It looks good," Nashashivi admitted.

More silence, amid clouds of cigarette smoke. The tobacco smell clung to the bare walls.

"Nashashivi?"

"What?"

"Maybe we're wrong?"

"About what?"

"Maybe, if we kill him, Mother will move even further from us."

"Maybe."

"Then maybe we should rethink the whole idea?"

"No!"

"Why not?"

With a vigorous flick of his wrist, Nashashivi threw the remains of his last cigarette into a corner of the room. With his other hand, he grabbed his younger brother's chin and snarled, "No. You know why? Because I don't even care anymore about our Jewish mother. Did you see the way she begged us not to do what we planned? And you know something else? I'm also angry at her brother for taking our mother away from us. Even if it will hurt Mother, I don't care."

Nashashivi sat back. Though Saib sensed that they were going too far, he did not dare oppose the big brother he had summoned back in such haste from Kuwait. Nashashivi had always been the dominant one, and this balance of power had remained intact despite their two years apart.

"Saib?"

"Yes?"

"I do think, though, that it would be a good idea for us to go into hiding for a few days. To get out of this room, and waste no time about it."

"Where to?"

"Anywhere. Twelve hours have passed since last night. That's more than enough time for those accursed Israelis. I have a feeling they're looking for us."

"So what do we do?"

"I told you — we look for another place. You're the one who knows the city these days, not I."

Silence, cigarette smoke, dry coughing.

"All right," Saib said presently. "I've thought of a place. In Kasava."

"Let's go now!"

"We need to clean up this room."

"No. Now! This minute!"

As usual, Saib yielded to his brother. He stood and followed Nashashivi to the door. They opened it — and recoiled. Three masked men pushed them back into the room, overpowering them quickly; the brothers, in their total shock, barely offered resistance. They felt the cold clasp of handcuffs around their wrists. Then they were led outside to a car that waited with its engine running. The moment the five men were inside, the driver hit the accelerator and sped out of Shechem.

Samira woke up. For a moment, she had no idea where she was. She lifted her head in confusion — and saw that she was lying on a couch in a corner of her own hotel lobby.

How, she wondered, had she gotten here? She had not the slightest memory of entering the hotel or of lying down on this couch. Daylight had already come to the streets of Shechem. Sunlight crept into every available crack in the heavy drapes that partially covered the lobby windows. What time was it?

She sat up, rubbing her eyes slowly as she opened her mouth in a wide yawn. Then, curiously, she surveyed the lobby. This was the first time she had ever passed the night here. It was becoming increasingly clear to her that she had been asleep on this couch for many hours.

All at once, she remembered.

Her head began to pound. All the previous night's fears returned with a vengeance. She stood up hastily, casting looks in all directions to see whether anyone was there to see her in her ignominy. The lobby was quiet and deserted at this early-morning hour.

Or *was* it morning? Somehow, she sensed that the morning had already passed, and that this was actually afternoon.

Very slowly, she walked to her own room. She passed the reception desk, hoping that the clerk sitting there would not notice her. This being impossible, she smiled wanly at the young woman, who returned a smile just as uncomfortable. Had she seen Samira asleep on the couch?

Samira turned away and entered her room. In a flood, the memories flowed back: her sons and their frightening threats against her brother; her own race after the Israeli half-track, her screams, her loss of control. But how had she ended up back in the hotel?

Try as she might, she could not remember.

She flung herself onto the bed, helpless and resigned to her bitter fate. There was nothing to be done. A horrible guilt invaded her at the thought that she had been unable to prevent her sons from carrying out their plans. Had they done the job already? Avraham, her baby brother —

She wanted to cry, but the tears refused to come. Deepest despair numbed her with a black totality. And yet, through the darkness, through the despair, she heard an inner voice crying out, *G-d! Help me!* The cry rose from some hidden place inside, a place of whose existence she had not been aware.

The phone rang.

Listlessly, she got out of bed. It was not so much that she was interested in hearing what anyone had to tell her at the other end of the line; she just wanted to end the annoying ringing.

"Samira?" a voice asked excitedly.

"Yes." Her reply was nearly inaudible.

"Samira," the voice said, speaking with such agitation that she could not recognize the speaker. "Samira, they took them!"

"Who?"

"The Jews!"

She became more alert. In moments like these, as she steeled herself for bad news, she was usually very capable of masking her emotions. For a moment, she regained that old self-control. "Whom did they take?"

"Your sons. Saib and Nashashivi!"

The words hit her like a fist, knocking the breath out of her. Wild scenes ran through her mind in frenzied procession. *Her sons, caught in the act, after murdering* — She did not dare ask where they had been arrested. *In Petach Tikvah? Before — or after?* A deathly fear prevented her from demanding from the anonymous caller the facts she so desperately wanted.

At last, the caller supplied the information himself. "Samira, I saw them, the Jews, pushing your sons into a small car. Right out of their room they were taken. I saw them!"

Carefully, she asked, "From where? From here, in the city? From their room here?"

"Yes, yes, from here! From the room! I saw them! They had handcuffs on their wrists. They were pushed into the car, which sped away and disappeared. Do something, Samira!"

She answered with a calmness that surprised her: "All right. May Allah have mercy." She hung up.

She had not asked the caller to identify himself. The voice was familiar, but at the moment she was unable to match it with the face of any one of her many acquaintances in town.

It was 5 o'clock in the afternoon. Avraham was getting ready to leave the office for his mother's house. Rachel was still at her sister's, where she had been holed up in the house with her daughters all day long.

"Avraham," the receptionist called as he passed her on his way out. "Phone for you." She held out the receiver.

"Avraham?" a quiet voice asked in his ear.

"Yes."

"Binyamin asked me to pass on the news that everything is okay now."

"What do you mean, 'okay'?"

"We arrested those two. They're in our hands right now, being interrogated."

The Envelope / 367

Though he knew exactly whom the caller was referring to, Avraham could not resist blurting, "Which two?"

There was no answer for a moment. The caller must have been wondering whether he had reached the right party. "I understood from Binyamin that you would know what I'm talking about. Your two Arab relatives — the ones who've been threatening your life!"

"Ah! Of course," Avraham said quickly. "In your opinion, is it safe for me to return home?"

"I think so. Still, be careful."

"Thanks!" After a beat, Avraham added, "Please send my regards to Binyamin. Tell him I'm very grateful."

"I'll tell him. But Binyamin did say he plans to call you today. This is a great opportunity."

Avraham did not understand. "Opportunity? For what?"

"He didn't tell me. But he'll be calling."

"All right. Goodbye."

"Goodbye!"

❊

Samira sat huddled and preoccupied in her chair, behind the desk in her office. She was trying to organize her confused thoughts, trying to figure out where she might turn for accurate information about her sons' arrest.

At precisely 1 o'clock in the afternoon, she turned on the radio and fiddled with the knobs until she found the Israeli *Kol Yisrael* station. She listened carefully, but there was no mention of a Jew murdered in Petach Tikvah.

She sat down by the phone. Whom to call for information? Name after name came to mind, but none of them seemed likely to supply what she needed. Finally, she phoned Abu Bachar, who had connections with the Israeli military governor. Maybe he would know something.

"No, Samira," he whispered into the receiver. "I don't know anything. Do you want me to find out?"

"No, no," she said quickly. "Don't bother. I'll call you again later, just in case."

With both hands resting on the phone, she laid her head on them. For just an instant, she toyed with the notion of calling the Israelis directly. They knew her — though not always in a complimentary fashion. In the context of her opposition activities, she had forged various odd connections with the Israeli authorities. More than once, senior IDF officers had been guests under her hotel's roof, often conducting long political discussions with her. Not all of them knew her background; they saw her merely as a shrewd Arab woman who spoke logically and with conviction. Maybe, she thought now, I should turn directly to them to find out what happened to my sons.

And, she thought, to my brother.

At length, she gathered the courage to dial the number of Major N., Shechem's assistant military governor and a longtime acquaintance.

"Samira? Good afternoon," he said to his unexpected caller.

"I need your help!"

N. was surprised. "My help? Help in advancing your intifada, maybe?"

"That would make me very happy," Samira answered. "But let's talk seriously, now. They've arrested my sons!"

"Hmmm —"

"The way I heard from an eyewitness, it happened a few hours ago."

The man at the other end of the line did not reply. Samira waited, then continued, "One of my sons doesn't even live here. He lives in Kuwait. He came here for a visit — and was arrested."

"What do you want from me? Shall I set them free, in return for all your wonderful service to the State of Israel?"

"No, no," she said impatiently. "All I want is information. Why? What have they done? What false accusation has been leveled at them?"

"You make many demands, Samira. I'll try to find out. Okay!"

"Just a minute. There's something else."

"Yes?"

The Envelope / 369

"Did anything happen in Israel during the night?"

"What do you mean?"

"I don't know — Were there any clashes between Palestinian freedom fighters and Israeli soldiers?"

"Still at it, I see. Yes, if it makes you happy. There was some stone-throwing in Ramallah, and a few other minor incidents here and there. We took care of all of them."

"I heard about those on *Kol Yisrael*."

N. laughed. "Are you a regular listener?"

"I listened today, anyway," she said. "Were there any other incidents in Israel? Was anyone killed, or injured?"

For a long moment, N. was silent. Samira grew nervous.

"That's a strange question, Samira," N. said finally.

"I know that, too."

"Do you have something to hide?"

"If I had anything to hide, I wouldn't ask you a question like that."

He laughed. "You're right. But the question is still strange."

"You don't have to answer."

"I don't have to do anything."

"Just find out exactly why my sons were arrested. I tell you, they are innocent."

"As you know, the G.S.S. generally operates on the basis of solid intelligence."

"That's true. And that's *our* tragedy. Please, find out for me."

"I'll try, Samira."

"Thank you very much, Major N."

The major got back to Samira two hours later.

"Yes, the news is true. Your sons were arrested by the G.S.S."

"Thank you. My question is: Why? What did they do? The older one is a chemical engineer, the younger a student."

"I'm not sure. But I believe they're accused of murdering a Jew."

Samira began to shake. Her head swam until she was afraid of losing consciousness.

"Which Jew?" she asked, her hand gripping the receiver so tightly that her hand ached.

Major N. sensed her agitation, and became suspicious. "Calm down, Samira. As far as I know, they're talking about the murder of an Israeli soldier near Elon Moreh, two years ago."

At first, Samira was overwhelmed with relief. So her sons had not murdered her brother, after all. What a miracle!

A second later, she was reeling from another thought. If the present case went against her sons, they might spend years in jail. They were all she had left in the world.

She made sure to keep these thoughts from N.

"Thank you very much for this unfortunate information," she said. "But I also asked if something happened in Israel."

"Samira, if you ask me that again, I'll make sure they drag you in for an interrogation! What's this supposed to mean? You're suddenly interested in the fate of Jews in Israel?"

Samira was quiet for a time. Then she said, "The day may come when you will understand."

"I'm curious!"

"I can imagine," she said quietly, and hung up.

❦

On his way home, Avraham dropped by to see his mother in Bnei Brak.

"Look, Imma. I hope this is all behind me now. The police have arrested Samira's sons, I don't know on what pretext. But I'm pretty sure that the case is closed."

She looked at him with eyes that were wise and pain filled.

"For me," she said, "it is just beginning."

"What do you mean? Are you afraid that something will happen to you?"

"To me? To *me*?" She raised her voice. "I explained to you last night that something is happening to me all the time!"

Then, into the uneasy silence that followed her outburst, she added, "My grandsons are sitting in jail as terrorists, and he asks if something is happening to me!"

Avraham realized that he had not expressed himself well, but he had no words just then with which to comfort his mother. He stood up, wished her a good night, and hurried home to Petach Tikvah. He knew that his wife and children had already returned to the apartment. He was looking forward to resuming a normal life with them again.

But that night, Binyamin of the G.S.S. called.

Avraham answered the phone hesitantly. He recognized Binyamin's voice.

"Good evening, Binyamin. I got the good news. Thank you very much."

"Yes. It wasn't a very complicated operation."

"I hope you didn't link me to the arrest," Avraham said anxiously. "After all, they are family, those two Arabs."

"No, no. We spun a tale about an old case, a two-year-old murder of an Israeli soldier near Elon Moreh. We actually know who committed that murder, but he's in hiding. Maybe if word spreads in and around Shechem that we've arrested Samira's sons for the crime, the real perpetrator will become less cautious and we'll be able to grab him."

He paused. "Meanwhile, you got what you wanted."

"Thanks again!" Avaraham said warmly.

"Still, be careful. It's impossible to know whether or not your wonderful sister will send others to do the job in their place."

"I'll take care."

Another pause. Then, "Avraham?"

"Yes?"

"I didn't only call about that."

Avraham was confused. "What else, then? Mahmoud?"

"No, we're taking care of him. He's all right."

"Then what is it?"

"Your two precious nephews won't answer a word in the interrogation room. They insist on meeting with you first."

"With *me*?" Avraham said in a panic. "What do they want with me?"

"I don't know."

"But — but you said you didn't link their arrest to their threats to me."

"That's right. We didn't mention your name at all."

"Then —"

Binyamin cut him off. "I don't have the answer. They're being very stubborn. The only way to advance this investigation is to let you meet with them."

Avraham did not care for the idea one bit. After Shechem and all its attendant dangers, he dreamed only of returning to normal life and his former, safe routines. But apparently the saga was not yet over. What did those two scoundrels want from him? Did they think he had turned them in? Were they going to get their friends to avenge them? Suddenly, Avraham was very frightened.

"When should I pick you up?" Binyamin asked.

"And — if I refuse to see them?"

"You have no choice, Avraham. We've done so much for you already. I think you owe us this one."

"But why is this so important? You'll manage to get whatever information you want from them, without my help!"

"Don't try to teach us our work, Avraham. We have our methods. And one of those methods says that we bring you in to see them."

Avraham felt powerless to stop the chain of unfolding events. A representative of the Israeli establishment was demanding something that was clearly beyond his emotional capacity. He did not have the resources with which to meet his two nephews from over the hills. Somehow, he sensed, the encounter would prove detrimental to him. What would his nephews tell their friends back in Shechem? What were they plotting against him? Why wasn't the G.S.S. being more careful?

"When?" Binyamin pressed.

"Let me think."

"When?" Binyamin demanded again, almost immediately.

"Why do you care? Give me a couple of days to think it over."

"Fine. I'll call for you at 8 o'clock tomorrow morning. Good night, Avraham."

"But —"

The line had gone dead.

Samira nervously cracked the knuckles of both hands. What to do? What to do? Her sons were in prison, accused of a murder they had not committed — the killing of an Israeli soldier two years before! She knew they were innocent of that crime. But how could such an error have come about?

Suddenly, she stood up. *Maybe*, she thought, *this is just another dirty G.S.S. trick*. Could her sons have actually tried to act against Avraham, and been caught? And if that were the case, why wasn't anyone telling her the truth?

She had to know what was happening. Energy flowed back. Though she was genuinely glad that her sons' arrest prevented them from carrying out their threats against her brother, she was still prepared to protest with all her capabilities against their imprisonment on false pretenses. They did not deserve a lengthy prison sentence for a crime they did not commit.

Samira left the room with a confident step, radiating her old quiet confidence. In fact, she exaggerated the confidence, in an attempt to erase the memory of the pitiful state in which she had found herself the day before. Let them all know: Samira was back!

Leaning her elbows on the reception desk, she met the young receptionist's eyes squarely. Tentatively, Soah asked, "How are you, Samira?"

"Fine, fine," Samira replied. Briskly, she added, "Send for Abdul Rachman. Tell him I want him here for a conference. Also Mahmoud Aziz. Okay?"

"Yes, sure."

Samira turned back toward her room — then stopped and called back, "Soah?"

"Yes?"

"I also want Ibrahim Turak. All right?"

"Will do, Samira."

An hour later, the phone on Samira's desk rang. She had been trying, unsuccessfully, to nap. She snatched up the receiver. "Yes."

"Samira?"

"Yes." It was Soah.

"Samira, I let them all know." Soah sounded distressed. "All three refused to come."

Samira was stunned. The three men were active in the local Fatah organization and, like her, struggled against the Israeli occupation. Their relations had always been cordial and cooperative. They had always displayed total loyalty toward her. What had happened to change that?

"Samira, what do we do now?"

"Nothing. Just smile and be nice to our guests." Samira disconnected.

Her eyes, unfocused at first, found themselves staring at the picture hanging on the wall, that of her late husband. She stared at it, as though willing Abu Daoud al-Razak to explain to her why her old friends had abandoned her just when she needed them most. She wanted advice about how to deal with her sons' arrest. Instead, she had met with point-blank refusals.

"Why are they distancing themselves from me now?" she wondered aloud. "Is it all because of Avraham's visit here? How could they know about that already?"

She tore her eyes from the picture on the wall. For the umpteenth time in the last few days, she flung herself onto the couch with both arms covering her face.

She lay there for no more than a few seconds before a thought struck her. Was it because of the two men who had dissuaded her from running after the Israeli half-track? Had they managed to spread the word so soon?

As though trying to dispel the shreds of a nightmare, she rocked to and fro. Then she buried her face deep in her pillow.

In the silence, she felt a sudden terror — and an unendurable loneliness. She found herself suddenly and inexplicably isolated — completely alone in the world. Her sons, who had served as her mainstay after her husband's death, were in jail. Who knew what fate awaited them? Her friends and supporters in the city had abandoned her unexpectedly, refusing even to meet with her. Alarm bells shrieked inside her head. What would happen to her tomorrow?

She tried to doze, but sleep eluded her. Hours passed as she lay tormented, a prey to wild and disordered thoughts. Night fell. Darkness spread to fill every corner of the room, until it became impossible to distinguish the outlines of the furniture. But the darkness failed to bring the relief she sought. Every plan she tried to devise to help Saib and Nashashivi was brought up short and stamped "unrealistic."

Finally, she got up and turned on a light. The clock on the wall told her that the hour was late: It was 3 a.m. Without hesitation, ignoring the time, Samira picked up the receiver and dialed. She heard ringing at the other end. Both hands gripped the receiver tightly, to combat the sudden surge of emotion that threatened to overwhelm her.

The phone rang and rang, but no one answered.

She hung up and tried again. This time, the phone rang only a few times before Avraham picked up. He, too, had not been able to sleep.

"Yes?" he whispered.

"Avraham?"

"Yes?" he said again.

"This is Samira!"

Mrs. Rosenbaum tossed and turned in bed, but sleep continued to elude her. The wellspring of her tears had long since dried up. The knowledge that her own grandsons, children of her wayward daughter, Rivka, wished to kill Avraham — their uncle — had drained her last reserves of stoicism. All through the long, dark hours she lay awake, letting her imagination roam freely over past events. Even Auschwitz, much against her will, sprang up in horrible memory.

And wasn't what she was living through now another Auschwitz? Arab grandchildren! Murderers! A daughter who supported the Palestinian cause! Was this not a smaller version of that earlier hell?

All at once, she remembered her dear, departed husband. What was left of her heart contracted with an almost unendurable pain. Her only consolation was that he had passed away before all these revelations had occurred. Enough that he had punished himself all his life for what had happened to his beloved Rivka'le, the renewed light in his life after the horrors of the Holocaust. Better that he died when he did —

But what will become of me? she wondered in the darkness. *How can I bear all this? Why have I been punished so? Why? Why? Why?*

She threw back the covers and got out of bed, making for the kitchen to fix herself a cup of tea. She sipped the hot brew slowly, to draw out the time before there would be nothing left to do but return to bed.

It was 3 a.m. by the kitchen clock when she shut the lights once more and walked cautiously through the dark to her bedroom. Her eyes were wide open for a long time — a measureless time. Gradually, as she lay awake, several things became clearer to her.

Just the other night, Avraham had explained his reason for going to Shechem. If Heaven had decreed that he stumble upon his parents' secret, he had decided, then Heaven wanted something from him.

In that case, his mother thought now, maybe it wanted something from her, as well. Maybe Heaven had indicated as much by giving her the terrible news about her grandsons.

Slowly, a resolution formed in her heart. Minute by minute, it grew clearer and stronger.

First thing in the morning, at 7 o'clock, she would call Avraham and tell him of her decision. She would ask him — No, she would demand! She would insist!

At long last, her eyes closed. It was nearly dawn.

Despite her exhaustion, and despite the short sleep, she woke punctually at 7 o'clock. Avraham would still be home at this hour. With clear eye and confident hand, she picked up the phone and dialed his number.

Avraham stood still as a statue, holding the phone pressed tightly to his ear. His shock was total. Words rose up in his throat and stuck there. He simply could not speak.

"Do you hear me? It's Samira!"

Her voice was cold and hard. Feeling the old terror wash over him, Avraham managed, "Yes. I hear."

A violent trembling seized him. He had hoped — how he had hoped! — that his nephews' arrest would bring a return of peace and security to his life. In time, he had planned to contact his sister again; and hoped that time, too, would calm her sons and make them drop their murderous plans toward him. Now, here she was at the other end of the line, rejection in her every syllable, just the way she had been when they met for the first time. Why had she called? What new information did she have to impart? That revenge was on its way, at the hands of the band of assassins with whom she consorted?

"Avraham, I apologize for the late hour. But I must speak with you, urgently."

He felt slightly relieved. Her voice had become more human somehow. His instinct signaled something else: There had been a pleading note there as well. Gathering his wits, he tried to speak with quiet calm. "Now? At 3 in the morning?"

"If you can, it would please me greatly."

He switched to the telephone in the living room. Avraham was growing more confident. "Why? To make more threats against my life?"

"What are you hinting at?" she asked angrily.

"It's no hint. I'm speaking plainly. You've been stalking me, and I don't know why. You sent a gorilla here with a letter and a bullet. That bullet did not have to enter my heart in order to wound me. Believe me, it hurt."

"But —"

"Just a minute." Avraham raised his voice. "Hear me out, please, before you answer."

"But I want to explain —"

"Explain all you want, afterwards. That letter with the bullet wasn't enough for you? It wasn't frightening enough for me, so you had to send along your two sons to threaten me. What have I done to you? Tell me!"

He was still trembling, from anger this time. Now that she had called him, he intended to have it out with her. He would pour out everything that had accumulated inside over the past two days since he returned from Shechem — reeling from the frostly reception he had been accorded by the sister he had gone to such lengths to seek out.

"You ask what you've done to me? I'll tell you what," Samira said furiously. "I sent you off from Shechem in peace. I sent along two of my most trusted men to escort you. Where are they now? We found the body of one of them. Where is the other corpse? Why did you kill them — you and your G.S.S. friends? Tell me that!"

Avraham was too stunned to speak. From the bedroom, Rachel called sleepily, but with a definite note of alarm, "What's going on? Who are you shouting at in the middle of the night?" Her head appeared at the bedroom door.

He raised a finger to his lips in the classic request for silence. All at once, he understood what had happened. When Nawil and Mahmoud had failed to return to Shechem, Samira had instituted a search and discovered Nawil's body. Apparently, she believed that he, Avraham, had been responsible for Nawil's death. What a horrible mistake! She knew nothing of Mahmoud's fate; logically, she had jumped to the conclusion that he, too, had been murdered at Israeli hands.

"So," he said sarcastically, "that's why you decided to have me killed?"

Her answer came quickly. "You'll be surprised to learn that I did not. Blood is thicker than water."

"What about the Kalishnikov bullet and the threatening letter? What were those about?"

"To frighten you! To show you how ungrateful and despicable you are. To murder those who were sent to help you —"

"And your sons?"

Samira took a deep breath. "What did they do?"

"What did they do? They phoned my house. They wanted to settle the account with me."

"And what did you tell them?"

"Luckily, I wasn't home when they called. My wife spoke to them. She was terrified."

"I can understand that. And if I tell you that I did not send my sons to you, would you believe me?"

Avraham smiled. "And if I tell you that I did not kill Nawil, will you believe me?"

"If you didn't," Samira demanded, "then it was them. The G.S.S."

"And if I tell you that it wasn't them, either, would you believe me? I'll add something else. If I tell you that Mahmoud is alive, would you believe me?"

Samira was surprised, but it was crucial that she mask that surprise and maintain her equilibrium. Coolly, she said, "Suppose you explain yourself."

"I'd prefer if you'd explain first what you meant when you said you didn't send your sons to threaten me. That will help me explain exactly what happened."

"I don't see the connection. But — all right! I tell you truthfully and honestly that I did not send them. I did everything I could to try and stop them. I knew of their plans, but they refused to listen to me. You can believe me or not, as you like, but I was broken hearted at the awful prospect that they would kill my — my brother, who had been born to me again!"

The last words were like a flame of warmth directly to Avraham's heart. Seeing the broad smile on his face, Rachel whispered, "Tell me what's going on. Please!" He hardly heard her.

"Samira," he said, a bit shakily, "now I understand the terrible mistake that nearly led to tragedy. I understand why you thought I killed them."

"What really happened?"

"I'll tell you." His voice grew stronger. "It wasn't me who killed Nawil. He wanted to kill Rachel and me, but Mahmoud managed to get to him first. Mahmoud saved our lives. That's the whole story."

Samira did not know what to think. The story sounded strange, even dubious, but she tended to believe it. After she had bared her heart to her brother, she sensed that he felt the same toward her. But it was an unlikely story all the same, and hard to digest.

"Then where is Mahmoud?" she whispered. "Why hasn't he returned? Is he afraid of me?"

"Yes, he is. But that's not the only reason."

"What do you mean?"

"I hope you're sitting down, Samira." Avraham fought to suppress a note of pride as he continued. "Mahmoud has decided to return to the Jewish people. To live as a Jew."

Samira said nothing. She was wondering in a vague, detached fashion just how many shocks a person could sustain without falling apart. Mahmoud had crossed over. She had never suspected him of Jewish tendencies. On the contrary — she had believed that his mother's death at his grandfather's hands, intentionally or accidentally, had fostered a heightened hatred of the Jews. And now, it seemed, the opposite was true. Incredible!

A deep sadness descended. *He had the courage to choose,* she thought suddenly. Then she heard Avraham's voice on the phone — and her sadness turned to fury.

"Obviously you can't know this," Avraham was saying, "but Mahmoud was a G.S.S. informer, operating out of your hotel."

This time, Samira really did look for a chair to sit on. The last tidbit had undone her. No! She could not believe it.

"Why do you want to make me angry?" she demanded. "Haven't I been through enough, these last few days?"

"No, Rivka. From now on, I'm going to call you Rivka. I don't want to make you angry, just to explain the situation as it is to you. That's all."

"And where is Mahmoud now?"

"He's in good hands. He's taking a brief vacation at the moment. Everything will be fine with him." Avraham paused. "I only hope the same can be said about you and your sons."

"Me?" Samira laughed quickly. "After the way my parents hated me? Never. That's a lost cause."

Quietly, he said, "You're mistaken there, too."

Curiosity overcame Samira. "What do you mean? Do you think I don't know exactly how my father felt about me? Just the way you discovered in that envelope. I have an envelope, too. An envelope with a very cruel letter that Abba wrote me in Shechem, immediately after I arrived here. If you had read that, you wouldn't be sprinkling salt on my wounds the way you did just now."

Avraham understood now the reasons for his sister's distance, and her cold, harsh attitude toward her family. A letter from their father — that he had not known about. Who knew what his father had written in his first rage and grief?

But Avraham had a different picture of the evolving relationship between his father and sister.

"Rivka!"

"My name is Samira." All her old pain and anger had revived again, at the memory of her father's letter.

"All right — for now. Samira. Just last night, Imma showed me a whole stack of envelopes, each with a letter to you. Letters that Abba wrote to you."

The Envelope / 385

She was taken aback. "They never reached me!"

"I know. He kept them himself."

"I only care about what he wrote me!"

"That's true. But what he wrote and kept to himself is equally valid. They were letters to his wayward daughter, Rivka. Letters filled with love, with powerful longing for his Rivka'le, as he called her on those pages. I had tears in my eyes as I read them. They're kept in a plain wooden box. Imma keeps guard over them."

"I don't believe you!" Samira's voice rang, sharp and cold, in his ear.

"A pity, Rivka. Come here, and I'll show you. We'll read the letters together. We'll read them slowly, and see how, despite the deep rift between the two of you, the fundamental inner bond was solid and strong. You didn't sense it. Your own connection with Abba was based on the angry letter he wrote you. But hatred is also a form of bonding, you know."

Samira felt as though she had imbibed a whole bottle of wine. Her brother's words were like hammers pounding at her brain, blow after relentless blow. She honestly did not know whether or not to believe him. Silent tears coursed down her cheeks. The last thing she wanted was for Avraham to sense how broken she was feeling at this moment.

"So you'll come to my house and read Abba's letters?" he asked. The question was a trial balloon, sent up to test his sister's state of mind. Her long silence encouraged him to believe that she was wavering. That was a vast improvement over her initial reception, that night in Shechem.

At last, she said, "Maybe I'll come. My condition for considering it, though, is that you free my two sons."

"I wasn't the one who arrested them."

"I'm sure you didn't. But I'm positive that you were the one who set the authorities on them!"

"Not exactly."

"What do you mean by that?"

"I informed the G.S.S. that I'd been threatened. That's all."

"I see. But they were no doubt interested in knowing who had made the threats, right?"

"True."

"And then — you told them!"

"I had no choice."

"I don't accept that excuse," she snapped.

"But I," he said softly, "kept myself alive."

"Anyway, do something for them — now that you believe I didn't send them to you, and I believe you didn't kill Nawil. Will you help me?"

"What's wrong with letting them stew in jail for a while? Are they the first men to sit in an Israeli prison?"

"No. But they are being accused of murdering an Israeli soldier near Elon Moreh two years ago. It's a trumped-up charge, of course — but it could land them a life sentence. They're my sons. I owe it to them to do something on their behalf."

"They didn't tell me about that," Avraham said. "I'll check it out, I promise you. I'll also ask them personally."

"Ask whom?"

"Your sons!"

"How can that be?"

"For some reason, they've refused to answer any questions until they talk to me. I don't know what they want from me, but the G.S.S. is insisting that I meet with them. It's not a pleasant prospect, but what can I do?"

Samira thought a moment. "Do you know where they're keeping them?"

"In the Sata prison."

"That awful place?"

"So it seems."

"And when are you going?"

"I'm to be picked up at 8 o'clock in the morning. I didn't want to go, but I have no choice in the matter."

Samira did not answer. Inwardly, she resolved to be there at precisely that time.

52

Consulting his watch, Avraham saw that it was 4 a.m. He had spoken with his sister on the phone for a full hour. In the grip of the strong emotions their conversation had roused, he doubted he would fall asleep again. Amazing, how a short talk could turn a situation around so completely —

Rachel had been waiting, more or less patiently, for him to hang up. Quietly, so as not to waken their children, she asked, "What happened?"

"It was Rivka."

"I gathered that. What did she want?"

"She wants my help in freeing her sons."

Rachel shook her head vigorously in the negative. "That's all we need! Let those murderers sit in jail!"

"Calm down and hear me out, Rachel."

"Calm down, you say? I still haven't calmed down from that awful call from them. When was it — only yesterday? It feels like it happened a year

The Envelope / 389

ago! She sent them here to hurt you, and then she has the nerve to ask you for help in setting them free? 'Calm down,' he tells me!"

Avraham laughed lightly. "I'll say it again: Calm down, and hear me out to the end."

She fell silent, though still visibly agitated. Fury and hatred, both directed at her sister-in-law, shot forth from her eyes.

"It seems," Avraham said, "that it was all a big mistake."

Rachel couldn't stop herself. "I agree!" she cried. "And the mistake was our going to Shechem!"

Now it was Avraham's turn to grow impatient. "Rachel, please! I am not prepared to share the details with you. There has been a tremendous change which resulted from my phone conversation with Rivka just now. It's enough that I know about it, and I'm very calm. Good night!" He started for the bedroom.

Her voice floated over to him. "All right, tell me. I'll be quiet."

Avraham turned back to the living room. Taking a deep breath, he said, "She didn't send her sons to hurt me."

"You believe that?"

"Yes. It all arose from a misunderstanding. She thought that we killed Nawil and Mahmoud. Her men found Nawil's body in the hills, and were convinced that I, or G.S.S. agents, killed him. That's the whole story, and the basis for the whole misunderstanding. Do you see? When people talk to each other, things become clear."

"And what do you intend to do now?"

He shrugged. "Nothing. Binyamin is coming in a few hours to take me to meet with them. We'll see what happens. Maybe I'll be able to convince her sons that I did no harm. Maybe my Arab nephews will believe me."

There was a brief silence.

"Avraham?"

"What?"

"I'm afraid."

"Afraid of what? They're in jail."

"I'm afraid because you're going to see them in jail. I know what they're capable of doing to you."

Avraham's reply was a dismissive wave. "I'm not looking forward to this visit. But there's nothing to be afraid of." He glanced at his watch again. It was nearly 5 o'clock. "I'm going to try and get a little more sleep. I want to be fresh when I meet with Samira's worthy sons. Good night!"

For a time, his rest was disturbed by nervous and troublesome thoughts. Avraham had finally sunk into a deep sleep, when he was abruptly roused by the ringing of the phone.

"Good morning, Avraham."

"Good morning, Imma." He stifled a yawn. What could she possibly want so early in the morning?

"Did I wake you?" Mrs. Rosenbaum asked politely, in the time-honored fashion of early callers.

"Of course not," he replied equally politely.

"Avraham, I couldn't sleep all night."

"What happened?"

"'What happened?' he asks!"

Cautiously, he ventured, "Could you tell me what's on your mind, anyway?"

"You know very well why I couldn't sleep, Avraham. My two grandsons are in jail. And not just any grandsons — half-Arab grandsons. And —"

"According to Jewish law, they are fully Jews," Avraham interposed. "Their mother is Jewish."

"What do I care about that? Their father was an Arab! And they are not just any Arab, they are killers! Then you ask why I couldn't sleep."

"I understand," he said softly.

"Do you know why I'm calling?"

"No."

"I want to meet them."

Panic gripped Avraham. What had happened to his mother?

"Whom do you want to meet?" he stalled.

"What do you mean, whom? My grandsons! My Arabs! My murderers!" Her bitter sarcasm came through clearly over the telephone wire.

"Rivka'le, now," she added, in a different voice, "I don't want to meet."

"Why not?" he asked curiously. His talk with his sister a few hours earlier had dramatically changed his attitude toward her.

"I just don't want to. A sister who, for my sins, happens to be my daughter, sends her sons to murder her own brother — my son. I don't want to have anything to do with her, ever!"

Her philosophical standpoint interested him. "But you do want to meet her sons, the murderers?"

"Avraham," she said firmly, "what is it, exactly, that you don't understand? They are victims of their wicked mother. Intentionally she did everything to anger her father, *alav hashalom*, and me."

The word "wicked" struck Avraham painfully, like a physical blow. For the first time, he realized, he was firmly on Rivka's side. This surprised him.

"Imma, I have some news for you."

"What kind? Good news, or bad news?"

"I don't know. You decide. Rivka did not send them to hurt me."

"How do you know?"

"She told me."

Mrs. Rosenbaum was astounded. "You met her? But just yesterday evening you were here with me, and you never said a word! Did you meet her in the middle of the night? Don't tell me you went back to Shechem?"

"No, Imma. It's a lot simpler than that. She called me up just a few hours ago."

His mother's astonishment grew. "Called? You? In the middle of the night? After what you told me, what's that supposed to mean?"

"She called about her sons, who are locked up in jail."

His mother's laughter was cynical and pain filled. "Aha. Now she knows how a mother can suffer! Very nice! That's what our *chachamim* called *middah k'neged middah* — a measure for a measure. Believe me, Avraham, what she's suffering now is nothing compared to the pain and suffering she caused your father and me. Believe me."

"I believe you," he said quietly.

"And what did she want, my precious daughter?"

"She wants my help in obtaining the release of my nephews."

"Is that so? She has remained *chutzpadik* to the end, I see, just as she was as a young girl! She sends them to kill you — and then asks you, the chosen target, to help them. Very nice!"

Avraham hesitated. "Imma, she didn't send them to kill me. That was their own idea. Tonight she told me that she did everything she could to stop them."

His mother laughed again, dismissively. "And you believe that?"

"Yes."

"You don't even suspect that she might be lying to try and spare her sons the punishment they deserve?"

"No!"

There was a short silence, which Mrs. Rosenbaum broke with a question. "Why do you believe her?"

"I can sense the truth when I hear it."

"Even when it's spoken under such pressure?"

"Yes, Imma." He paused. "Imma, I told her about the letters that Abba wrote to her but never sent."

Mrs. Rosenbaum was gripped by emotion. Those unsent letters had always broken her heart. She struggled to keep her voice light and uninflected, as she asked, almost casually, "Well, what did she have to say?"

"She didn't say anything. She was quiet."

Mrs. Rosenbaum was disappointed. "That's all?"

"I think she was crying."

A deep sigh escaped his mother. "If only that were true —"

They fell silent again, both sensing the heavy and unspoken emotion quivering on the line between them. Mrs. Rosenbaum was the first to speak. "Can you get your new friends to arrange a visit to the jail for me? To see my grandsons?"

Avraham became very uneasy. "Imma, why? Your heart will be broken when you see them. They most probably look like any young Arabs you might see in the street. It's not good for you."

"I want it. That's all!"

Avraham sensed that she was on the verge of tears. "What will you talk to them about?"

"I don't know."

"Then what do you hope to get out of it?"

"I don't know that, either. Maybe, when they see me, their Jewish grandmother, something will tug at their Arab hearts. Maybe."

This seemed nonsensical to Avraham. Impatiently, he consulted his wristwatch again. 7:30! In just half an hour, Binyamin was coming to fetch him for the trip to the prison. He barely had time to *daven* and grab a bite to eat.

"Imma, don't be angry at me. There's no point."

"Will you try?" she persisted. "You're obligated. There is a mitzvah of honoring your parents!"

"All right, I'll try. I'll talk to the people involved. But I can't promise anything."

"I didn't ask for promises. I asked you to try."

"All right, Imma. I'm sorry, but I have to hang up now. I'm in a rush."

"Where are you rushing off to?"

Avraham lost the last of his patience. Contrary to his previous intention, he blurted out, "They're taking me over to the prison. Your grandsons refuse to answer any questions unless I come to see them first. I don't know what they want, but the G.S.S. is insisting that I meet with them. They'll be here to pick me up soon. So, excuse me, Imma."

Mrs. Rosenbaum's heart leaped up as if attached to a spring. "You mean to tell me that you're going to the jail *now*?"

"Yes. What choice do I have?"

"Where is it located?"

"Somewhere up north. It's the Sata Prison."

"Aha —"

At that moment, Mrs. Rosenbaum decided that she, too, would make the trip up north. She would meet Avraham at the prison, and force him, on the spot, to speak up on her behalf to his G.S.S. friends.

To his satisfaction, Avraham managed to finish *davening* and grab a piece of cake before the horn of Binyamin's Mitsubishi sounded downstairs. He said goodbye to his wife and raced down the stairs, too impatient to wait for the elevator.

Binyamin greeted him pleasantly. A second, taciturn man sat in the car. He bobbed his head briefly in greeting, but not the faintest glimmer of a smile appeared.

The car took off quickly. Suddenly, Avraham thought of something.

"Binyamin," he said urgently, "tell the driver to stop!"

Binyamin was astonished. "What's the matter? Have you changed your mind?"

"No. I know I have no choice in this matter. I just want to take Mahmoud along."

"Why?"

"I had a long phone conversation with Samira last night. Now I understand just what was going on."

"Tell me!"

"They thought I killed Mahmoud. If he comes with us, they'll see for themselves what really happened. That might affect the outcome of the investigation."

Binyamin did not answer. He peered at Avraham through narrowed eyes. Then he turned away, murmuring into his cell phone.

He turned back to Avraham. "All right. He'll be waiting for us at the prison gates."

※

Mrs. Rosenbaum's decision infused her with a new energy. She dressed in Shabbos clothing, so her grandsons could see their grandmother at her best. She *davened*, then added several chapters of *Tehillim* in honor of the upcoming occasion and its hoped-for success. As she stood near the door, ready to leave, she whispered to herself, "I don't even know how to get to that prison. What do I do?"

She returned to the apartment and sank into an armchair, her mind whirling fruitlessly in search of a solution. At last, inspiration struck. She reached for the phone and dialed hurriedly.

"Nachum, good morning."

"Good morning, Adina. What brings you to call so early in the morning?"

She went straight to the point. "Nachum, do you know where the Sata prison is?"

"Yes, more or less."

"Good. Now, listen. I'm going to hire a taxi. I should be at your house in approximately an hour and a half. You will escort me to the prison."

"What happened all of a sudden? What crime have I committed that makes you want to throw me into jail?"

"Nachum, I'm serious. You know very well that I have no desire to lock you up in jail. Until this morning, I never even heard of the Sata Prison. I'll tell you the whole story. My grandsons, Rivka'le's sons, wanted to kill Avraham. So —"

"Why?"

"Why? That's not important at the moment. I'll tell you on the way. The point is, they've been arrested, and Avraham is now on his way to meet them, at their request and the G.S.S.'s. I want to meet them, too. Maybe it will have an impact on them."

"*Oy*, you're just as naive as you've been all your life!"

"Maybe," she said crisply. "But naivete will sometimes succeed where wiser men fail." She paused. "You're coming with me, you hear? I haven't asked you for much in my life, Nachum."

"It's crazy," he sighed. "But, okay."

"Crazy — but truth can sometimes be found in what the world calls 'crazy.'"

Nachum did not respond immediately. It was only a moment later that he burst out uncontrollably, "How I tried to warn your foolish son not to go to Shechem! How I tried to explain to him that the trip could only bring trouble." He caught himself. "Okay, okay, if that's the way it is. What time should I expect you here?"

"In about an hour and a half."

※

Samira woke at 8 a.m.

"I'm leaving!" she told the receptionist. "If anyone looks for me, tell them I'll be back this evening."

"All right," the receptionist replied. "Have a good trip."

She did not ask where Samira was going, and Samira offered no details.

Samira drove her own car. She did not want to make this trip up north in anybody's company. By her calculations, she should arrive at the Sata Prison at just about the same time as her brother, Avraham.

It was a tense ride for Avraham. For a long time he did not utter a word, leaning back in his seat with his eyes closed. Up front, Binyamin sat beside the youthful driver, equally uncommunicative. The coastal road disappeared beneath the wheels of the Mitsubishi as they passed Herzliya, Netanya, and other towns. When they reached Chadera, the driver turned right, onto the road leading to Wadi Ara. The only sound in the car was the roar of its engine.

Suddenly, Avraham opened his eyes. "Binyamin?"

"What?"

"What am I supposed to be doing there?"

Binyamin considered before replying. "Doing? First of all, you listen."

Leaning forward, Avraham asked, "Just listen?"

"Yes!"

The car approached and passed the village of Uhm al-Facham and inched uphill toward the Meggido intersection. Presently, Avraham spoke up again. "And afterwards?"

The Envelope / 399

"After what?"

"What happens afterwards? After I listen to them, do I ask them questions? Or do I tell them something?"

Binyamin twisted in his seat so that he could look his passenger in the eye. "You're much too tense, Avraham," he said with a touch of impatience.

"You can understand why, surely."

Binyamin did not answer.

"I'm just an ordinary citizen. I've never found myself in a situation like this." He waited, but Binyamin still offered nothing. "So, I'm a little tense," Avraham went on. "Isn't that understandable, under the circumstances?"

Binyamin's long silence began to irritate him. "Look, Binyamin," he said. "I'm worried. I'm afraid that I won't meet your expectations in this meeting. I've never met face-to-face with terrorists before."

Binyamin laughed lightly. "And certainly not with Arab terrorists who are your own nephews."

Once again, Avraham leaned back and closed his eyes. That was when Binyamin decided to offer some reassurance. "Why worry? Let's wait and see what happens. Do you think I know, at this moment, how you ought to begin the conversation? I don't. But I'll be right there with you — so don't worry!"

Rows of eucalyptus trees partially concealed the verdant green fields they were passing. At the end of the straight road lay Afula, capital of the valley. Avraham could not remember when he had last visited this beautiful section of the country. He checked his watch; it was already 10:30.

He worked valiantly to maintain a modicum of calm. It was not physical fear that he felt at the upcoming meeting with his nephews, Samira's sons. They were in prison, after all, and doubtless restrained in some fashion. His fear was more nebulous, buried in an urgent desire to find some way to influence them spiritually. This would be their first encounter with their Jewish uncle. What sort of reception would they accord him? Hostility? Curiosity? A desire for mutual understanding? Would this meeting lessen their desire to kill him — or, Heaven forbid, have the opposite effect? They were grandsons of his departed father, a Radomsker chassid — but they had been raised with violence and steeped in hatred against the Jews. That hatred was doubtless operating on all cylinders now, particularly because they had to live with the knowledge that they were half-Jewish. Silently, Avraham prayed for salvation.

In Afula, they turned right again, moving eastward in the direction of a sign proclaiming "Beit She'an." In just another three-quarters of an hour, Avraham calculated, the hour of reckoning would be upon him. His tension reached a new high. They passed Kfar Yechezkel, Geva, Ein Harod. On the road to Beit Hashita, not far from Beit She'an, they pulled up to the entrance to the Sata Prison.

Avraham climbed out of the car and lifted his eyes to take in the tall gray walls, liberally studded with watch towers that girded the prison. It was a forbidding-looking place. The coldness of gray stone penetrated his heart.

※

Samira drove recklessly, her old Ford careening out of Shechem's northern exit. She had decided to cover most of the trip over Arab-populated territory rather than take the more direct east road to Beit She'an. The fewer Israeli cars she met on her way, the better. She turned onto the road that would take her past Tobas, Kabatia, and Jenin. Just north of Jenin, she was forced to stop at an Israeli military checkpoint. Soldiers in IDF uniform checked her identity card. They spoke to her in Arabic, never dreaming that this woman who spoke and looked like an Arab was actually an Israeli like themselves.

She made an unplanned stop in Afula. For some reason, the sight of that city staggered her with an inexplicable sense of shock. It had been more than twenty years since she had set foot in Afula. In fact, this was the first time she had set foot over the Green Line since that day, when she had bolted from her home in Ramat Gan to take up a new life in Shechem. She wanted suddenly to breathe the air of a Jewish city.

Pulling up at a kiosk, she bought herself a bottle of soft drink. Just for the sake of speaking a few words of Hebrew — a strange and unexpected pleasure.

Then, hastily, she returned to her car. For a moment, she had allowed herself to forget her intent in making this trip.

She pointed her car eastward, following the signs that said "Beit She'an."

❧

Binyamin strode unhesitatingly up to the prison entrance. Cautiously, Avraham followed. Binyamin pulled out his identity documents and passed them over to the guard at the gate, who spoke into a phone. The gate opened. Avraham and Binyamin were swallowed up within the forbidding gray walls.

They passed several additional checkpoints before they finally reached the administrative offices. A prison official rose to greet them, then led them to a small side room.

Avraham looked around. The room was very simply furnished. A wooden table stood in the center, and several chairs were scattered throughout the room. The walls were bare, save for a portrait of the Israeli Prime Minister.

Binyamin and Avraham sat down beside the table. Anticipation charged the air and made Avraham's pulse race. Suddenly, he asked, "Where is Mahmoud? Find out if he's arrived! His presence is crucial."

Binyamin nodded. He left the room, returning a moment later to say, "It's all right. Mahmoud is due here any minute. When he comes, he will be taken directly into the next room."

❧

Mrs. Rosenbaum was forthright with the taxi driver. "We're going to Haifa first, and afterwards to some prison whose name, if I'm not mistaken, is Sata. I'm not sure exactly where it is."

The driver grinned. "What does a nice *savta* like you want in that terrible place?"

But Mrs. Rosenbaum was in no mood for joking. Grimly, she said, "It's not funny for me. Believe me, I have no pleasure in making this trip."

The driver looked as if he wished he could swallow his words. Silently, he started the engine.

An hour and a half later, they were in Haifa.

Nachum was waiting at his front door. The whole thing seemed like a foolish undertaking to him, but his sister's authoritative manner over the phone had made refusal out of the question. He stepped into the taxi, saying, "Hello, Adina. *Nu*, so two old-timers are going out to see the country a little?"

"Nachum!" she snapped. "I'm not going sight-seeing. I'm a broken woman, I'm suffering, and you're laughing at me?"

"Laughing at you? Of course not! But what does amuse me is the idea that you really expect them to let you see your grandsons. That's one. And, two, the idea that your grandsons will pay any attention at all to you. And, three, even if you do get in and get to talk with your grandsons, what makes you think there's even the remotest possibility that you will have the slightest influence on them? But" — He spread his hands in the classic gesture of surrender — "my sister's wish is my command."

The taxi sped on past Afula and continued on toward Beit She'an.

The door to the small room opened. Two men clad in prison uniform were shoved into the room. Avraham studied them with immense curiosity and a pounding heart.

The men were young, sturdy, and black eyed. They boasted nearly identical black mustaches. With an intensity equal to Avraham's, they scrutinized this uncle who threatened to steal their mother from them.

The guards led the prisoners to two chairs at the table, facing Binyamin and Avraham.

"Take off their handcuffs," Binyamin ordered quietly.

The handcuffs were removed. Saib and Nashashivi flexed their wrists with pleasure. No one said a word, though four pairs of eyes darted ceaselessly. Finally, Binyamin broke the silence once again. He said to the brothers, in Arabic, "You wanted to speak to your uncle. Well, here he is!"

"Does he understand Arabic?" Nashashivi asked.

"No. Speak in English."

Nashashivi said to Avraham, "We're in jail because of you. We know that!"

Avraham said nothing.

"You reported us to the authorities!"

"Who told you that?" Avraham asked. "Did you call me here in order to give me this information?"

"Yes. You'll soon understand why. We're not naive. They arrested us exactly one day after we tried to meet you, just in order to talk to you. The story about some Israeli soldier that we allegedly killed two years ago is just a camouflage — an unsuccessful camouflage. Not up to the G.S.S.'s usual standard."

Avraham stirred uneasily. "You wanted to talk to me? Just to talk?"

The brothers exchanged a fleeting glance. Nashashivi said, "Yes, to talk. Or, more accurately — to warn you."

"That's all?"

No answer.

Avraham pressed, "Maybe, just by the way, you also intended to kill me?" He gathered courage from their silence. "I'm waiting for an answer."

"That's not important now," Nashashivi said finally. "We're already sitting in jail. But, even from here, we can and want to warn you."

"Warn me about what? That your friends outside are planning to kill me?"

"We want to know why you came to Nablus. Why did you come to disturb our lives? And," Nashashivi inhaled deeply, his black eyes boring into his uncle's, "we want to insist that you stop disturbing us. Or else —"

Avraham sat up straighter in the hard chair. His chin jutted forward proudly. "She is my sister, as you are well aware. It's a hard pill to swallow, I know. But those are the facts. I'm sure it's not a pleasant situation for you." Ironically, he continued, "I ask your forgiveness for the fact that she's my sister. I bear no guilt for that."

He saw his nephews grind their teeth in silent frustration.

"Yes," Nashashivi said. "We are aware of that fact, to our grief. But first and foremost, she is our mother. You can't steal her away from us. Let that be very clear."

Avraham suddenly understood. Apparently, his visit to Shechem had triggered an emotional response in his sister — a response that rang a warning bell for her sons. They sensed some deep evolution taking place deep within their mother's heart, and had decided to avenge themselves on him. For an instant, he rejoiced. His trip to Shechem had not been in vain.

"Does it threaten you?" he asked gently.

Nashashivi shrugged. "Interpret it as you will. I'm also curious about something. Can I ask you?"

Reluctantly, Avraham nodded. "Ask away."

"Why did you, or your G.S.S. friends, murder Nawil and Mahmoud?"

"I didn't kill them."

Pointing at his brother, Nashashivi said, "Saib found Nawil's body. What's the point of denying it? Where did you bury Mahmoud? In some Jewish cemetery, because he's half-Jewish?"

"I repeat: I didn't kill them. Your mother already knows the truth."

Both brothers reacted as though some button had been pushed. "You were in touch with her?"

Avraham nodded calmly. "Yes. We spoke last night. We spoke about you."

Instinctively, they tried to leap to their feet. The guards stepped in, bearing down on the prisoners' shoulders with all their weight until the brothers remembered where they were.

"Please stay calm," Avraham said. "With the guards' permission, the man who killed Nawil will now walk into this room."

Binyamin motioned to one of the guards, who left the room. A moment later, he returned leading a beaming Mahmoud. Saib and Nashashivi's eyes almost popped out of their sockets. The surprise was total. With one voice, they shouted, "Mahmoud!" in the tone of those who do not quite believe the evidence of their own eyes.

Samira reached the prison gates at exactly 11 a.m. She presented a letter from Shechem's military governor, requesting permission for her to visit her sons — who were still in the category of administrative detainees. She was ushered into a waiting area.

"They are undergoing questioning right now," someone told her. "Afterwards, we'll see."

※

Ten minutes later, it was Mrs. Rosenbaum's turn to arrive at Sata Prison. She turned to the guard and asked to see the warden, or some other senior official.

"My son is inside, and also my grandsons," she explained. "They — the grandsons — are Arab terrorists."

The guard stared at her. "You're Jewish, aren't you?"

"Yes, I'm Jewish. Life can be strange, young man."

He picked up the phone. Some minutes later, a prison official emerged to hear Mrs. Rosenbaum's strange and confusing story. He knew at once which prisoners she referred to, and summoned Binyamin from the interrogation room. To his surprise, Binyamin gave his consent to Mrs. Rosenbaum's entrance. Her presence might actually turn out to be useful to his own plans.

"**M**ahmoud?" Nashashivi exclaimed in obvious bewilderment. "Is it really you?"

"No," Mahmoud grinned. "It's someone else."

Still reeling from the shock, the brothers missed the irony in the answer.

"You're alive?" Saib asked pointlessly.

"Can't you see that I am?" Mahmoud laughed.

Slowly, as their initial surprise receded, the brothers turned to Avraham. He smiled slightly, and there was a victorious intonation in his voice as he said, "I told you I didn't kill him." Then, to Mahmoud, "Tell them what happened, the night we left Nablus."

Nashashivi and Saib waited in silence. Mahmoud, in the grip of emotions of his own, seemed reluctant to break that silence. Finally, Avraham decided to do the explaining himself.

"Nawil wanted to kill us. For no reason — we hadn't done a thing to him. At literally the last minute, Mahmoud saved our lives."

All at once, Saib and Nashashivi understood the implications of what Avraham was saying. Their eyes met and darkened. Nashashivi looked at Mahmoud again, and hissed, "Traitor!" And Saib added quickly, "Filthy worm!"

Saib clenched his fists and half-rose from his seat. Immediately, the guards pressed down hard on his shoulders. He subsided, though sparks of hatred and fury continued to fly from his black eyes.

Mahmoud paled. He looked around for a chair and sank into it. For their part, Avraham and Binyamin were quiet, watching with interest the interplay between the cousins.

Sitting down had helped Mahmoud regain some of his equilibrium. He faced down the prisoners, saying, "Traitor? Me? Why?"

"You betrayed us! You betrayed the Palestinian people! You returned to the *Yahud*!"

"True, I returned. But I am no traitor."

"Yes, yes! You are!"

"The Palestinians are my people?" Mahmoud asked.

"What else? Where were you raised? Who is your father? He is an Arab!"

"Have you forgotten who my mother was? She was a Jew!" Mahmoud's voice strengthened with each word.

Saib smiled cynically. "Have *you* forgotten who killed her? A *Yahud*!"

This infuriated Mahmoud. He knew very well that his maternal grandfather had, according to the stories he had been told, been responsible for his mother's death. But this fact, painful as it was, could not deter him from his decision to return to his mother's people.

"I have forgotten nothing, Saib," he answered. "But I remember what you, apparently, have failed to remember — that you also belong to the Jews. Your mother, Samira, is Jewish!"

Avraham felt an urge to intervene. He opened his mouth to speak, but Binyamin stopped him with an urgent tug on the sleeve and a gesture for silence. He had not anticipated the turn of this interrogation, but it interested him all the same. These young men were undergoing an agonizing identity crisis. Binyamin was anxious to see how the conflict would be resolved.

"What does that have to do with anything?" Nashashivi demanded. "A man can choose to whom to belong."

"Very nice," Mahmoud said approvingly. "So, I've chosen. Does that make me a traitor? Maybe the opposite is true? Maybe it's you two who are the traitors. Traitors to your mother's roots!"

"But our mother has stayed with us, on the Palestinian side."

Mahmoud stood up. His eyes burned with a fierce fire as he pointed at Avraham. "Why did you want to kill him? I'll tell you why! You are afraid that Samira, your mother, will return home to the *Yahud*. I was a witness at her meeting with her brother. I saw how she reacted. Admit it — you are afraid!"

The brothers hung their heads, seeking an answer to their traitorous cousin. They would not admit openly to having planned their uncle's murder. That would only incriminate them in the Israeli courts.

"We just wanted to warn him," Nashashivi said at last. "Not kill him."

Mahmoud grinned. "Ah, to warn him! An Arab doesn't warn. He kills. Period."

Saib and Nashashivi lifted their heads. Without warning, Nashashivi shot to his feet, trembling with anger. After a few tricky minutes, two of the guards managed to subdue him.

"Are you not ashamed?" Nashashivi screamed. "Ashamed to dishonor the people you came from? What has happened to you?"

Mahmoud stood stoically facing the furious prisoner. "I did no dishonor, Nashashivi. I merely stated a fact that both of us know to be true. Why are you so angry?" He waited a beat, then added, "Avraham told me about your phone call to his home. You did not warn his wife. You only asked where Avraham was, saying that you wished to speak with him. True or false?"

"True. Just speak with him," Nashashivi said.

"You could have warned his wife," Mahmoud said. "She would have passed the warning on to her husband. No, you wanted to meet him for other purposes."

"Not true! Whether we like it or not, he is our uncle. We wouldn't kill an uncle."

Mahmoud's grin turned into full-bodied laughter. "You wouldn't kill an uncle? Do you remember what happened to the Arikat family? The wonderful sons killed their own dear father. I'm an Arab, like yourselves. I know the truth — just as you do."

He turned to Avraham. "Did you hear, Avraham? They wouldn't dream of killing an uncle. Such polite young men, these nephews of yours."

Binyamin pulled a plastic bag from the briefcase he had placed on the table. Carefully, he drew a folded page from it. All eyes watched him, momentarily distracted. With patience and care, he unfolded the paper, lifted it up to the prisoners' eyes, and asked, "Recognize this?"

They did not reply — though their eyes answered for them. They recognized the paper. Addressing Avraham and Mahmoud, Binyamin said, "Do you see? It's a street map of Petach Tikvah. How they got their hands on one of these I don't know yet. But, trust me, we'll find out. Come closer."

Mahmoud approached the table. Avraham leaned forward. Binyamin spread out the map. "Here, do you see? Your house, Avraham, is marked with an 'X.' These red arrows designate the streets to be used for the getaway, after the planned murder."

"Not true!" Saib shouted.

Binyamin did not even glance his way. Picking up the plastic bag, he pulled out two used stocking masks and waved them in front of the prisoners.

"You only wanted to talk to your uncle, eh? Very nice! What were these intended for?"

Saib did not answer. Nashashivi stared coldly at Binyamin. From the bag, Binyamin pulled out other items.

"Here are two nice toys. Two small pistols, complete with silencers. A pleasant chat you wanted to have with your uncle, hey?"

Binyamin's voice hardened. "Do you know where we found all these interesting things? In your room! True? I'm sure you'll admit that much, at least!"

They admitted nothing. Saib ran his fingers through his raven-black hair. Neither brother said a word.

"Maybe you can answer me?" Binyamin prompted.

Nashashivi hesitated. Then he said, "I want a lawyer."

"Never fear," Binyamin said. "You'll get one."

The waiting room was crowded with Arab women in black, all with white kerchiefs framing their faces. Samira was dressed in similar fashion. She found a place to sit between two women who were glumly staring straight ahead. Others were chatting with varying degrees of animation. Most whispered. All waited for a brief meeting with a son, husband, or father who had been imprisoned on security charges.

From time to time, a name was called and a woman was led away to a different room inside the prison compound. The others followed her with their eyes until she disappeared. After a moment, the murmured conversations resumed.

Samira looked at her watch. She had been sitting here upwards of thirty minutes, and still no sign of anyone to call her name. Who knew what was happening in the interrogation room at this very moment? Resolutely, she subdued her fears. She would not allow such thoughts to weaken her. With steely patience, she set herself to wait as long as necessary.

The outer door opened to admit Mrs. Rosenbaum and her brother, Nachum.

They stood for a moment just inside the doorway, surprised at the size of the waiting crowd. It seemed strange, almost threatening, to take their places among the Arab women — wives and mothers of the enemy.

But they had no choice. They found seats in a corner of the room, trying to ignore the scores of curious eyes that watched their every move. They sat on a wooden bench and did not look at anyone.

Samira, too, studied the newcomers curiously. They did not fit into this setting. The elderly woman, and the man accompanying her, were Jews. What were they doing here? Wild speculation filled her brain, but not even her most outlandish conjectures targeted the truth.

Some deep instinct in her heart made her glance again and again at the elderly Jewish woman. Samira did not understand what it was that drew her attention to the woman. She continued to ponder why the woman was in this place. It must be unusual circumstances, Samira thought, that brought her to the waiting room of a grim prison populated almost entirely by Arab security prisoners.

Binyamin signaled the guards to replace the handcuffs on the prisoners' wrists. When Saib and Nashashivi were secured, he addressed them directly.

"You wanted to talk to your uncle. We agreed to let him come and talk with you. Are you satisfied?"

They did not answer. Both faces were obstinate.

"Well, I'm satisfied, anyway," Binyamin continued. "We've progressed very nicely with our investigation. You will be brought before a judge tomorrow to have your imprisonment extended."

Still the brothers said nothing. The guards raised them to their feet and began to hustle them from the room.

Quickly, Mahmoud said, "Saib, Nashashivi, I want you to understand our strange and unbearable lives. Mine, and yours. We are not *Yahud*, nor are we Palestinians. We are both. We are nothing, and we are everything. Our parents, may they forgive me, brought us into the world and saddled us with a lifetime burden. We have no identities of our own. I am not a traitor if I chose the *Yahud* option, because I am already half-*Yahud*. From my perspective, I believe I have made the right decision. I just want you to understand." He was visibly emotional, though at the same time angry with himself for trying so hard to obtain his cousins' understanding or approval.

Nashashivi was already at the door. He twisted his head around and sneered one word: "Traitor!"

The blood rushed to Mahmoud's face. "Your own mother, in her heart, has already betrayed you, too. I saw her on the night she met your uncle. And now, you are about to betray her."

He was not certain if they even heard him. The brothers passed through the door, and it closed behind them.

Binyamin, Avraham, and Mahmoud were alone in the room. Each stood quietly, lost in his own thoughts. Binyamin smiled faintly. "Well, that was pleasant."

Avraham shrugged. "Pleasant? I don't know. I thought it was exhausting."

Mahmoud said nothing.

"Avraham," Binyamin said, "despite all the angry rhetoric, seeing Mahmoud alive and well shocked them and altered their attitude toward you. Perhaps you can get their mother, Samira, to desist from her Fatah activities. Then we can consider releasing her sons on her recognizance."

"I understand," Avraham nodded. "But my sister is very stubborn. She is full of hate and resentment."

"Do what you can," Binyamin said firmly.

They turned to go. Their path took them past the waiting area. Avraham was the first to enter. He stopped short, stunned.

"Samira! What are you doing here?"

Then he caught sight of an even more extraordinary vision. "Imma? Uncle Nachum? How did you get here? And why? What's going on?"

55

Samira leaped up as though she had been stung. She could neither move nor speak. She stood like a rock, utterly paralyzed. Even her heart seemed to have turned to stone. She was incapable of thinking coherently. Her existence seemed to have narrowed down to the utterly still place in the eye of the storm.

With uncomprehending eyes she stared at the short woman seated opposite her on the bench. She was slightly bent, and seemingly prematurely aged. Was this really her mother?

Slowly but surely, amid the lines and creases that time had etched on that face, Samira began to discern familiar features — features she had last gazed upon more than twenty years before. She closed her eyes. The enormity of the shock made it almost impossible for her to maintain her equilibrium. Her head pounded as it exploded with sudden pain.

The Arab women around them did not comprehend what was happening. At first, they gaped in silence at Samira, who appeared on the point of collapse. They saw the elderly Jewish woman — so out of place in this setting — stand up amid a violent trembling, eyes wide and fearful. They saw the way the Jewish woman stood, as though carved of marble, her only movement the kneading of her fingers under the pressure of an inner agony. She did not move from her place. In whispers, the Arab women began to speculate at the reason behind the unfolding drama. What would happen next?

As though seeking an escape, Samira squeezed her eyes shut. An Arab woman stood up and with small but hurried steps left the room; the tension was too much for her. Seconds later, a second woman followed her. Then another, and another —

The waiting area quickly emptied. Only Samira stood there, facing her mother. No more than a dozen feet separated them.

Suddenly, — it happened — Both of them moved at once. With a strangled cry, they ran headlong into each other's arms. The impact of their collision was so forceful that it nearly toppled both women. Their embrace was intensely powerful, its warmth melting in an instant the walls and the distance that had stood between them for so long —

"Imma! My Imma! Why did this happen to me?"

As she said the words, Samira/Rivka felt a stab of pain, sharp as an arrow, penetrate her heart. They had emerged from some deep recess of her heart, to erupt out of her with volcanic force.

"No! Rivka'le, you are not to blame! We were the guilty ones. Your mother and father are to blame!"

That was all. No other words were possible after that. With that brief interchange, the tragedy ended. Neither woman could speak for the tears that clogged her throat. Behind them, hardly breathing from the sheer unexpectedness of it all, stood Avraham, Binyamin, Mahmoud, and Uncle Nachum. They listened to the inarticulate murmurings of mother and daughter as they clung to each other, swaying back and forth as though unable or unwilling ever to be parted again.

Avraham wiped away tears. *Too bad Rachel's not here to see this*, he thought. *She'd know that our trip to Shechem was not a waste of time, after all.*

Hesitantly, he walked toward his mother and sister. Once again, Binyamin stopped him. Grasping Avraham's arm, he said in an undertone, "Wait! Don't."

Avraham turned in surprise. "Why not?" What business, his manner seemed to imply, was this of Binyamin's?

"Give them a chance to calm down. Let them get all their emotions out, all the pain and turmoil. Then we'll get what we need from your sister."

Avraham stared at Binyamin blankly. With a weak smile, Binyamin said, "Yes, I understand you, Avraham. You are in the grip of perfectly understandable emotions. But I must remind you of reality. It seems to me that your sister's two sons are sitting in this jail by your invitation. True?"

With a start, Avraham remembered where he was. He remembered his nephews, and remembered what the G.S.S. wanted from his sister. Slowly, he said, "After this emotional meeting, you think it will be easier to persuade her. Is that it?"

"That's what I'm saying. I believe so. That's why I'm asking you not to go over to them now. Leave them with each other for a little while longer."

"I understand," Avraham whispered.

The two women paid no attention to the small group of men watching them. With their arms locked around each other, they moved slowly to a bench and sat down, whispering softly to one another, the sounds mingling with their tears.

From his pocket, Binyamin pulled out a pack of cigarettes. He offered one to Avraham, and another to Mahmoud and Nachum.

"Who's the gentleman?" he asked, nodding at Uncle Nachum. Once a G.S.S. investigator, always an investigator.

"Me?" Nachum answered for himself. He pointed at Avraham. "I am his mother's brother."

"You came here with her?"

"Yes. She asked me to."

Avraham extended a hand to his uncle. "Uncle Nachum, forgive me. In all the confusion, I didn't notice you."

Nachum smiled. "I understand. And I forgive you."

"Thanks. What brought you and Imma to this place? Did you know I was here?"

At that, his mother broke off her whispered talk with Samira to say, "What's with you? Don't you remember that you told me yourself?"

Nachum added, "Your mother requested — or rather, insisted — that I come along. So I came."

"Yes, but why did she want to come? What did she hope to accomplish here?"

"Believe me, Avraham, I don't have a clue. She said she wanted to see her grandsons in jail."

"What a crazy idea," Avraham murmured.

"Yes. But once a person becomes fixated on an idea, crazy or not, it's impossible to talk her out of it. Your mother pulled me along with her."

Avraham shrugged. His uncle added, "Does your mother's sudden urge really surprise you? After all, you believe in Divine Providence, which causes surprising and moving encounters" — he gestured at the two women on the bench — "like that one. No?"

From the moment he laid eyes on his uncle, Avraham had been wondering how to introduce Mahmoud, the only grandchild from Nachum's only child, who was no longer among the living. How to do it without arousing his uncle's anger? Now, he realized, Uncle Nachum had handed him his opportunity on a silver platter. The platter of Divine Providence.

Enthusiastically, he agreed. "True, true! I believe in Providence. It was that Providence that brought both my mother and my sister to this place, at exactly the same time, without either one knowing that the other was here. How right you are, Uncle!

"And I also believe," Avraham continued, "that Providence brought me to this room for the totally unexpected shock of seeing both of them here in the last place in the world I'd expect to meet them. And that the surprise made me blurt out words that both of them, my mother and my sister, heard — words that made them realize they were seated just a few feet apart. It's an extraordinary turn of events, something that only Heaven could arrange."

He paused. For a brief moment, he closed his eyes and composed himself. Lightly at first, and then with pounding insistence, his heartbeat accelerated. "Uncle Nachum?" he asked in a choked voice.

His uncle looked at him curiously, noting the sudden change in Avraham's demeanor. "Yes, what is it? What's happened?"

Avraham attempted a smile. "The turn of events is even more impressive than you think."

"What do you mean?"

"I mean that I know why you had to be here today. Why you gave in to Imma and came along with her."

Nachum was amused. "Well? Let's hear."

Gathering his courage, and speaking quickly so that he would not have a chance to turn back, Avraham said, "*HaKadosh Baruch Hu* wanted you, Uncle Nachum, to meet your only grandson!"

And he pointed a quavering finger at Mahmoud.

The words hit Nachum like the proverbial ton of bricks. He shifted his gaze to Mahmoud. For an instant, their eyes met. He opened his mouth to say something, but the words would not come. Until now, Nachum had seen himself as an observer at an unusual and moving spectacle. Now, to his shock and amazement, he had become a central player. He stood in the center of the room, at a total loss.

Mahmoud had not gathered the import of what Avraham was saying to the elderly man standing a short distance away. But the man's sudden glance, and the intuition of his own heart, told him that they were speaking about him. More — his intuition insisted that this man must be his own grandfather! The grandfather who refused to know him — He was overcome by a deep sadness and confusion.

Avraham saw the anger suffusing his uncle's face. Nachum's cheeks took on a tomato-red hue. His lips tightened and his eyes narrowed. Avraham tried to subdue the inferno before it raged out of control: "Uncle Nachum, this is a moment for reconciliation. Look at Rivka and Imma. The boy has come to us, to *Am Yisrael*, on his own initiative."

"Out of the question!" Nachum snapped. Rage at his daughter's defection still flowed strongly in his veins.

"But this is all you have left, Uncle Nachum!"

Nachum averted his face and did not answer. Mahmoud hung his head. Avraham pressed on, "Uncle Nachum, listen to me. The boy is asking to get close to the family, at any price. We are his family! Remember: According to Jewish law, he is a Jew. Look how much he wants to be part of us. Just half an hour ago, he asked me what his great-grandfather's name is — that is, your own father. I told him that it was Efraim. And do you know how he reacted?"

Nachum was not interested in Mahmoud's reaction. He refused to look at either Avraham or Mahmoud.

"Listen well, uncle Nachum," Avraham said. "Mahmoud said, 'From today, don't call me Mahmoud. From this day on, I am Efraim.' Do you hear, Uncle? You have an heir, someone to continue your line. Accept him. It can only benefit you!"

This proved too much for Nachum. His heart burst open like an overripe fruit. Though he would not openly surrender, he was deeply affected. His father had merited a great-grandson to carry on his name! Not exactly the kind of offspring he might have dreamed of — but offspring nevertheless! Deep down he knew that Avraham was right: He had an heir! But pride and obstinacy refused to allow him admit it.

Avraham sensed the change. He saw his uncle totter over to a bench, sit down on it, and bury his face in his hands. Mahmoud/Efraim whispered, "I'm going out for a few minutes. I need some air."

Mrs. Rosenbaum and her daughter had calmed down somewhat. Still holding each other's hands, they sat quietly together. Neither one so much as glanced at Avraham and Binyamin, standing to one side in the empty room.

The door opened, and a kerchiefed head peeked in. The Arab woman looked around to see the outcome of the drama, then timidly walked in and found herself a seat in an unobtrusive corner. Gradually, others came back into the room.

"Now," Binyamin whispered to Avraham. "Go over to your sister and introduce me. This is our chance."

Avraham walked over. "Rivka, this man would like to talk with you."

She lifted her eyes and looked at Binyamin. With her finely tuned instinct, she knew immediately who he was and what he represented. At the moment, however, she was without ability to resist. She felt as weak as a patient recovering from a long and terrible illness, calm but depleted. Her head nodded in assent. Binyamin approached.

"I am Binyamin, of the G.S.S.," he began without preamble. "Your sons are jailed here on administrative detention. Their case has not yet reached a judge. They can be freed in minutes by my order."

"What do you want?"

"As I said, you can have your sons back right now. There is just one condition. You cease all underground activities against the authorities. If not —"

He did not specify the alternative. Rivka, he noted, grasped his meaning very well.

For several minutes, there was silence. Then Rivka nodded her head again, in the affirmative.

"Thank you very much," Binyamin said quietly. "In just a few minutes, your sons will be joining this family reunion." He left the room.

True to his word, ten minutes later he returned, accompanied by Nashashivi and Saib. Catching sight of their mother, they rushed over to her. She gestured at Mrs. Rosenbaum and whispered, "This is my mother. Your grandmother."

The brothers threw the elderly woman a hard, indifferent glance. Hostility was stamped clearly on their faces. They were certain that their mother had arranged this meeting. In other words, she had begun her journey toward her Jewish family.

"I'm not interested in her," Nashashivi said sharply. "We are returning to Nablus, and you're coming with us. Understand?"

Samira/Rivka recoiled at his tone. After great hesitation, she stood up. Mrs. Rosenbaum called plaintively, "Rivka'le, where are you going?"

Rivka seized her mother's thin hand. "Imma, I'm going home. To Shechem."

Mrs. Rosenbaum did not understand. There was a note of hysteria as she said, "What do you mean? I thought that our family was finally reunited."

"Yes, but I can't destroy my own family. My sons."

"And what about your mother?"

Rivka began to cry. "What will become of my sons?"

Saib and Nashashivi started for the door. "Come on already!" they called back harshly. For their grandmother there was not even a momentary glance. Rivka trailed in their wake without a backward glance.

The room was rent by a sudden, piercing shriek. "Rivka'le! Don't go!"

Mrs. Rosenbaum wept bitterly and long.

56

At the sound of his sister's anguished scream, Nachum lifted his head and lowered the hands that had been covering his face. What he saw alarmed him. He got to his feet and ran to Mrs. Rosenbaum, holding her firmly to prevent her from fainting.

Avraham had the same thought. He sat down beside his mother on the other side and spoke softly to her, offering words to soothe and comfort. But his mother's eyes, darting restlessly to and fro, showed no sign of comprehension. Avraham and his uncle exchanged a discouraged glance.

Suddenly, Nachum began to sweep the waiting area with his eyes. He was searching for something or someone, but there was nothing to be seen but waiting Arab women.

"Where is he?" Nachum asked abruptly.

"Who?"

Nachum hesitated before answering. The fact that he had an Arab grandson who bore his own father's name was still difficult for him to digest. His father had been a chassid in Poland and Nachum, despite the fact that he had strayed from his childhood upbringing, had revered him. Witnessing his sister's profound pain now, the thought flashed through his mind that his own situation, at any rate, was improving. His Arab grandson wanted to be Jewish, while his sister's grandsons desired only to distance themselves as much as possible from their Jewish roots. The situation had most definitely taken on a whole new cast. Unexpectedly, he found himself warming to Mahmoud/Efraim. He actually wanted to see him. But where was he?

"You know who!" he said.

For a moment, Avraham was at a loss. He did not fathom whom his uncle was referring to.

Then his eyes lit up. "Ah, I get it! You mean Efraim!"

"Yes," Uncle Nachum answered in a near-whisper. "I mean him."

"Don't be embarrassed," Avraham said. "Say 'Efraim.'"

With a slight smile, his uncle admonished, "Avraham! Leave that alone for now. Where is he? Where has he disappeared to?"

Avraham gave in. He sensed a shift in his uncle's position toward his newfound grandson. "He hasn't disappeared, Uncle Nachum. He felt stifled by your insulting reaction to his presence and decided to step outside briefly. That's all." He watched his uncle's face, curious to see his response to this straight talk. But Mrs. Rosenbaum chose that moment to slip out of their grasp and slide slowly, effortlessly, to the floor.

They picked her up again, setting her firmly on the bench and holding on to her arms for support. Binyamin fetched a cup of water, but she refused to drink. Although she was no longer limp and lifeless, she sat immersed in her own thoughts, not responding to her son's and brother's questions. Emotionally she was not present in the room at all.

Avraham resumed his conversation with Uncle Nachum. "I see that you are interested in your grandson after all."

Nachum nodded. "True. I won't deny it."

"In that case, what's your decision about him?"

Nachum took a deep breath, then exhaled slowly. "Let time take care of that."

"Anyway, say something nice to him. He's thirsting for some sign, some mark of attention, from you. Show him that you are pleased!"

"I told you," his uncle said with a trace of impatience, "it's still too early for me to behave the way you want me to. You tell him. Tell him that — that it will come soon. I need time to get used to the idea. It's hard for me — very hard."

"So what do you want me to do?" Avraham asked, disappointed.

"I told you! Tell him to get in touch with me in a few days. I hope that things will straighten out by then."

Avraham nodded gravely. "Okay, I'll do that. Let's hope it really will straighten out."

He turned to Binyamin. "I'm not going back to Petach Tikvah with you. I'm taking my mother home."

"Fine," Binyamin acquiesced. "Let's stay in touch. I'll take Mahmoud in my car."

In the taxi, after they left Nachum at his home in Haifa, Avraham finally induced his mother to speak. He realized in what state her emotions were and took pity. She was a broken vessel, trapped in a profound sense of despair.

"It's a pity I met her at all," she whispered brokenly. "All through the years, I wrapped myself inside steel armor. The armor protected me from the knowledge that I had a daughter out there, past the borders. It made it possible for me to go on living, even though the pain didn't leave me for an instant. I constantly reinforced the armor, telling myself that a person has to learn to accept Heaven's decrees with love."

She fell abruptly silent. Then, with a heavy sigh, she burst out, "And now, everything's gone! Destroyed. Exploded!"

"What is?" Avraham asked curiously.

"What? 'What?' he asks. What do you mean, 'What?' Don't you realize what's happened?"

She waited for his answer, but he had decided that silence was the more prudent course. Impatiently, she said, "All right, I'll explain it to you! When I met Rivka'le, I let the armor slip. It simply melted away when I hugged my daughter as tightly as I could. You can have no concept of the amount of pain, suffering, heartache, and pangs of conscience that burst out of me at that moment." Her eyes went to the window, where golden sand met the blue Mediterranean on the outskirts of Haifa. Avraham made no attempt to break the silence. He waited.

"Why did I need to meet her?" she cried out heartrendingly. "Why did all the old wounds have to open up? Now my suffering is starting all over again." Her voice dropped to a whimper. "I don't think I can bear it."

"Imma, be calm. I beg you, calm down! All is not yet lost. Her way back is going to take time. But, Imma, she will return!"

Even as he said them, he did not really believe the words.

Neither did his mother. She turned her head away.

"But you must have sensed yourself that Rivka is feeling regret. You saw what strong feelings she had for you, how much longing burst out of her when she hugged you. The way you spoke to one another. Wait a little. Let time do its work. Everything will turn out all right, you'll see."

Mrs. Rosenbaum made a despairing gesture. "No! There is no future. No hope."

It was hard not to feel rejected by her reaction. With restraint, Avraham asked, "In other words, I'm not the future? Or Rachel? Or the two sweet granddaughters that Hashem has given you?"

His mother did not answer. Her devoted son was hurt, hurt by her own words, but she did not make any effort to repair the damage. There was just no strength left in her.

She leaned back, rested her head on the back of the seat and closed her eyes. Her breathing was so low as to be scarcely audible. Avraham was deeply troubled. In all his imaginings, he had not pictured this kind of crisis.

Days passed, and turned into weeks. The weeks lengthened into months, without any shortening of the distance between Shechem and Bnei Brak or Petach Tikvah. Once in a long while, Samira/Rivka would pick up the phone and dial Avraham's number. Their conversations were generally short and to the point: "How are you? Is everything okay? Good. Take care." She never came to visit either him or their mother. For his part, Avraham had no intention of traveling back to Shechem.

More often, it was Avraham who phoned his sister, but she did not always take his calls. He did not understand her behavior. Why the almost solid wall she insisted on maintaining between them? Were her sons exerting pressure on her to stay away?

Mrs. Rosenbaum had taken to her bed. The emotional encounter at the Sata Prison, and its traumatic conclusion, had undermined her health. Avraham tried to tell Samira about it when they spoke on the phone, but all he heard in response was the sound of muffled sobs. What was going through his sister's mind? Avraham could not even hazard a guess.

Finally, he began to entertain the idea of going back to Shechem and placing himself in danger's way just to see her again, face-to-face.

"You are not obligated to do so," his rabbi told him, when Avraham went to him for guidance. "The Chazon Ish said that the Torah is not a poor beggar who has to go around pleading for a handout. If a person doesn't want the Torah, then he won't have it! There is no reason in this case to endanger yourself. Even the first time you went, there was some doubt whether your actions were consistent with the laws of *'pikuach nefesh.'* But you went! We can't undo the past. However, you are not obligated to go again now. This time, her sons would find it easier to harm you, Heaven forbid."

"But my mother is ill because of all this. There's an element of *pikuach nefesh* here, too."

The rabbi considered this. Slowly, he replied, "One of our *gedolim* used to say, in the name of earlier Sages, that there is a question and a lesson to be found in the following verse: 'Go, my sons, and listen to me, and I will teach you fear of Heaven. Who is the man who desires life, who loves to see good all of his days? Stop your tongue from speaking evil...' It seems, he said, that the second sentence is unnecessary. It should have

The Envelope / 427

said, 'Go, my sons, and listen to me, etcetera,' followed immediately with the advice, 'Stop your tongue from speaking evil.' The explanation he gives is very insightful. Only the man who desires life will heed words of *mussar*. Only if he desires life can you tell him, 'Stop your tongue from speaking evil.'

"Your sister, evidently, does not want to, or cannot, embrace the 'life' you're offering. She will not listen to you. Therefore, you are exempt from the obligation of trying to teach her.

"As for your mother —" the rabbi ended soberly, "pray."

※ ※

There was one ray of sunshine for the family. Uncle Nachum had established a relationship with his only grandson. It irritated him that Efraim had become very close to Avraham, and through his influence gradually began accepting the mitzvos on himself — while Nachum was still leading a secular existence. Nevertheless, he was close to Efraim and acknowledged him as his full heir in every way.

※ ※

The year passed. Elimelech Rosenbaum's first *yahrtzeit* was upon them. Mrs. Rosenbaum stubbornly insisted on leaving her sickbed and going to the cemetery. Avraham asked some friends from the Radomsk *shtiebel* to be part of a *minyan* at his father's grave. He instructed them to meet the family at the cemetery. Then, quiet and sad, the family set out. Avraham held his mother's arm on one side while Uncle Nachum, who had traveled down from Haifa for the occasion, took hold of the other.

At her front door, Mrs. Rosenbaum paused. Silent tears rolled down the drawn cheeks. "I so much hoped that Rivka'le would be here with us today, at least."

Neither her son nor her brother offered an answer. In silence they continued to lead her toward the waiting car. Behind the wheel sat Efraim. Rachel was waiting in the backseat.

They reached the cemetery gates and climbed out of the car. Slowly, the small group began to makes its way toward the place where the patriarch of the family was interred.

Suddenly, Rachel let out an excited cry. "Avraham, look!"

He stopped walking. "Where?"

She pointed at her father-in-law's grave. "There!"

Following the direction of her pointing finger, Avraham saw a figure standing motionless at the grave. It was a woman's figure, and she was holding something that looked like a *siddur*.

Efraim narrowed his eyes, the better to see. "It's Samira," he called softly. "I'm sure of it!"

Rachel squinted, too, then whispered, "Yes. I think he's right. It's Samira."

A rush of emotion filled Avraham's chest and throat. He wanted to call her name out loud, to run toward her. But Rachel hissed, "Quiet! Don't do it. Let's all stay back. Let her be alone for a while."

They stood together without speaking. The cemetery was deserted under its blanket of eternal silence. Samira, reunited with her father, was unaware that she was being observed by her family. Mrs. Rosenbaum rested her head on Avraham's shoulder and whimpered softly, "Rivka'le. My Rivka'le —"

Very quietly, Rachel said, "I feel there's been some sort of reconciliation. She's come to ask her father for forgiveness — I'm sure of it. I can't bear this." Tears of emotion welled in her eyes and spilled over.

The figure at the grave leaned close to the headstone and rested her forehead on its cool marble surface. It seemed to Avraham that the figure was shaking slightly. Was she crying? His own eyes were definitely moist.

Avraham saw his sister placing something on the gravestone.

"What is she putting there?" he wondered in an undertone. "Flowers?"

Rachel peered ahead. "Flowers? I don't think so." No one else offered any other suggestions.

Then, in a flash of intuition, Avraham understood. "Yes, I see!" he said, deeply moved. "It's — the envelope. The envelope with the letter!"

"Which envelope?" Rachel asked. "What letter?"

"I told you about it," he whispered. "About the letter that my father, *alav hashalom*, wrote to her in his initial anger, and that she held onto all these years as proof that he hated her. I convinced her that she was mistaken. Now, apparently, she's returning the letter to Abba." He turned to his wife, eyes shining. "You're right — it's a reconciliation! Do you see, Rachel? Our trip to Shechem was not for nothing!"

The figure pressed her lips to the marble stone and kissed it. Then she began to move slowly away from the grave, head down. The rest of them watched every move intently.

Suddenly, she lifted her head — and saw them watching.

Her eyes widened in shock. She saw her mother, Uncle Nachum, Avraham, Rachel, and Efraim. For an instant, she stood stock still.

Then she spun away and began to run with all possible speed, down the path to where her car was waiting.

Efraim spoke first. "See who's sitting in the car? It's Nashashivi and Saib. It's them! I'd recognize them anywhere."

The car sped off at once, as though intent on fleeing.

❦

This proved too much for Mrs. Rosenbaum. She fainted dead away into her son's arms, there in the cemetery, as the car bearing her Rivka'le disappeared back to Shechem. Avraham and Nachum laid her tenderly on the ground. Efraim raced to a nearby water fountain and brought back a cupful of water. Cold water on her face, along with a couple of light slaps, courtesy of her brother, were sufficient to rouse her. Avraham stroked his mother's thin hand and spoke softly in her ear.

"Imma, be strong. This is a great day for us! Rivka came home! Even though she did not come to Bnei Brak, she came home, Imma. She came to see Abba. I'm sure she came to ask his forgiveness. To reconcile with him. Abba is surely very happy right now, in the next world. Imma, be strong!"

Mrs. Rosenbaum did not answer, but she inclined her head as a sign that she took in what he was saying. Encouraged, Avraham continued,

"There's hope, Imma! Now I'm positive that she will return home to us. And the fact that her sons — your grandsons, Imma — came to the cemetery with her is a very good sign, too. They must likewise have undergone a slight change of heart. What did I just say — a good sign? No, it's an excellent sign! *Mazal tov,* Imma! You've given birth to a daughter. Go on, say *'mazal tov'!"*

Mrs. Rosenbaum was silent. Then she whispered something, though he could not catch the words.

But the smile that suddenly lit her eyes provided Avraham with all the answer he needed. She understood. She believed.

A Postscript

The story that comprises this book first appeared in installments in *Mishpachah*, a Hebrew-language magazine published in Israel.

One day – during the period the story was being serialized – we received a letter. The letter was unsigned and bore no return address.

Understandably, the letter caused a stir in our editorial offices, and had a dramatic impact upon me, the author of the story. A translation of the letter appears below.

I succeeded in contacting the letter-writer, who did not have the words to adequately convey how *The Envelope* had saved her from losing her connection with the Jewish People.

We never know the full impact of our words.

Chaim Eliav

Tuesday, 13 Elul

Dear Chaim Eliav,

I would like to extend my heartfelt thanks to *Mishpachah*, particularly for the story entitled "The Envelope." This story deeply influenced my life, as I will explain.

I am a 17-year-old girl who lives in the North. I am a bookworm, and I am particularly fond of your books. I own – and have read – all of them. Every one of the books is a treasure, and I have found valuable lessons in each. But *The Envelope* hit particularly close to home.

Several months ago, an irreligious-looking teenage boy began following me around. It seems that one day he saw me and decided that I was "his."

He passed me his cellular number, and for weeks I debated whether or not I should call him.

I am, after all, observant, and he was irreligious. Finally I could no longer hold out – I called him, and we began to speak often. He impressed me as being a very intelligent young man.

Soon he asked that we get together. Though I initially refused, I later agreed to meet him. It was during that meeting that I learned he was, in fact, an Arab.

By then it was too late, though. He had strong feelings for me, and I for him. Though I knew that I *should* end our relationship, it was too difficult to simply cut off contact with him.

It was at that time that I was reading the serialization of *The Envelope* in the magazine.

At first, I didn't sense the parallel of my own situation to the one described in the book. But as you began to describe the emotions that haunted Rivkah/Samira over her father's throwing her out of his house, as you portrayed her torment — I saw myself. Though it was Shabbos, I could not stop crying.

It was then that I decided to absolutely cut off all contact with the young man I was seeing.

That evening, *Motza'ei Shabbos*, I traveled to the grave of Rav Shimon bar Yochai. I prayed from the depths of my heart to be given the help and the strength I needed to leave "my friend" without having any problems.

By Sunday morning, however, I reconsidered my decision and called him.

It was then that I clearly saw the Divine intervention afforded to those who want to do what's right: He was selling his cellular phone that day, and he said he would call me when he got a new phone.

It was the perfect opportunity for me to disengage myself from him.

For the past month I have had no contact with the young man, and I no longer have any desire to do so.

Thank you, *Hashem*, for giving me the inspiration to want to do the proper thing – and the assistance to do so.

Thank you, Chaim Eliav, for writing the story that motivated me and that led me to be saved.

May *Hashem* help all others in similar circumstances as well.